The *Man* Who Wrote the *Book*

Also by Erik Tarloff:
Face-Time

The *Man* Who Wrote the *Book*

a   n   o   v   e   l

ERIK TARLOFF

Crown Publishers • New York

Copyright © 2000 by Count Leo, Inc.

All rights reserved. No part of this book may be produced or transmitted in any form or by any means, electronic or mechanical, including photocopying, recording or by any information storage and retrieval system, without permission in writing from the publisher.

Published by Crown Publishers, New York, New York.
Member of the Crown Publishing Group.

Random House, Inc. New York, Toronto, London, Sydney, Auckland
www.randomhouse.com

CROWN is a trademark and the Crown colophon is a registered trademark of Random House, Inc.

Printed in the United States of America

Design by Leonard Henderson

Library of Congress Cataloging-in-Publication Data
Tarloff, Erik.
The man who wrote the book : a novel / by Erik Tarloff.
1. English teachers—California, Northern—Fiction.   2. Erotic stories—Authorship—Fiction.   3. California—Fiction.   I. Title.
PS3570.A626 M3 2000
813'54—dc21   99–057839

ISBN 0-609-60468-6

10 9 8 7 6 5 4 3 2 1

First Edition

For Laura and Elliot

Acknowledgments

With thanks to early readers James Carroll, Richard Dimitri, Ronald Goldfarb, Stephen Greeblatt, and Robert Reich. And, as before, with special thanks to Kate Lehrer and Wendy Lesser.

Part 1

Still Life with Chrysalis

A deep dispiriting despondency, an oppressive enervating angst, settled over Ezra Gordon around the time Dr. Jacobs put her hand up his ass.

Or so Ezra reconstructed it eight days later, a hundred miles from home, hurtling down Highway 1 in his beat-up Toyota Tercel at eighty miles per hour, twenty-five of them illegal, escaping from . . . well, from everything.

He had gone to the Beuhler College infirmary because of a nagging pain in his left shoulder and chest which had troubled him for weeks. Certain it was his heart, confident he was a corpse waiting to happen, he had put off doing anything about it until one of his students, Henry Ng, innocently asked him why he was walking funny. That's when he decided to be a grown-up, or at least act like one; for the first time in his employment at Beuhler, he availed himself of the college's niggardly faculty health plan and went for a checkup. Within minutes, Dr. Jacobs had her hand up his ass. Opting, apparently, for the scenic route to his upper torso.

"What's this got to do with my chest?" he had gasped, much too late to influence her plans.

"It's been years since your last checkup," she said. "It's important to do this periodically." And then, with a note of asperity, "Would you *please* relax?"

"Relax? You want me to relax? *Your hand's up my ass!*" The sheer indignity of the situation was already inducing a certain melancholy, but he didn't pay it much attention yet. It was hard to focus on something as insubstantial as a mood when a hitherto unknown—and not especially prepossessing—older woman was violating him so intimately. She had already forced him to pee in a cup and had held his testicles while he coughed. Where would this madness end?

It ended in her small bare office, less than a half-hour later. Seated behind her desk, primly leafing through his file, acting as if she didn't know his prostate from a hole in the ground, she assured him without conspicuous enthusiasm that she had found nothing.

"But what about those pains?" he demanded. "They're getting worse."

She hesitated a moment. She looked down at his file. She adjusted her glasses. Then she met his eye and said, "Pains. How old did you say you were, Professor Gordon?"

"Thirty-five."

"Thirty-five. Yes. And are you married?"

"Divorced."

"But you've been married. Any children?"

"A daughter. Seven years old. I've never met her. She lives with her mother in Switzerland. But what does that have to do with—?"

Dr. Jacobs held up a hand, demanding silence. "Look, Professor, you're a reasonably healthy man, and I'm sure you still have a good many active years ahead of you, but—" She shrugged, and smiled an odd conspiratorial smile. "It's just, you've reached a stage in your life where things don't have to hurt for a reason anymore. They just . . . hurt. Do you see? You've done your part. And now, *nature is through with you.*"

■   ■   ■

So Ezra wasn't in the best of spirits when he drove Carol home from their dinner date that same night. Nature was through with him. The words reverberated, of course, but they did much more than that: They explained absolutely everything about his current life. I had my chance and I muffed it. I misplayed the hand I was dealt, and nature, that fat arrogant fuck, couldn't care less. Nature has dropped me like a moist, unraveling cigar butt. Failed husband, failed father, failed poet, failed scholar, and any minute now, failed lover. A safe prediction, surely. Wherefore should this night be different from any other?

This "relationship" with Carol—it was impossible to think of the word without quotation marks—was one of the ongoing mysteries of his current life. Not unlike those inexplicable chest pains. Did they see each other only because they had nothing better to do? Or was there, buried within some deep emotional cave somewhere, a small stalactite of genuine affection remaining between them? Well, he didn't have the energy to go spelunking tonight. How could he? Nature was through with him. So, in all likelihood, was Carol. How else to interpret her sullen taciturnity throughout dinner?

Dinner that set him back almost $60, which came to approximately $5 a word out of her, if you discounted her relatively lively exchanges with the obnoxious French waiter.

"Do you want to come in?" she suddenly asked, breaking the oppressive silence. They were strolling up the paved walk which bifurcated the rolling front lawn of her house.

He was startled by the sound of her voice and taken aback by the invitation itself. Why extend the charade? Why not agree there was no purpose in continuing to see each other, why not concede that nature was through with him, why not get on with the pointless remainder of their absurd lives?

"Sure," he heard himself say, "that'd be nice." Sheer inertia. He could think of no other explanation for so readily accepting.

They climbed the three steps to the antebellum-style veranda. While Carol fumbled for her keys, Ezra took a deep breath. The moon was fat and full, the night air was deliciously soft and balmy, the jasmine growing near the porch wonderfully sweet-smelling. Nature in full-court press, if you ignored the human component.

She finally located her keys in the nether reaches of her purse and opened the door. Although the porch light was on, within the house was dark. "I think Daddy's gone to bed," she whispered, turning on the light in the foyer.

"He sleeps?" Ezra responded incredulously. It suggested there were hours in the day when the man wasn't spoiling things for someone else, and that seemed out of character. Ezra stepped inside gingerly, anxious to avoid any creaking floorboards which might rouse the ogre slumbering upstairs, then eased the front door shut behind him and followed Carol across the foyer into the huge handsome country-style kitchen, which was marred only, but decisively, by plaid linoleum flooring of mid-'50s vintage.

"Coffee?" she asked, after flicking on a light.

"Not for me." The espresso he'd stupidly drunk with the crème anglaise he'd stupidly eaten figured to keep him awake half the night all by itself.

"I think Daddy has some apple wine around here somewhere," she said.

"Really?" It was an odd offer, since Carol had declined all but half a glass of the rather good, or at least rather pricey cabernet he'd ordered at dinner. She had decorously brought the glass to her mouth once or twice, but no liquid got past the bolted gates of her pursed lips. Rather than waste the stuff, he'd done a fair bit of damage to the bottle all by himself.

"His sister makes it. Sends him a couple of bottles every Christmas. It's not too bad. Better than you'd think."

"Won't he miss it?"

"Nah. He only brings it out for special occasions." She laughed. "My wedding and my divorce are the times I recall. Once to celebrate and once to grieve."

Ezra smiled, remembering—distantly—that Carol was capable of a certain droll irony about herself and her world, or at least had been once upon a time. Before the ice age set in, before he had been accused of sexual harassment and things had gone to hell between the two of them. They hadn't laughed together quite so freely since.

But he was also at a loss for an answer. That Carol was a certified divorcee was one of many facts about her which failed to fit, along with her still living with her widowed father in this weird gothic Victorian manse, along with her odd and unpredictable alternation of school-marmish priggishness and girlish high spirits, along with her willingness, however grudging, to go on dating him. His own divorce some eight years back struck him as exactly appropriate, an unpleasant but predictable consequence of an ill-considered impulse, irrelevant to his present existence except that it produced a child he didn't know and never saw. But Carol, so detached from, so above life's messy fray, Carol was something else.

"Are you going to have any?" he asked.

After a moment's reflection, "Sure. Why? Thought I might pull a Lucrezia Borgia?"

"I just don't care to drink alone."

She inclined her head, accepting the rebuke, and then disappeared into the pantry—a room substantially larger than his own kitchen—rattled around in there for a minute or so, and returned with an unlabeled bottle of brownish-yellow liquid, which she handed to him. "The corkscrew's in that drawer over there."

He eyed the bottle suspiciously, but proceeded to open it while Carol produced two heavy, faceted, green-stemmed goblets. "You're certain this is the right bottle?" he asked while pouring. "The alternatives are too ghastly to contemplate."

"Don't be silly." Claiming one of the glasses, she led Ezra through the foyer and into the parlor, turning on one dim table lamp before kicking off her shoes and joining him on the overstuffed sofa. She took a moment to adjust herself, settling in sideways, sinking down, her knees tucked under her on the cushion, her right arm lying along the sofa back, and then faced him, holding up her glass.

It struck Ezra for only the second time that night—the other was when she'd first appeared on the stairs, while he'd been struggling to make conversation with her patently disapproving father—how pretty she was. She was wearing a baby-blue cotton print summer dress which showed off her slender figure and exposed the constellations of freckles bestrewing her shoulders, her reddish hair was in some new gamine-style do which flattered her neat features, and she held herself with a tomboyish country-girl poise he occasionally found sexy, when the less appealing aspects of her personality weren't on display. There had been a time when he'd found it very sexy indeed. There had been a time when she seemed to enjoy his finding it so. The more appealing aspects of her personality made more frequent appearances in those days.

"Well," she pronounced with an unfamiliar wry smile, "cheers."

He sipped. Jesus! The acidity of the brew was staggering. "Unpolished," he pronounced, "but you have to respect its audacity." He puckered and took another sip.

"Aunt Goldie swears it's excellent for the digestion. Digestion's a very big topic with her. She finds her own insides endlessly fascinating."

"Gee, I'd love to meet her some day. She sounds like a swell gal."

Carol shifted her weight to get nearer to him. "Why do you always make fun of my family?"

He considered. "Maybe because you're such easy targets."

Her smiling face came very close to his. "You're a real jerk, Ezra, you know that?" And then, without warning, she kissed him.

Was it the cabernet he'd had earlier, or the apple-accented astringent he'd just sipped, or the warm pillowy spring air, or some combination of all of these? The kiss made him dizzy.

"You're a puzzlement," he whispered.

Still smiling, she took another sip of wine, and then deposited her goblet on the black lacquer coffee table. Evidently she meant business. He followed suit. She leaned in close and kissed him again, less tentatively this time. Aunt Goldie's concoction was more palatable on her tongue than direct from the glass. He slipped an arm around her bare shoulders and pulled her body against his.

"It's even better when you help," she murmured into his neck. The words sounded familiar, although he couldn't quite place them. June Allyson in her pre-diaper phase? No, it was Bacall to Bogie. Hmmm. Promising.

He put his mouth back on hers and kept it there, feeling a strange sensation in the pit of his stomach as she sighed and her body went limp and yielding. In the melee, she had slid down low on the sofa, and he now had the advantage of height. He leaned over her, kissing her wetly, and her arms went around his neck and pulled him close. Could the unfamiliar sensation be . . . arousal? He cupped her small pert breast—her body was a lovely combination of the taut and the spongy—she sighed, and he found it easy to slide his hand under the flimsy fabric of her dress and over the gentle swell of warm bare skin. No bra. Another anomalous fact about Carol. The sensation was unexpectedly, disproportionately pleasurable; not since high school had a bare breast had comparable impact.

"This is lovely," she breathed, echoing his sentiments exactly. Her voice sounded different, coming from some distant and unprotected region inside her.

"Isn't it?" Ah, spring. Man's best friend. His index and middle fingers found her hard little nipple, and in response she moaned softly and positioned herself across his lap. As he pressed against her, she said directly into his mouth, "Um . . . you should know . . . I can't tonight."

He ceased pressing. "You said the same thing two weeks ago."

"This time it's true."

Her prohibition against sex during menstruation was absolute. One of the many absolute prohibitions in her code, which was slightly more stringent than Hammurabi's.

Nature wasn't letting him down easy.

But the impossibility of anything definitive happening seemed to embolden her. One of her hands found its way onto his inner thigh. He had the impression she was trying to bring it into contact with his erection without quite seeming to intend to. I really ought to get out of here, he told himself, I'm much too old for these games, at the same time shifting his position to help the accident along. Eureka! It was only the back of her hand, just a casual sort of unwitting proximity, but she was beginning to apply some pressure, not, of course, on purpose or anything, just sort of—

A shadow suddenly fell across them. Even with their eyes closed, in a room illuminated by a sixty-watt bulb under a thick shade on a remote corner table, there was no mistaking the shadow of something dark and cold and immense.

Her hand edged away from his crotch. Their mouths separated. Their bodies inched apart. But extricating his hand from her bodice proved to be no easy matter, despite the marvelous ease with which it had slid in. And so they sat on the sofa, his hand down the front of her dress, staring up bleary-eyed and slack-jawed at the housecoated, Brobdingnagian figure of the Reverend Mr. Dimsdale.

The name was no longer a source of amusement to Ezra; familiarity, plus the sheer bleakness of the man's personality, had seen to that. Not to mention his position as Beuhler College chaplain, and hence his ex officio seat on the college Board of Overseers, which in turn gave him a voice in Ezra's frequently postponed tenure case. No, it was no longer possible to find anything funny about the minister. Stout, red-faced, with thinning yellowish-white hair in tufts on the crown of his large head, Dimsdale stood now in the gloom, staring down in dismay at his daughter and her despised suitor.

Ezra managed to free his hand. Liberation was accompanied by the rude sound of ripping fabric. The Reverend Mr. Dimsdale blinked very slowly and then said, "Is that Goldie's wine?"

"I hope you don't mind," Carol answered, her voice a tiny piccolo.

Dimsdale shook his head, not in response to Carol's hope, but in despair at man's fall. "You should've asked," he said.

Ezra, his recently freed hand asleep and tingling, stretched and forced a yawn. "I'd better be running along," he announced. "Busy day tomorrow."

This was greeted with silence. He rose, hoping his incompletely detumesced penis was unnoticeable amidst the multitude of wrinkles in his corduroy trousers.

"So . . . good-night," he continued. "Thanks for a lovely evening."

It was insulting, the way no one even acknowledged his effort. He surely deserved points for trying. Feeling hideously self-conscious and graceless, he started out of the parlor. But a second or two later, before he could draw an easy breath, he became aware of footsteps behind him. The elephantine tread left no room for hope. But he didn't turn around until he reached the front door, when a plaid flannel-covered arm reached around him and opened it.

"Well," he began, as he stepped through it onto the porch, feeling the sort of exhilaration Cold War–era East Berliners must have felt as they made their terrified escape across Checkpoint Charlie, "I guess—"

"Listen, son."

Brightly: "Yes, sir?"

"You're lucky I came in when I did."

A dubious proposition from almost any point of view. But this didn't seem a good time to explain that, owing to the vagaries of the lunar calendar, the man's daughter's virtue hadn't been in jeopardy. "A thought-provoking suggestion, sir."

Dimsdale frowned. This time, Ezra's irony wasn't lost on him. It was a challenge to remember that this complete and utter fool was no fool. "You'd better watch yourself," he said. "A man is judged by the enemies he makes. And when those enemies *include* his judges . . . I'm sure you understand me."

Ezra understood him perfectly.

■   ■   ■

His foot was getting heavy on the pedal. On his tape deck, the Eagles were promising him, at full volume, a heartbreak tonight—in his present situation, an empty threat—and his bare left arm was absorbing an abundance of carcinogenic rays, the sky above him was eyeball-blue and cloudless, the air was crystalline and clean-smelling, with just a soupçon, a cunty tang of sea salt for seasoning, and down below to his right the vast indifferent Pacific glinted and sparkled.

He took a deep breath, felt his chest expand. Could he be feeling better? Could his depression be lifting? Could his spirits be rising?

Do weasels play the tuba?

It could only be an illusion, a momentary response to the mocking beauty of the day and a fugitive's fleeting sense of freedom. Too much was profoundly wrong.

Like his tenure case, for example. There. That took care of that. The words "tenure case," as soon as he thought them, collapsed his chest, deposited an immense weight right between his shoulders, restored the natural order of things. It was oddly comforting, having the familiar malaise settle in and make itself comfortable, like a visiting in-law.

■   ■   ■

When Bob Dixon casually uttered the words which sealed his fate, Ezra's attention was elsewhere, out the window, observing a golden butterfly alight briefly on a golden wildflower, disappear amidst the accidental camouflage, and then take wing again. The effect was magical: The flower seemed to have effortlessly produced a butterfly from some template hidden within its folds, to have shrugged and released its creation into the perfumed spring air.

"Your publications," Professor Dixon was saying, " lean rather heavily toward the, er, creative side of the ledger. These poems and so on. Not much in the way of research."

Ezra reluctantly turned back toward the department chairman, who looked up from the c.v. on the desk before him—Ezra's c.v.—and regarded him with eyebrows raised interrogatively. Some reply was evidently expected. "Well . . ." Ezra said, his heart suddenly racing, "I do have several articles in the hopper."

"Do you? That *is* encouraging, even at this late date. When will they appear? *Where* will they appear?"

"No," said Ezra, "I meant *this* hopper." He tapped his head.

Dixon frowned. He was a large man, tall and beefy, with a big pasty face and a prognathous jaw, and even with his tie loosened and his shirtsleeves rolled back, his grudging concession to spring, he looked more like an old-fashioned small-town banker than a well-regarded expert on romantic poetry.

"Ah. I find that troubling."

"You do?"

"Your case would be stronger if there were more scholarly publications. Not this, this, this verse of yours."

"I thought my poetry was part of my appeal."

"Well, initially, perhaps. But it hasn't quite worked out, has it? To be blunt. I mean, you're not exactly . . . you know."

Ezra did know. To call him obscure was to pay him a compliment.

"There have been some articles," Ezra pointed out. He glanced toward the chairman's window. The butterfly had fled. If I had wings, Ezra mused, I'd do the same. It was a lovely day. Through with Ezra, nature was otherwise going about its accustomed business at full throttle.

"Yes," Dixon readily, too readily, agreed. He was prepared for this line of defense. "A few. Most of them dating from your first year here. And they're—what's the word I'm searching for? They're rather *traditional* in approach."

Ezra smiled. "Like the department."

Dixon didn't smile back. "Yes, that's why we hired you. You and Susan. To provide some modernity. Susan covers the, the, what is it, the *multicultural* end of things, literature as colonialism, and, and, you know, the feminist stuff, the canon as an expression of patriarchal fascism—I believe I've got that right—and we were led to believe you did this other nonsense, this French sort of business, what's it called? Decomposition?"

"Deconstruction." Of course, Dixon knew perfectly well what it was called. He was signaling his disapproval even while reprimanding Ezra for not being a practitioner.

"Yes, that's it, we expected deconstruction from you. You were meant to give the department a little reflected chic. Although that stuff has more or less passed out of fashion lately, hasn't it?"

"Not quite."

"You *did* deconstruct once upon a time, did you not?"

"A youthful indiscretion." Of which there were far too few, and all of which had ended badly.

Dixon frowned again. His full lips, his generally heavy features, the huge jaw, made his frowns especially eloquent. Perhaps if he ever smiled they would magnify that expression too, but Ezra had no data upon which to form such a judgment. "Your teaching evaluations are excellent, and you're a good colleague, and some of these letters, while of borderline relevance, are fairly positive. But problems remain."

"Other than the dearth of publications, you mean?"

Dixon coughed. "That's the main thing, of course. But there was also that unpleasant business last year . . ."

Ezra, for the first time during the interview, was conscious of anger bubbling up from the pit of his stomach. His other derelictions, unpleasant though it was to have them displayed for inspection, were fair game, but "that unpleasant business last year," an accusation of sexual harassment from one of his students, an unstable junior named Mindy Dunkelweisse, had no place on the table.

"The charges were dismissed, Bob," Ezra said, his voice steely.

Dixon looked up mildly. The steel in Ezra's voice didn't faze him. "For lack of proof," he said, his tone equivocal. "It was your word against hers."

"There was no proof because nothing happened." Well, almost nothing. Mindy had come to his office one afternoon and unceremoniously raised her tee shirt and bared her breasts. Although they were of unequal size, each was in its own way a handsome specimen, and Ezra was not unstirred. But she was his student, and Beuhler had strict rules about that sort of thing, and Mindy struck him even then as being a tad unreliable; self-restraint was a basic no-brainer. He had good-naturedly suggested that her action could jeopardize their professional relationship and she really ought to cover herself up. She seemed to understand, complied promptly, and left his office with every appearance of good cheer. But in the ensuing days she evidently began to brood, then decided she'd been scorned, and all of a sudden Hell had no greater fury. A week later, she filed her complaint.

"I was under the impression that the Fourth and Fifth Amendments still apply at Beuhler," Ezra added. "I guess I was mistaken."

It had been very embarrassing. The school newspaper had run a series of articles about it, admirably even-handed and factual, but no less humiliating for that. "Look," he'd told the student reporter who came to interview him, "this isn't ideological. Sexual harassment is a real issue, and I'm as opposed to it as the next man" (a lazy choice of words that would come back to haunt him). "It's just, in this case, I was *there,* I happen to know what happened. And what happened happens to be *nothing.*" He sounded pretty convincing to himself while saying it, with the (female) reporter nodding encouragingly and so on, but when he saw it in print he realized it looked pretty damned hollow on the page.

So, here he was, now, henceforth, and forever a suspected sex offender. He, Ezra Gordon, who wouldn't have a clue how to commit a sex offense even if it was demanded of him at gunpoint, whose very fantasies, even at their most extravagant, were PG-13: Boy meets girl, boy pleads with girl, boy disappoints girl.

A week or so later, there was a preliminary investigation, conducted, most uncomfortably, by an unsmiling Carol in her capacity as college counsel. Inspired, evidently, by the fear that Mindy might instigate a lawsuit against Beuhler. For over an hour, Ezra had to confirm and deny, explain and defend. Carol's manner gave no hint of any personal relationship, let alone any personal trust, having ever existed between them, and her questions were unremittingly hostile, her tone skeptical. So much for having a friend at court. A jealous and suspicious enemy at court is what he had. And even though she ended up recommending the charges be dismissed, things hadn't been the same between them since.

For a brief time, his classes were picketed by outraged students. Even worse, the local chapter of some neo-con outfit had rallied to his defense. His students had treated him peculiarly, and to a certain extent still did. And Carol, now acting in a private capacity, kept repeating the same questions over and over, never entirely satisfied that he was telling the truth, perhaps because, despite his protestations of wronged innocence, he did feel a niggling trace of guilt: He had done the right thing, but not, he had to concede to himself, for the most honorable of reasons, and not without a regretful pang. T.S. Eliot, that tight-ass, would have said he'd committed "the greatest treason," and Carol must have sensed this scintilla of ambivalence. And worst of all, Mindy had perversely, or maliciously, chosen not to drop his class, and—damn her!—had written such a good term paper he felt compelled to give her an A. Which of course reinforced everybody's suspicions.

Dixon sighed. "We're, as you yourself pointed out, a conservative institution. We were founded by Baptists, for Pete's sake. And as you know, we still haven't completely severed those ties. Now, of course you're innocent until proven guilty, here just like anywhere else. But if there's a whiff, a taint, of something *irregular,* it can have a negative influence."

"Thanks for explaining that. Now I know how to deal with any colleagues who oppose my promotion."

Dixon sat back in his chair. "I'm not saying this Dunkelweisse affair—I'm sorry, affair is the wrong word—I'm not saying this *incident* will tip the balance. But your tenure case is problematical regardless."

"Problematical? Can you tell me what that means?"

The chairman looked unhappy, but not nearly as unhappy as Ezra felt he ought. This interview should have been outright agony to him, not merely a tiresome chore that went with being chair. "You still have a year to get some serious research into, as you say, the hopper. That might help. But failing something major along those lines, well . . ."

"Stick a fork in me?"

"You might consider looking elsewhere, is how I'd put it."

Elsewhere? Once you failed at a shithole like Beuhler, there *isn't* any elsewhere.

"Okay, Bob, thanks. I appreciate your candor."

■   ■   ■

"I appreciate your candor, you egg-sucking horse's ass," Ezra said now, out loud, as rage at the memory of that awful interview rose like acid reflux in his chest. On the tape deck, the Eagles were advising him to take it to the limit, and perhaps unwisely, he was following their advice. Exceeding it. Usually a careful and unadventurous driver, he was being a little reckless on this curvy stretch of highway with the precipitous plunge off to his right. But why not? If nature was through with him, why be cautious?

Not that he wanted to die. He didn't think he'd mind being dead very much, but dying was another matter. Dying might hurt.

Teaching, he was beginning to think, was not a good profession for someone with whom nature was through. All those students, nature just beginning to take them up and toy with them, were a daily taunt, a constant reminder of his inanition. Not that he was fit for anything else, but not being fit for anything else didn't prove he was fit for teaching. The department seemed to have reached the same conclusion, albeit for different reasons. The department didn't really care about students very much. Or nature either.

Which brought him with a sigh to Henry Ng. To his conference with Henry three days ago. Nature was far from being through with Henry Ng. Nature had just begun taking an interest, and Henry was flirting back, leaving provocative messages on nature's answering machine, casting mischievous glances in nature's direction across a crowded room.

An engineering major until last summer, Henry had suddenly, alarmingly discovered literature. This epiphany was probably a consequence of getting laid, was Ezra's jaundiced guess. Now the former computer-whiz had located wellsprings of passion and sensitivity within himself, had joined the editorial staff of the campus literary magazine, had taken to smoking Gitanes, God knows where he found them, and had traded in his ridiculous sports jackets and bow ties for Levi's and tee shirts. He had also, since the previous June, tried to swallow Western civ whole; with an engineer's systematic diligence he had read the *Iliad* and the *Odyssey*, the *Divine Comedy*, ten Shakespeare plays, several poetry anthologies, six

Dickens novels, five Henry James, three Dostoyevski, all of Proust, great
gobs of Mallarmé, Rimbaud, and Baudelaire, and *Ulysses* twice, once with
the Gilbert trot, once without.

His parents must be appalled. What had become of their bright, docile,
ambitious boy? Heedlessly leapfrogging right over their traditional second-
generation American aspirations for him, to thrive in one of the profes-
sions, he'd plunged waist-deep into assimilated decadence. He smoked
those Gitanes, he wore his fine black hair in as disheveled a manner as it
would permit, he moped around like a Chinese avatar of young Werther,
he would have drunk absinthe if it were available in Seven Hills. His folks
hadn't left Taiwan for *this*.

He had also, without much reciprocal encouragement beyond good
manners and a threadbare sense of professional duty, adopted Ezra as his
mentor. This wasn't so bad in itself, except as a result he expected Ezra to
read and critique his massive work in progress, a sort of Bildungsroman,
already 537 pages long and growing ceaselessly, about a sensitive, over-
sexed Chinese boy coming of age in the San Joaquin Valley. A boy whose
parents want him to be a proctologist but who yearns to paint. Ezra had
glanced at it once or twice, but the thing was much too daunting to *read*.
Ezra's failure in that regard elicited many a hurt, reproachful glance from
Henry.

Henry had come to his office three days ago for a chat. He did that frequently, assuming a community of interest with Ezra, taking for granted a
certain unspoken affinity. Ezra usually tried to handle him with gentle
irony—Henry was either immune to it or oblivious—but on this occasion,
he caught Ezra at a vulnerable time. It was a week when all of Ezra's waking hours were vulnerable.

"I need a vacation," Ezra had sighed. A non sequitur. They had been
discussing William Gaddis only moments before.

Henry glanced around Ezra's windowless, airless cubicle and nodded
sympathetically.

"What are *your* plans for spring break, Henry?"

"Paris."

The ensuing spasm of envy was almost unbearable. "Paris, France?"
Paris, Texas, would excite marginally less envy, but the odds were against.

"Isn't April a good time to be in Paris?"

"The best. Think of the song."

"What song?"

Henry's autodidactic cultural immersion evidently omitted the Vernon Duke canon. "You're a lucky fellow."

"Yeah. My mom and dad came through."

"Whatever possessed them?"

Henry looked ever so slightly abashed. "I kinda lied a little. Told them there was this big international computer expo at the, what's it called, that place. I sorta let 'em think I was gonna give it one last shot."

Ezra smiled with what he hoped looked like avuncular disapproval, indulgent tolerance for the foibles of youth. That was as far as he could go.

"Paris justifies desperate measures, doesn't it?" Henry pressed.

"Hitler thought so." Realizing this came out more harshly than he intended, and in response to the fact that Henry had just produced a cigarette, he added, "You'll have a chance to stock up on those."

"You mind?" Henry inquired, holding up the cigarette.

"Not in principle, Henry. But California law—"

"Say no more." Henry worked the cigarette back into its crumpled blue package. "Listen, why not come along? We'll have a blast. Dinners at Deux Magots—you can give me notes on my novel while we ogle the existentialists."

Wasn't there a time not so very long ago when this sort of familiarity with a professor was unthinkable, when some vestige of the class system resisted all the epoch's democratizing tendencies and remained in effect on university campuses? Oh well, no point in fighting the tide. "I'm not sure there are any existentialists left, Henry. Or anarchists or socialists. All the groovy notions have been discredited." He sighed. "Anyway, it's financially out of the question." Along with everything else. Like *food,* practically. He was two months in arrears on his rent and owed small sums to various people all over Seven Hills.

"That's rough."

"Yes, well . . ." Ezra suddenly found himself discomfited, telling his troubles to an undergraduate. Of course, he was hardly in a position to stand on his dignity this week—he had already been discovered in quasi-flagrante by the Reverend Mr. Dimsdale, been threatened with denial of tenure, and been informed on the highest medical authority that nature was through with him. But the line had to be drawn somewhere.

"So you're sticking around Beuhler over the break?"

"Don't really have a choice." Ezra stood. This had gone quite far enough. Henry, surprised at the abrupt termination of their chat, had no option but to do the same.

"Enjoy Paris," Ezra said, opening the door for his visitor. "The first time is special."

"Like sex?"

"Better. Paris lives up to expectations."

■   ■   ■

Life, Ezra thought as he tooled along Highway 1, is like one of those speeded-up nature films. We're just usually too horrified at the implications to admit it—it makes our mortality too palpable. Once, not so long ago, you were *that,* and then, when your back was turned for a second, you became *this.* The inevitable corollary is that any day now you'll look in the mirror and staring back at you will be . . . Gabby Hayes.

I'm thirty-five years old, and my doctor says I'm in reasonably good health, but let's not kid ourselves—I'm definitely on the back nine.

■   ■   ■

Two days before, Ezra had made his determined way to Beuhler Hall, the college's administration building. Carol's office was in the basement. He hadn't spoken to her in almost a week, not since her father had surprised them in the act of foreplay (a misnomer, since no *play* was in the offing). It was impossible to phone her at home, except on Sunday morning, the only time he could be sure Dimsdale would be out (unfortunately, so would she; it was convenient to forget she was a confirmed churchgoer who attended her father's services, so to speak, religiously). But he'd phoned her at work four or five times, leaving a message in her voice mail each time, and she hadn't called back. At first he didn't mind, but as the days went by, her silence began to rankle. And even more galling, he discovered he missed her.

What the hell was *that* about?

As he pushed open the door leading to her office—she had no personal assistant to prevent him—she was behind her desk, talking on the phone. She gave him a look of such annoyance that he wanted to back out there and then, but when she gestured toward the chair in front of her desk, he really had no polite choice but to take it.

Here it was. The scene of his interrogation. His first time back. Sweat started to form in his armpits. Had John McCain experienced something similar on his return to Hanoi?

She held a finger to her lips to enjoin his silence, and said into the phone, "Germany? But that isn't definite, is it? This whole thing could just be a foul-up, right?" She rolled her eyes impatiently while listening to the lengthy answer. He obviously hadn't caught her in the best of moods. But then, Carol and the best of moods weren't the best of friends these days.

"Look," she finally said, and it was Ezra's impression that she was interrupting the person on the other end of the line, "this could involve the college in *catastrophic* litigation. Our vulnerability is enormous. I need hard facts. I can't make decisions based on guesswork. Get me something definite."

After she slammed the phone down, Ezra said, "The computer business?"

"I can't talk about it, okay?"

Sometimes she couldn't talk about it and sometimes she did talk about it, sharing some shred of information with him. What he knew, based on the few tidbits she'd let slip in the past, was that the college computer system had been behaving wackily for several months, and that it apparently didn't have anything to do with the Y2K bug, that cybernetic Edsel. No, instead, sabotage, possibly of international origin, was strongly suspected.

"When did you get so secretive?" he asked.

"I should never have told you anything."

"You don't trust me?"

The look she gave him spoke volumes. She was thinking of Mindy Dunkelweisse—it was so obvious she might as well have had a cartoon balloon above her head. Well, this exchange wasn't getting them anywhere, so Ezra shifted his shock troops to the other flank and demanded, "Why haven't you returned my calls?"

Carol tried to abort the conversation by staring at the phone, but it uncooperatively refused to ring. "I've been awfully busy," she finally said, lamely.

"Ah," said Ezra, "that explains it."

The silence hung there for a moment. "And besides," she added, taking the bit between her teeth, "Daddy thinks I shouldn't see you anymore."

Ezra nodded. Now we're making progress. "And you? What do *you* think?"

"Well . . . he may have a point." After six days of unanswered calls, it didn't come as a complete surprise. "Anyway, it isn't only what I think. Daddy won't permit you in the house. You can't imagine what it was like after you left the other night. Daddy was, was—"

"Shitting bricks?"

"Something along those lines." She didn't seem to know whether to laugh or scold him for his vulgarity.

"For God's sake, Carol, why don't you just move out?"

She was startled. "Of my house?"

"His house."

"I live there too."

"Exactly. It's unhealthy. It's, it's like some creepy Tennessee Williams deal."

"It is not."

"Jesus, Carol, you're twenty-nine years old."

"Thirty. You forgot my birthday two months ago."

Damn. I'm batting a thousand. "Well," he went on, pretending not to be fazed, "that's even worse. You should be on your own."

"He needs me. He's all alone except for me. And he was gracious enough to take me in after Buddy and I . . . you know."

"So wait, let me get this straight: Was he gracious, or does he need you?"

"Anyway, it won't last forever. Besides, where should I move to?"

"You could move in with me." This was farther than he had intended to go. A lot farther. Sometimes a conversation generates a momentum of its own; you find yourself riding a wave, just trying to keep your head above water.

She was taken aback, which made two of them, but unlike Ezra, she had no reason to dissemble. "You mean like live in sin?"

"They don't call it that anymore, Carol."

"But it's what you're suggesting?"

"I'm just tossing it on the table for our mutual consideration." And tap-dancing away from my own insane proposal. Whatever possessed me?

"Golly, Daddy would, would—"

"Shit a brick?"

"Stop saying that!" She leaned across her desk. "Have you thought this through?"

"No."

"That's what I figured. Is it what you really want?"

"Does your question suggest you're actively considering it?"

"I asked you first."

Ezra sighed. "I don't know what I really want."

Carol nodded vigorously: Annoyed, but relieved to be annoyed. It made things so much easier. "That's it exactly. It's what Daddy was saying about you."

"Oh, I think he suspects there's *one* thing I really want."

She granted him a sidelong glance before continuing, "See, if you were passionate about this, about living together I mean, that would be one thing . . ."

"It wouldn't make the slightest difference."

"It would. I probably wouldn't do it, but I'd consider it. Even though Daddy would, would . . . Don't you dare!"

In spite of everything, Ezra laughed. Carol did too, but only for a moment. Then, after the briefest of intervals, she went on, "But this half-hearted drifting into something 'cause nothing better's on offer . . . it isn't for me, Ezra."

He waited for something mitigating. It didn't come. "So is this . . . the end?"

"I don't know. Maybe it is."

Ezra nodded. Maybe it ought to be. They had begun dating soon after she'd returned to Seven Hills, and to her father's house, from her brief marriage; Dimsdale called in some chits and arranged for her to be Beuhler College counsel. The job sounded impressive for someone who'd passed the bar less than three years previously, but, in fact, in the ordinary course of things it was largely free of serious responsibilities. Within a couple of months of her coming aboard, however, the Justice Department found Beuhler in noncompliance with Title IX of the Civil Rights Act, and suddenly her responsibilities were very serious indeed.

And she'd risen to the occasion. She'd formed a faculty committee to redress the problem—Ezra had volunteered to serve on it—and she'd impressed everyone with her energy and intelligence and commitment. Many people, surely including Beuhler's president, James Matson, had hoped for a few minor cosmetic proposals that would buy off the Feds but leave Beuhler fundamentally unchanged. That isn't how it worked out. Modified budgetary priorities, a community outreach program, a new hiring policy, revised admissions criteria, new scholarship funds, new courses:

These were all fundamentally her handiwork, the faculty committee merely acquiescing after the fact. And she conducted the subsequent negotiations with the Justice Department single-handedly, since she had no legal staff. Worse, she had to win over the chagrined President Matson and the recalcitrant Board of Overseers, including her own father. It was altogether a virtuoso performance. And in the short time since, minority attendance at Beuhler had almost doubled.

Ezra, watching her in action, was first impressed and then smitten. He asked her out, she declined, he asked a few more times—uncharacteristic persistence demonstrating how very smitten he was—and eventually she agreed. Probably because it was easier than continuing to say no. After a few dates, they were sort of going together.

And now they were apparently sort of breaking up.

The moment, here in her office, felt incomplete, lacking the traditional rituals. No solemn regrets, no speeches about needing more space, no assurances they'd always be friends. But maybe that was appropriate too. Drift in, drift out. Nothing momentous in any direction, just laconic finality.

First nature, then Carol.

■   ■   ■

As he neared Santa Barbara, the air grew heavier. Ezra, pretending everything was normal, slipped some Poulenc into his tape deck. But something odd was going on: A little voice was murmuring at him. It wasn't a psychotic thing, wasn't, say, a barking dog urging acts of mayhem. The voice came from inside himself, spoke for some long-buried, long-forgotten part of his being.

"Take it easy," the voice was saying. "Let go of your victim's irony, an imperfect defense at best. Just drop it. If only for the novelty, and only for spring break. Consider: The view is lovely. The air is superb. The *Gloria* is glorious. And Beuhler is far away, infinitely far, its very existence seems implausible right now. How can a universe boasting this view and this air and this music contain an abomination like Beuhler College? It can't. Therefore it doesn't."

Whatever you say, pal, Ezra answered the voice.

"See?" said the voice. "That's what I'm getting at." And then it added (gratuitously, it seemed to Ezra), "Asshole."

■   ■   ■

Back in his apartment after the understated donnybrook with Carol—a three-room dump unfit for an impoverished graduate student, let alone an impoverished professor—Ezra decided to get drunk. This wasn't a normal diversion for him, but he couldn't devise an alternate plan that met his needs nearly so well. Sitting in his underfurnished living room contemplating the vast arid expanse of spring break looming before him and the hopeless hash he'd made of his life, intoxication, even unto insensibility, was an attractive proposition.

After downing a couple of tumblers of supermarket vodka in his kitchen, he couldn't tell if he felt any better, but he felt different. And given the circumstances, different was better by definition. But, he realized with dismay, only five minutes had elapsed, and he still had an empty evening in front of him. How to fill the void? Drinking steadily for hours was beyond his capabilities, not to mention his purse. What videos haven't I seen? he wondered. What books remain to be read? What (with an inward shudder) articles need to be written?

It was this last question which made him feel as if the ground had opened up beneath him. A hideous helpless panicky feeling, the kind usually reserved for 2 A.M. night sweats. Why the hell did I become a professor?

It was as if, over ten years before, callow and emotionally retarded, he had set his course in an ill-considered direction—as much for lack of a viable alternative as anything else—and now rudderless, oarless, engines coughing impotently, he continued, and only from attenuated vestigial momentum, to drift in that same direction, but purposelessly, joylessly, with no destination in sight and no particular desire to arrive anywhere anyway.

That it was too late to do anything about it was self-evident. He was unfit for any other line of work—twenty-eight years of schooling had seen to that. He wasn't fit for *this* line of work either, but at least, and for the time being only, he enjoyed (what a word) not-quite-gainful employment practicing his not-exactly-chosen profession.

The vodka was kicking in. Big time. This, alas, wasn't signaled by elation, merely distant nausea and dim intimations of stupidity, plus an odd sort of self-pity, languorous and maudlin. What next? A few slurred choruses of "Melancholy Baby"?

But through the encroaching fog, through the gathering misery, his thoughts ineluctably moved on to, seized onto, his closest friend in grad school, Isaac Schwimmer. Because unlike Ezra, Isaac *had* escaped. It was a major scandal at the time, Isaac's breakout.

Back at the University of Michigan, Isaac was considered the most promising candidate in the doctoral program, but after having passed his orals brilliantly, and having completed most of the research for his dissertation on Robert Herrick, he proclaimed one day that he'd had enough. "It's rosebud time," he announced. People assumed he was joking, but the next week he absconded on his Harley and never returned.

Of course, Isaac's freewheeling ways were the stuff of legend around Ann Arbor well before he'd cut and run. Among the cloistered monastic literary adepts laboring in their carrels in the university library, Isaac was regarded as an alien presence, a voice of the instincts, a creature of impulse, an antic full-throated bard of the unbridled id. But still, to abandon everything he'd worked for, so long and so hard and with such distinction . . . it left people flabbergasted and shaken. Many claimed to be outraged. Isaac never seemed to mind if people were outraged. Their disapproval was a matter of indifference to him. As was their approval. Isaac was blessed somehow, Isaac possessed a great soul, Isaac, for all his crudity, existed in a mysterious state of grace.

Ezra reached for the phone.

Isaac had abandoned his books and his sizable CD collection and his furniture, which he'd schlepped from one Ann Arbor apartment to another over the years, giving everything away to friends and colleagues, none of whom believed he would really go through with his crazy scheme, all of whom promised to return everything once he came to his senses. He'd fled to New York, where for a while he'd swanned around in ways unthinkably Boho, waiting tables, driving cabs, hustling chess games in Greenwich Village, constructing sets at various fringe theaters. Then he somehow had migrated to Boston and landed a respectable job at the *Atlantic Monthly*. Typical Isaac, who had a knack for sowing the wind without reaping any discernible whirlwinds.

Maybe the bold ones are bold because fate rewarded their boldness from early on. They never discovered how fate enjoys sandbagging those it doesn't favor.

They maintained a desultory correspondence for a while, then lost touch. The last Ezra heard—and because everyone who'd known Isaac told stories about him, he couldn't remember where—Isaac had moved to Southern California and gotten into publishing.

Ezra dialed 310 directory assistance, hoping he had the right area code. He gave Isaac's name to a recording, spelling the surname slowly, and seconds later, a live human came on the line. "I have an Isaac Schwimmer Press in Marina Del Rey," the live human said.

His own press! Pretty sharp! Without giving himself time to reconsider, Ezra dialed the number he was given.

"The Isaac Schwimmer Press," spoke a well-modulated woman's voice.

Jeez. This was almost too easy. "Mr. Schwimmer, please."

"Who should I say is calling?"

Ezra toyed momentarily with hanging up and abandoning the whole thing, but steeled himself and gave his name. A few seconds later, Isaac was on the line. "Ez? Ez Gordon?"

"Ike?"

"My God, it's really you!" The voice sounded the same, as warm and friendly as if they'd spoken the day before yesterday.

"You have a press named after you, Ike."

"Pike has his peak, Hodgkins has his disease, I've got my press. Are you in town?"

"No, I—"

"I mean, how've you been? Jeez, it's been so long. You married or anything?"

"Was. Briefly. To Helga. Remember her?"

Isaac groaned. He remembered. "Mistake."

"Immense mistake."

"I could've told you."

"You probably did. So what about you?"

"Nah, I slept with her a couple of times, but I never married her."

This was news to Ezra. He took a moment to process his emotions, and finally decided he wasn't terribly bothered, or at least wouldn't let himself be bothered. It was ages ago, and the honor of enjoying Helga's favors hardly made Isaac unique.

"God, I'd love to see you," Isaac went on. "You say you're in town?"

"No, I—"

"Wait just a second, I'm gonna have to put you on hold."

Click. After a two- or three-minute interlude involving a lushly orches-
trated version of "Skylark," Isaac came back on the line, demanding
gruffly, "Who is this?"

"Ezra." This was greeted with a silence that felt uncomprehending, so
he added, "Gordon. Ezra Gordon."

"Oh yes! Great, great! Hold on." Ezra then heard, through muffling
suggesting a hand covering the mouthpiece, "Thanks, honey, I'll call you,"
and then, once more at full volume, "Okay, now I can focus. Are you in
town?"

"No, I'm not."

"You're not? Well, anyway, how you been, buddy?"

"Oh, I've . . . Well, the truth is, not so hot." Is this why he called? To tell
somebody how bad he felt? Is this why he'd drunk the vodka, to free up a
confession? "Not so—" To his horror, he heard his voice strain and then
crack. That wild panicky desperate feeling in the pit of his stomach had
returned. His head was reeling.

"You okay, Ez?" Isaac sounded concerned.

"I'm, no, I—" And then, to his immeasurably greater horror, a sob
escaped him, and then another, and then wave after wave. God, how mor-
tifying! He hadn't cried since he was a kid. An oddly voluptuous sensation,
not entirely unpleasant. He surrendered to it, his left hand covering his
forehead from temple to temple, a long series of wracking sobs, hot tears
flowing freely. He could hear Isaac's voice, emerging tinnily from the
receiver, which he'd dropped on the floor, asking him what was wrong.

After a few minutes, like a fire with nothing further to consume, the cry-
ing began to die down. When he could trust his voice, he said, "Jeez, Ike,
I'm sorry. I didn't call with this in mind."

"That's good to know. What *did* you have in mind?"

Ezra considered. "Nothing, really." He laughed self-consciously. "It was
an impulse call. I got drunk, and I was feeling like I've hit the wall, like
there's no escape. And I recalled the guy who *did* escape, so I took a flyer.
Guess I hoped some of the magic would rub off."

"Magic doesn't do that. But you might as well tell me what's wrong."

"Why do you think something's wrong?"

Isaac snorted his amusement. "Let's go, buddy, start talking."

"You've got the time?"

"My name's on the building, Ez."

"But I mean—"

"Look, there's no point trying to save face. You don't have any face left. I'm asking, you can't embarrass yourself further, you might as well tell all."

"This is awfully good of you."

"Yeah, I'm a prince. Now start already. You wouldn't be stalling if I charged."

So Ezra explained his situation. His career and his tenure case, money, Carol, nature being through with him. When he finally ran down, Isaac said, "When's your spring break?"

"Two days. Why?"

"Get the hell out of there."

"I can't. I'm broke. I'm in debt. My credit card was confiscated two weeks ago." At the campus bookstore, with students watching. *That* was pretty fucking humiliating.

"Yeah . . . hmmm . . ." There was a pause. "You'll just have to come visit me. I should've thought of it immediately. We'll have a ball."

Ezra was startled. "But Ike, you don't even know me anymore."

"We were best friends. Have you changed a lot?"

"Kind of bowed down by failure. I'm not as much fun as I used to be."

"You weren't that much fun before. Fun was *my* department. Anyhow, it'll be great to talk books again with someone who isn't a complete idiot on the subject."

"But you're a publisher."

"It's different from grad school. You'll see." He seemed to assume it was all arranged.

"You seem to assume it's all arranged."

"Isn't it? What more do you need to know?"

What indeed? It was an unexpected offer, but what did he have to lose by accepting? Anything had to be better than moping around the town of Seven Hills for the next week. "Your address."

"Right, right. Got a pencil?"

■   ■   ■

As L.A. neared, Ezra accelerated. I'm a fugitive slave on the underground railway, he thought, and freedom is just across the river.

"That's more like it," said the little voice.

Yeah, Ezra told the voice, okay, let's make a deal: As long as we understand it doesn't mean anything, as long as you can accept it's merely a few days' respite, a furlough, I solemnly swear that while away from Beuhler I won't dwell on my troubles, won't whine, will be only minimally sardonic, and will try to enjoy myself. And even though there's no way I can regard myself as invincible, neither will I consider myself . . . well, hopelessly vincible.

The voice shook on it.

Newly audacious, Ezra pressed his foot down on the accelerator, gritting his teeth in terrified exhilaration. And then, perhaps because his heart was beating so fast, he suddenly noticed that for the first time in weeks his chest wasn't hurting.

Part 2

Deut.

Chapter 1

His speeding ticket on the seat beside him, Ezra braked to a halt before a city-block-size, sand-colored stucco structure with a narrow stretch of unnaturally vivid green lawn and two hefty palm trees in front. NO PARKING ANY TIME warned the red letters on the white sign stuck into the curb just by his right fender. Okay, pal, no problem, just taking a sec to get my bearings. A larger sign, thrust into the lawn, announced apartments of various sizes to let at various prices, all of them astronomical, and promised in return a state-of-the-art security system ("Armed Response" was the chilling claim), an Olympic-sized heated swimming pool, and a sauna and a Jacuzzi. Clearly, Isaac was doing well for himself. Even the cheapest studio on offer cost more than Ezra's entire Beuhler salary.

Ezra reignited his trusty Tercel and set off in search of a parking space. Those damned NO PARKING ANY TIME signs seemed to be everywhere.

He finally found one—well, it was *sort of* a parking space, his rear end did jut out just a bit into a nearby driveway—perhaps half a mile away. He parked, got his two bags out of the trunk, and trudged back to Isaac's building. His body felt stiff from the long drive, his bladder uncomfortably full, but it was something of a relief to be moving after all that enforced idleness. The brilliant sunlight and the sea air were invigorating. Things looked different here, they had a crispness of outline, a sharp bright clarity. Colors were more intense, too. Indeed, so extraordinarily green were the lawns Ezra passed, he began to suspect some sort of artificial turf, and finally dropped his bags and knelt down to palpate a stretch of putative grass. And it proved real. Amazing. Apparently, the laws of physics and biology behaved differently here. No problem. Any change could only be an improvement.

When he reached Isaac's building again, he located the buzzer to his friend's apartment—among the columns of literally hundreds of names and buzzers, fortunately arranged alphabetically—and rang. And waited, whistling a snatch of Poulenc. And continued to wait. There was no response from the mouth-level intercom.

Puzzled, although refusing to allow himself to acknowledge displeasure, he tried the heavy glass door. Which opened. So much for the lethal security system. His unsanctioned entry provoked no armed response, on the whole a good thing. He held the door open with his foot, hoisted his suitcases, and stepped through.

The capacious lobby was sponge-painted pastel blue, had veined marble flooring and lots of potted fronds. Off to one side were two elevators. In front of Ezra were two open glass doors leading to the central swimming pool area, around which the entire four-sided complex was built.

I've died and gone to heaven, thought Ezra.

Still lugging his suitcases, he headed through the doors to the pool area. To his immediate right was the Jacuzzi, currently unoccupied. Around the mammoth pool directly in front of him were arrayed countless plastic yellow-and-white chaises longues, many of which *were* occupied, by men and women uniformly gorgeous, uniformly tanned, and in uniformly superb physical condition, all of them apparently in their twenties and thirties. There were a few people splashing about and schmoozing in the pool itself, and one blond Adonis in an absurdly skimpy, absurdly bulging bikini swimsuit was perched on the high diving board. Just as Ezra looked up, the man leapt into space, hung there a heart-catching second, and executed a perfect swan dive.

I've died and gone to heaven, sure, but heaven ain't my kind of town. There's been some celestial screwup. The whole spectacle before him looked like an elaborate tableau vivant advertisement for a sybaritic way of life. What's wrong with this picture? Why, *I* am.

Just then, he noticed, with a momentary coronary arrhythmia, what could only be called an apparition: Coming his way was quite simply the most beautiful woman he had ever laid eyes on, in the barest string two-piece he'd ever seen outside the pages of *Sports Illustrated,* constructed of some loosely knit tan fabric. Her skin was the color of a perfectly roasted

Thanksgiving turkey, her copious cascading hair the color of butter. Her body was at once so firmly toned and so bounteously voluptuous it seemed to belong to some other, more evolved species of primate than the people he knew; her abs alone were sufficient to force any thinking person to reconsider the eugenic advisability of passing on his own DNA. And she had a moist honeyed patina, probably consisting merely of tanning lotion and perspiration, which nevertheless lent her a radiantly lubricious aura.

Ezra stood there, frozen, literally breathless, his mouth suddenly dry, trying not to stare too obviously, hoping she would take her own sweet time about passing him by and continuing into the lobby. Simply to be in the vicinity of such a presence was an intensely erotic experience, and, frustrating as it must ultimately prove, he didn't want it to end. Ever.

She smiled. At him. Although he recognized that this was no more than an act of social charity, his life now felt complete. He succeeded in offering her a twisted rictus in return.

And then, her mouth started to move, and sounds seemed to be issuing from it. "Are you Ezra Gordon?" was what the sounds, impossibly, sounded like.

"I beg your pardon?"

She repeated the question. There could be no doubt.

"Yes. Yes I am. Ezra Gordon is my name." And being a total zhlub is my game.

"Hi. I'm Tessa. Isaac asked me to keep an eye out for you." Responding to his pop-eyed look of blank idiocy, she added, "Isaac *Schwimmer.*"

"Oh yes. Isaac *Schwimmer.*" Glad we got that straightened out. "So you know Isaac, then?" Before she could answer—and the question was so stupid she was momentarily flummoxed—he stammered, "I mean, of course you do, otherwise he wouldn't have asked you to, to keep, I mean, gosh," shrugging helplessly, cheerfully abandoning any pretense to competence, "I'm sorry, it's just, it's just you're so gorgeous, I'm not really, I can't really think too clearly."

She laughed. Even her wide brown eyes laughed, but then, still twinkling, they also suddenly seemed to be taking inventory, sizing him up. "Isaac had to go to the office," she meanwhile explained. "Some sort of emergency. Said I should let you in and tell you to make yourself at home."

"Do you, do you *live* with Isaac?" For God's sake, boy, crank your tongue up off the concrete and back into your mouth.

She laughed again. "No, no. We're just neighbors. I'm in 348, he's in 346."

That this creature was somebody's, *anybody's* neighbor, that she actually occupied ordinary living quarters next to somebody else's ordinary living quarters, seemed to Ezra a profound spiritual mystery, an eerie brush with the occult. "Oh yes, that's the girl next door, name's Aphrodite, spends weekends here when she's not visiting her folks up on Mount Olympus." And that she was *Isaac's* neighbor . . . It was suddenly clear to Ezra that he had not merely traversed several hundred miles, he had stumbled into some dislocation in the space-time continuum.

"He gave me a key," Tessa was saying in a blandly friendly tone of voice, stubbornly pretending that nothing out of the ordinary was occurring. "Come on, I'll let you in."

So saying, she lifted one of his suitcases. He tried to dissuade her, but she insisted with another laugh. And she was such a superb physical specimen there was obviously no reason, other than obsolete notions of chivalry, that she should not carry one of his bags, or indeed both, although, perhaps out of solicitude for his beleaguered manhood, she made no move to take the second. "Follow me!" she called cheerily.

Anywhere, thought Ezra. Her buttocks, totally exposed by what was laughably regarded nowadays as socially acceptable swimwear, had uncanny muscle tone. Her glutes didn't jiggle, they *rippled* as she walked. What it must be like to have those cheeks in one's hands . . . For the first time since she had entered his ambit, Ezra felt a direct sexual stirring rather than mere sexual awe. Somebody, presumably more than a few, had made love to this woman at one time or another. Had dared to commit all manner of indecencies with her. Ezra's heart was beating a Highland tattoo as he followed her into one of the two elevators.

She pressed the button marked 3, and the doors closed.

They were alone together in a small enclosed box. Ezra's heart started pounding harder.

"Why is it," she asked, breaking the oppressive silence (oppressive at least to Ezra, but then, everything about this experience was unendurably, if also deliciously, oppressive to him), "that everybody always stares at the indicator in an elevator? Ever notice that?"

"I can only answer for myself."

"Okay."

"Right now, I'm afraid to look anywhere else." He reluctantly turned his gaze from the indicator, and his eyes met hers. He fought the urge to look away.

She was grinning, flattered again. Evidently he had struck the right note. But surely a woman like this must be beyond flattery. "That's silly," she told him. "I don't wear a suit like this 'cause I'm ashamed of my body."

"I should say not."

"Although I like that you're looking me in the eye. Lots of guys, they seem to be focusing a foot or so lower, but not you."

"You have no idea the effort it's costing me."

The elevator came to a halt with a pinging noise, and the door opened. "You're funny," she observed.

Ezra shrugged self-consciously. Is funny good? Did she mean funny ha-ha, or funny ridiculous?

"Tell you what," she said, "why don't you take a good look now, you have my permission. No hard feelings. Get it out of your system."

He smiled with embarrassment.

"Go on. I'm giving you a free pass."

Under the circumstances, it would have been rude to decline. His eyes traveled down to her breasts and back again in approximately a nanosecond.

"That hardly counts," she said with a laugh. "You still have a good ogle coming."

"I'll save it for a rainy day."

"Big mistake. It's gonna be dry and sunny for months." So saying, she lifted one of his suitcases and led him out of the elevator. He followed her, able to ogle with unfettered awe now that her back was to him. They walked down the carpeted corridor, around several twists and turns, and then she stopped and announced, "Here we are."

"This is all a little overwhelming."

"Yeah, Isaac said L.A. would fuck your head."

"He did?"

She nodded. "That's my place over there," she said, pointing. "348."

"Right next door."

"That's how come we're neighbors."

"Now I think I understand."

She unlocked the door to Isaac's apartment and opened it, said the obligatory "Ta DA," and motioned for him to enter. He stepped inside, and she followed after, closing the door behind her. "So this is it. Your bedroom's down there to the left, it's got its own bathroom. TV and stereo's in here. Killer system. Home theater and everything. Liquor cabinet's over there. Kitchen's down that hall. Dope's in the cookie jar on top of the refrigerator. Isaac said you should help yourself to whatever you want. Is there anything else you need to know? How come you're not saying anything?"

Ezra found his voice: "It's a palace!" he exclaimed. The apartment was beyond anything he had imagined. Huge, beautifully decorated and furnished, with a striking collection of paintings on the walls, charming tchotchkis on shelves and other surfaces, a shiny ebony Bösendorfer grand piano, a luxuriously deep carpet, a mammoth fireplace, the place was—he didn't even reprimand himself for the cliché—fit for a king.

"Yeah, it's neat. Mine's only a one-bedroom. And he really kinda went to town with it, didn't he? Brought in a decorator and everything. Well, you know what they say: When you got it, flaunt it."

"I had no idea he had it. At least so much of it."

"I thought you two were old friends."

"When I knew him, he didn't have it yet." Ezra shook his head. "This is staggering."

"At first I figured he's gotta be a dealer. When I found out he's a publisher, I was like, that's really neat, you know? Getting rich by bringing books into the world."

Ezra nodded.

"Well, anyway, you okay here?"

"I guess."

"Anything else you need?"

"Nothing I can think of." Or that I'd dare utter out loud, anyway. Do guys still get their faces slapped at the millennium?

"Okay, here's the key. I'll be down at the pool, if you want anything."

"Great."

"Or, you know, after you freshen up and everything, you can come take a dip."

"Yeah, well, the truth is, I didn't bring a suit." He gestured self-deprecatingly, palms out. "Stupid me, right?"

Tessa pointed down the hall. "He keeps his swimsuits with his underwear in the top left-hand drawer of his dresser. I think you're about his size, only smaller. I'm sure he won't mind. So maybe I'll see you down there."

"Okay. Thanks a lot, Tessa."

He closed the door on her reluctantly, and then, on impulse, opened it a fraction and watched her walk away. Holy shit.

He shut the door and carried his bags to the guestroom. Which didn't disappoint. It was spacious, done in various soothing shades of gray, and had, in addition to a queen-size bed and a dresser, a television, a radio, and a telephone extension. The attached bathroom—which he immediately and gratefully put to use—was larger than his own living room.

He made a half-hearted stab at unpacking. But before getting very far, he decided he was hungry, and walked to the kitchen.

It was no longer a surprise to find something out of an interior design magazine, large, sunlit, black- and silver-surfaced, with clean lines, high-tech appliances, and a sizable granite-topped island in the middle. Ezra was beginning to get the range: Isaac had gone for broke.

The phone rang. Ezra was unsure whether to answer or not, and then heard Isaac's answering machine click on. The outgoing message went, simply, "Talk!" Then Ezra heard Isaac's voice: "Ezra, if you're there, pick up the damn phone."

He crossed to the phone, on a counter near the refrigerator. "Hi, Ike. This is some place you got."

"A poor thing, but mine own. Tessa make you comfortable?"

"She made me *un*comfortable."

"Good sign. Proves you're not terminal."

"Oh, I bet she's caused more than one spontaneous remission in her time."

"Did you say 'remission' or 'emission'?"

"It'd be true either way." Ezra was pleased to note they were falling back into their old rhythm. "What's up?"

"Last-minute hassle with a manuscript. Too boring to explain, but it'll take a while. So have a dip or a sauna, have a drink, watch TV, whatever. The pot's in the cookie jar."

"Tessa told me."

"Good girl. I should be finished around six. Why not meet me here, I'll give you the grand tour, and then we can get some dinner."

"Fine."

Isaac gave him directions to his office and then rang off. Ezra checked his watch. It was a little after three. His first thought was, Jeez, three long hours to kill. And then, for the third time that day, he heard that mysterious voice, saying, "Jeez, will you please stop bitching already, you've got three free whole hours to do *whatever you want.*"

And while he was processing this, it added, obnoxiously pushing its advantage, "I mean, what's your fucking problem, Bozo?"

Chapter 2

Ezra hunkered farther down, hoping the churning bubbles would hide his etiolated, unprepossessing flesh.

"Isn't this great?" said Tessa.

And it might have been, except he couldn't help feeling self-conscious, a Nibelung among all these blonde bronzed Walsungs. "Nobody cares," the little voice murmured in his ear, thereby sacrificing some credibility; around here, people obviously did care, bodies undeniably mattered. "It's very, it's very relaxing," he lied.

"Yeah." Tessa's eyes glinted mischievously. "After a hard day lounging around the pool, nothing calms your jangled nerves like a soak in the hot tub."

She reached for the bottle of chablis by her elbow and held it up, tacitly offering Ezra a refill, along with a Patron's Circle view of her extraordinary breasts. So he was getting his ogle after all. In the busy water, her skimpy knit halter had shifted position sufficiently so that he even had a brief, diaphragm-wrenching peek of lavender nipple. He held his glass out to her, and she poured, filling it so high that the wine sloshed over the rim into the hot bubbling water.

"Whoops! Now it's like poaching broth," she said.

He smiled. Was it the wine, or the Jacuzzi, or just having grown accustomed? He found he was able to look right at her without instantly becoming a moron. "And we're salmon?"

"Exactly."

He was about to say, "That must be why I feel an urge to spawn," but he didn't have the guts. Looking at her was one thing—a major accomplishment in its way—but flirting quite another, well beyond his capabilities.

"Wuss," said the little voice.

"Do you, do you have a job or anything like that?" was the pathetic alternative he came up with.

"Not exactly. I mean, I have a *career.*"

"Modeling? Acting?"

"Bingo. Both." She poured some wine into her own glass. "But I'm unemployed at the moment. As you see."

"But you, you . . . ?"

"Get work now and then?" She laughed when his silence confirmed she had guessed right. "Yeah. Commercials mostly. Some trade shows. Couple music videos. And I had a spread in *Penthouse* last February." She went right on, as if this were not a conversation- and heart-stopper, "I'd really like a real part in a movie or a series or something, but, well, everybody says that, and I'm certainly not complaining."

Wait! Wait wait wait! Rewind! *Penthouse?* A spread? What issue did you say that was? What exactly got spread? Are copies available? Gimme gimme gimme!

"Have you had acting lessons?" He managed to keep his voice remarkably steady, given the circumstances.

"Oh sure. I'm in a workshop right now. I mean, not *right* now, but . . ." She smiled toothily and then took another sip of wine. "And I was in a film last year, as a matter of fact."

"You were?"

"But I don't imagine you saw it." She gave him a wry little smile. "*Flight Attendants in Heat,* it was called."

"I missed that one."

"Caused quite a stir at Sundance," she said, and then, seeing his confused reaction, quickly added, "That was a joke. It went straight to cassette. I had a couple of lines, but it was mostly a T-and-A sorta thing."

"I'm sure you were great in it."

Her smile broadened, her pert nose twitched, and once again she had that disconcerting assessing look in her eye. "It drew on my talents, you mean?" she said, and laughed. "I guess I should say thank you. Anyway, it's a living. For the time being. Till everything starts to sag. Isaac says you're a professor."

"Uh huh. But everything's already sagging, I'm afraid."

"And a poet, he said."

"Oh, I just dabble."

"Will you tell me one of your poems?"

He took a sip of wine, trying to figure out how to get out of this one gracefully, when suddenly, another woman slid into the Jacuzzi between him and Tessa.

"Wow, it's boiling! But great! Um! So . . . who's your friend, Tess?"

Ezra put his glass down and turned to look at the new arrival. It was too late—drat!—to tell much about her body, except for her shapely neck and shoulders, but she was certainly pretty, red-haired and wide-mouthed.

"My name's Ezra."

"Lucy. Nice to meet you." She offered her hand, above water level, and Ezra shook it. "New blood is always welcome."

"Ezra's a friend of Isaac's," Tessa explained. "He's just visiting for a few days."

"Where from?"

The question was directed at Ezra, but Tessa answered: "He's a professor. At some college up north. He writes poetry."

"Really? I love poetry." This too was directed at Ezra. "I write poems myself."

Tessa frowned.

"I just dabble," Ezra repeated. Not even, anymore. The poetic impulse must have sprung from some sort of hormonal activity which nature no longer wasted on him. "All I have in common with any *real* poets is abject poverty." He retained the presence of mind to observe whether any obvious diminution of interest followed this confession. As far as he could tell, it did not. They must have already rejected the eccentric billionaire hypothesis.

"Isaac said you'd won some prize or other," Tessa said.

"Oh, oh yeah, well . . ." Jeez, what a memory Isaac had. Ezra had himself half-forgotten winning the Boyle Prize for Poetry back in graduate school. It had seemed like a pretty big deal at the time. "It was a long time ago. No big deal."

"Are you married?" Lucy asked.

Tessa laughed. "Honestly, Luce . . ."

"Just asking."

"He isn't."

Ezra turned to Tessa in surprise. She shrugged. "Isaac happened to mention it."

"Did he provide you with a beaker of my urine too?"

Both women giggled, and then Tessa explained, "He was just reminiscing. He said you guys were tight."

"Isaac's an amazing guy," observed Lucy.

"Yep," Ezra agreed. "He was kind of a legend back in Michigan."

"He's kind of a legend around here too," said Lucy, and both women laughed again. Snickered, actually. Hmmm. What could that mean? Lucy continued, "How long did you say you were here for?"

"He didn't," Tessa said. "And Luce . . . ? I was here first."

She said it lightly, and Lucy dutifully laughed, but it struck Ezra as extraordinary nevertheless. Not that he dared dream Tessa was interested. But even for mild feelings of territoriality to have been aroused . . . It was obvious that being Isaac's friend conferred some sort of legitimacy on him, and that Tessa's visible willingness to spend time with him extended the circle of presumptive legitimacy outward, so that now Lucy too regarded him as being, considered merely as someone for whose attention she might vie on a slow afternoon, not completely *infra dig*.

Well, fine. Guess who isn't going to argue.

Lucy took his wine glass from out of his hand. "You don't mind, do you?" she asked, and immediately took a healthy swig from it. And then, handing the glass back to him, she said to Tessa, "God, babe, you're really pruning up."

Tessa's answering frown possessed less humor than her previous frowns. She stole a quick glance at her wrinkly fingers en route to directing her gaze at Ezra. "Aren't you supposed to be meeting Isaac at six? 'Cause it's five-thirty."

"Gee, is it? I better get going."

"You probably better."

"Well . . . this has been terrific." He smiled at them both.

"Listen, do you know your schedule yet?" Tessa asked. "Has Isaac scheduled you every waking moment kind of thing?"

"I don't really know."

"'Cause maybe we could do something together."

"Yeah, maybe we could *all* do something," suggested Lucy.

Ezra was already climbing out of the Jacuzzi. As he reached hurriedly for his towel, he said, "That'd be nice. I'll talk to Isaac about it."

He waved good-bye, and proceeded to dry himself off as he headed back into the building. He didn't feel like lingering with so much of his body available for inspection. *He* wasn't the stuff of *Penthouse* spreads, after all.

God, that was fun, he nevertheless decided, after he'd successfully made his getaway and was walking, still dripping a little, from the elevator down the corridor to Isaac's apartment. Is this what it's like to be Leonardo DiCaprio or one of those guys, where desirable women actually compete for your attention and interest? Go out of their way to catch your eye? *Audition?* A fellow could get used to it. An all-volunteer seraglio, every boy's dream.

He took a quick shower, washing his hair with the salon-quality shampoo smelling like tropical punch that Isaac had thoughtfully provided. Then, while poking around, he also found a blow drier. Ezra didn't ordinarily use one, but his hair was wet and he was due at Isaac's office in less than fifteen minutes, so he gave it a try. Not bad. His hair, for the first time ever, had . . . what was the word? *Body.* His hair had body. "My hair has body," he told himself, "and beautiful women are fighting over me. I am da bomb."

He dressed quickly, trusting that his pitiful wardrobe and Marina Del Rey casual were more or less in accord. Khaki pants, blue denim shirt, moccasins. How wrong could this be? Especially when your hair has *body.* When your hair has body, you write the dress code.

As he emerged from the apartment building into the fine almost-gloaming, he experienced a momentary twinge of panic. I've lost my car! he decided for no good reason, I can't remember where I left it! And his new friend, the little voice, said, "Will you please look for the fucking thing first?" The little voice was making better sense now that it wasn't urging him to press his luck with women who were absurdly, stratospherically out of his league. He managed to swallow the panic rising in his throat and set off in the direction he believed he had come from earlier that day. Earlier that day, back before his life had been transformed, back before his hair had body.

The Tercel was where he'd left it. And, despite the fact that it was jutting into the nearby driveway considerably farther than he'd been willing to admit before, it was unticketed and unbooted. Of course, this observation brought to mind his speeding ticket from earlier that day, which he certainly couldn't afford to pay, but still, relief at finding the car outweighed despair at recalling the citation. Before climbing behind the wheel, he silently addressed the little voice: "Yes, I *do* trust Isaac's directions. I do *not* actively anticipate spending the rest of my life lost on the L.A. freeway system." Just to shut the thing up.

The drive to Isaac's office took under three minutes. The building was two stories tall, undistinguished, a generic commercial structure, newish, stucco and glass, close to featureless. But it gave Ezra a thrill, because, in large letters over the entrance were written the words THE ISAAC SCHWIMMER PRESS. Isaac, the dropout, had made it, and "in publishing." Pretty good. Better Isaac than one of the lifeless grinds who, like great white sharks unable to change course, unreflectively pushed forward through the doctoral seas, staying on course simply because no alternative existed for them. Like himself, to pick a great white shark at random.

Although there was a space on the street directly in front of the building, Ezra elected to use the parking lot in the rear. He wanted the complete Isaac Schwimmer Press experience. There was only one other car on the lot, a large shiny blue BMW, and Ezra pulled in beside it. It figured, for any number of reasons, to be Isaac's, but if it was, the vanity plates were a puzzlement: DB 1. Whatever could that mean?

After he got out of his car, he paused to savor the twilight. It was still warm, probably in the upper sixties, and the light was dying slowly. And there was that ineffable sense of the ocean's presence somewhere nearby.

He crossed the small parking lot to the rear door. He opened it and stepped through, and found himself at one end of a short corridor. To his left was a bathroom. To his right was a room with a Xerox machine. Farther along was an alcove with a water cooler, a small refrigerator, a coffee machine, and a microwave oven. Through a door at the far end of the corridor was the reception area, the room to which the front entrance led from the street. It had functional furniture, industrial carpeting, a window giving onto a receptionist's cubicle—empty at the moment—and a magazine rack. That was about it. The walls were bare.

"Hello?" Ezra called out. He went to the foot of the carpeted stairway. "Anybody here? Isaac?"

Isaac, beaming, suddenly materialized at the top of the short flight of stairs. "So," he said. "You made it."

Ezra, staring up at his old friend, found himself smiling broadly, and it was the best kind of smile, entirely involuntary. "Jeez, Ike, how're you doing? You look great."

Isaac had often been called handsome in the old days, but to Ezra's mind the adjective didn't really fit. Isaac was tall, about six-three, he was lean and muscular, he had thick black hair, olive skin, and large soulful brown eyes; he was an attractive man. But he wasn't exactly handsome; the word suggested to Ezra a refinement of feature that the large-nosed, thick-lipped Isaac did not possess. Nevertheless, right now, in white shirtsleeves with rolled-up cuffs, a loosened maroon-and-black figured tie, and pleated chalk-stripe trousers, he had the sheer *vividness,* handsome or not, of a movie star.

"You look just great," Ezra repeated.

Isaac laughed. "Wish I could say the same, buddy. You look like shit." He squinted. "Except for your hair."

"Yeah, I know, it's got body or something. I'm starting from the top down."

"You got a lot of ground to cover."

Ezra's smile faded.

"Hey, if I meant it, would I say it? You look fine, except you maybe could benefit from an attitude make-over. And that's why you're here, right?"

"I guess."

"And you've come to the right place."

"The Isaac Schwimmer Press?"

"I meant Southern California. But the Press ain't chopped liver either." He gestured, a kind of grand beckoning. "Come on up, I'll show you around."

Ezra, his hand on the beveled wooden banister, bounded up the steps. When he got to the top, he shook Isaac's hand warmly. "I've missed you, Ike."

"Yeah. Grown-up friendships suck, don't they?"

"I wouldn't know."

Draping an arm unselfconsciously around Ezra's shoulders (it was one of Isaac's virtues that he could do such a thing; he was so intrinsically physical a man, on such good terms with his own body, that he never had any difficulty touching or being touched), he guided his friend down the corridor. "My office is at the end of the hall here."

"You had some kind of emergency, Tessa said?"

Isaac waved a hand carelessly. "Every book's an emergency."

"You're doing well for yourself, aren't you?"

"Yup. And I'm having a ball."

He gestured for Ezra to precede him into his office. The first thing that struck Ezra's notice was how much more elegant this room was than everything else in the building.

"Wow."

"It's an old story, pal. Name on the door, Bigelow on the floor."

There was indeed fine carpeting, blue-flecked oatmeal Berber. There was also a sleek steel kidney-shaped desk with a computer and an elaborate telephone console on it and a black leather high-backed reclining chair behind it, a stereo and television unit in a corner, a gray leather sofa-and-loveseat combination facing each other with a low marble coffee table covered with magazines and books between them, and, off in another corner, one of those electronic easy chairs that give you a massage.

But what seized Ezra's attention was the art on the walls. Handsomely framed, it was a series of lurid, crudely rendered paintings of a grossly sexual nature: One portrayed a bosomy, sneering, black-haired, black-lipsticked woman in some sort of skin-tight leather jumpsuit, holding a whip in one hand and a thick, grotesquely twisting python in the other; another showed a long-haired nude woman from behind, squatting before a grimacing athletic blonde Marine with his tunic in place but his trousers around his ankles, obviously (although not quite explicitly, her shaggy head blocking the view) fellating him; a third featured two unnaturally nubile girls, one chained naked to a dungeon wall in cruciform posture, the other, in boots and hot pants, sucking on the nipple of her companion's gargantuan right breast. And there were four or five more, all along similar lines.

Ezra turned to Isaac, who was smiling expectantly. "Collect Renoirs, do you?"

Isaac laughed. "Not bad, huh? Wouldn't have them in my house, of course, but they've kind of grown on me."

"But, but what *are* they?"

"Well, that one's called 'Bondage Ho'. Over there is 'Booty Bait.' 'Dungeon of Delight.' 'Rotten to the Corps.' This one here's my favorite, it's—"

"No, I mean, what *are* they? We're not talking limited-edition seriographs."

"Oh." Isaac laughed. "I see. I thought it was obvious. They're book covers. The originals. Guy named Winkler does most of 'em for us."

"'Us?'"

"He's great, isn't he? I mean, he's lousy of course, he can't draw worth shit, but he's got that certain something. Bypasses the eye, goes straight for the groin."

"But who's 'us'?"

"Why, the Isaac Schwimmer Press. Obviously. You know, in this business, it's the cover that sells the book. We can't rely on *Publishers Weekly* or Amazon.com to give us a boost."

"'This business'?" Ezra rubbed his eyes. "Isaac, are you a pornographer?"

"Of course I am!" Isaac affirmed happily. "And business is booming! I'm king of the fucking dung-heap!"

■   ■   ■

As they emerged from Isaac's BMW at the entrance to a glass-and-weathered-wood restaurant in the Marina called, predictably, The Breakers, and Isaac reluctantly handed his car keys to a young Hispanic parking valet, he said to Ezra, "You're surprised, aren't you?"

They hadn't spoken much during the drive; Isaac's CD player, playing Lauryn Hill at full blast, with Isaac providing a falsetto descant, had seen to that. But Ezra knew what Isaac was referring to. "Well, I am, a bit. When I heard you were 'in publishing,' I . . ." He shrugged.

"Were thinking *literature*?" He pushed open a heavy oak door with a burned-in anchor emblem. "Wake up, pal. It's a new millennium. The good books have all been published."

They stepped into the restaurant's reception area. It was dark and cozy, with lots of wood and acres of earth-toned carpeting. There was a bar-room to the right, with anchors and fish-netting for decor, and in front of them the dining area proper, boasting wall-to-wall windows looking out over the water. Isaac approached the maitresse d' at her rostrum and gave his name, then turned back to Ezra. "So you disapprove?"

"Not at all. I'm a sucker for a nautical motif."

"I meant, of my chosen profession."

"Oh. Uh, I wouldn't say that."

"Your lips say no no no, but there's yes yes in your eyes."

A pretty young woman in a ruffled serving-wench uniform revealing lots of leg and considerable cleavage appeared with two menus. As they followed her, Ezra said, "Maybe it's Beuhler. You know, it's a Baptist cow college, very uptight. And then, we've had this influx of feminists lately. You've been away from university politics for a long time, you may not realize feminism's a whole area of scholarship now, an important niche market. Of course, these different types disagree about a lot of stuff, it's a volatile mix on campus these days, but they do seem to concur that pornography's bad news. So maybe some of that's rubbed off."

"You should be ashamed of yourself," Isaac said flatly. "Letting yourself get bullied like that. Never apologize for having a cock."

They took their seats at a small table by a window. Night had fallen, but the moon was almost full, reflecting in a shimmering yellow line along the undulant surface of the water, so the view wasn't wasted. And although the restaurant was still quite empty, the table adjacent to theirs was occupied by two young women. Isaac inclined his head toward them and gave Ezra a little smile whose exact meaning was obscure.

"Enjoy your dinner," said their guide, gliding away.

"So, you think your books make a positive social contribution?"

"I could make that case, in fact. But why should I? What other businessmen have to defend themselves that way? The schmucks who make video games? Arms merchants? Dow Chemical? If I wanted to make a social contribution, I'd join the Peace Corps. I'm doing this 'cause it's fun and I'm making a pot of money. You want to split some paella? It's pretty good."

A waitress, also turned out in serving-wench regalia, had appeared. "Good evening. Can I get you anything to drink?" she asked encouragingly.

"A bottle of dry sherry," Isaac said, and then turned to Ezra for his approval. "Good with paella. That authentic touch."

After they ordered, and the waitress gave them the third-degree about their salad-dressing choices and withdrew, Isaac demanded, "Now where was I?"

"The Peace Corps."

Isaac gave a twisted smile. "Right. Look, you think this business is easy? With all those videos out there? With the crap you can download right off the net? Man, I tell you, it's a fucking uphill battle, the Isaac Schwimmer Press is one of the few profitable houses left. Companies are going belly-up all around me. People don't read anymore. The NEA should give me a medal for promoting literacy. Or even a grant."

"Yeah, right."

"And I mean, I run a classy operation."

"Of course. I saw those covers."

"I'm serious. For a publisher like me, it's a buyer's market these days, so we can pick and choose, we use only the best writers. We vet the manuscripts really carefully for spelling and grammar and so on. Not that anybody cares, but *I* care. Isaac Schwimmer puts out a quality product."

"You must be very proud."

"Hey, is this 'tude?" Isaac was smiling, but Ezra noticed a moist wounded look in his eye.

"Nah. I'm happy for you, Ike. Really. And for what it's worth, I also envy the living crap out of you."

"I'm not forcing anybody to read my stuff. And you have to be eighteen to buy it. Which is bullshit in my opinion, but it's the law."

The waitress arrived with their sherry and their salads.

"So, this Carol person," Isaac said, after an interval in which they ate and drank in silence, "I'm still kinda confused. You porking her, or what?"

Ezra glanced up and encountered Isaac's friendly, concerned gaze. It was impossible to take offense when that face was staring back at you. "It's been known to happen."

"But not as a regular deal?"

"Not recently, no. Every date is a journey into uncharted waters."

Isaac shook his head. "Sounds bad, chum."

"Well, you know, I wouldn't want her to feel *obligated* or something." For some reason, he felt a need to defend Carol. Or was it himself he was defending? "She has the right to her preferences."

"Boy have they got *you* by the balls," Isaac said disgustedly. "Of course she has the right to her preferences. What's disturbing is that *her* preferences aren't the same as *yours.*"

"Sometimes they are."

"Fine. Only you don't make it sound that way. You make it sound like every once in a while she lets you satisfy your nasty urges. And that ain't my idea of a good relationship."

Ezra took a bite of salad and a sip of sherry. It was hard to explain his relationship with Carol at the moment—the restaurant had filled up and grown noisy in the last few minutes, so that they had to raise their voices to be heard—and besides, it was just about impossible to explain the situation under *any* circumstances without a serious loss of face.

"It's probably my fault too," Ezra heard himself shouting. "I don't exactly set her on fire, if you know what I mean. I'm kind of at sixes and sevens when we're in bed."

The two young women having dinner at the next table turned around to look at him. Ezra blushed and stared down at his plate, but Isaac smiled at them and nodded a hello, whereupon they quickly turned their attention back to their meals. Then he addressed Ezra: "One of those numbers is out of place in that particular setting," he said.

"Right." Ezra stared out the window and watched the glinting water lapping at the wooden piling in the moonlight. "This place is great," he said. He didn't want to discuss Carol anymore; he preferred to forget his Beuhler life altogether for the time being.

"Not bad. Food's only so-so, and the décor is pretty cheesy, but they did a great job with the ocean." He refilled Ezra's glass. "So. Anyway. What're we gonna do with you this trip? I don't want to dictate an itinerary."

"I just want to cool out, Ike. I don't really need an itinerary."

"Which I don't in any case intend to dictate."

After hesitating, Ezra said, "Tessa mentioned maybe getting together some time."

Isaac's eyebrows went up. "She did, did she? Does that interest you?"

"Scares me to death."

"Then you ought to do it."

"No, it wasn't really like that. She was including you, too. And Lucy kind of hinted she'd like to be part of it as well."

Isaac whistled. "Luce too? Luce by name, loose by nature, as we say. You work fast, buddy. Two conquests in one afternoon. No flies on you."

Ezra smiled. "Nah, I'm telling you, it wasn't like that."

Isaac leaned across the table, his face suddenly very earnest. "I want you to pay close attention, Ez. There's something I need to show you." He held up a finger to indicate he would need a moment to prepare himself, took a sip of sherry, and then turned toward the neighboring table. "Excuse me," he said, loudly enough to be audible over the general din.

Both of the women at the table swung around, surprised, to face him. "Yes?" one of them said.

"My name's Isaac Schwimmer, I'm a publisher. Dirty books, if you must know. This here's my friend Ezra, he's a professor of English literature and a very good poet. I guess you could say we're sort of an odd couple." He flashed his patented charming smile, and the two women smiled back, although, it seemed to Ezra, a little warily. "Ezra's visiting from out of town," Isaac went on. "I'm trying to show him a good time. He's been kind of depressed."

"Isaac!" Ezra hissed.

Isaac ignored him. "Would you possibly be interested in joining us for the evening? Going dancing, maybe, or I know of a really nice jazz club in town?"

The two women exchanged a look. "No, thank you," said the one who had spoken before, crisp and definite if not exactly vehement.

"Okay," said Isaac pleasantly. "It was just a thought. Enjoy your dinner."

The women still looked somewhat puzzled, but they returned to their dinners again, and Isaac turned back to the mortified Ezra. "You see?" he said.

"See *what?* They turned you down cold!"

"Of course they did. They're not crazy. The point is, that's *all* that happened. They turned me down cold. It's a pity—maybe—but is it the end of the world?"

"No, but—"

"Was it your impression they were offended?"

"Not particularly."

"There you go. And I even told them I publish dirty books, which I don't think honor strictly required."

Ezra laughed, regarding Isaac affectionately, and then asked, "Okay, so what's your point?"

"My point, my friend, is that Tessa probably *wasn't* including me in her invitation. And neither was Lucy. Which is fine. I've been included in their invitations before, *both* their invitations, and I'm delighted to see a friend of mine similarly honored. That's *one* of my points. The other is, let's say I'm wrong, let's say I've misinterpreted the situation in some way and they really want to go out on the town as one big happy mob. *It doesn't really matter.* You see? Nothing irretrievable will have been lost. No harm done, no skin off anybody's nose. That's my other point."

He sat back in his chair with every appearance of satisfaction and took a long pull of sherry. Then he noticed that Ezra was laughing. "Why are you laughing? What's so funny?"

"I was just thinking, if Carol ever saw you in action, she'd think you were the devil incarnate."

"Yeah?" After Ezra nodded, Isaac suggested, "Maybe she'd mean it admiringly."

"Uh uh. Hardly. You don't know Carol."

"That's true. But . . . now don't get offended, Ez, but, but neither do you. Not fundamentally. Ah, here comes our dinner. Looks good."

Later, after they'd eaten, when the check came, Ezra reached for his wallet, whereupon Isaac held up an admonishing hand. "Uh uh. This week, everything's on me."

"But Ike—"

"Please. This is easy for me, I'm rolling in it these days. You wouldn't believe how rich I am. Besides, I can lay you off on the Press, make everything deductible."

"How can you do that?"

"Oh, my accountant'll figure out something, that's his job. Come on, we're supposed to pay at the register."

Ezra waited by the pay phone near the bar while Isaac paid. When he finished and joined Ezra, the two women who had been at the table near theirs suddenly, as if on cue, emerged from the bar. Had they been lying in ambush?

"Listen," said one of them, "you know what you said before? About going dancing? We sorta changed our mind, if that's okay."

Isaac smiled, showing no surprise. "What do you think, Ez? Feeling charitable?"

Ezra followed Isaac's lead. "There were mitigating circumstances. You gave them a lot of data to absorb." But he was thinking, Jeez, this is a pickup. We've picked these women up. We're pickup artists. Then, to his own chagrin, he found he was also thinking, I wish they were more attractive. Not that they're *un*attractive, they just aren't . . .

"Yes," Isaac was saying, "your point is well taken."

They just aren't, well, *Tessa*. They aren't the stuff of which *Penthouse* spreads and movies called *Flight Attendants in Heat* are made.

The woman who talked, the business-suited one, introduced herself as Barbie and then her companion, who wore a white summer skirt and red chamois blouse, as Bitty.

"Barbie and Bitty," said Isaac. "Boy, that's really something."

"We're sisters," explained Barbie. "That's how come."

"Ah. Ah ha." He and Ezra exchanged a glance, and Ezra encountered a how-did-we-ever-get-into-this? expression staring back at him, which made him laugh out loud. He turned away and managed to stifle it.

They all went outside together and handed their parking tickets to two white-coated valets. While waiting for their cars, Isaac explained to Barbie which club he had in mind, and Barbie, who knew of it, expressed her enthusiastic approval. Of course. Isaac would know the current hot place to go. After a couple of minutes, the women's gray Civic was driven up, followed, moments later, by Isaac's Beamer.

As Ezra followed Barbie toward the Civic, he heard Bitty cough once, as if to locate her voice, and ask Isaac, "'DB 1?' You said your name is Isaac." She sounded vaguely accusing.

"'DB' aren't my initials. I told you, I'm a pornographer. 'DB' stands for *dirty book*." Apparently in one fluid motion, he slipped a bill into the valet's hand, slid into his seat, pulled the door shut, put the car in gear, and zoomed off into the night.

Chapter 3

Ezra had a headache. All the chrome crap in Isaac's high-tech kitchen reflected the brilliant Southern California sunlight painfully into his photophobic eyes. He sipped the cup of coffee he had brewed in Isaac's Mr. Coffee and munched, with distaste, a green apple he had found in the refrigerator, and tried to read the *Los Angeles Times* without much in the way of comprehension. Tony Blair did *what?* Gore went *where?* The Fed was trying to *which?* The words made no sense, and the effort to find some wasn't doing his headache any favors.

It was almost half-past nine and Isaac had yet to emerge from his room. Ezra didn't want to wake him. But sitting there thinking about his headache, and about last evening, and trying to read the newspaper, and trying to swallow and digest the apple, which was just about as flavorless as it was crispy, wasn't exactly time spent profitably either.

He had tried, during these meditations, to slip that bit about "last evening" into the middle of another, designedly more complicated thought, enclose it, one might almost say, build a *cordon sanitaire* around it in the form of a catalogue of woes, of which last evening itself was meant to seem merely a minor and incidental appendix, an afterthought, a trivial annoyance; but unfortunately the stratagem availed him not at all. You couldn't let last evening in through the door and hope it would just blend in with the wallpaper. Last evening was assertive, last evening aggressively proclaimed its existence, last evening made its presence known and its primacy felt. Last evening last evening last evening. Ezra groaned.

Last evening had been a glimpse of hell.

Last evening he had learned the meaning of the word *torment,* last evening he had discovered the limits of his courage and endurance, the outermost boundaries of his very manhood.

Last evening—

He heard the front door to Isaac's apartment opening. Curious, he rose, which caused a considerable twinge of pain in his cranial region, and, carrying his coffee mug, trekked down the corridor. Coming through the front door, chalk-striped jacket draped over his left shoulder, was Isaac.

"'Morning," he said cheerily.

"Ike? I thought you were still . . ." He gestured toward Isaac's bedroom.

"'Fraid not. 'Fraid I never made it home. Coffee smells good. There enough for me?"

"I think."

The two of them strode back to the kitchen together. Ezra resumed his seat at the kitchen table, and Isaac made a beeline to the Mr. Coffee machine. "Ever wonder about Mr. Coffee's first name?" he asked as he got a mug down from the shelf and filled it. "One of life's conundrums. And another thing: Has it ever occurred to you what a snooty son of a bitch he must be, still going by 'Mr. Coffee' after all these years, after everything we've been through with him? It's so fucking *elitist* it just makes my blood boil."

"I think his first name is Joe," Ezra said, but listlessly. He wasn't in the ideal frame of mind for whimsy.

"Yeah, that kind of rings a bell." Isaac put the coffee pot back in the machine and joined Ezra at the table. "Military slang, isn't it? Cuppa joe. I guess he's on more familiar terms with soldiers. Hard to take issue with that. They're out on the front line of democracy risking their lives so we can enjoy the blessings of liberty. Even a pompous ass like Mr. Coffee has to appreciate their sacrifice." He took a sip of coffee. "So." He smiled. "Last night, speaking only for myself here, last night I got screwed, blued, and tattooed. I underestimated that Bitty, big time. She is *hot*."

"That's right, you're speaking only for yourself."

Isaac's smile widened. "Nothing, huh?"

Ezra groaned.

"Now listen, buddy. I was kind of otherwise engaged last night, even at the club, I mean perhaps you noticed that Bitty kept kinda practicing her scales under the table, and the amplification system at that place was deafening and all, but I sorta couldn't help, I thought I, *did* I hear right? Did you buy $250,000 worth of term life insurance from Barbie?"

Ezra groaned again.

"Oh, Ez."

"I wasn't myself," Ezra moaned. "First she got me drunk—I mean *real* drunk, Ike, *frathouse* drunk—then she started in. It was like spending six months in the Lubyanka with a team of KGB interrogators. Had I planned for my old age, had I given sufficient thought to the financial security of my loved ones, getting in on the ground floor, waiving the physical 'cause I'm such a good risk, peace of mind, some business about the policy being convertible at maturity, and meanwhile the room is spinning like one of those miserable rides at the goddamn midway . . ." Ezra shook his head and, when Isaac laughed, looked up with only dimly amused and very bloodshot eyes. "I mean, no long-term sweat, I'm gonna stop payment on the check. But it was absolutely hideous, a glimpse into the abyss. I must have acquired some really bad karma in a former life."

"Plus you didn't get laid."

"Oh man, the last thing in the *world* I wanted was to spend any more time in her company. For all I know, she makes it a general practice to fuck all her clients after selling them a policy. Sort of like giving them a calendar, only with that personal touch. She probably quotes actuarial figures when she comes. But I had two, no, three things on my mind, and they were *urgent*: I wanted to get away from the sound of her voice, that's one; I wanted to be somewhere I could throw up without attracting any attention, that's two; and I wanted to get to bed. Alone."

"She wasn't bad looking, I didn't think."

"I'd rather do it with Phyllis Schlafly. With all the lights on. And no sheets."

"You didn't drive home, did you? Please tell me you didn't. Lie if you have to."

"Uh uh, my car's still in the Isaac Schwimmer parking lot. She dropped me off here. It was dangerous enough I had to navigate the elevator."

Isaac frowned thoughtfully. "I hope her feelings weren't hurt. That you didn't ask her in, I mean."

"*Her* feelings? Who cares about *her* feelings?"

"She's a fellow human being, Ez."

"She made my night a journey through Dante's Inferno! *She sold me*

$250,000 of life insurance under duress! I don't even have a beneficiary, for God's sake!"

"Yeah, that's pretty bad all right. Maybe we can have her indicted in The Hague. So how are you feeling now?"

"Terrible! I haven't had a hangover like this since college." Ezra pressed his fingertips against his forehead. "What pathological moron invented Long Island iced tea?"

"That's what you were drinking?" Isaac sounded both awed and scornful.

"Several. She did the ordering."

"It's a miracle you lived to tell the tale."

"Only hate keeps me alive. I owe it to posterity. To bear witness."

Isaac snickered, and then said, "Well, please don't think me callous, but *I* feel *great*. Like my dick's been to the car wash. And you wanna hear the funny part? Back at the restaurant, I was hoping I'd end up with Barbie. I thought *she* was the one who showed promise. What an eye, huh? I guess the joke's on me."

"No, Ike, I don't think so. I don't think the joke's on you."

Isaac regarded his friend with amused sympathy. "You're a real hard-luck case, you know that?"

"Thanks for pointing it out."

"But it's true, isn't it?"

Ezra shrugged. "Things keep happening to me."

"There's your problem in a nutshell."

Ezra looked up alertly, sniffing significance. "What are you driving at?"

"'Things keep happening to me.' You're a lit scholar. Deconstruct that sentence." Then, before Ezra could respond, Isaac said, "You maybe want a virgin mary or something?"

Ezra groaned.

"They say it does the trick," Isaac urged.

"They say all sorts of things that aren't true. They say it's fun to leap head-first off a bridge with a rubber cord around your waist." He shook his head. "The only thing that does the trick is *time*. I'll feel better eventually. In about, about a hundred years or so."

"You might consider taking a sauna. Sweat out the poison."

"It's too hot."

"It must be rough, things keeping happening to you and all. Listen, you're probably not going to like this, but I'm *famished*. I burned up a hell of a lot of calories last night, and what I ate, although it certainly hit the spot, wasn't what you'd call *nutritious*. I'm going to make myself an omelet, maybe some bacon, some toast. I don't suppose that appeals?"

Ezra grimaced. "I'll be in the living room with the *Times*."

"Leave the Book Review section, okay?"

Isaac was already squatting in front of the pantry, clangorously assembling a variety of pots and pans. Ezra grabbed several sections of the Sunday paper and exited into the living room.

Over the next hour and a half or so, as he read the paper, listened to a Bruckner symphony on the radio, drank his way through several cups of coffee, his hangover began imperceptibly to recede, until at last all that remained was a dully throbbing but manageable headache and a slightly sour stomach. Given how he'd felt, it was a miracle worthy of a trip to Lourdes.

Finally Isaac appeared in the archway dividing the living room from the main hallway. He had showered, shaved, and put on jeans and a tight yellow sweater. He was barefoot. Ezra was struck again by how attractive Isaac was, how big and athletic and loose-limbed.

"Well," Isaac announced grandly, "I'm pleased to report that my kishkes and I are on the best of terms. This is gonna be a great day!"

"You sound like one of those commercials."

"What can I say? The kishkes are a window into the soul. And today I know my soul is pure. My Redeemer liveth." He stepped farther into the room, then stopped and wrinkled his nose. "Bruckner? Fucking Bruckner?"

"It's the radio."

"Bruckner? The idiot who never made it to savant?" He ambled over to the sofa and plopped down, lying supine, his head against one armrest and his bare feet on the other. "You feeling any better?"

"I am, a bit."

"Glad to hear it. Dee-*light*ed to hear it." He locked his hands behind his head, and then, after studying the ceiling's bare beams for a few seconds, swiveled his head to the right so that he was looking directly at Ezra. "I have a proposition for you."

"I'm all ears."

"Write me a dirty book."

"Huh?"

"I lost a writer last week. One of my best. He finally sold his screenplay. I never thought it would happen, the fucking thing's been kicking around for it seems like decades, but, well, go know. Made 400 K, got a handsome back-end, which is movie talk by the way, I'm not referring to his tush, which frankly I don't go in for that sort of thing. So anyway, suddenly he's too important, he's too classy to write for old Isaac and his press. So I've been on the lookout for a replacement. It just hit me this morning, while I, while I was—"

"Jeez, I don't think so, Ike."

"It's not a bad deal. Ten thou, five on commencement, five on delivery. That's the standard fee, which I'll pay you, even though first-timers usually get seven-five. It won't make you rich, but it'll wipe out your debts and leave you some change. Lots of writers grind out a book in less than a month. Approximately 65,000 words. I don't pay royalties, but let's face it, we're not talking *Great Expectations* here, we're talking low expectations, a dumb-ass d.b."

Ezra shook his head. "Not really up my alley. I appreciate the offer, but, I mean . . . "

Isaac held up a hand, like a traffic cop signaling a car to halt, even though Ezra had already run out of steam on his own. "Just think about it while you're here. You don't have to answer me now."

"Shit, Ike, I've been stuck on the same *sonnet* for the past two months. Eight lines and I'm stumped. How the hell am I gonna come up with 65,000 words?"

"They don't have to rhyme."

"They just have to be spelled correctly?"

"There's maybe a little more to it than that. A lot of them should refer to body parts, for example." He stared at his friend. "It might help you out of your jam. *Some* of your jams, anyway."

"It's generous of you, Ike. But—"

"Say no more. I won't mention it again. The offer's out there, it's up to you. So. What's on your itinerary for today?"

"No itinerary, Ike."

An hour later, they were at Zuma Beach, lying on adjacent Teletubby beach towels. Isaac, like a concerned mother, had insisted that Ezra coat himself with sunblock, and now Ezra was discovering that the oily cream, melting into his perspiration, felt surprisingly pleasant. *Everything* felt pleasant; his hangover seemed to be oozing from his pores in the intense sunshine. The breeze off the sea was balmy and clean. Off to his right, a group of adolescents were playing volleyball.

"They could charge admission to this," Ezra said to Isaac.

Isaac lowered his sunglasses with his index finger and studied the game for a few moments. "Life is beautiful," he finally declared. "A fucking garden of earthly delights."

"So you don't think nature is through with ya?"

Isaac snorted. "Nature, my friend, has barely begun with me."

Ezra sighed, with a curious combination of contentment and longing. Without taking his eyes from the game, he asked, "You ever think about settling down?"

"As in, get married? Sure. Eventually. And in the meantime, I plan to fuck my brains out. Life requires these compromises of us, so we might as well be good sports about it."

Ezra sat up, took a handful of sand, and let it slowly dribble out of his fist back onto the beach. "I don't think I'm the fuck-my-brains-out type."

"You're really going out on a limb there."

"I mean, it sounds like fun in theory, but . . ." A new thought occurred to him: "Don't you worry about, about . . . ?"

"The virus?" Isaac finally took his eyes off the volleyball game. "Uh uh. It's like sunblock. You take precautions."

"Right."

"The precautions come in colors now and everything."

"I actually already knew that, Ike." He hugged his knees, staring out at the Pacific. "Even though my experience *is* fairly limited. Another reason I'm the wrong person to write one of your books. I'd have to make everything up. I'd probably get it all wrong."

"You could do a little research. You wanna go in the water? Get your feet wet, as the old expression goes?"

"Everything you say sounds symbolic."

Isaac laughed as he got to his feet. "The awful vestiges of grad school. Some day I hope to be free of them entirely."

"You've come a long way, believe me."

They walked together down to the surf. The sand soon changed from hot, dry, and granular, difficult to walk on, to moist and spongy; and then, a little farther on, the tide washed over their feet. The first contact with the water was so cold it literally set Ezra's teeth on edge, and revived, for a brief painful moment, his headache.

"Christ! It's freezing!"

"Nah, the Pacific's a warm ocean."

"Yeah? Tell my feet."

"It's fine once you get used to it."

"But why bother?"

"You're hopeless," Isaac said, and went bounding into the surf, screaming something resembling the comic book noise "Arrggh!" at the top of his lungs as he did so. Ezra watched with a rueful smile as Isaac, once the water was up to his thighs, dived in head-first, disappeared for a few seconds, and then reemerged a substantial distance out, treading water, buoyed up and down by the gentle waves, spitting and spluttering, his bushy hair now flat against his head. "It's glorious!" he shouted.

"I'll take your word for it," Ezra shouted back. He had waded in up to his shins. He reached down, cupped a little water in his hand, and sprinkled it over the back of his neck. Ghastly!

Isaac swam back toward shore, doing an easy breast stroke, keeping his head above water, riding the bosomy crest of a wave, which deposited him, conveniently, right at Ezra's feet. "You don't know what you're missing," he exulted as he rose to a standing position.

"That's true," conceded Ezra. "I've also never experienced the thrill of combat. Or childbirth—hey, wait a minute!"

Isaac had grabbed him about the waist. Isaac's skin was cold and wet and . . . and disconcertingly *skinlike,* and he was also immensely strong, much stronger than Ezra. Ezra resisted as much as he could, but Isaac was determined, Isaac continued to pull and wrestle him into the water.

"It's for your own good," Isaac grunted.

"Fuck you!" Ezra rejoined, unamused.

Ezra soon lost his balance and tumbled backwards into the water, which was in any case already above his waist, had already sent that first startling electric shock through his gonads. Because he fell backwards, seawater filled his nose as he went under. In the struggle, Isaac also lost his balance, and toppled over on top of him. It took a few moments under the water for them to get their limbs disentangled. Ezra fought his way back to the surface, and rose to a standing position, coughing and snorting and gasping for breath. Isaac was facing him, a broad grin on his face.

"I hated to do it, pal."

"That wasn't funny."

"You're angry?" Isaac was nonplused.

"Of course I'm angry!"

"Jeez . . ." Isaac bit his lower lip, surprised, perplexed, and contrite, and then said, "I thought you'd thank me." After hesitating, he asked, "Well, how do you feel otherwise?"

Ezra glowered. Both men were breathing hard from the recent exertion. A long, tense silence ensued, during which Isaac stared down at the murky green water, then looked up again. To find Ezra's face lit up with a great sunny smile of discovery. "I feel fabulous! Absolutely fabulous!"

Before Isaac could respond to this proclamation, Ezra was already plunging back into the roiling surf. "It *is* great once you get used to it! Just like they say! Come on! Surf's up!"

Laughing, Isaac scampered after him, battling against the incoming waves. "Hey, wait up, Ez!"

"Time and tide wait for no man!" Ezra shouted. "Carpe diem, Ike, that's the ticket!"

"Just call her, for God's sake! What are you afraid of?"

"That she'll answer."

"Look at it this way: After last night, no matter what happens, you're insured."

Ezra removed his right flip-flop and flung it at Isaac, who was laughing too hard to duck. It hit him on the side of the head.

"Nice," said Isaac. "A charming way to express your gratitude, after all I've done."

"Last night is out of bounds. Forever more. Capisce?"

"Hey, whatever you say."

"Anyway, I'm sunburnt. I'm in no condition for activity that entails physical contact."

"I told you, I *warned* you, put on more sunblock."

"I freely admit it, I have no one to blame but myself."

They were still in bathing suits and tee shirts, having returned from the beach only a few minutes before, and were in the kitchen drinking a couple of beers. Ezra's sunburn looked worse—or was it better?—than it felt; his skin gleamed bright red, he had what used, before dermatologists poured cold water on the notion, to be regarded as a *healthy glow,* but it wasn't very sensitive. He was leaning, one flip-flop off and one flip-flop on, diddle-diddle-dumpling, against the granite counter. Next to the telephone, whose receiver still nestled securely in its cradle. Isaac sat at the kitchen table, watching him with amused impatience.

"What are you afraid of?" he repeated. "For real."

"For real? That I'll make a fool of myself."

"That's so stupid."

"See? I've already done it."

"Pretty lame, Ez."

"Seriously, what if my attentions are unwelcome?"

"She'll say no."

"But what if she says yes 'cause I seem like an okay guy and she wants to be nice to a friend of yours, but my, my *ultimate* attentions, my *dishonorable* intentions, are unwelcome?"

"Then you won't get laid. I gather you've had some practice at that."

Ezra produced a moue at this thrust before beginning to protest, "But she'll—" only to be interrupted by:

"She won't be shocked, she won't think less of you. Besides, before any of that can happen, she'll be sending signals. Women do. It's a survival skill, developed over millions of years of evolution. If you pay attention, you'll be able to tell whether she's receptive or not. If she isn't, fine, let it slide. No harm, no shame."

"I'm not so hot at reading signals. Not unless it's something obvious, some monkey kind of deal, where her ass swells and turns purple."

"Uh, no, that isn't exactly what you'll be looking for. It's a *bit* subtler than that."

"Yeah, see, that's what I was afraid of. I'm a beginner at all this, remember."

"If you're your usual gentlemanly self, she'll consider you a fucking prince whether you make a move or not. You don't have a *clue* what a woman like Tessa has to put up with in this town. It's inhuman." He shook his head. "Men are such pigs."

"Including you?"

"There are gradations." His tone changed: "Now. This is a direct order, coming from the guy who introduced you, kicking and screaming I might add, to the joys of body-surfing: Make the damned call!"

Ezra obediently lifted the receiver, punched the first five digits, and then abruptly hung up again. "Can't we make it a double date? Get you and Lucy in on this?"

"No, Ez. That is, we *could*, but in the words of Richard Nixon, 'that would be wrong.' You've got to face this thing like a man."

"That's precisely what I'm afraid of."

"You'll have a great time. Word of honor. Tessa's got a great set of Kegels."

Ezra looked puzzled. "Kegels? Is that like . . . I mean, what're Kegels?"

Isaac eyed Ezra fondly. "You've got so much to learn, buddy! Why, you're embarking on a voyage of discovery! Oh, brave new world! Your life'll never be the same!"

This had the opposite effect from what Isaac intended. Ezra put the receiver, which he had been holding in his hand, decisively down, and crossed back to the kitchen table. "Forget it. This ain't gonna happen. I'm not like you, Ike."

"They should put that on a campaign button," Isaac put in.

But Ezra had a full head of steam, and kept going: "I admire what you are. I envy what you are. But I can't *be* what you are. And I can't just imitate you, it wouldn't work. You, you have, there's a kind of vitality . . ." He sat down across from Isaac, and regarded him with a shrug and a forlorn smile.

Isaac didn't smile back. "At Bollocks College or whatever it's called, do they ever condescend to consult the Old Testament? Or is that too Jewish for 'em?"

"What are you getting at?"

"The Bible, buddy. Deuteronomy. 'I have set before you life and death. Therefore choose life.' Man, it's all there. That's the whole story, that's all anybody needs to know. It may be messy, it may be unruly, it may confound all our notions and intentions. None of that matters. It's the only game in town. Like the bearded guy says, the other choice is death. Therefore choose *life*."

"Yeah. Fine. I understand. Only, the thing is, *you* didn't, Ike, you didn't *choose* life. You, you, it's different, what happened is, life chose *you*. Life *bestowed* itself on you."

Isaac, for the first time Ezra could remember, looked embarrassed, seriously, painfully embarrassed. Ezra immediately regretted having said it, regretted pointing out something so salient about him, so fundamental it simply didn't bear saying. So he hastily added, to cover, "Anyway, it's a hell of a thing when a fucking pornographer quotes the Bible at you. I mean, if they ever heard about this at Beuhler, they'd hop into their pickups and come after you."

Isaac's answering smile looked a little wan, but he said, "With shotguns and burning crosses?"

"With cowshit, of which Beuhler possesses copious quantities. Beuhler has pretty much cornered the market." Ezra drained his beer. "Anyhow, forget Deuteronomy, *I'm* gonna set before you the sauna and the Jacuzzi. Therefore choose the sauna."

Isaac shook his head. "Nah, I've done enough sweating lately. I'm referring to last night, incidentally, not the beach today. But if you think your skin can stand it, be my guest."

"Maybe I will. I'm feeling kind of hedonistic."

"That'll be the day. But go on, spoil yourself. I'll whip up some margaritas for when you get back."

"Perfect."

"The sauna's on the top floor. I don't know why they didn't put it down with the pool and the Jacuzzi, but they had some reason. Probably something to do with hygiene, that's a big deal in singles complexes these days. Take care of the cold germs and the chlamydia will take care of itself must be the philosophy. When you get off the elevator, make a left, go to the end of the hall. The door's marked. There's a shower there too. To wash off, after."

"Splendid."

"Don't overdo it. It's dehydrating."

"I swear, Isaac, with you as a friend, I don't feel deprived about not having a Jewish mother. You out-yenta the best of 'em."

Isaac smiled crookedly, and Ezra rose from the table, put on the flip-flop that was on the floor, clopped back to the guest bedroom to grab his robe and towel, and left.

He took the elevator to the top floor, which was the thirteenth, but, in deference to superstition, marked fourteen, and stepped out. He turned left, followed the hallway around several corners, and finally came to a dead end, with a doorway marked SAUNA. He opened the door and stepped through, finding himself in a tiled shower room. At the far end of this room was another door. Since there was still sand between his toes and in various intimate places within his bathing suit, he decided to shower before using the sauna. He hung his towel and his robe on a hook on the door, stepped out of his flip-flops, peeled off his bathing suit, and turned on the water. It was tepid, which was ideal, exactly what his angry skin wanted. He rinsed off his flip-flops and his bathing suit and flung them into a corner, then washed himself quickly, paying special attention to his toes, which still felt scratchy from the adherent sand.

Satisfied, he opened the door to the sauna room and stepped in. The heat almost knocked him backwards. He could feel it on his sunburn, he could feel it in his lungs when he inhaled. But, he decided after a few seconds, it was okay, even pleasant. He took a couple of gingerly steps over the slatted wooden floorboards and seated himself on one of the wooden benches, which were arranged in tiers against one wall. The boards were hot against his bare buttocks, but tolerable. After a few moments, he lay back on the bench, closed his eyes, and let himself drift. In seconds, he was coated in sweat, a uniform sheen over his entire body. And all his muscles seemed to relax, to *unclench*. Those Swedes, their celebrated suicide rate notwithstanding, were on to something. This was terrific.

Then he heard the door to the sauna room open. He was too relaxed to feel *alarmed* precisely, but he was startled enough to raise himself up on one elbow and open his eyes. Standing in the doorway, regarding him with a quizzical smile, was Tessa. She was wearing a floral-print Lycra two-piece, almost as skimpy as the knit she had worn the day before.

"Oh," she said. "Hello there."

She stepped fully into the room, letting the door shut behind her.

He felt a hot rush of embarrassment, and briefly wondered whether covering his genitals with his hand would be worse than leaving them exposed and distended in the heat. He compromised by raising his right knee slightly, which accomplished precisely nothing other than urging them an inch or two to the left.

She said, "I see you don't believe in signs."

At first he thought she was referring, in stereotypical Southern California fashion, to some obscure occult message she had picked up from the ether and assumed everyone else had received too, but then she pointed to an actual physical sign posted on the wall which he had failed to notice until now: BATHING SUITS TO BE WORN IN THE SAUNA AT ALL TIMES, it insisted, in large red block letters.

He was mortified, he was appalled. Even with his angry sunburn, even in the raging heat of the sauna, he felt himself blush, felt himself grow even hotter, felt the blood rush to his face and a new wave of perspiration instantaneously ooze from his armpits. "I, I didn't see it," he explained lamely. He rubbed the sweaty back of his hand over his sopping forehead; sweat had begun to dribble stingingly into his eyes.

"Stupid, isn't it?" she said brightly. "I mean, a swimsuit in the sauna's like, like, like what's the point, right?" Upon which, she unhooked her halter and dropped it on the floor, a moment of awe and wonder. "There, that's much better."

It was like confronting some hitherto unimagined incarnation of perfection, it was like encountering the Platonic ideal, the phenomenological absolute, of breastness. Ezra's mouth fell idiotically open, but she didn't notice. She was occupied stepping out of her bikini bottoms, saying, "If you're in a sauna, the last thing you want is to sweat into your clothes. You want to wear the *heat*." She tossed the shorts on top of the halter. "God, this feels great." She stretched, going briefly on point, spreading her arms akimbo. Her breasts moved; contrary to the skeptical promptings of common sense, they were as nature had sculpted them, not the product of a cosmetic surgeon's artistry. Ezra managed to force his jaw shut, but he couldn't take his eyes off her, even though he knew he shouldn't stare. This is a *Penthouse* spread, I've *got* to stare. I'm in a sauna and there's a *Penthouse* spread not ten feet away from me. In three dimensions, *four* dimensions if you count personality as a dimension, and without any folds or creases God didn't intend.

She smiled at him. It can be dangerous to interpret smiles, but Ezra thought this smile, unlike its predecessor, was deliberately provocative. He immediately chastised himself for harboring such a notion. But then he noticed with a tremor of terror—was it terror? It was definitely a tremor— that she was staring at him as frankly as he was staring at her. Her smile faded, her lips parted slightly. His heart began to pound. The steamy air was suddenly thick with possibility.

"You're not looking me in the eye anymore," she said, her voice husky and insinuating.

He couldn't find his own voice, nor think of an answer. Which was perhaps just as well, since an apology was struggling to find articulate expression in his roiling, static-filled brain. He was pretty sure that would have struck the wrong note.

"Anyway," she went on, "I guess I owed you an ogle, didn't I? We had a bargain. Is it okay if *I* stare too?"

"I suppose," he said. "Sauce for the goose . . ."

"Exactly. I want a gander." She took a step toward him. "Impressive."

Startled, he looked down at his penis, lying fat and heavy along his thigh, and coughed, in order to pinpoint for himself the exact location of his larynx. "Must be the heat," he explained. "I'm about average, if high school gym class is a reliable gauge."

Her eyes went bright with amusement. "There aren't many guys who would argue the point," she said.

Before he could devise an answer, she rapidly crossed the tiled floor to where he was lying, squatted beside him, and sucked him into her mouth. Instead of a bantering rejoinder, all he managed was a groan of surprised pleasure. The same blood that had filled his cheeks with shame a few moments ago flooded his erectile tissue. His heart continued to pound violently, but the tremors he felt had nothing to do with terror.

A minute later she came up for air, and said, "Still impressive," with a sweet smile.

"You're seeing it at a flattering angle."

"Some guys just can't take a compliment."

"Right now," he said, sincerely, "your being here is all the compliment I want or need."

"Well, you know what they say: The proof is in the pudding."

He laughed. "When did you get so clever?"

"Sexual excitement does that to me."

"It makes *me* stupid."

"Yeah, well . . . guys and gals are different that way."

"You are *so* beautiful." He sat up, put his hands under her armpits, and pulled her up onto the bench beside him. "You're, you're, you're so exquisite, I just want to *drown* in you." He began to touch her. "Never in my wildest dreams. Did I ever think. I would be with someone so beautiful."

"Notice how I'm not arguing? Let that be a lesson."

"You're a feast."

"And big portions, too."

He snorted his amusement as he knelt down on the wooden floorboards and began to lick the sweat from her skin. I don't want this ever to end, he thought. "I don't want this ever to end," he murmured.

Now it was her turn to moan, and it was a relief, much as he enjoyed her playfulness, for her to surrender to pleasure under his ministrations. As he slid his left hand under her right buttock—it was everything he had dared imagine, all pliable yielding muscle—and separated her legs with his other hand, and pressed his mouth against the smooth firm sweat-bathed skin of her inner thigh, she sighed, "I've never done it with a poet before."

He paused, and looked up at her. And elected not to discuss his poetic limitations. He was learning. "Is it different?"

"You make me feel . . . what's the word? I feel *savored*. Like nothing is escaping you."

"Listen—what I'm feeling now—if I could get it on paper—if I could capture this, this, this absolute *distillate* of joy, I'd be the greatest fucking poet there is."

"And vice versa."

She just couldn't help herself, he guessed.

"Kiss me," she said. "I want you to kiss me."

"That's what I am doing."

"No. Up here."

He crawled—slid—up her sweat-slick body, pressed every part of himself against every part of her, and kissed her. It was vertiginous, as if his whole being, his soul, his lost soul, had somehow been compressed and encompassed within his mouth. He moved against her importuningly, and she whispered, "Do you, do you have a, a *thing?*"

An unpoetic injection of millennial reality. "No. No. All I expected was a sauna."

She nodded, and opened her eyes. The two of them remained locked together in each other's arms, frozen, motionless, suspended, for several long seconds. "I have some in my apartment," she said. Then she sighed and said, "Oh well . . ."

"I know I'm all right," he breathed. "Honest. It's pathetic how certain I am."

"Yes, I trust you." Kissing him again, she raised her knees, shimmied her hips downward on the bench so that the small of her back became her center of gravity, wrapped her legs around his waist, and pulled him inside her.

Chapter 5

"I'm sorry about the margaritas, Ike. Kind of left you in the lurch, didn't I?"

"No problem. Lucy came by and helped me drink them."

It was a little after 7 A.M., and they were running side by side through the almost deserted palm-lined streets of Marina Del Rey. Ezra was in nearly good enough shape almost to keep up, and Isaac, considerately, was holding himself back. This is a real male bonding experience, Ezra thought. We're bonding this very minute, even while running side by side. I'm panting, yes, but I'm bonding too. I can bond and pant at the same time.

"Were the margaritas *all* Lucy helped you with?"

"No," said Isaac, "she also lent a hand with my prostate."

A surprised bark of laughter escaped Ezra. Isaac elevated indelicacy to the status of performance art.

"And except that she kept asking about *you*," Isaac went on, "we had a fine time."

Ezra was startled. "Are you making this up?"

"You made quite an impression, pal. And when I happened to mention where you were—in response to an inquiry from her, I hasten to add—well, that seemed to add to your luster."

"Yes, *that* I can believe. Tessa's like the sun, she exalts whatever she elects to shine upon."

"That a poem you're working on?

"Hardly."

"Good. 'Cause it stinks."

Ezra looked over toward his smiling friend and felt a renewed rush of affection for him. More than affection. Something closer to love. Isaac had such abundance about him, such abundance of energy, appetite, spirit, life, that he doubtless could afford to be profligate with it. But that didn't make his emotional generosity any less noble, didn't detract from his boisterous eagerness to share the bounty of his own expansive temperament. Ezra had always liked Isaac, would certainly have called him his closest friend back in graduate school; but over these last few days, he had come to realize that their friendship had not merely survived a long hiatus, it had achieved something new. Solely as a result of his finally recognizing what a large, what a *magisterial* soul Isaac—Isaac the unrepentant pornographer—possessed.

"You're a good friend, Isaac. Don't think it's escaped my notice."

"Can you manage another mile or so?"

Isaac didn't like having his attention drawn to his own attributes; perhaps like the centipede unable to walk after being asked in what order it moved its legs, Isaac feared for his best qualities if he was forced to confront them.

"Maybe. Just."

"You're doing pretty good there. Exceeding my expectations."

"I run in Seven Hills," Ezra said. "Couple times a week."

"Even if you do daily marathons, I'm still amazed you've got reserves left. You know, after last night." It was, by Isaac's standards, a discreet, an oblique query, and its intended delicacy made Ezra laugh again.

"Oh, the bill'll come due eventually. But right now, I never felt better."

"Had a good time?"

"The best. She's fabulous, Ike. I mean, not just, you know—"

"I certainly do."

"'Cause she's also really quite an interesting woman."

"Yep."

"Terrific sense of humor."

"Absolutely."

"And sweet."

"Not a malicious bone in her delicious body."

"And I'm pretty sure I figured out what the Kegels are."

It was Isaac's turn to laugh. "Those miraculous Kegels. Among Aquinas's ten proofs of the existence of God." Then he asked, "Get any sleep?"

"Not much." He looked over at Isaac again, torn between an adolescent male urge to brag and an adult fastidiousness. He finally compromised:

"Set a record, actually. Not *Guinness Book* or anything, but a, you know, a personal best. I even think *she* might have been impressed. You know, what with my being a geeky prof and all."

"She doesn't think of you as a geeky prof, she thinks of you as a sensitive poet. But I'm sure she was impressed regardless. Sensitive poets aren't expected to come eighteen times a night either. They come once, prematurely, and then they write a sappy ode about it."

"It was somewhere between one and eighteen."

"I don't really need this information. Closer to one or eighteen?"

Ezra smiled.

"So where'd you leave things?" Isaac looked away. Evidently, this was the question he'd been leading up to.

"With Tessa?"

"No, Ezra, with Bitty and Barbie. Of course with Tessa, numbskull."

"That's an odd question."

"And also none of my business. So. Where'd you leave things?"

Ezra considered. "Well, I was tempted to pledge my eternal troth, but somehow I doubt I can lure her up to Seven Hills to be the consort of a junior professor with a dubious promotion case who brings in twenty-five thou a year at an agricultural college run by Baptists."

Uttering this sentence while running almost brought him to his knees. Which had its good side: He was too busy gasping for air to continue talking, and the interval gave him time to reconsider what he was about to tell Isaac next. The truth was, some hint of just this issue, this where-are-we-leaving-things issue, had seemed to come up between them in Tessa's bedroom last night, or was that simply Ezra's naive benighted misinterpretation? In any event, now didn't seem like a propitious time to share his no doubt ludicrous suspicions with Isaac.

For Tessa had murmured, as she nuzzled against him in the impenetrable blackness sometime between their fifth and sixth bouts (the fifth was the final one to go the distance, the sixth resulting in a TKO), "Tell me about the San Joaquin Valley. What's it like? Beautiful?"

"Awful."

He felt her hair brush against his cheek as she shook her head. "Uh uh, L.A.'s awful. Any place else on earth is an improvement. You can't imagine how they treat you here. How they treat *me*. I've been trying to get away for years."

"What's stopped you?" He leaned forward and flicked the summer-weight blanket down toward their feet, leaving only the cotton sheet covering them. They had generated a lot of heat over the last few hours.

"Look at me, Ezra. I mean, I know you can't actually see me right now, but—"

"It's okay. I remember. Vividly. And my hands are keeping the memory fresh."

"Um, I've noticed. See, a girl like me . . . Girls like me don't *leave* L.A., they leave other places *for* L.A. And they can make a good living here. Too good to turn their backs on."

"So you could do worse, right?"

"Not really," she responded, her voice bleak. "Not a whole lot worse. A good living isn't the same thing as a good life. But you get spoiled here. In all the bad senses of the word." And then, a little more brightly, "I bet where you are is nice and bucolic."

"You're half-right."

"Not nice?"

"Very not nice."

"You think I'd find it dull?"

"I doubt you'd find it at all."

"You could draw me a map."

That's when the possibility occurred to him. Unsure what to make of it or what to do about it or whether to trust it, he said, "Let me give you directions to *this* local point of interest instead," guiding her hand downward. It's rare for sex to get you *out* of a tight spot.

"Oh my God," she giggled.

"We'll write to Mr. Ripley tomorrow."

"You're amazing."

"The credit's all yours. This is unprecedented."

"Then it'd be a shame to waste it." Which put an end to any further discussion for some time.

But was it possible she'd really been angling for an invitation to Seven Hills? It hardly seemed likely, and the thought of her laying eyes on, let alone occupying, his apartment (if the apartment would even *be* his after next month) was too horrible to contemplate. But could such a thing have been on her mind? Nah, he decided now, not a chance. He felt like a jerk for even entertaining the notion that she might have entertained the notion.

"I just don't want to see you get hurt," Isaac was saying. "What went on between you two last night might have a different significance down here from up in cow country." It was almost as if he had been reading Ezra's thoughts.

"Different as in . . . none whatsoever?"

"I'm just saying it's possible."

"Yeah, I know. And don't fret, there isn't time for anything drastic to happen. I mean, sure, I can see myself falling in love with her a little before I leave tomorrow, but not enough to abandon everything I hold dear, head south, and start to languish in one small Mexican village after another where I'd be known as the gringo loco and never shave and shack up with a succession of señoritas who try to soothe my wounded soul but know they can never possess me completely, I'll stay a while and eat their tortillas and their frijoles and then move on, and I'll end up drinking myself to death on cheap tequila, bought with pesos cadged from American tourists horrified to see a compatriot reduced to such a pitiful state, and the last words on my lips as my liver goes belly-up are a terrible hoarse rasping, 'Tessa, my dearest darling, your Kegels are with me still.' Is that the sort of thing you're getting at?"

"Close."

"If I was staying an extra day there might be a problem, but I'm getting out in time."

"Ready to turn back?"

"If you insist." All the muscles in Ezra's legs had apparently taken a vote and unanimously decided to do some serious aching. As they turned around and ran back toward the apartment complex, Ezra said, "Don't get me wrong, I don't mean to minimize the Kegel side of things, but there's lots more to the woman than . . . you know, *that*."

"Hey, you don't have to tell me, I'm half in love with her myself. She's a doll."

"What's the state of play between you two, anyway?"

Which won him a sidelong glance from Isaac. "Tess and me? We're like brother and sister nowadays. Only I still harbor incestuous feelings."

Sex *wasn't* the only thing that had passed between them last night, Ezra decided. There'd been more. There had. It wasn't *entirely* his imagination. It may not have been *Tristan und Isolde,* maybe not even a Harlequin romance—certainly nothing to tempt Tessa to trade in her *Penthouse* spreads and softcore movies for a life in the academic boonies—but there'd been something sweet and genuine and rather melancholy all the same. Under that riot of golden hair and that bounty of tawny skin dwelt a vaguely disconsolate young woman with perplexing dissatisfactions and inchoate yearnings for other lives she knew she would never lead. And she was shrewd enough to know the world would never take these seriously. And astute enough to recognize and appreciate that Ezra did.

And there were also those incredible Kegels.

After running in silence for several minutes, Ezra suddenly muttered, "Ten thou, huh?"

Isaac instantly understood, answering, "Yep. Five when you sign, five on delivery."

"No royalties?"

"Never. That clause is non-negotiable. But I'm not singling you out for a screwing. It's my standard contract."

"The money could come in awfully handy."

"I figured."

"I'm not committing myself yet."

"Understood."

"I hope we're almost there."

"Just around the corner."

"Thank God."

Later, after both had showered and dressed, Isaac proposed a deli breakfast. Ezra, upon hearing the suggestion, realized he was famished. He and Tessa had never quite gotten around to dinner last night; he hadn't eaten in almost twenty-four hours, and even then only a solitary apple.

"It's not too far," Isaac said. "Shall we walk?"

"Not a chance."

The delicatessen Isaac had in mind was indistinguishable from any other glass-and-plastic Southern California coffee shop, complete with pink-clad waitresses, laminated menus, and weak coffee. Only the food on offer distinguished it from the multitude of places with diminutive possessive male names, Art's and Norm's and Mel's and Jerry's. This one was called Hymie's.

"I'm ordering," Isaac announced after they sat down in a vinyl booth, just as Ezra was reaching for a menu. "An ethnic prerogative."

When the elderly waitress in her ruffled pink dress (obviously designed with a younger sort of waitress in mind, some sort of ingénue, say, who had taken the job while waiting to be discovered by a fat producer with severe gustatory nostalgia) finally came for their order, Isaac requested the smoked fish platter. "And a couple of extra bagels. Toasted."

"I don't really care for smoked fish," Ezra said.

"You'll eat it and like it. We're going traditional today. In any case, I think you'll be agreeably surprised. Have I steered you wrong so far?"

"Don't get cocky."

After the waitress had brought their coffee, and Isaac had taken his first sip, and grimaced with distaste, he said, suddenly all business, "Okay, here's the deal. Sixty-five thousand words. The fundamental requirement is, if you throw the manuscript up in the air and let the pages scatter, any page you pick up should have a sex scene on it. I call that the Schwimmer Test."

"Hold on a minute—"

"We're a classy operation, as I told you before, so I won't be satisfied with a bunch of cardboard characters getting into bed with other cardboard characters. I want to see three-dimensional flesh-and-blood people getting into bed with cardboard characters."

"Wait up—"

"You'll be tempted at first to treat the whole business humorously. Resist that temptation. Respect the conventions of the genre, and don't think of your reader as a wanking foil for your sophomoric satire. When you write a book for Schwimmer Press, you haven't only made a contract with me, you've made a solemn covenant with your audience."

"Good God, Ike."

"Plot is up to you. Some semblance of story is helpful, it gives you a clothesline to string the dirty bits on, but it isn't *de rigeur.* Just remember we publish with the one-handed reader in mind. You'll find the most difficult challenge is finding synonyms. For 'buttocks,' for example, that one seems to give everybody—"

"Hey! Stop! I didn't say I was going to do it. I'm thinking about it, that's all."

"Get real, Ez. Let's end the charade. Of course you're gonna do it."

Ezra smiled, but not without annoyance. Before he could answer, though, the waitress arrived with a huge platter of various smoked fish, cream cheese, lemon wedges, olives, sliced onions, tomatoes and lettuce as garnish, and, on a separate plate, four toasted bagels.

"There you go, darling," said the waitress to Isaac. She must have already identified him as the landsman of the table.

After she withdrew, Ezra said, "What makes you so sure I'm going to do it?"

"'Cause you'd be nuts not to. It's that simple." He reached across the table and began to dole out slices of fish. "Wait till you try this. It'll change your life." He put several slices of lox, several slices of sturgeon, and a chunk of whitefish on a plate and passed it to Ezra.

"You keep promising me that."

"And I keep delivering, in case you haven't noticed. Now start eating, bub, and under no circumstances neglect the onion. This is a festival of halitosis, the terrible taste in your mouth afterward is an integral part of the experience."

As if to prove this last point, after they had finished, and they were back in the BMW, Isaac reached into the glove compartment and produced two large cigars.

"I don't think so," Ezra said.

"You gotta."

Ezra laughed. "Why?"

"Well, first of all, it goes with the breakfast. Every couple weeks I find I have to get in touch with my roots by following my dad's Sunday morning routine, and the cigar's part of the package. Since you're Dante to my Virgil here, you have to follow my lead. Unless you want a reputation as an anti-semite. Anyhow, these are Havanas, you can't even buy them in this country, they're contraband, I got 'em on my last trip to Canada, I'm offering you a very special treat. That's two. The third thing is, we're celebrating."

"Celebrating what?" And then Ezra noticed that they had driven right past Isaac's apartment complex. "Where are we going?"

"The Press. We'll fire these up when we get there. All my employees will complain tomorrow, but fuck 'em, with the fringe benefits I provide, they'll sniff and swear it's Arpege."

Once they were in his office, Isaac removed a cigar clipper from his desk and tossed it to Ezra, seated on the love seat across the room. Ezra caught it, figured out how it worked, and circumcized his cigar. "I hope this cigar doesn't make me sick," he said.

"There's the old frontier spirit." Isaac opened another desk drawer and withdrew several sheets of paper, which he carried across the room, taking a seat across from Ezra.

"What're those?" Ezra asked.

Isaac flicked an onyx cigarette lighter toward Ezra, who smiled and held his cigar to the flame. Once it was lit, he said, "Now, will you please tell me what we're doing here?"

"Signing a contract. I had it drawn up the other day."

"Has anyone ever told you you're kind of pushy? Also a little presumptuous?"

"Nope. Never."

"Well, you are. Both."

Isaac lit his own cigar, rotating it in the flame, took several puffs, and leaned back against the cushions of the sofa. "Your observation may have merit," he said. "Now, initial here and here and sign there, at the bottom. You can read it first if you want, but I've told you everything you need to know."

"I'm not ready to sign this."

"Why not, for God's sake? You need to have it vetted by an attorney? You want an agent to negotiate? That'll set you back ten or fifteen percent, and it won't change a thing."

"You're impossible, Ike."

"I'm the best friend you ever had."

"That too." Ezra took a puff of cigar. "Let me think for a minute."

"You like your Havana?"

"It's . . ." Ezra saw the hopeful, expectant, puppy-dog look in Isaac's eye. "It's very good." Okay, so Isaac wasn't quite batting a thousand. He'd come pretty close, his record still inspired trust.

Isaac stood and went to his desk. He put on a pair of half-moon reading glasses and began leafing through documents, occasionally making a notation in the margin of one page or another. Perhaps it was an act, but it looked to Ezra as if he were making a genuine effort to stay out of Ezra's hair—his hair with *body*—while he considered the offer.

At one point, Ezra broke the silence by inquiring, "Is it now or never?"

Isaac looked up, startled, from what he was doing, and peered at Ezra over the rims of his glasses as if trying to place him. Eventually, he said, "The contract? Of course not. I'm not *strong-arming* you, for heaven's sake. I'm just making an opportunity available. There's no deadline and there's no pressure. The last thing in the world I want to be is pushy, and the next-to-last is presumptuous. This just seemed like a good time, since you're here today and you're gone tomorrow." His face relaxed into a smile. "Which, you might say, is the position we all find ourselves in, taking the cosmic view."

"'Therefore choose life?'"

"'Therefore choose life.' Precisely."

"What if I just asked you for a loan instead? Would you lend me the money?"

"Of course. But I'd be a little disappointed in you."

Ezra nodded and settled back against the loveseat. Isaac's eyes stayed on him for a few moments, and then drifted toward the papers he was holding in his hand. He soon seemed lost in thought, made another marginal notation with his fat Mont Blanc fountain pen, and appeared to have forgotten Ezra's presence entirely.

After another few minutes, Ezra spoke again. "I have a few conditions of my own."

Isaac glanced up, suddenly very alert. "Yes?"

"I want them in writing. A codicil to your standard contract. We both have to initial them."

Isaac laughed. "Good to know I've earned your trust."

"It isn't a question of trust. It's a question of, it's . . . Look, if Beuhler finds out about this, I'm dead meat. Not just my tenure case. Everything. Immediately. It's a religious institution. And they have a very broad morals clause in their contract."

"I don't have any in mine."

"I'd be out on my ass before I could draw a breath. My career would be over. So I need protection. I need to *ensure* I'm protected."

"Go on."

"First of all, I want to sign it as 'Anonymous.'"

"Are you out of your mind? If you hope to stay anonymous, the last thing in the world you should do is sign the book 'Anonymous.' Remember Joe Klein?"

Ezra considered. "Okay, that's a point. How about some sort of pseudonym?"

"All my writers use pseudonyms, genius. Did you really think there's a guy out there named Jack Gough? A woman named Charlotte Russe? You think Tranh Long Dong is a real name?"

"Tranh Long Dong?"

"His real name's Nguyen Dinh. Former government official in Saigon. Got out in '75. He has some hair-raising stories—one day he'll write them down, it'll be a bestseller, and I'll lose one of my best writers. He must've picked up a lot of idiomatic sex talk from the GIs."

"Jeez."

"So anyway, there's no need to put that in writing."

"No harm either. Put it in."

"Fine. Next?"

"No one at the company other than you can know who I am. It's your responsibility to keep my identity secret from everybody. No exceptions."

Isaac shrugged. "Okay."

"I'm in earnest."

"I already agreed, Ezra. Let's move on."

Perhaps this was the professional Isaac Schwimmer, the one with the press, the one who dealt with writers and printers and distributors and retailers: snappy, sharp, tough, alert, decisive. Ezra found he liked this guy too.

"I want my paychecks made out to 'Cash.'"

"Whoa." Isaac leaned forward and tapped some ash into the ashtray. "Not sure about that one, kiddo. My accountant's not going to like it. Neither will the IRS, who make it an annual rite of spring to comb through our books."

"I need these layers of insulation, Ike. For you it's just pocket money, for me it's my whole life. I won't give way on this."

Isaac nodded thoughtfully, blew out a mouthful of smoke, and said, "Done. Next?"

"I don't want any correspondence, and that includes my payment, sent to my home address. I'll rent a post box. Everything gets sent there, addressed to 'Occupant.'"

"You sure you want thousands of dollars, for all intents and purposes in cash, sent to a blind post box? That's a risk."

"It's a bigger risk the other way."

Isaac nodded. "Have you talked to a shrink lately, by any chance?"

"You think I'm nuts?"

"Something like that."

"I just need to cover my flanks."

"There you go! A synonym for buttocks! I knew you could do it!"

"You agree to all this, Isaac?"

"You drive a hard bargain, I'll say that." Eyes twinkling, Isaac rose from his desk and walked toward Ezra, his right hand extended. When he reached him, they shook warmly. "Now sign the fucking contract," he urged.

He handed Ezra his pen. Ezra hesitated for a moment, and then announced, "I'm not signing anything."

Isaac blinked, once. "But what about all your codicils and the rest of it?"

"I wasn't thinking. The arrangement still holds, but you'll have to be content with a handshake. I can't leave a paper trail. Who knows who goes through your files? Starting with the IRS, like you just said. I need deniability."

"You're a fucking lunatic." Isaac grimaced. "Well, given the context, the phrase 'oral contract' has some resonance. Welcome aboard. Now you know why we're celebrating."

"What if I'd decided not to do it?"

"I'd be out one Havana. But I figured you'd come round. How could you refuse?" So saying, he produced a checkbook and wrote out a check for $5,000, the payee denominated as "Cash." He handed it to Ezra. "There you go. You will take a check, won't you? You don't insist on singles with nonsequential serial numbers?"

"A check is fine. What do you think I am, paranoid?" Ezra took the check. Holding it in his hand was a modestly extraordinary sensation. Here was a small piece of paper which represented, at least temporarily, salvation.

"Thanks, Ike."

"Notice it's a *personal* check. That'll save me some bookkeeping problems. Declaring it on your taxes is between you and your conscience. The contract stipulates delivery of a manuscript within three months, but take as much time as you need. I mean, don't dawdle, but don't sweat the deadline. We all know what performance anxiety can do to a guy."

Ezra continued to stare at the check. "I feel as if the ground has shifted under me."

"All things considered, not perhaps the best metaphor to use in Southern California."

■　■　■

Back at the apartment, after Ezra had brushed his teeth five times, gargled with half a bottle of Listerine, and consumed two packs of Tic-Tacs, he joined Isaac in the living room.

"Somehow I don't feel we've celebrated sufficiently," Isaac said.

"One cigar a year is just about all the celebrating I can handle."

"Let's get Tessa and Lucy over tonight, make an evening of it. After all, you're splitting tomorrow. And it isn't every day a guy undertakes to write a book."

"Yeah, great, only . . . we're not going to mention the book part, right?"

"Why not, for heaven's sake? The girls'll be thrilled."

"It's supposed to be a secret, remember? Nobody's supposed to know?"

"Aw shit, I forgot."

"Ike—"

"Anyway, Tessa and Lucy don't have anything to do with that dumb college."

"Ike—"

"I mean, who could they tell?"

"Ike, you shook on it! Total secrecy!"

"You're serious about this, aren't you?"

"Never more so."

"I hope I don't get careless."

"Ike—"

"Okay, relax. My lips are sealed." He mimed locking his lips and throwing away the key, then said, "I'm gonna call up Luce and Tess and issue the invitations, then let's hit the beach, okay? And you be more conscientious with the sunblock this time, whuddaya say?"

■　■　■

Isaac and Lucy were on the small patio that overlooked the pool, tending the Weber, urging the coals, with imprecations and threats, into flame.

Ezra watched them for a moment, and then turned back to Tessa, seated beside him on the sofa. "So," he said, taking her hand.

"This is kind of sad," she said quietly.

Ezra had been unable to figure out how to allude to their night of love-making, how to incorporate it into their quotidian social relations. Things were different in daylight. Was she providing an entrée into the taboo? "Yes, it is."

"You had a good visit?" Apparently withdrawing what she'd been proffering.

"Great. The best. Unbelievable. I'm going to have to try to hold on to it when I'm home. Not let it slip away. Not let it come to seem like a nice dream I once had." I'm talking about you, Tessa, I hope you realize that.

"Write a poem about it."

"Well . . ." Ezra couldn't suppress a smile. "I imagine it'll have an impact on my work."

"I'm glad." Then she added, "Lucy was really jealous." Her voice changed when she said it, finally and decisively breaching the barrier.

"Come on."

"She was. Also curious. She wanted details."

Ezra smiled uncomfortably. "Did you supply them?"

"See, you're different from the guys around here."

Sure, he thought, I'm a repressed little schlemiel with a bad sunburn, and they're all bronzed sex-machines. I can see how that might excite some curiosity. The allure of novelty, even when it involves trading down.

"Do your poems rhyme, by the way?" she suddenly asked.

"Some of them."

"I believe poems *should* rhyme. Lucy's never do."

"You've read them?"

"They're crappy."

Just then, Isaac and Lucy stepped in off the patio. "Ladies and gentle-men, we have achieved ignition," Isaac announced grandly. "Four years in the Boy Scouts and I finally have something besides mosquito bites, poison oak, and an injured rectum to show for it."

"I'll go get the tuna," Lucy offered, crossing toward the kitchen.

"Let's just concentrate on dinner for the time being," said Isaac.

They were far enough gone on tequila and ricocheting vibrations that they all found this amusing, especially Lucy, who laughed so hard on her way into the kitchen that she had to brace herself against the door post, coloring deeply, and then slowly slid to the floor. Luckily, she didn't drop the platter of fish on her way down.

Isaac was a great host; the simple dinner of ahi tuna, corn on the cob, and salad was unpretentious but excellent, and he kept a good cabernet flowing freely. And he regaled the women with stories of his and Ezra's grad school days, which he somehow contrived to distort, or at least *shade,* in such a way that, even though no outright untruths were uttered, Ezra had all the best lines and the boldest schemes, which was anything but the way Ezra recalled them. It was a virtuoso turn of such transcendent and unobtrusive generosity that Ezra once again felt actual love for his old friend.

When dinner was finished, after everyone had pitched in with the table clearing and the dishwasher loading, Isaac brought out the fabled cookie jar, rolled several joints, and set them in motion around the table. Ezra took only the occasional cautious sociable toke, but Isaac, Tessa, and Lucy gulped down smoke by the lungful. When everybody finally staggered from the dining room into the living room, they were completely looped.

Isaac quickly put a CD reissue of old Sinatra recordings on the stereo, offered Lucy his hand, and began to lead her around the room to the strains of "Dancing in the Dark," in an exaggerated but surprisingly graceful parody of Arthur-and-Katherine ballroom terpsichore.

Ezra smiled at Tessa, who smiled back; there was unmistakable invitation in her eyes, and, although he was an awkward and self-conscious dancer, he was drunk enough not to care. He rose and extended his hand, she took it and rose in turn, and glided smoothly into his arms. The feel of her body against his added deliciously to the sensation of intoxication. They began to dance.

The song ended, and was succeeded by something faster and brassier, and they changed partners and whirled around in a silly frantic laughter-filled extravaganza; Isaac dipped and spun Tessa, and Ezra climbed over chairs and sofas with Lucy. But when this was in turn succeeded by another romantic ballad, Tessa moved purposefully back toward Ezra, effectively cutting in, put her arms around his neck, and pressed herself against him hard. He locked his arms around her waist, their faces touched, he pulled her even closer, they took little steps in place, not really doing more than shifting their weight from one foot to the other, and the mood was suddenly and magically transformed.

Out of the corner of his eye, he noticed that Isaac and Lucy were also standing locked together, swaying in place, kissing.

"Let's go back to my room," he murmured.

"Um."

They left the living room, their arms around each other, walking/stumbling down the hall to the guestroom. Once inside, they kissed again, and as he began to remove her sleeveless sweater, she said, "I'm a little sore from last night." She sounded oddly shy, almost coy.

"I'll be gentle," he promised her. And then said to himself, Here am I, Ezra Gordon, poindexter extraordinare, promising this fabulous sexy woman I'll be gentle. Who is zooming who? And it was only then that he realized his friend the little voice hadn't spoken in over twenty-four hours, because all of a sudden it started talking a blue streak: "She *likes* you, idiot. The two of you made love all night last night, what more do you need? Did you catch the look in her eye when she showed up tonight? Do you hear how her voice sounds when she speaks to you? Stop arguing and accept it. What's it gonna hurt, hah?"

It struck Ezra that the little voice had a speech rhythm remarkably like Isaac's.

When he entered her, it was like a homecoming. "Baby," she breathed, her voice thin and tender, and she pulled him against her. It occurred to him that this was the only time in his life anyone had addressed him as "baby," at least since he had *been* a baby. He liked it.

He wasn't as gentle as he'd planned to be, but it wasn't all his fault, her responses encouraged him in the opposite direction. And he had the odd notion that, for the first time in his life, he was actually doing this right, the way it was supposed to be done. As if he had stumbled upon a skill known only to the elect, a closely guarded cabalistic secret. An odd thought: As if, after an unsuspecting lifetime as a cocktail bar tinkler, it were suddenly given to him to understand what it was like to be András Schiff. Every movement and gesture felt right, he could trust his instincts, an invisible force was guiding him.

Zen and the art of humping.

Later, lying behind her with his arms wrapped around her shoulders, he found the courage to say, "Isaac warned me against falling in love with you, you know." Was it courage, in fact? Or was the impulse irresistible?

Her body stiffened slightly. "Did he?" Something in her voice sounded wary.

It was too late to pull back. "Uh huh. I think he was being funny. You know Ike."

"Yes, I know Ike." Still wary, as if unsure where this was leading, unsure whether, and how far, to follow.

"But, for what it's worth . . . I mean, I'm not the type who falls in love overnight, so don't panic or anything, but it's probably a good thing I'm leaving tomorrow."

"It doesn't feel that way, though, does it?"

"No. No it doesn't." He hesitated, then went on, "But there's something sweet about the way it hurts. This is all very new to me, Tessa."

"Tell me something . . . You have a honey up where you live?"

Ezra hesitated. It wasn't an easy question to answer; wouldn't have been a week ago, and was even more difficult now. "Not really. I sort of did, and now I guess I sort of don't."

"Not that it matters." She turned around till she was facing him, a major navigational undertaking, and then kissed him deeply. "This has been . . . You make me feel . . . I mean, being with you, it's like, it's like you're Keats and I'm an urn."

"My God," he said, "wherever did you dredge that up from? You're just full of surprises."

She pulled away from him. "Hey, buster, I had a couple years of college. Everyone expects me to be an ignoramus. I may not be a rocket scientist, but—"

He pulled her close to him again. "No, Tessa, I think you're, you're—"

"You know what it is? Everyone's so sure someone like me has to be an idiot, they're impressed with *anything*. Anything beyond counting to five and knowing the Alphabet Song."

"Anyone who thinks you're an idiot is a fucking idiot himself."

"It's not just hims," she said. "It's hers too. The hers are usually worse, in fact."

"Whatever. I mean it, Tessa."

"Yeah, I know." She kissed him. "I know you do. It's one of your nicest qualities. Anyway, it isn't exactly they think I'm an idiot. It's more they'd *prefer* it." She laughed. "And look, it's probably my fault too. I play along. I know I shouldn't, it just digs the hole deeper, but it's a way of coping with the world. *This* world. It reassures people. Like, I heard somewhere that a sociologist or psychologist did a study comparing bust measurement with IQ. And he found they were, they were . . . what's the right way of saying it?"

"Negatively correlated?"

"There, see? If my tits were smaller, I'd know that."

He laughed. "How can you be *so* adorable?"

"I've spent my whole life working on it, Ezra."

He pulled her close and kissed her again. When she kissed back, he essayed a probing caress. She gasped, and he immediately desisted, but then she reached for his hand and put it back where it had been. "I don't want you to stop," she whispered. "We just have to be—"

"Gentle. I know."

And so they began to make love again, on their sides, face to face, with an almost Tantric minimalism, the barest suggestion of movement, when there suddenly came a discreet tapping at the door, which then squeakily opened a crack, admitting a thin shaft of light. Without disengaging, both turned toward the noise, and were startled to see Lucy as she stuck her head in, her naked body backlit, a study in chiaroscuro.

"Hi, guys," she announced brightly. "How's it going?" When neither answered, she continued, "Isaac and I were wondering if, if, you know, if you had any interest in switching."

Ezra looked into Tessa's eyes, which glowed back into his own. Yesterday he might have been tempted. "We're pretty content with the present arrangement," he said.

"Just a thought," Lucy answered graciously. "Sorry to interrupt." She remained in the doorway perhaps a second more than was strictly required, and then withdrew, shutting the door after herself. And against what seemed at that moment to be insuperable odds, Ezra and Tessa recaptured their mood of tender valedictory ardor almost immediately.

■   ■   ■

"I hope you didn't mind that business with Lucy," Isaac said the next morning. He was helping Ezra load his bag into the trunk of the Tercel. They were standing in the street a couple of blocks from the apartment complex. "I mean, I knew it was kind of crass, and, you know, I saw you and Tess dancing, it didn't take clairvoyance to realize it was more than just a sex deal with you two. But Lucy was hot to trot—it was her idea, you do realize—and I figured you could make up your own mind."

"No harm done."

"You're annoyed."

Ezra threw his arms around Isaac and embraced him tightly. "How could I possibly be annoyed with you, Ikey? You're my best friend. I can't imagine a better."

"You did have a good time, didn't you?"

"I'm getting out in the nick of time."

"Mexican villages and cheap tequila?"

"One more day and I'd be heading for the border." They faced each other, smiling. "I'll start working on the book right away, that's a promise." Ezra slammed the trunk shut.

"Picked a pen name?"

"I was thinking of E. A Peau. P-E-A-U."

"And E. A. as in Edgar Allan?" Isaac looked thoughtful for a moment. "E. A. Peau. I like it."

Ezra opened the car door and leaned on it, not quite ready to climb in. "You know the amazing thing?" he said. "I've been thinking about it all morning. That Tessa came to the sauna when she did. I mean, I would've had a fine time here anyhow, but . . ." He shrugged.

"It made a difference."

"A *big* difference," Ezra confirmed as he slid behind the wheel. "Took a great vacation and transformed it into a mind-bending sojourn in paradise. Just an amazing coincidence, her showing up like that."

"Yeah." And then, a moment later, "Well, not exactly." Isaac shut the car door.

Ezra stared at his friend inquisitively—or was it suspiciously?—through the open window. "What do you mean?" he demanded.

Isaac put his hand through the window onto Ezra's shoulder. "You have a safe trip home, kiddo. Buckle up. And don't forget to write, ha ha."

He stepped away from the car, turned on his heel, and strode back in the direction of his building.

"Isaac, get back here this instant!"

Isaac waved once, but kept on walking.

Part 3

Every Inch a Lady

Chapter 1

Ezra's first full day back in Seven Hills was devoted to chores. Not slopping the pigs and milking the cows, not those Seven Hills kind of chores, but chores all the same. He paid back the fifteen or so people from whom he had cadged small loans over the years. Their universal surprise at being repaid could almost be considered insulting: What sort of deadbeat did they take him for? He changed the oil and oil filter in his car, which, after over five years or 50,000 miles, he couldn't remember which had come first, was presumably overdue, he paid his utility bill and his phone bill in person—everything would be reconnected very soon, he was assured—he rented a post box at the campus post office, and he paid his back rent to his landlady, Mrs. Anthenien, who was delighted, even (it wasn't going too far to say) overjoyed, and who forced some rather dry apple cake and a cup of translucently weak coffee on him.

He still needed to buy a computer—his old one had crashed almost a year ago but still sat on his desk, a cybernetic memento mori—but Isaac's advance would take him only so far. He would have to write the way they wrote in paleoliterary times, by hand.

Now all he had left on the list was to buy some legal pads and he'd be set. Oh, except for preparing the syllabus for the seminar he was teaching this semester. A little afterthought. A seminar on the Victorian novel. Well, coming up with some plausible books for *that* shouldn't be too daunting a task. Victorians wrote novels the way we consume potato chips. Even one of their prime ministers wrote novels, only moderately bad ones too. Ezra toyed briefly with the notion of including *Fanny Hill,* as a small collegial salutation, Peau to Cleland, across the centuries, but that was obviously a nonstarter from any practical point of view, fun as it was to imagine the ensuing commotion. The question was, who would be most upset? The department? The Board of Overseers? The Alumni Association? The campus feminist organizations? Even as a mental exercise, it was a breeding ground for thrashing insomnia.

In any event, other than his syllabus, he had taken care of business, he was ready to proceed with his life. His *double* life. By day, a citizen in good standing of the bucolic hamlet of Seven Hills, California, gainfully employed, solvent, law-abiding. Professor, gentleman and scholar, molder of young minds, timely payer of rent.

While by night . . . heh heh heh.

He liked having a dirty little secret. Interesting, that. Unexpected, really. He'd never been much good at keeping his own dealings secret—had never had dealings worth *keeping* secret—and he usually found other people's confidences a difficult burden to bear, since it seemed so ungenerous to withhold them from his other friends. Now, however—

Heh heh heh.

Now he found himself fairly bursting with guilty pleasure, in his car, at Jiffy Lube, the post office, the phone company, virtually everywhere: I know something you don't know.

I'm E. A. Peau.

That, he had to admit, that and efficiently discharging unpleasant obligations, were virtually the only gratification available to him upon returning to Seven Hills. Let members of the Grange extol the virtues of country life, the manicured lawns and upthrusting palms of Marina Del Rey were his new yardstick for scenic beauty. Oh, he could see that spring was an attractive time of year in Seven Hills, what with the birds and the wildflowers and so on; but once you factored in his job, and his awful apartment (paid for through May), and his students and colleagues and miscellaneous acquaintances, the whole package lost its allure.

Which, circuitously, brought his thoughts exactly where he didn't want them to go, to a miscellaneous acquaintance named Carol.

That was one bit of unfinished business he didn't have on his list, one bit he planned to leave unfinished. He didn't trust his judgment, he didn't know his own mind anymore, not that he ever had. It was only a week since he had left Seven Hills, but it seemed a lifetime. And although he'd been home less than a day, Southern California now resembled Brigadoon, legendary and remote and perhaps illusory. With so much disorientation, he'd demonstrate judicious restraint by not trying to resolve a major source of confusion in his life.

Or maybe he'd demonstrate cowardice.

Whatever.

Thinking about Carol—even deciding *not* to think about Carol—led inescapably to Tessa, the impossible memory of whom made him sigh.

Just let it ride.

He turned onto Main Street, chose to use the metered municipal parking lot—why not? He could afford it, couldn't he?—and strolled over to the town stationer's. I know something you don't know, he thought. "Ten pads of legal paper," he told the owner, an old codger who'd had this store since way back in the Bronze Age, back when obscenity laws had teeth. And I want them to write a dirty book on, he continued to himself. Which is something I know and you don't, and you never will, because it's my secret and not yours.

This must be the pleasure espionage provides, he thought. Every trivial activity the spy engages in is suffused with a special quality, an I-know-something-you-don't-knowness. He was quite taken with the insight, until he recalled that John LeCarré had mined that vein for just about all the ore it had in it. Oh well, doesn't matter, I'm not going to write a spy novel anyway. That is, *E. A. Peau* isn't going to write a spy novel. Which is a good thing, seeing as how the Cold War is a distant memory. E. A. Peau is going to write a *dirty* novel. The Cold War's over, but fucking is in its heyday, and E. A. Peau is going to write about it. And Isaac and I are the only ones who will ever know it.

Heh heh heh.

Not that he had given the projected book serious thought. He hadn't even given it *frivolous* thought, unless basking in the fact that he knew he was going to write it and nobody else did qualified as thought. And even this basking carried with it a certain subterranean undertone of unease. He hadn't admitted the fact to himself until this very moment.

The old codger plunked ten shrink-wrapped legal pads on the counter with a resounding thump. "That's a lot of paper," he observed. "Gonna write a book or something?"

Ezra felt a spasm of paranoia. "Ha ha, what a thought," he said, laughing with grotesque falseness. Trying to undo the weird impression he knew he was making, he went on, "Me? Write a book? In my dreams, maybe."

Hey, mind your own fucking business, gramps. Although maybe in my dreams is the only place my book *will* get written. In truth, he wasn't feeling as sanguine about his book as he was trying to make out to himself. The question of how to go about starting it—let alone *finishing* it—had been nagging at him since he had maneuvered his car onto Highway 1 yesterday. It was something he was reluctant to admit to himself. Better to pretend to feel anxious about Carol and tenure and the meaning of his life and other relatively peripheral matters. *Displaced anxiety,* Freud called the phenomenon. He didn't know how to write a book, that was the long and the short of it. Despite Isaac's confidence in him, he doubted he could do it. Sixty-five thousand was a lot of words. Looking up "buttocks" in *Roget's Thesaurus* would only carry him so far. There would still be approximately 64,000 more to come up with.

Optimistically. If he was a lot kinkier in print than in life.

For reference, Isaac had given him a stack of books bearing the Isaac Schwimmer Press imprint. Perhaps reading them would give him a few ideas.

Back in his car, baking in the stifling late-afternoon heat, he headed home. The only way to confront the problem was head-on. No point letting it fester in a remote corner of his consciousness, subtly poisoning every other aspect of his existence (even though none of *them* was any bed of roses either). He was a scholar, wasn't he? He'd been trained to analyze texts, to subject them to minute examination in order to determine how they had been put together, to probe them for meaning and for resonance. It was time to put these skills to practical use, time to apply them to the collected works of belles-lettristes with names like Jack Gough, Charlotte Russe, and Tranh Long Dong. It was time to see if twenty-eight years of schooling had taught him anything useful.

He had a long night ahead.

Chapter 2

Her magnificent ~~bosom~~ chest heaved with ~~arousal~~ desire as his hands sought her ~~gaping moist distended gorgeous pussy love sleeve~~.

Christ.

Something told him he didn't quite have it.

Sitting in his living room at the rickety wooden table that now served as his work station, the cold remains of a mug of coffee at his elbow, his eyes aching from staring at the same almost-blank legal page for almost three hours, he felt raw, soiled, and headachey. An ashtray full of cigarette butts would have completed the picture nicely; maybe he should take up smoking for the aesthetics of the thing.

He glanced away from his desk—a ghostly afterimage of scored pornographic scrawl remained in his eyes—and consulted the Casio on his wrist. Four-thirty A.M. He felt like an undergraduate with a paper due the next day. The same panic-scrambled brains, the same mixture of unfocused energy and bone-numbing exhaustion.

He was being foolish. Isaac had said not to worry about the deadline, and tonight, after all, represented only his first stab at the thing. But he wanted to make a good start, wanted to build up a head of steam, generate momentum, feel he was getting somewhere.

A page and a half was where he had gotten, virtually all of it unusable.

And as if that wasn't bad enough, he was *horny*.

It was demeaning, really, to be turned on by the crap he'd been plowing through until about 1 A.M., when he'd finally abandoned his research and taken his chances with the *creative act*. But, looked at in a certain way, Isaac had a right to pride in his product: Those writers of his—especially

Charlotte Russe, clearly the brightest star in the Isaac Schwimmer firmament—had a special knack for this stuff, for conveying the tactilia of unconfined sexual omniverousness, for contriving extravagantly, enviably, unimaginably concupiscent situations that didn't *altogether* beggar credibility, for inventing characters whose carnal appetites and achievements, while awesome, weren't *entirely* outside the realm of some remotely, optimistically glimpsed possibility. Someone whose life bore no resemblance to Ezra's might have enjoyed some of these things once upon a time.

Not only had Ezra painstakingly combed through nine or ten of the books Isaac had given him, paragraph by paragraph, sentence by sentence, in some cases even word by word, virtually deconstructing them, in a vain attempt to figure out how the various authors had, in their various ways, succeeded in achieving their effects. He had also masturbated twice.

Which may have been a mistake, he was prepared to acknowledge. He may have sacrificed that fine edge you need to write this stuff. Balzac might have been onto something, was his rueful, albeit conditional, conclusion. I've lost that lovin' feeling.

I'm also getting giddy.

He pushed his chair back from the table, picked up his ceramic mug, and headed into the kitchen. Taster's Choice. It worked for that attractive trans-Atlantic couple a few years back, didn't it? They even fell in love drinking the stuff. But it wasn't quite they same; they weren't trying to grind out a dirty book when they could barely keep their eyes open.

After dumping the remaining inch of cold coffee into the sink, he turned on the gas flame under the kettle and shoveled a granular spoonful of instant into his mug. When the crystals hit the moisture at the bottom, they began to run a little, oozing into a muddy goo. Yum yum, any minute now, pornographer's ambrosia.

He rested his hips back against the sink and closed his eyes. Images of naked body parts danced in his brain, but they didn't seem sexy at all, they seemed like something out of a medical text. Carnal, but not prurient. Well, maybe that was the right approach. Cold and methodical. Ecstasy recollected and recreated in tranquillity. Or even distaste. Just the mechanics, ma'am. Tabs into slots. Protuberances and concavities. Hairless rutting primates going at it under bright fluorescent lab lights. Himself in a white coat, transcribing their shenanigans with his indifferent Papermate.

What, after all, was sexy? To him, to Ezra Gordon, right now, right this minute? Was there anything?

Well, Tessa, of course. But Tessa . . . she was so close to being a fantasy in real life, he couldn't imagine transmuting her further into fantasy. Besides, even granting the limited plotting appropriate to the genre, there wasn't really any way she could change or develop in the course of a book. She was already perfectly realized. It would just be one damned thing after another, like life.

Steam was beginning to rise from the kettle. He turned off the flame, lifted the kettle, which produced a sizzling sort of noise, and poured boiling water into the mug. As he stirred it, a dusty smell rose with the vapor. Just consider it medicine, he told himself. And buy yourself a Chemex tomorrow. You're allowed, you're entitled.

He took a sip. Too hot. He put the cup on the yellow Formica counter; it felt like a reprieve. What about Carol? he mused, reverting to his earlier train of thought. Carol used to be sexy, back before the Deep Freeze set in. Sweetly, artlessly, innocently sexy. But that was once upon a time. Except for those rare recent occasions when she became aroused in spite of herself, the result of some chance confluence of circumstances he was never able to identify. And what made that sexy was the *unexpectedness* of it, his awareness that she herself was surprised and probably dismayed by her physical reactions, his sense that buried somewhere within that proper young lady was an appetite, a potentially *unruly* appetite, an appetite she couldn't order into nonexistence. If somebody like Carol ever discovered passion, ever let go, ever overcame her inhibitions sufficiently to become sexually selfish, sexually greedy, sexually *voracious,* well, that would be quite an event. That would be something else. Worth buying a ticket to, just for the chance to see it firsthand.

His quickened heartbeat alerted him. Could he be onto something? Let's keep our head, he told himself, let's examine this coolly. How would it be if a young woman *began* as Carol and gradually *became* Tessa? Not the real Tessa, of course, not the complicated and conflicted young woman of whom he'd caught glimpses in bed, in conversation during the interludes between lovemaking, but an idealized Tessa, a fantasy Tessa, a beautiful young hedonist obsessed with her own pleasure and fearlessly aggressive about achieving it. To impel and then monitor such a character's burgeoning awareness of her own sensuality, and her growing embrace of her own sensuality, to follow her progress as she becomes a pilgrim of pleasure, a disciple of desire, a fleshly ecstatic off on a carnal hegira . . . Now *that* might worthily generate 65,000 words of well-wrought prose.

Ezra essayed another sip of coffee. Tolerable, at least insofar as temperature was concerned. Dandy. Time to take pen in hand.

He walked back to the living room with a spring in his step. As he was sitting down at his desk, a title came to him: *Every Inch a Lady.* Perfect. He felt something, something that wasn't merely his central nervous system's response to caffeine, rising up from deep within his thorax. It was *certainty.* He knew he could write this book.

As if to demonstrate his confidence to himself, he tore off the page he'd been working on, crumpled it up, and tossed it onto the floor. Don't need it. On the wrong track. I'm starting clean. I'm starting clean to write a dirty book.

So confident was he, he next did something his instinctive, superstitious prudence urged him not to do until the book was completed: He wrote a title page. *Every Inch a Lady by E. A. Peau.* There. Don't stop. Next page. *Nora patted her hair into a perfectly concentric bun,* he wrote. He could visualize her, standing in front of the bathroom mirror in her cramped Upper West Side Manhattan apartment, dressed in a no-nonsense pin-striped business suit, fixing her make-up, preparing to start her well-organized day, unaware of the extraordinary events that would soon transform her life, oblivious to the erotic Odyssey upon which she was about to embark.

When he next remembered his own existence, more than two hours, and almost seven pages, had come and gone. The birds were singing outside his window, the sun had risen, there wasn't a cloud in the sky. Never would be heard a discouraging word. It was going to be a beautiful day.

His double life had well and truly started. He felt like Maclean, Burgess, Philby, and Blunt rolled into one.

With a *hard-on.*

Chapter 3

O ne week and 19,000 words later, Ezra, his right hand now chronically swollen and cramped, faced the first session of his Victorian novel seminar. The turnout was distressingly large, SRO in the undersized seminar room. It had been Ezra's understanding that undergraduates, even upper-division English majors, had an aversion to long novels with stilted diction, large numbers of characters, and convoluted plots. But then, Ezra's classes, regardless of their subject matter, were usually well attended. He suspected this was one of the reasons for the tenuousness of his tenure case: pained jealousy on the part of his senior colleagues. Oh, his dearth of publications might have *something* to do with it, but on the whole it was less unsettling to blame collegial envy.

After passing out copies of the syllabus, he announced, "We won't be reading anything particularly heretical. Dickens, Thackeray, a quantity of Brontë, a dollop of Trollope. *The Picture of Dorian Gray* is about as risqué as we're going to get." He hoped this would discourage potential thrill-seekers who believed his relative youth, his reputation for heterodoxy, and the lingering echoes of the Mindy Dunkelweisse case might suggest this class would be livelier than the standard fare on offer at Beuhler. There was no profit in their having heightened expectations before the semester really began, not when they still had the option of dropping the class without suffering consequences.

But then he made a tactical blunder: "I'll probably be called on the carpet for *Dorian Gray*, as a matter of fact." The quality of their attention suddenly changed; they immediately sniffed controversy in the air, their faith in his covert subversiveness was restored. Shit. Looking away from the eager, hopeful, vaguely prurient stares of the students who had succeeded in finding seats at the seminar table, his eye encountered that of Mindy Dunkelweisse herself, twinkling a message of amusement and shared secret knowledge. He hadn't noticed her before, he'd been spared that particular piece of good news until now. She was one of the crowd of students standing around the periphery of the room. Double shit. Mindy was his own personal bad penny, minted just for him.

Tearing his eyes away, hoping his face hadn't registered any emotion, he moved quickly to lull the students back into their former lassitude. "As some of you may know, there have been some problems with Beuhler's computer system." The problems had become so pervasive that it was no longer possible to keep them secret. "Therefore, for those of you who elect to stay in this class despite my warnings about how boring it'll be—" This was greeted with the kind of dutiful laughter after-dinner speakers receive when they've made their obligatory opening joke—"I must warn you, your attendance here has to be regarded as provisional." He glanced around the room (gliding quickly past Mindy), hoping for signs of incipient distress. Seeing none, merely the same bovine passivity one normally encounters in mid-April, he decided to rub their noses in it a little more. "And I'm afraid that includes credit for time served. Until the college can figure out who belongs where, the whole situation is up for grabs. I'm mentioning it because I know how much you'd hate to learn you've read *Little Dorrit* for nothing. Which is the assignment for next week. That's all for today."

The students rose, milled around briefly—they always seemed to have a hard time recognizing the show was over—and began to file out. There were so many of them in this tiny room that watching them leave put Ezra in mind of the Tokyo subway, even though he'd never been to Tokyo and even though they weren't especially polite about navigating the bottleneck. The advantage of so large a crowd was that he at least missed Mindy's exit, merely noting with relief that it had taken place. He remained in his seat at the table which took up most of the room's floor space. Usually, three or four students had questions, and today it was in his interest to remain behind to answer them as discouragingly as possible.

First up was Henry Ng. Typical.

"No I haven't, Henry," he said, before Henry could pop the inevitable question. "I'm sorry. How was Paris?"

"Fabulous. Everybody thought I was Vietnamese."

"That made it fabulous?"

"No, it was an independent observation I thought you'd find interesting." Henry smiled. "It was fabulous because it was Paris, because it's spring, because the Tuileries are in bloom, because—"

Ezra noticed that the two other students waiting their turn were beginning to grow impatient. "— And so on," he interrupted. It wasn't fair to them to sit through an entire travelogue. Nor, for that matter, to himself.

"And so on," Henry concurred, unoffended. "Can I walk with you wherever you're headed?" he asked. "After you've talked to, to . . ." He gestured toward the other students.

"I don't see why not," Ezra lied. And then suddenly realized he might finally be able to derive some benefit from his acquaintance with Henry at long last, might actually introduce the barest hint of reciprocity into their dealings. "Wait outside. I'll find you."

Five minutes later, as they strolled past the malodorous campus breeding pens, Ezra launched a conversational preemptive strike: "I've started working on some articles," he said. "In earnest. Making up for lost time." It was a lie chosen to secure Henry's immediate interest, thereby deflecting him from his own agenda. A delaying tactic only, of course, but if Ezra's concern wasn't the first item on the table, it would never get addressed at all. "A few hesitant stabs at deconstruction."

"Uh huh," Henry responded, the two bare syllables awash in votive fascination.

"And they're, they're going, they're going quite well."

"Uh huh."

"But the thing is, Henry . . ." He held up his swollen right hand. "I think it's time for me to match the modernity of my literary discourse with an appropriate medium of production."

Rather frighteningly, Henry understood without further explanation: "You've been working longhand? You want to switch to a computer?"

"Terrible writer's cramp," Ezra confirmed.

"I can't believe you don't use a computer."

"Well, I *did*. The thing died on me."

"Why didn't you replace it?"

"I'm a pauper, Henry."

"Wow. I had no idea you were as broke as that."

Ezra resisted the urge to say something bitter about parents and largesse. It wasn't Henry's fault that his parents were generous, nor was it his fault that he was still young enough to be legitimately considered their dependent. Nor that Beuhler paid its junior faculty in so niggardly a fashion.

But the boy had just been to Paris, and that *was* his fault.

"So what *do* you want?" Henry prompted.

"Well, I have an account on the college system. Which I've never used. Part of my laughable remuneration. I just want some advice."

"Jeez, Ezra, it's been a long time since I was anywhere near the college system."

"But you used to use it, right? Before you changed your major? And you must still know how it works." What a nerve! For Henry to be resistant about helping, after everything Ezra had done for him (or rather, *not* done for him, but at least *promised* to do for him). "You can give me a quick explanation, right?"

"Oh well, sure, is that all? You just want to use it for word processing, right?"

"Exactly."

"You don't need me. I mean, if you can use a word processor, it's pretty self-evident. UNIX is a friendly system. What you should do—I'm not trying to wriggle out of anything, it really would be simplest—is just go to the bookstore, get the manual. It'll tell you what you need to know. The only warning I'd give you is, with all the problems they've been having, make sure you back everything up on disk really often. Every paragraph or so."

Ezra felt a small tremor of incipient terror. "But the system's secure, isn't it?" Perhaps, all things considered, it would be safest to write the book in cuneiform.

"Oh sure," Henry said airily, "security's no problem. Just the survival of your data. That's why you should back everything up. Otherwise, you're in serious danger of losing it."

I'm always in serious danger of losing it, Ezra thought. And then, more charitably, Well, maybe Henry isn't being uncooperative, maybe he's simply being realistic: The only way to master anything is autodidactically. Lessons are just for the companionship.

"If there's anything you don't understand, call me."

"Right. I will. Now, what's on your mind, Henry?"

Henry hesitated a decorous moment or two before replying. "There's a favor I'd like to ask you. It's a little delicate."

Ezra suppressed a sigh. "You can always ask. But in case you've forgotten, my record with you isn't exactly exemplary."

Henry grimaced. "You don't have to read the damned book if you don't want to."

"It's mainly a question of finding time."

"Whatever," Henry answered with a toss of his hand. "This is a little more pressing."

Henry had stopped walking, and now withdrew a pack of Gitanes. He suddenly seemed uncomfortable. Ezra, waiting while Henry lit his cigaratte, couldn't resist observing, "You really do smoke too much, you know. I mean, there aren't two sides to the debate." He disliked himself for saying it, knew he wasn't telling Henry anything the boy wasn't already aware of, but the words slipped out.

"At least my nicotine stains aren't too obvious," Henry said lightly. After he got his cigarette lit, and they resumed walking, he went on, "I have a problem with my parents."

Ezra waited. But Henry was waiting too, if not for a reaction exactly, then for some sort of conversational punctuation. So Ezra provided it: "Go on."

"They found out there wasn't any computer show."

"Ouch. Still, you must've realized you were taking a risk."

"They made inquiries." He shook his head. "Just when you're convinced your parents are total meatballs, they take it on themselves to prove they experience something resembling consciousness."

"This generational stuff is always hard, Henry. And I'm sure it must be exacerbated when there's a cultural gap of some kind."

"Gap? It's the Grand Canyon."

"Were they very angry?"

"Worse. They were *hurt*. You know that wounded look mothers give you, they probably teach it at Lamaze classes or something?" He shook his head again. "It's a mess."

Ezra wasn't thrilled with the tendency of the conversation, but he knew he was in too deep to extricate himself. "So how were things left?"

"They want me to, to redeclare my major. Go back to engineering. They sort of threatened to cut me off if I didn't."

"Ah." Ezra positively dreaded what was to follow.

"They're coming to visit next week. I'd like you to talk to them."

Yep, right on schedule. "What am I supposed to tell them, Henry?"

"That, that you think I should stay in English."

"On what basis?"

Henry, uniquely since their paths had first crossed the previous June, regarded Ezra mistrustfully. "On the basis that you think I'm doing what I should be doing. God, Ezra, are you going to treat me like the rest of the department? Like, except when it's time for me to pay my fees, I don't exist? On the basis that I have a, a talent or whatever for literature. That's kind of the basis I had in mind."

"Talent as a critic? As a creative writer?"

Henry frowned, dropped his half-finished cigarette on the grass, and ground it in with the toe of his Nike. "You know what? Forget it. Just forget it. I'm sorry I asked."

And Ezra was suddenly sorry he had answered, or at least *how* he had answered. "Don't be silly. I'd be happy to talk to them, Henry. Let's set up an appointment."

"Really?" The hopeful, wary, boyish look on Henry's face was touching.

"Absolutely. How's Tuesday?"

"Perfect!"

"My office? Two-thirty?"

"Just perfect! Thanks a lot, Ezra! I really appreciate this!"

Henry scampered off across the field as if he were floating. Ezra wished he knew whether he was doing the right thing. It was like with the boy's smoking; it wasn't at all clear to him where his responsibilities lay. Was he the older generation's ambassador to the young, still young enough himself to be a persuasive, trustworthy advocate for maturity and prudence? Or was it rather his role to counsel them to resist the encroachment of adult solemnity, to stay young, to nurture their adventurousness, to guard closely their precarious, beleaguered access to their own instincts and impulses?

I'm too old to be the Catcher in the Rye, he told himself. How can I encourage Henry to leap if I won't be there to grab him when he topples?

Feeling oppressed by these reflections, he proceeded to the Student Union Building. At least I have almost 19,000 words, he thought, and his mood instantaneously brightened. The peculiar thing was that over the last week, *Every Inch a Lady,* and the dizzying dazzling exploits in which his dear darling Nora was engaged, had become more real to him than his own life. He was like a sleepwalker these days, competently but not altogether consciously negotiating his existence, except late at night while sitting at his desk scribbling, scribbling. Those were the only times he felt fully alert.

There was, miraculously, no line at the Automatic Teller Machine, merely one girl who was completing a transaction. Ezra stepped up, inserted his new card, and indulged himself in a soliloquy about how much money he should request. "Sixty is enough, but maybe I'll take eighty just because I *can*." He finally decided on a hundred; that way he wouldn't run out so quickly, which meant he wouldn't have to return so soon, which meant less time in the Student Union, which translated into more time available for the book.

Next stop was the bookstore in the basement, predictably deserted. Ezra found the UNIX manual, helped himself to a box of floppy disks, and took the items over to the cashier with a feeling of exaltation. If I was going fast before, watch my dust now!

He climbed the stairs to the ground floor two at a time and entered the Cabbage Patch, the health food cafeteria, for lunch. Grabbing a tray, a napkin, and plastic cutlery, he moved along the counter, took a salad—rather heavy on the sprouts today—a cup of tomato soup, a whole-grain roll, and a glass of water. Can't get any healthier than this, he thought, I'm a lean mean porn machine. He paid at the cash register—traffic was light, considering it was the first day of a new semester—and moved into the main part of the restaurant. Scanning the room for a table, he encountered the searching gaze of Carol Dimsdale.

Hmmm.

Well, it was obviously bound to happen sooner or later. He smiled a tentative, neutral, no-hard-feelings smile in her general direction. She waved at him, with what could almost be called enthusiasm. Uh oh. That upped the ante, rather. It would be impossible to maintain a tentative, neutral, no-hard-feelings stance and *not* sit with her after receiving such a wave. But perhaps it was for the best. Get the air cleared, reestablish their relations on a sensible, mature, friendly basis. He crossed to her table.

"Well, hello, stranger," she said.

"Hi, Carol. How have you been?"

"Sit down?"

"Pleasure."

"So how was L.A.?" she asked, as he put his tray on the table and seated himself across from her. "That's where you went, right?"

"Yep. It was great."

"Had a good time?"

"Very."

She looked him in the eye and nodded. He had the definite impression she was fighting another, more wicked smile. "Know somebody there, do you?"

"An old grad school buddy."

"Ah ha." She took a sip of milk, then wiped the moustache off her upper lip with her napkin.

"How've things been around here?"

"Well, the computer business has been giving us no end of trouble. Other than that—" She shrugged. "Nothing much. Daddy's asked after you once or twice."

"Has he now? Was he packing heat?"

"Silly. He sounded, he sounded sympathetic and concerned, is how he sounded."

"Absence makes the heart grow fonder."

"I suppose it does at that." She regarded him fondly. "I expected you to phone."

"I sort of got the impression—"

"Oh, we girls are temperamental," she interrupted. "Don't you know anything about women?"

"Less and less."

"I mean, surely there's no reason we can't be friends, is there?"

He dipped his fork into his salad and came up with a bundle of sprouts. No good. Try again. "I have the definite feeling you're sending me mixed messages, Carol." Ah, a cherry tomato, one bite of which will send seeds scattering in all directions and red gunk dribbling down my shirt. Maybe the third time will be lucky.

"And *I* have a feeling you're breaking the rules by pointing that out." The tip of her tongue peeked through her lips and her eyes danced.

Maybe she's on drugs, he thought. "You're acting mighty strange, Carol."

"Yes, well, you know how we were both supposed to take a little time and try to figure out where our relationship is heading and everything?"

"Uh huh."

"Did you come to any conclusions?"

"Uh uh."

"Same here. So I guess that's why I'm acting strange."

"I'm afraid I need another hint."

"It's like this. Every time I tried to puzzle things out, I kept deciding our relationship doesn't make sense and isn't going any place. But . . . Tell me something. Did you miss me?"

Careful, boy, this could be a trap. "Sometimes," he hazarded.

"You didn't, did you?" All her pertness seemed to drain away in an instant, like air escaping a punctured balloon. "You know what I was about to tell you? That I missed you a lot." She looked very upset. "I bet you had intercourse while you were in L.A., didn't you?"

"Carol—"

"You did! I can tell! I can see it in your eyes! It's so easy down there, isn't it? Everybody has intercourse with everybody else, it's like shaking hands. 'Hi, nice to meet you, let's have intercourse.'"

He had to resist the temptation to shush her. She was talking rather loudly, and a number of students at neighboring tables were looking their way.

"Our timing is really lousy, you know that?" she continued. "Here I spent like the whole last few days thinking about you, hardly even sleeping, and I get the feeling you haven't thought about me at all."

"What was I supposed to think? About my host of failings, the ones that make our relationship so pointless? I was on vacation. It was a vacation from examining my problems and my flaws as much as anything else. And it did me a world of good."

"Vacation's over."

"Not necessarily. Not that part."

Carol took a long moment to regroup, regarding him speculatively. "She must have really been something," she finally said.

"Who?"

"You know who. Your soup's getting cold."

He automatically dipped a spoon into his soup and took a sip. Not bad.

Even the Cabbage Patch couldn't completely ruin tomato soup. He said, "Okay, look, you know what I just realized?" He was surprised to recognize a new emotion: cold clear cleansing choler.

"What?"

"That without knowing it, I *have* been thinking about us, about you and me, over vacation. You know how I know? Because I realize I don't want to have this conversation."

She looked very hurt. "Ezra—"

"Did you ever read Eldridge Cleaver?"

"Who?"

"Sixties writer. Died a few years back. Had a very checkered career, from convict to street activist to born-again Republican. He was very hot for a while there. He said, 'If you're not part of the solution, you're part of the problem,' that's his contribution to American folk wisdom. Not bad, is it? Well, I'm prepared to admit I've got problems, Carol, but what I realize is, you're not part of the solution."

Tears sprang into her eyes. "This isn't how this conversation was supposed to go," she said, her voice small and quavering.

A sudden torrent of regret. But he had momentum now, he felt some strength, his feelings were crystallizing, it was no time to backtrack. He rose. "This just doesn't work for me anymore," he said quietly. "And it never worked for you. So let's be grown-ups and admit it. We've just been marking time. Good-bye, Carol. Take care of yourself."

He walked quickly out of the restaurant, and out of the Student Union Building. Well, that was that. As he crossed campus, he tried not to assess his own reactions. The image of her crumpled teary face remained uncomfortably vivid in his inner eye; he had the unpleasant notion it would persist for a while.

In the parking lot, as Ezra was opening the door to his Tercel, Professor Dixon's big Buick rolled up into the adjacent space. As Dixon effortfully emerged from his car, he said, "Ezra! Well met! Did you have a good break?"

"Just fine, Bob. And you?"

"Excellent. Put the finishing touches on my book."

Dumbfounding: The man had tenure, why did he bother? "That's very exciting," Ezra offered. Dixon's book examined the various drafts and

revisions of Wordsworth's *Prelude,* and word around the department suggested it would be ground-breaking in some indefinable way, might actually put Beuhler on the lit-crit map.

"How's *your* research coming? Get any work done during the hols?"
Evidently, his visits to the Lake Country had left their mark on Dixon's
diction.

"Oh, pushing ahead," Ezra said.

"Let me urge a certain amount of *speed* on you. Even *urgency.* The
sooner we see some results, the better."

"I'll bear that in mind." Ezra felt a sudden outbreak of flop sweat in
every cranny and crevice of his body. Even in the midst of mind-splattering
panic, he found himself noting how speedily perspiration can be secreted
when the right cues are activated. Ivan Pavlov could have designed this
conversation for one of his experiments.

So let's see, he said to himself as he drove home, let's take stock. The
chairman is giving me warnings even more direct, even less hedged, than
all his previous warnings; I've irreparably broken up with Carol and
reduced her to tears; her father—this just occurred to him—has never
liked me and enjoys an influential position on the body which makes the
final decision on promotions. Of course, the effect of the break-up with
Carol on her father's attitude needn't be straightforwardly negative; there
was always the hope that he'd be so relieved to see the match ended that
he'd regard Ezra in a more benign light.

Fat chance. The man hates me. I'm no more acceptable to him as
despoiler of his college than despoiler of his daughter.

Pulling into his garage, Ezra felt a sudden wave of relief. The world outside might be a miserable place, but *Every Inch a Lady* was waiting within,
ready to welcome him into its warm protective embrace. It offered solicitude, solace, shelter.

This wave of relief was followed immediately by a wave of excitement.
Everything about the book was great. It would even get him off his ass and
onto the Beuhler computer system, something he'd postponed for years,
literal years. Pornography was a character-builder, that much was inar-
guable. He was growing as a scholar and a man, and doing it while nestled
in Nora's welcoming arms. Who could ask for anything more?

■   ■   ◪

Six hours later, he was sprawled on his living room couch, a half-eaten roll and a half-drunk Diet Coke on the rickety table in front of him. Having combed through the manual he'd just bought, he knew he could write his novel on the college computer. At the speed of light! He pulled himself upright. No time like the present. This wasn't his usual approach to life— any time but the present was more his line—but pornography was transforming him into a better, more responsible individual.

The college computer facility was open all night, in deference to those fanatics whose afflatus might visit at unconventional hours. Fortunately for Ezra, their existence was entirely theoretical. The large room in the basement of the building was empty. Indeed, as far as Ezra could tell, the whole building was vacant except for the guard who manned the entrance. Ezra flashed his ID, signed in—with some misgivings, for, despite his perfectly plausible cover story, he didn't like leaving a written record—and proceeded down the stairs and through the double doors to the computer room. He felt like a character in a Hitchcock film, oppressed by vague (and, he preferred to think, irrational) guilt, entering an alien and hostile environment. His pulse was elevated, his mouth felt dry.

He picked a cubicle, sat down, placed his manual, his floppies, and his yellow legal pads on the desk, and addressed the monitor. Here goes nothing.

```
UNIX
Login: Gordon
Password: 1G2O3R4D
```

The password he typed in had been issued to him a couple of years before, when Beuhler opened an account for him unasked. He'd obviously have to change it, and soon. The manual he had read promised him ironclad security, and he wasn't so paranoid as to doubt it, but still, a little extra caution couldn't hurt. Nevertheless, that would have to wait. Right now he didn't dare stop what he was doing for fear he might never resume.

```
Last login: None
Welcome to Beuhler College Computer System
>
```

Holy smoke! Just like the manual promised! His first task, and a boring task it was, involved transcribing what he already had. But, dreary and mechanical as this would be, it conferred some incidental benefits. Not merely getting his work to date on disk, but also providing useful practice with the system before he essayed original composition.

Well, here goes. Be still, my heart.

■　　■　　■

By 3 A.M., bleary-eyed, with a pounding headache and a triumphant sense of accomplishment, Ezra had succeeded in transcribing more than half his work in progress. A good night's work. Resisting the impulse to rush home to bed, he forced himself, like the double-agent he still imagined himself to be, to follow security procedures punctiliously. Consulting the UNIX manual before each operation, he copied what he'd done onto a disk, eradicated his files from the system, and then, still not letting himself flag, altered his password. Can't be too careful. Then he dragged himself to the printer room down the hall to make hard copy, so he'd be able to line-edit at home. Only then did he head for the exit.

As he paused at the front desk to sign out, the guard gave him a twisted smile. "Working hard tonight, mm?"

"Yep."

"Productive session?"

"Not bad," Ezra said.

"Haven't seen you here before, have I?"

"No, I shouldn't think so."

"Not one of our regular night owls?"

"Not usually. But I may be changing my ways." And then, unaccountably feeling that he owed the man an explanation, "I'm trying to write some articles. For my tenure case."

"Publish or perish?"

"Exactly."

The guard nodded. "You guys have it rough. But working at night's nice. Nice and peaceful."

Nice maybe, Ezra thought as he exited the building. But I don't expect much peace.

"You yourself publish poetry, Professor Gordon, do you not?" inquired Dr. Ng.

Dr. and Mrs. Ng were both compact, conservatively dressed, and of indeterminate age. Dr. Ng's first name was unintelligible to Ezra when Henry introduced them, and although Dr. Ng, seeing Ezra's confusion, had suggested graciously that his friends addressed him as "Biff," Ezra decided that this familiarity, though implicitly sanctioned, was best left unemployed. Dr. and Mrs. Ng would remain Dr. and Mrs. Ng for the purposes of the interview.

"Yes, I do. Or, that is, I have done."

The four of them were sitting in Ezra's office—Ezra had borrowed two chairs from Hannah Jenkel, whose office was next to his own—and claustrophobia had set in almost immediately. To cross one's legs in this setting was a delicate and dangerous operation, risking both injury and intimacy.

"You are working on something else at present?"

"That's correct."

"Something other than poetry?"

"Er, yes."

"But of a creative nature?"

"Well . . . it's not a distinction I'm comfortable with, Dr. Ng."

"I see. Criticism can also be creative, you mean to suggest?"

"Something like that." Ezra didn't actually believe this for a second, but it was current lit-crit gospel, and there was no reason to air the profession's dirty linen. Let alone his own.

"And . . . may I ask a rather impertinent question, Professor Gordon?"

"By all means."

"When you do write poetry, does it bring you appreciable income?"

Dr. Ng's English was so lightly accented it was impossible to tell whether he was an immigrant or a native-born American who had first learned the language from immigrant parents while growing up in an immigrant community. But there was something in the combination of elaborate soft-spoken courtesy and sharp purposefulness that struck Ezra as very Chinese. Mrs. Ng, on the other hand, could be so characterized only on the basis of her recessiveness: After saying hello and shaking his hand with a little bow, she hadn't uttered a word. Neither had Henry, sitting in a corner as far from the other three as the room allowed, suffering silently and very visibly. The change in his demeanor was remarkable; even his posture had altered, stiff and controlled, at attention, every muscle in place, instead of the loose shambling American slouch he customarily adopted.

"Appreciable?" Ezra echoed. "No, I wouldn't say so."

"Perhaps it was unfair of me to use the word 'appreciable.'"

Ezra smiled modestly. "The answer would be the same either way. I don't write poetry for money, which is just as well, since it's never brought me any."

"Yes, I see. And so you pursue a profession which brings you adequate income?"

Christ, this is like being on *The Practice.* "Well, I might cavil at 'adequate,' but I teach here at Beuhler, yes." If I pursue a profession, so far it's managed to elude me.

"You've found you can do your, your creative work while earning a salary, yes?"

Ezra glanced over at Henry. He didn't look happy. Ezra imagined that dialogue of this nature had been a fixture of the Ng household while Henry was growing up.

"Yes. But a poem is—"

"Forgive me for interrupting, Professor Gordon, I only wished to observe that this is something you and I have in common. Although I practice internal medicine, I also paint as an avocation. Water colors, primarily, although I have also attempted oils on a few occasions. It affords me the greatest pleasure. My life would be greatly impoverished without it."

Jeez, this guy was good. Ezra looked over toward Henry again. Henry looked back beseechingly. Ezra opened his palms to signal, "What more can I do?" and then noticed out of the corner of his eye that Dr. Ng had caught the gesture. Not much escaped him, was Ezra's guess. The man must be a superb diagnostician.

Mrs. Ng broke the silence by saying something to her husband in Chinese. He answered with a short harsh syllable.

"Please, Professor," he then said a moment later, "you were about to make some remarks about poetry, and I rather rudely interrupted you."

"Not at all." Ezra had once, during a brief adolescent infatuation with chess, read an article in which Bobby Fischer disputed the apparently common idea that it was Capablanca's skill as an endgame player that had made him such a formidable champion. According to Fischer, the Cuban played "with such brilliance in the middle game that the game was decided—even though his opponent didn't always know it—before they arrived at the ending."

Ezra was put in mind of Fischer's observation by this conversation with Dr. Ng. Was there really any point in playing it out? Only to Henry, who was watching its give and take unblinkingly. He was one of those who didn't realize the game had been decided before the endgame. Oh well, might as well offer a show of resistance. Don't want him to think the match was rigged. Ezra took a deep breath. "I was going to say, in our country, in our culture, poetry is a notoriously unremunerative activity. There are almost no poets who do nothing else. Most have other jobs. Many, like me, are teachers."

"It is not a happy situation," Dr. Ng offered, and Mrs. Ng clucked her tongue in what Ezra interpreted as a mixture of sympathy for him personally and disapproval for the Philistine culture which denied him support.

"No it isn't," Ezra agreed. "But things are somewhat less bleak for writers of fiction."

Dr. Ng's eyes opened a little wider. He hadn't seen this one coming. But he wasn't worried, he still believed his position impregnable. "Only at the very highest levels, no?"

"No, Dr. Ng." Ezra noticed that the older man winced; he was probably unaccustomed to, and offended by, direct contradiction. Keep your tone nice and respectful, Ezra cautioned himself, before continuing, "Reasonable livings are to be made, although of course the market for engineers is on the whole healthier." Before Dr. Ng could speak—and it was clear that he intended to, that he felt he had given Ezra rather too much leeway—

Ezra rushed into the dangerous part of his pitch: "In any event, I'm reluctant to present the case to you on that basis. I believe Henry has a very large talent. I believe he has a potentially major contribution to make. And so I believe it would be a shame not to permit him some period of time in which to try to fashion a career as a novelist. He might make you very proud."

He was piling it on pretty thick. Let's just hope they don't ask me directly whether I've *read* Henry's book. The master diagnostician sitting across from me can probably spot a barefaced lie from way over the county line.

Meanwhile, the Ngs were engaged in a rather animated conversation in Chinese, which Henry was straining to hear, or possibly straining to understand. In this conversation at least, a conversation unintelligible to outsiders, Mrs. Ng was an active participant. After they stopped talking, and nodded at each other once, Dr. Ng said, "This is really true?"

"Dr. Ng, in these matters, no one can say something is really true. It isn't like diagnosing disease."

"It may be more similar than you think."

"As a sometime patient, I'd prefer to think not." He *had* to think not; Dr. Jacobs had put her hand up his ass. Was he now to understand this was merely part of a medical guessing game? "All I can give you is my opinion. I think Henry has something important to say. I think he's an artist. I'm honored to have been entrusted with his education."

Why am I doing this? he asked himself. When Henry's out on the streets panhandling for spare change, will he thank me? But then Ezra caught himself: Henry's a bright fellow, he's young, he can take a year off to finish his book, then go back to school and study engineering. At least he'll have given the thing a try, at least he won't spend the rest of his life feeling cheated and deprived, feeling there was an artist imprisoned within him who had never even been granted a work furlough, feeling resentment toward his parents and himself for that excess of caution and good sense that never let him go for broke. Besides—and this was most comforting of all—these Ngs are obviously pretty tough old birds, it's unlikely they'll pay the slightest attention to a word I've said.

Dr. Ng rose. Mrs. Ng rose. Ezra rose. Then Henry rose. Dr. Ng extended his hand. "We don't wish to take up any more of your valuable time, Professor Gordon. Thank you for your candor, sir."

"My pleasure, sir."

After ritual farewells, repeated several times in increasingly courteous formulas, Ezra opened the door for the Ngs. He was surprised and touched to see Biff Ng tousle his son's hair affectionately as the family exited the office, and amused when Henry whirled on his heel and flashed him a grin and a thumbs-up sign before resuming his trek down the corridor two steps behind his parents.

Maybe, Ezra told himself as he stepped back into his office, there are enough voices out there counseling prudence, maybe it's good—for me too, not just for Henry—that I didn't add my voice to the timorous chorus. Maybe if Henry doesn't take some calculated risks when he's young, he'll end up taking some desperate risks when he's not so young.

Maybe also, he considered, seeing as how I've gone out on a limb, maybe it's time to give Henry's book a read. Just to see how idiotic I'll feel if the Ngs solicit a second opinion.

But that would have to wait. First he had to finish his own book. The thought provided a thrill; the Ngs were instantaneously forgotten, and beautiful lithe insatiable Nora usurped their place. On something like automatic pilot, he set about preparing to leave his office for the day. Sure, it was a little early to go home, before lunch and everything, but what the hell, there was text to edit, which entailed savoring Nora's previous exploits, and then, an even more enticing treat, after dinner he could look forward to a nocturnal visit to the computer center, a private tryst, a cerebral liason, with his lovely wanton.

He slipped a few books into his briefcase, locked his office, and started down the corridor. But just as he reached the door leading to freedom and, soon thereafter, bliss, he heard Bob Dixon's voice: "Oh Ezra!"

Ezra turned and saw Dixon's massive figure angled out of the doorway to his office, the fat slab of unsliced bacon at the end of his wrist waving him back.

Just what I need: another conversation about my tenure case, another official warning going onto the record and into my file. Dixon was playing this by the book, protecting himself and the Department against any potential legal liability—as if Ezra would ever let himself get into litigation with Carol representing the opposite side—covering his ass with skill and care, and doing nothing in the process to make needless enemies. Even Ezra himself had to concede that Dixon had behaved like a gentleman in their dealings, an upfront and honest broker. No wonder they had begged the man to accept a second term as chairman. He possessed an indispensable, unacademic slyness.

"Do you have a minute, Ezra?" the chairman asked as Ezra approached.

"Of course," Ezra answered cheerfully.

Dixon beckoned him into the office. Standing there was a square-jawed man about Ezra's age, an inch or two taller than Ezra, in an ill-fitting black suit, with neatly trimmed light brown hair and an ugly mole on his cheek.

"Ezra," the chairman said, "this is Daniel McGruder. FBI. The Fresno office."

Ezra was puzzled. "FBI?"

"He'd like to ask you a few questions," Dixon went on. "Agent McGruder, Professor Gordon. The one I was telling you about."

Ezra shook the man's proffered hand and smiled as pleasantly as he could manage under the puzzling circumstances. McGruder's grip was firm to the point of crippling, and while applying it he gave Ezra a searching gaze, whether because he thought there was a reason for it or because it was his habit Ezra was unable to tell. But there was certainly nothing friendly in the fellow's demeanor; if anything, it bordered on the insolent.

"Please, sit down, Professor," McGruder said. "This shouldn't take long." He pronounced the word "Professor" with the exaggerated courtesy that invariably implies disdain.

Ezra glanced at Dixon and took a seat.

"Are you aware Beuhler's computer system has been the target of sabotage?"

"I've heard something about it, sure. I guess everybody has by now."

"Can you tell me what you know about it?"

What little he knew he had heard from Carol, and she had sworn him to secrecy. "Nothing much. I gather some records have been scrambled or something."

"How do you know it *is* sabotage, then?"

"I don't. I was taking your word for it."

"Are you aware English Department records are among the more seriously affected?"

"No, I hadn't heard that."

McGruder and Dixon exchanged a glance. "Do you own a computer, professor?"

"Uh uh. Not a functioning one."

"Do you ever *use* a computer?"

"I've begun using one recently, yes."

"The college system, by any chance?"

"Right."

"So you're familiar with its operation?"

"Just for word processing. What is this? Am I supposed to be a suspect?"

"We're talking to a number of people, Professor." McGruder sounded insufferably smug. "Do you have any friends or relatives in Germany?"

"None that I know of. My daughter and ex-wife are in Switzerland, but I have no contact with them."

McGruder frowned. Was it skepticism or disapproval? "You don't?"

"I don't. As I just said." He turned to Dixon. "What's this about, Bob?"

"It's just routine," McGruder said, peremptorily reclaiming Ezra's attention. "Would you object to our examining your computer records, your time sheets and files and whatnot?"

Oh shit, perfect timing, an investigation begins the moment I start writing a dirty book. Thank God I erase my files every night! "I certainly would."

McGruder nodded happily, one interim hypothesis confirmed. "And why is that, would you say?"

"Because they're my business and nobody else's. Because Americans are supposed to be secure from unreasonable search and seizure."

"People might disagree about what's reasonable and what isn't."

"That's perfectly true. Which is why I feel comfortable relying on my own judgment."

"You don't want to cooperate with our investigation?"

"Sure. Until it infringes on my rights."

"Aren't you eager to demonstrate your innocence?"

"I don't have to demonstrate my innocence. That's not how it works."

McGruder processed this for a moment, then continued, "Do you have any feelings of resentment toward Beuhler College?"

"More now than a couple of minutes ago." And in fact Ezra did feel an exhilarating surge of anger going through him, and he surrendered to it joyfully. It lifted him right out of his chair into a standing position, where, seething with rage, he wheeled around to confront Dixon. "This is a fucking outrage, Bob." He was trembling, but he didn't think anyone would mistake what he was feeling for fear. "How do you justify this shit?"

Dixon was mild. "We're stumped, Ezra. No leads lead anywhere. We have to look into every possibility, no matter how remote."

"And you regard me as a possibility?"

"I said, *no matter how remote.* And with your tenure case in jeopardy and all . . ." He shrugged. "No one seriously suspects you. We have to touch every base, that's all."

"It's wonderful to have the support and trust of my department."

McGruder looked alert. "You don't feel you have the trust and support of your department?"

Ezra turned to him. "Let me say this as clearly as I can. I have not messed with the computer system. Even if I wanted to, which I don't, I wouldn't have a clue how to go about it. I deeply resent being suspected. And since it's clear the chairman of my department is the one who fingered me—" Here Ezra turned back to face Dixon again—"I have to conclude I don't have his trust and support. Now, is there anything else, or can I get on with my job?"

"Go on, you can go," McGruder said with a wave of his hand. "We may want to talk to you again later."

"Oh goody."

"In the meantime, if you hear anything, let us know."

Wordlessly, Ezra strode out of the office. When he was a few paces down the corridor, he heard Dixon call, "Ezra!"

He stopped and turned around. "What is it?"

Dixon was leaning out his door into the hall. His face was even more rubicund than usual. Perhaps he was blushing. "I'm sorry, Ezra. I don't blame you for feeling irked. But we're in a tizzy over this thing."

"Ah, that makes it okay, then."

Still furious—and furiously happy that he could now resent Dixon with a clear conscience—he clomped down the hall, down the stairs, and out of the building. A suspect, he thought to himself as he crossed the lawn to the parking lot. I'm a fucking suspect. Thank you, Beuhler College. I gave you the best years of my life, and this is how you repay me.

It was only as he was pulling into his own driveway that the full implications of this intelligence hit him, the practical as opposed to the emotional implications: It would be nuts to keep using the college computer system. One way or another, legally or not, they were bound to monitor his work. He exhaled a sigh of gratitude to E. A. Peau for being so conscientious about erasing his files every night.

Four sessions on UNIX and now he had to cease and desist. The problem was, in those four days, he'd irrevocably turned a corner. Not only was he comfortable using the computer, he'd come to depend on it. The notion of returning to longhand was unthinkable. Which meant he'd have to fork over big bucks for a computer for himself, and a printer too. Thank you, Agent McGruder. Thank you, Chairman Dixon. Almost all of what remained of his advance would be gone.

I'm a victim of harassment, that's what I am. A patriotic, hard-working American pornographer on the receiving end of a bureaucratic vendetta. Get me the ACLU.

Of course, it was past time he had a functioning computer. But that didn't alter the principle. He was being smeared and his finances laid waste by a government probe. It was what Hamlet meant by "the insolence of office." What was next, Kenneth Starr breathing down his neck? Even though he'd never invested in real estate or engaged in sex acts in his office, unless the brief, involuntary glance at Mindy Dunkelweisse's breasts qualified.

He was sufficiently incensed by this new development that it took him an unaccustomed five minutes before he was entirely absorbed in editing his manuscript.

Four hours later, though, he was still at his desk, going strong. Editing wasn't an adequate word to describe the process he was engaged in, didn't begin to cover the modifications he found himself making. Barely a sentence escaped some emendation, and whole new scenes and episodes suggested themselves, and were promptly interpolated longhand in the margins, great inky efflorescences which spilled over onto the backs of the printed pages. Oh, he'd have to buy himself a computer all right, and soon. Right now, except he couldn't bear to tear himself away. Even while fixing coffee, while peeing, while taking off the odd minute or two to rest his eyes or to stretch, his brain kept turning over, kept churning out material, kept devising more intricate situations for Nora, and more rhapsodic ways to describe her sensations. His awareness of himself was sporadic and unwelcome; when he thought of himself, when he knew his name was Ezra Gordon and he was sitting in a certain place in a certain position feeling a certain way, he wasn't thinking about his book. And his book was all that mattered.

And then his doorbell rang.

It took him a moment to identify the sound. And another moment to realize it required some sort of response from him. And a few more moments, while he was crossing to the front door, to wonder who it could be. Nobody ever came to his apartment. And finally, as he swung the door open, it occurred to him it might be a burglar and he probably should have demanded that the visitor identify him or herself before he so freely admitted said person.

Said person was Carol. In torn faded jeans, a plain white blouse, and sandals, looking very serious and very determined.

"Carol!" His mind was still in Venice with Nora. He felt as if he should give the side of his head a sharp rap in order to bring it back to present reality.

"May I come in?"

"Of course. Please." He stood back and let her enter. She had been to his place only a handful of times before this. Considering how long they'd been going together, or whatever it was they'd been doing, and the zeal with which he'd tried to arrange it, it was astonishing how rarely she visited.

The same thought was evidently on her mind. "Gee, it seems like years since I've been here," she said. "I forgot how crummy it is."

"Well, make yourself to home," he said, the folksiness an inevitable consequence of contemplating the cornpone family Dimsdale. Only then did he remember that there was a sheaf of papers on his desk, and that the page at the top of the pile contained a detailed description of outlandish improprieties performed by Nora and two gondoliers drifting along the Grand Canal by moonlight.

"Oh, you're writing something!" she said. "What is it?"

She was steering straight for his desk.

"Nothing!" he said hastily, dashing after her. "Nothing nothing nothing!" Quite rudely, he managed to get past her, elbowing her aside rather roughly in the process, and reach the rickety table. He quickly stuffed the sheaf of papers into the top drawer. Just in time, as she loomed up beside him.

"My goodness!" she exclaimed. "What's the big mystery?"

"'Big mystery?'" he echoed, somewhat out of breath, but gamely aiming for puzzled innocence. "No mystery. No mystery. Neither big nor little."

"Is it some sort of love letter or something? What *are* you hiding?"

"Hiding?" He laughed, and his own laughter sounded falser to him than any other sound he had ever heard in his life. "Hiding? How absurd!"

"Well, then what is it?"

"Oh, it's just, it's just a—"

"I mean, you obviously *were* writing something."

"Well, yes, that's true, I suppose."

"So?"

"It's, it's . . ."

"Are you working on another poem?"

"Yes! That's it! You hit the old nail on the old head! A poem!"

"Well, gee, it's good you've taken that up again, isn't it?"

"Yes, yes, it certainly is. Been way too long."

She looked at him quizzically. "You're sure it *is* a poem, though?" And, off his nod, "Then why didn't you just say so?"

"Well, I, I . . . What are you doing here, Carol?" The best defense, his old chess books used to say, is a good offense. "I mean, you're not exactly in the habit of *dropping in*. It was hard enough to lure you here back when we were, we were . . ." He gave up the search for a satisfactory verb; they had never agreed on a vocabulary to describe what they'd been up to when they'd been up to something, even if it admittedly had been very little.

"I just thought I'd pay you a visit."

"You were in the neighborhood?" This was a little joke: Ezra's apartment was in a neighborhood no one in his right mind would "just be in;" it was as close as Seven Hills came to having a slum, it was literally on the wrong side of the tracks, although no trains had used those tracks in over forty years.

"Nooo." She wrinkled her nose at the notion. "I thought we left things a little unsettled before." This was a brave, if transparently false, claim; the one way they *hadn't* left anything was unsettled. "I think we ought to talk."

Ezra sighed. The last thing in the world he wanted to do was repeat the same conversation they'd already had at lunch several days ago, but with variations, the variations mostly consisting of lexicographical inquiries on her part (as in, "What do you mean by 'unsatisfying'?") whose real purpose was to probe the wound in order to see how painfully it could be made to throb.

"But first, tell me what you're working on. Why is it a secret?"

"You know I don't like to talk about unfinished work," he asserted.

"I don't know anything of the kind."

"You don't?"

"Come on, Ezra, you always used to call me when you got a good first line, you'd read it to me over the phone, remember? And you'd read more if you got *past* the first line."

"Well, yeah, that's true, but, but, this is different."

"Apparently."

"This is, it's sort of an experiment."

"Okay." She waited.

"It's sort of a, a . . ." His mind was racing. In circles. Sort of a what? Sort of a pornographic book? No no no! "It's sort of an *epic*. Sort of a *saga*. You know, in the old style. Kind of, kind of, you know, *Icelandic* in tone."

Huh?

"Sounds like fun," she said.

"It does?"

"Yes. Can I hear a little?"

Oh God. Suddenly, a long circuitous inconclusive conversation about the good and bad points of their former relationship struck him as desirable. "Didn't you want to—?"

"Oh," she interrupted airily, as if she hadn't been weeping about this very subject only a few days ago, "that can wait. Let me hear your poem."

What radar did she possess, what killer instinct, that told her that, despite her original intention of subjecting him to a painful, a *mutually* painful grilling about their break-up, this thing of his, this unknown thing dwelling in his desk drawer, was more promising quarry?

"I'd really rather not, Carol."

"Jeez," she said, her voice steely, "I'm not going to plagiarize it! I'm *interested*, okay? I'm a *fan*. I'm glad you're over your writer's block. Let me hear it. The opening, at least."

Oh God oh God oh God.

"Okay." This felt like very deep shit. "But sit over there." He gestured toward the sofa at the other end of the living room.

"Why, for goodness sake?"

"Because, because, uh, because the epic tradition is an *oral* tradition, I want you to *hear* it, I don't want you reading along. That would ruin it. Okay? This is the most authentic way to experience this, this, this experience. Word of honor."

"You're not going to read me something *in* Icelandic, are you?"

"No, no, it's in English," he said, and immediately regretted having done so. If he could convincingly fake his way through a series of quasi-Nordic nonsense syllables . . . No, the execution would clearly be beyond him, the very idea was simply a measure of his desperation. "Now go sit over there. Go on. Sit."

"Sounds silly to me," she said, but, blessedly, while crossing to the sofa. "I just want to hear what you're working on, is all."

"Right, right." He reached into the drawer and retrieved the top couple of pages of his manuscript.

Now what?

He cleared his throat. She looked up at him expectantly, her hands in her lap, a good girl, polite and attentive and quiet. He pretended to read from the page in his hands, in a grandly declamatory style:

"Oh ye daughters of Goldruning,
Of the golden tresses and the silvery bodices,
Of the, the golden tresses,
Oh ye daughters and, uh, and sons of, of Goldruning—"

He stopped and glanced at her. She was still looking at him attentively. "You don't want to hear this," he assured her. "It's really, it's really intended for a, a specialist audience, it actually kind of stinks in a way."

"I'm finding it very enjoyable," she said.

"You are?"

"I'm curious to see where you're going with it."

He nodded, and resumed declaiming:

"Oh you children of Frig and Fredda
Guide me on this my journey
Guide me on, uh, on this my journey—"

He looked up at her. "Repetition is a very big deal in these things," he assured her. "You know, gives it a kind of incantatory quality."

"It certainly does. Go on."

"This journey to the shores of Trip—,
—uh, of *Tripgash,*
Where the Brampsons gather berries,
Gather berries ripe with sweetness,
Gather berries, uh, sweet with ripeness,
And await the coming hero.
Await the hero and the, the warrior
In whose hands lies their salvation."

He was bathed in sweat, his eyes were beginning to blur. How much longer could he keep this up? "I, it, uh, still needs work," he said.

"Isn't there any more?"

The note of disapproval in her tone—a "you-mean-this-is-all-you've-got-to-show-for-yourself?" inflection—caused him to reject, recklessly, unthinkingly, the life preserver she had extended to him. "Sure, of course, quite a bit more. But, I don't know, I'm not sure I've really captured the, the elegiac sort of, sort of *processional* feel I'm aiming for." That's it, boy, scatter the bullshit around, blind her with it. She's probably had enough too.

"Well, no, I think, I think it's very nice, in a way. I mean, it's certainly *different.*"

"Yes, it is that."

"Has a kind of, of, inexorable feel to it, somehow."

"Ah, you caught that, did you?"

"So how does it come out? Does the hero finally arrive at the Brampsons' and eat berries and everything?"

"Carol—"

"Unless you'd prefer for me to be surprised when I read it?"

"That might be best."

"Sagas and epics are narrative forms, aren't they? The story *counts,* right?"

"Yes indeed." He took a deep breath, a grand sigh of relief. He couldn't help himself; he discerned a ray of light in the middle-distance.

"Well, that's good. I've always liked stories. I know it's unfashionable for you literary people, but I enjoy wondering what's gonna happen next."

"It still needs a lot of work. It's very rough." He put the thing back in his desk drawer. It felt, all of a sudden, *radioactive.* He shut the desk drawer firmly. Maybe a little too firmly. Maybe he sort of slammed it. That might be the reason she jumped.

"Anyway . . ." he said. It was an invitation for her to begin. The next ordeal. No rest for the weary. But she didn't say anything, just sat on the sofa looking at him. After a brief wait, during which it became clear she wasn't going to initiate anything, he said, "Carol, you're always welcome to stop by, but, but I got the impression you came with a purpose."

"Oh, that," she said. "No biggie. I just, the way we left things, I just wanted to say I've thought it over, and, well, maybe you've been more right than me about, you know, things."

"Ah."

"It can't have been much fun for you, having me on your case all the time, trying to make you something you're not. You can get that elsewhere."

"And how."

"And I was also wrong about, you know, about—"

"Things?"

"*Sex,* I meant." It must have taken an effort, but she got the word out without stammering. "You obviously had—"

"Needs?" he suggested, oddly pleased to provide the awful cliché.

"Expectations," she corrected. "Expectations. And it was wrong of me to, to treat them as being *unreasonable.* We have really different backgrounds and attitudes, obviously, and mine, I mean in addition to how I feel about, about—"

"Sex," Ezra prompted.

"Things. In addition to that, mine have, I mean I guess mine have a pretty large dollop of self-righteousness too, so I took the difference between us and turned it into an attitude where I'm right and you're, you're—"

"Wrong?"

"—disgusting. And that's just something I need to get over. It's how I was brought up, but that's my problem, not yours."

How true, Ezra thought. But where was she heading with this? "Where are you heading with this?"

She hesitated. "I don't want it to be awkward when we run into each other. We can be friends. In a town like Seven Hills, in a community like Beuhler, our paths are gonna cross, and, and, when that happens I don't want you to think ill of me or think I think ill of you. 'Cause I don't. I respect you a lot, and I admit a lot of our problems were, were my . . . were caused by me."

This was a rather handsome concession. Ezra was touched. But while he tried to find the right words to express this sentiment without patronizing her or seeming to rehearse his grievances all over again, the phone rang. As he rose, he said, "I'm sorry, Carol."

"Don't be silly. Go answer it."

He nodded and scurried to the telephone table in the hall just outside the arched entry to the living room. "Hello?"

"Ezra?"

The sound of the voice on the other end of the line caused an immediate, Pavlovian stirring in his loins.

"Tessa!"

"How are you, honey? I've missed you."

He lowered his voice. "Really? I mean, I have too."

"Have you?"

"More than that. You've inspired me." Ezra was thinking: Women like Tessa don't call guys like me "honey," and they surely don't miss us when we're gone. They barely notice when we're there.

"How have I inspired you?" she was urging. "Tell me."

"Oh, I can't do that."

She laughed, low and dirty. God, she was fabulous!

"I must say, I didn't expect to hear from you again," he told her.

"I *did* expect to hear from you. There's this thing called manners."

"I didn't have the guts," he admitted.

"Guts? I mean, we—"

"Yes, I haven't forgotten."

"You'd think it took guts even if I sent you an embossed invitation."

"You're right."

"I know. It's why I'm breaking the rules and calling you."

"I'm delighted you did. Flabbergasted, but delighted."

"Does that mean I can be even pushier?"

"Push to your heart's content."

"I'm paying you a visit this weekend."

"What?"

"You heard me. The only way we're gonna make progress is if I take the reins."

"I'm not into that kinky stuff," he heard himself saying.

"I'm on a shoot now, we wrap Thursday, and—"

"Uh, Tessa," he interrupted, "I don't know what that means."

"It means I've got some time and I'm gonna spend it with you. And in case you were wondering, you don't have any say in the matter." She hung up without another word.

Ezra, abashed at the clownishness of the gesture but unable to refrain, stared dumbly at the receiver for a moment, and only then replaced it on the cradle. Life was taking a turn for the weird.

And then he remembered Carol. Whoops. He scampered back into the living room.

Empty. Carol was gone.

Chapter 5

"I mean, I don't get it," protested Jack Scheer with his customary undertone of personal grievance. "What is this tontine shit anyway?"

A seminar participant one actively dislikes is a problem most college instructors have to cope with sooner or later, and Ezra had encountered the phenomenon more than once in his career. Indeed, he sometimes suspected teachers and students were natural antagonists, like housecats and barnyard rodents. Even so, nothing had prepared him for Jack Scheer: Jack was the single most repellent human being Ezra had ever taught.

Out of the corner of his eye he noticed that Mindy's hand was raised. *She* knew what this tontine shit was.

Ezra sighed inwardly. This was turning out to be some seminar, all right. Mindy Dunkelweisse and Jack Scheer in the same airless little room. Two utterly impossibles out of seven enrollees. Well, at least Henry Ng had, against all odds, chosen to sit this one out.

"It isn't necessary to raise your hand, Mindy," Ezra reminded her. "Everybody should feel free to contribute in an informal manner. Just be civil."

This last caveat was for Jack's benefit, although there wasn't much hope he noticed. A bony, splotchily complexioned, scraggly bearded transfer from UC Irvine (who seemed to assume this last fact conferred some sort of academic cachet upon him), belligerent, obtuse, bullyingly ideological—both with regard to politics and lit-crit philosophy—and unrelentingly foul-mouthed, Jack couldn't be counted on to notice much beyond his own reflexive and ill-considered shibboleths and prejudices.

What surprised Ezra about all this was how particularly offensive he found Jack's profanity. He wasn't ordinarily the type who minded bad language. In fact, creative swearing was to Ezra one of the elements that gave American English its distinctive tang. And he was himself a pornographer these days, regularly excavating in the lower depths of the lexicon. But Jack's language was suffused with some deep-seated infantile fury—he used his favorite word, "shit," like a baby smearing feces over the walls of his nursery as a way of punishing his parents for some perceived injury— and with such loutish insensitivity to linguistic and social nuance that its constant iteration worked on Ezra like a throbbing toothache.

Still, he did what he could to hide his feelings. It would be unprofessional to let his animus show. Nor, he'd reluctantly decided, should he take his revenge on the boy by giving him a worse grade than he deserved; Ezra could only pray that Jack's term paper would turn out to be as awful as his comments in class promised it would be.

But the limitations he'd imposed on his own behavior notwithstanding, he *had* permitted himself to entertain hopes from the second session on that one of the other seminar participants, provoked beyond reason, would finally let Jack have it. Ideally Wesley Conrad, who was on the wrestling team, and ideally in the form of a physical assault. However, as far as Ezra could tell, neither Wes nor any of the other students objected to Jack's personality the way he himself did. His own revulsion and loathing apparently stemmed from one of those inexplicable idiosyncratic antipathies, from bad chemistry. The others seemed to accept Jack's bullying and his harangues and his *shit*s and *fuck*s as boilerplate academic discourse.

Mindy finished speaking. Ezra hadn't paid attention, but it was safe to assume she had given an accurate definition of *tontine*—that was the sort of thing you could count on with Mindy—that along with behaving like a complete mental patient—so he nodded at her. "Thank you, Mindy."

"Okay, fine, so who gives a fuck?" was Jack's considered response.

"Well, Jack," Ezra answered evenly, "it's a useful concept to grasp if you hope to follow the plot of *Little Dorrit*."

"Plot?" Jack replied with sneering incredulity. "You're telling us to read novels for the *plot*?" Apparently they were well past such puerilities at UC Irvine. "We're supposed to care about the *story*?" he went on sarcastically. "Like little children? 'But how does it end, Daddy? Happily ever after?'"

"Well—"

"Jesus, what're you gonna tell us next, we should care about *characters* too?"

Bill Scarcelli spoke up, innocently unaware he was approaching danger-
ously close to the whirling blades of Jack's doctrinal helicopter. "Of *course*
we care about characters!" he said. "Otherwise, why bother to read a
novel at all?"

"Well," Jack snorted querulously, "leaving aside your last question,
which may possess unintended cogency, the fact is, these characters aren't
real people, they're *words on a page.* You don't believe Little Dorrit is a *person,* do you?" He snorted again: the very idea! "She's a verbal construct.
Why care about a verbal construct, unless you're a complete moron?"

Oops, we're off and running, thought Ezra, another tired tirade with the
least interesting aperçu in all of literary studies as its theme. Poor Bill Scarcelli looked as if he didn't know what had hit him. Which served him right,
in a way; by now, if he'd been paying any attention at all, he should have
seen this one coming from miles up the pike. But alas, Jack was on the
right track about one thing: Bill Scarcelli *was* a complete moron.

"Okay, Jack," Ezra said. "I think we're all aware of your, your notions
about that. I'd like to stay with this tontine business, if you don't mind."

Jack rolled his eyes upward: You see what I have to put up with from
this fucking cow college? was the way Ezra interpreted the look.

And then, as he was trying to formulate his next question, and in the
process to get pretty little Linda Henry to say something, since she didn't
seem to realize yet that speech was actually permitted her in a seminar, he
heard a scraping sound behind himself. He would have looked to see what
it was immediately, except his attention was claimed by the faces of the
students around the table. Seven jaws dropped open simultaneously, fourteen eyes widened in shock or incredulity or horror. Feeling an anticipatory
shudder travel up his spine—was it Marley's ghost at the door behind him,
or Roskolnikov, armed and dangerous?—Ezra slowly turned around to
discover the source of this universal astonishment for himself.

And found—goodness!—Tessa, hovering uncertainly in the doorway.
Goodness gracious!

She wasn't due till early evening. He had planned to spend the rest of the
afternoon cleaning his apartment and brooding over his inadequacies in
preparation for her arrival. But, good Christ, here she was, hours early and
intensely, undeniably Tessoid.

There was something so intrinsically salacious about Tessa that her very
presence on campus seemed an infraction of the college rules. She was

wearing a very thin, very skimpy polka-dotted summer dress that had probably looked plausible hanging in the Banana Republic window, but draped over that impossible body was close to indecent. Her butter-colored hair poured down from her crown like lava from an erupting volcano. Her toothy smile—from self-consciousness, Ezra guessed, but such niceties were no doubt lost on his students—was dazzling.

Slightly flustered in this alien setting, she put a finger to her lips, ducked her head shyly, a self-abnegating please-take-no-notice-of-me combination of gestures that made zero sense under the circumstances, and then pivoted to shut the door quietly. It was a moment that single-handedly justified the phenomenon of static cling.

"Holy shit," said Jack Scheer.

She turned back, still hesitating by the door, engulfed in a golden nimbus, appealingly unsure of her ground. Ezra found himself smiling, and *not* from self-consciousness, although he felt some of that too, but from the simple honest pleasure of seeing her again, and surprise at seeing her here and seeing her now.

"I got here early," she explained. "I hope it's, I sort of asked around and they told me . . . Should I—?" Gesturing toward the door, she petered out with a shrug.

He rose, pushing back his chair, and she simultaneously started toward him. They met in a bear hug a few feet from the table. None of the seminar participants stirred. Then she kissed him. When her tongue slipped into his mouth, he knew this wasn't something that should be happening in front of an audience, especially this audience, but neither could he make himself pull away immediately. First he had to rally his faltering will.

When they broke, not so very long after beginning, Ezra took a step back and drunk her in. She was so shimmeringly beautiful that heat waves seemed to come off her; it remained impossible for him to apprehend that they shared the same planet, let alone had once shared the same bed.

Then Linda Henry coughed, bringing him back to earth, the planet they did share. He laughed uncomfortably and half-turned to face the room. "Class, we have a visitor," he said.

"Do tell," Jack Scheer muttered.

"My friend Tessa Miles," Ezra added.

"Hi," Tessa said, with a little wave. Marilyn greeting our boys in Korea. "Is it okay if I stay?" She seemed to be asking the class rather than Ezra.

Ezra surreptitiously checked his Casio. Still forty minutes to go. Oh Christ. Oh well.

Tessa had caught the gesture. "I can wait outside."

"Over my dead body," said Wes Conrad, and, when everybody laughed, the tension broke. At least for the moment. At least for the students.

"If she goes, *we* go," offered Darryl Paxton, typically taking somebody else's idea and presenting it as a fresh thought. But the class found such relief in laughing the first time they all laughed again.

"No, no, please, take a seat, Tessa," Ezra said. As he resumed his own, he snuck a glance at Mindy, a potential source of further trouble. But the look she was directing his way could only be described as *awed.* Indeed, that seemed to go for the seminar as a whole. Interesting. Even Jack's customary supercilious sneer had left his face. Professor Gordon's star was rising sharply.

Nobody looked especially *attentive,* however. This was going to be a very long forty minutes, reflected glamour or no. And after it was over . . . No, no, no! Don't think about it. That way lay madness.

"We were discussing tontines," Ezra reminded the class, and himself. He glanced over at Tessa, who was grinning at him goofily. Well, fair enough. It must be odd, seeing him in this ridiculous position of authority. And then, unbidden, the thought of possessing her entered his mind: a clear, intensely tactile sensation, his hands under that dress.

It was fortunate his lower torso was hidden by the seminar table. His body, perversely, stubbornly, refused to acknowledge his anxiety. And it insisted on secreting hormones which urged his brain, in the strongest possible terms, and right through the ongoing waves of emotional distress, to contemplate pleasanter possibilities. The result was a very odd, very unsettling mixture indeed.

My crotch is a darkling plain where ignorant armies clash by night.

He cleared his throat. "Would somebody care to delineate the way the tontine motif plays itself out in the novel?" When nobody said anything— was it the incredible pomposity of his diction or Tessa's presence that stunned them into silence?—he prompted, "Linda?"

Pretty little Linda Henry—who all of a sudden looked a whole lot plainer and unexpectedly undernourished—began to speak. As Ezra suspected, she was quite well prepared, which was good, because after her first couple of sentences he felt free to let his mind wander off in decidedly

unliterary directions. Not that they were *altogether* unliterary: Transmo-
grified by art, transmuted into words, they would eventually find their way
into a literary artifact called *Every Inch a Lady.*

When Linda finished, another silence ensued. Ezra forced a smile and
said, "Any comments, class? Come on now, don't make me look inept in
front of our guest." He hoped that by addressing the tension forthrightly,
he might succeed in cutting through it.

For that reason, or maybe because he wanted to show off, or simply
because he was an unstoppable monomind, Jack accepted the invitation
and launched into another of his monologues, liberally salting his remarks
with words like "text," "construct," "semiotic," and "trope," not to mention that old stand-by "shit." The upshot, insofar as Ezra could follow
him—difficult at the best of times, but especially hard when one was paying only desultory attention in between vivid sexual fantasies—was that
the novel wasn't about a tontine at all, wasn't about Little Dorrit, wasn't
about debtor's prison, wasn't about any of that obvious stuff, but was in
fact an encoded account of Dickens's fears of writer's block, which were
themselves in turn a sublimation of his more highly cathected fears of premature ejaculation. All of this with an air of weary ennui, as if it was
demeaning to have to explain something so crassly self-evident, but what
choice did he have in such company?

The worst of it was, if Jack ever got around to writing this horseshit
down, he'd have a pretty good shot at publishing it in a reputable journal.
He had mastered the lingo, certainly mastered it more completely than
Ezra ever had; awful as it was to acknowledge, Jack was probably going
places in the lit biz.

When Jack finally wound down some five or so minutes later, the class's
previous titillated silence had been replaced by what Ezra interpreted as
torpid silence. Not an improvement.

"Well," he said, trying to keep his annoyance in check, "what occurs to
me is, by your logic, when Lincoln rose to speak at Gettysburg, all he
needed to say was, 'Whoops.'"

Jack started to splutter into renewed life, and so, before the egregious
putz could get his intellectual gears engaged, Ezra added, "I think that's
probably enough for today. If you haven't finished the novel, please do so
by next session. We've got a lot of ground to cover."

The class took its own sweet time about filing out. They must have had an intimation that once they were gone things might get interesting. Which happened to be an intimation Ezra, with a revived sensation of panic, shared: He might have been able to fake his way through a few encounters with Tessa down in L.A., but the sort of exposure facing him now, the utter vacuity of his life here in Beuhler, his total lack of any of the qualities someone like Tessa must look for in a man, couldn't be kept hidden over a whole weekend of intimate proximity. Part of him, therefore, wanted to prolong the deadliness of the seminar for as long as possible, while the rest of him chose to hasten its finish merely to end the suspense and get the inevitable humiliating failure over with. All this despite his own spontaneous pleasure at seeing Tessa again, which struck him as a foolish and inconvenient irrelevancy.

Until the students had gone, Tessa remained in her little chair with its attached fold-down wooden desk, and Ezra, in an agony of apprehension, stayed at the seminar table.

"Nice to have met you," Jack Scheer, the last to leave, told Tessa with a leer.

"Um," said Tessa, in the most neutral tone Ezra had ever heard her employ. But of course a woman like Tessa must have early mastered a whole spectrum of neutral tones in order to discourage importuning males without having to resort to outright rudeness.

"What a creep," she observed after Jack, who somehow contrived to loiter even as he made his way out, had finally quit the room.

Ezra was delighted. "Isn't he? The worst!"

"After he graduates, he should go into the movie business. Ycch."

"The other students don't seem to notice."

"They only have eyes for you."

"I don't think that's it, really."

"They idolize you, it's obvious."

"Well . . ." What was there to say to that? He stood up.

While he began to gather his papers together, putting off, however briefly, a decision about what to do next, Tessa extricated herself from the seat-and-desk contraption she was in and came over to him. He felt himself horripilating: What was expected of him now? He kept shuffling papers, and then he noticed her hand sliding smoothly down over his buttocks and between his legs, cupping him through the thin corduroy of his trousers.

"Has anyone ever told you, Professor Gordon, you're a tall cool drink of water on a hot day?"

With her hand gently molded around his testicles, it wasn't so easy to turn to face her, but he managed it somehow—her hand did get somewhat dislodged in the process—and stared at her for a good long shameless interval. And the thought struck him: Maybe total personal disaster could be forestalled long enough to salvage something from this visit. Something resembling *pleasure,* perhaps. It was the first consciously optimistic rumination about her he'd so far permitted himself.

"Has anyone ever told you you look good enough to eat?" he heard himself replying.

She arched her eyebrows. "Can I have that in writing?"

Still self-conscious, but also thoroughly aroused, he kissed her. Within a few seconds it was clear this could easily get out of hand. He pulled back. "I have to stop by my office for a couple of things. It won't take a minute."

"Wither thou goest," she said, and, rather dramatically, blushed.

Daring to put his hand on the back of her warm bare neck, feeling the soft, almost invisible golden down against his fingertips, he guided her out of the room, out of the building, and along the broad sloping lawn toward Warren Hall.

"It's really pretty here," she said, surveying the undulant green grounds.

"You stop noticing that pretty damn quick."

"Maybe I can help you remember it."

"A waste of your talents."

She gave him a sidelong glance. "I've got talents you haven't dreamt of."

Which, among other things, provoked an immediate erection, a classic adolescent BOING! "You scare me," he said.

"Good."

This did nothing to deflate him. Nor did the look which accompanied the word. Fortunately, the people they were passing were taking no notice of him, one of the incidental benefits of walking alongside of a creature like Tessa.

When they got to his office, he motioned her into the chair in front of his desk. "This'll take about two seconds," he assured her.

But she remained standing. "You don't have any windows in here," she observed.

"Right. Take that as symbolic."

"I'd rather take it as an opportunity." She approached him purposefully.

"Wait," he said nervously.

"I've waited long enough." She sounded almost stern. "Weeks."

"Yeah, but—"

"Doesn't the door lock?"

"Well yes, but—"

"Then what are you worried about?"

"I just, I mean, don't you think, I mean, *in my office?*"

"Take it as symbolic." She unceremoniously began to pull her dress up over her head.

"Wait!" he insisted, moving out from behind his desk. "Please. Don't take it off."

"God, Ezra, don't be such a stick-in-the-mud."

"It isn't that," he assured her. "Not anymore. It's just, it's just, since I saw you today, I've wanted to—" He covered the distance between them in two quick steps and thrust both hands under her dress, the left hand behind, the right in front. "I've wanted to *this.*" Nirvana.

"Oh, well, that's okay then." And, a fraction of a second later, she exhaled a sound of slightly startled pleasure.

"And it's exactly how I imagined." Which wasn't completely true; his imaginings, vivid though they were, weren't vivid enough to conjure up the combination of tactilia, sights, sounds, and sweet odors confronting him now, and which, by some evolutionary imperative, banished all his previous anxieties and misgivings, subsumed them in pure lust.

"What is it about flesh?" he mused in a hoarse whisper. "It's a mystery, isn't it? Why does it feel so great?"

"Ezra, are you deconstructing pussy now?"

He snorted with amusement and resumed his explorations. While he nuzzled her neck, the fingers of both his hands met at her crotch and began to burrow.

"Let me take this off," she whispered.

He stepped back. For a brief instant, with her polka-dotted dress up over her head, wearing only bikini underpants, she looked to Ezra like the model for a painting by some perverted avatar of Norman Rockwell, a unique *Saturday Evening Post* cover portraying the famous farmer's daughter of folk myth. "Fun in the Barn," would be the Rockwellesque title.

She quickly removed her underpants, rolling them down over her hips and kicking them free. When he reached to embrace her, she strode past him toward his desk and gestured toward the various papers and journals resting on top.

"What's this stuff?"

"Work," he croaked.

She brushed it all onto the floor with one brisk sweeping gesture.

"Hey!" he protested.

"Take that as symbolic too," she said, and sat herself down on the cleared surface. "Come here. Hurry."

He did as she bade. She spread her legs so he could come between them, his thighs pressed against the edge of the desk. She worked on opening his trousers, which proved to be trickier than she expected, since they had a second, hidden button on the inside of the waistband. But she finally succeeded, and eased his pants down over his thighs. He stepped out of them, tossing them on the detritus of his work life lying in a heap on the floor.

Even in the groping excitement of the moment, he forced himself to stop, to look, to take stock of all the pleasures he was experiencing: They were too varied, too numerous, too *sanctified,* damn it, to let pass without conscious acknowledgment. Then he bent over her, she raised her knees, and as she reached down and guided him smoothly in, she whispered, "God I love this."

After a second to get his bearings, he whispered, "Whatever you do, don't pinch me."

"I was about to."

"No, please, it might wake me up."

Her smiling face was pointblank against his. "This is *real*. Why can't you accept it?"

"Because it doesn't make sense."

She reached for his hair with both hands and stared into his eyes. "I mean honestly, what do you think's going on here?"

"Something like noblesse oblige?"

"I'm not that noble," she said, "believe me." And then she came, as simple and quick as that. And it was just as well; he exploded a fraction of a second later. Which was her cue to remind him of her legendary Kegels, in response to which he found himself making a bit more noise than he meant to, and for a confoundingly prolonged interval.

A few minutes later, while they were putting themselves back together and he was picking his papers off the floor and slopping them randomly back on his desk, she broke the short silence by saying, "Feel okay now?"

"Never better."

"Good." She nodded. "I figured we should take care of that as soon as possible."

"You mean you weren't carried away by passion?"

"Well, sure, but I also . . . I mean, you seemed kind of nervous."

"It was that obvious?"

"Nah, you're a master of deception." She was slipping on her dress, and she suddenly said, "Do you have a Kleenex or something? I'm absolutely *swimming* in you."

"Take it as tribute," he said. Simultaneously relishing and rather disliking her casual, unselfconscious frankness, he tossed her a box of Kleenex, which was lying on the floor.

"Honey, it never occurred to me not to," she said, at the same time neatly catching the box of tissues with one hand.

When they left his office a minute or two later, the door to the adjacent office, Hannah Jenkel's office, opened, and the head of Hannah herself protruded into the hall. A woman in her sixties, silver-haired and petite, with a sweet grandmotherly manner combined with a no-nonsense bluntness (at least at faculty meetings), she had always been pleasant toward Ezra, and he had always liked her more than their purely professional relations warranted. But right now he felt threatened, exposed, *found out,* and the frankly curious expression on her face did nothing to assuage this feeling, nor the feeling of shame that followed hard upon it.

She pushed her glasses up on the bridge of her nose, perhaps in order to get a clearer view of Tessa, or because she didn't trust the evidence of her own eyes.

There was no denying this was taking place, no denying that Hannah's head was stuck out into the hall, no denying, even as a social fiction, that she had, at the very least, seen them, and that they had seen her; simply walking away wasn't an option.

"Hello, Hannah," Ezra said, trying (and no doubt failing) to sound natural.

Her eyes didn't leave Tessa. "Yes, hello, Ezra," she said. Only then did she turn her face to him, her eyebrows raised interrogatively.

He chose to pretend to interpret the look in her eye as amiable interest. It was the simplest course, the most comfortable for all concerned. "Hannah, I'd like you to meet my friend, Tessa Miles. Tessa, say hello to Professor Jenkel."

After they acknowledged each other, Hannah said, "It's nice to have friends pay a visit, isn't it?" And with that, she disappeared back into her office. It was impossible to tell what degree of irony, if any, she had injected into this observation.

"Do you think she heard us?" Ezra asked, as they proceeded down the hallway.

"I'd bet money on it." When Ezra nodded unhappily, Tessa added, "But I didn't get the feeling it bothered her."

Right, Ezra thought. Why should she care about one more nail in my coffin? There are already so many, so firmly embedded there.

So much for afterglow.

Chapter 6

Ezra filled a floppy plastic cup with wine from a jug of pale greenish stuff labeled "Mountain Chablis," and pivoted to face Susan McGill's living room, visible through an archway from the kitchen where he was standing, and aswarm with the usual English Department suspects. Here are the people I try to avoid all week, he thought, and yet here am I, socializing with them all on a Saturday night.

Here I go loop-de-loop.

Of course, it made sense from a careerist point of view—personal relationships weren't supposed to influence promotion decisions, but they inevitably did—and this was far from the first department party Ezra had attended on the simple assumption that every little act of ingratiation might bear fruit. But tonight his motives were more complicated.

He took a tentative sip of Mountain Chablis, which wasn't *quite* as bad as he'd feared, sweetish certainly, but you wouldn't necessarily want to pour it over pancakes. He drained his cup and refilled it. Turning back toward the table, he was suddenly reminded of the dull constant ache in his loins, which at rest wasn't altogether unpleasant, but in the event of any abrupt movement caused a rather alarming twinge, accompanied by a sort of ghostly pressure.

What he really needed now was protein, and plenty of it—he felt light-headed, and he doubted the sugary wine he was knocking back would improve matters over the long haul—but the two cheeses on offer looked dubious at best, sweaty and unnatural.

Surveying the living room from his post in the kitchen, the archway between framing it like a proscenium—as if he were witnessing an absurdist play, the dullest in the history of theater—unsure which little conversational knot to inject himself into, and how, and why, he thought, Okay, so instead let's take stock here. Let's consider where things stand. Let's coolly review the last forty-eight-plus hours.

Tessa has been here for forty-eight-plus hours. During that time she's cooked three excellent meals for me. She's washed—over my objections, be it said—at least twenty dishes, and mopped—over my *strenuous* objections—three floors, and hand-wiped every square inch of tile in my apartment. She's done—after I finally gave up even *trying* to object—a load of laundry, and twice gone to the grocery for provisions. Meanwhile, I've slept, at most, about eight hours, and written, at most, and only when she was doing those other chores, about a thousand words (funny how I've resented her presence after she's returned, even if only for a couple of minutes). We've ventured out of my apartment together four times. I've had nine orgasms during twelve varied acts of sexual intimacy, two of them previously unknown to me, either from personal experience or by reputation. She's had, by very rough estimate, fourteen of her own. We've shared six—or is it seven?—showers. I've brushed my teeth at least nine times.

And how do I feel about all this?

Before he could begin to answer this question—and he wasn't sure he could answer it even with the whole night available, and the assistance of a couple of out-of-work Stasi interrogators—Susan McGill, his hostess, glided up to him. Well, perhaps "glided" isn't *le mot just*. A Marxist-feminist, assuredly the only such specimen in the department (she'd been hired by Bob Dixon a couple of years before he'd hired Ezra, the opening move in his campaign to give Beuhler a soupçon of lit-crit pizzazz), she'd been tenured the previous year over the vociferous but impotent objections of some of the department fossils, had almost instantaneously gained at least thirty pounds, and had simultaneously become much louder, more outspoken, and (here was the joker in the deck) much jollier. All in all, a persuasive advertisement for tenure (not, God knows, that Ezra needed persuading); she was infinitely better company now than before her promotion, when she'd been tense, morose, wary, impatient, harshly judgmental, and anorectically thin. As far as Ezra was concerned, the change in her appearance, while certainly no improvement, was a small price to pay for those other changes; of course, it was her appearance, not his, and therefore the cost-benefit analysis wasn't his to make. But to return to the starting point of these ruminations, *gliding* was no longer her customary mode of locomotion.

"So, Ezra," she said to him, giving him a conspiratorial smile before she turned to address the cheese and Saltines she'd laid out for her guests, but which, thus far, few of her guests had gone near. Ezra waited; "So Ezra" wasn't sufficient to induce feelings of conversational obligation. Susan placed a square of waxy electric-orange cheese on a Saltine, put them both in her mouth, found a glass, filled it with wine, took a slug, swallowed everything with palpable effort, and then continued, "Okay, where'd you find her?"

Ezra didn't have to ask the antecedent of the pronoun "her." On the other hand, he suspected the question didn't really involve Tessa's geographical origins. So he waited.

"A Victoria's Secret catalogue maybe?"

"You've hit the nail on the head."

Susan nodded. "We're not used to gals like that in Seven Hills, if you know what I mean," she said, meanwhile foraging again amongst the cheese and crackers, and then, as if it were part of the same thought, adding, "I thought you and Carol Dimsdale were an item."

"We broke up," he said.

"I'm always the last to learn these things. When was this?"

"Spring break."

"Well, I can see why," Susan said, gesturing with her head toward the living room, presumably in order to indicate Tessa's presence there.

"It wasn't exactly like that."

"Like what?"

"Like what you were suggesting. Trading up."

Susan brushed this aside with a wave. "I'm flattered you brought her here. I mean—" She stopped to pop another cheese-and-Saltine open-face into her open face, holding her free hand up to indicate there would be a pause of relatively brief duration while she worked it down her gullet like a python swallowing a mongoose. When this was accomplished—her head went back, her eyes closed, her body shuddered, and the deed was done— she continued, "I mean, a gal like that, I'm sure she has guys, and I'm talking hunks, *GQ* fodder, elbowing each other aside to show her a great time. Gallery openings, clubs, happening restaurants, concerts with backstage passes in their pockets, you see what I'm getting at?"

"Indeed I do."

"Have some cheese."

"Uh, not right now, thanks."

"So I'm, like I said, I'm kinda pleased you included me on your itinerary."

"Well, Susan, I don't want you to take this amiss, but—"

"Go on."

"You may not have noticed, but here in Seven Hills we don't really *have* much in the way of galleries and clubs and happening restaurants and what not."

"There's Pierre's."

"Yeah, we were there last night, as a matter of fact."

"You were? What was the entrée?"

"Tornedos Rossini."

"Sounds scrumptious."

"It wasn't bad."

"Pâté under the steak? Everything on toast points?"

"Exactly."

"So anyway, what are you saying? About coming to my party, I mean."

He paid close attention here to the tone of her voice; the question could have been a straightforward inquiry or a belligerent challenge. He decided it was the former—a small gamble on his part—and so answered truthfully: "I'm saying I was grasping at straws. When you've had a guest here for forty-eight-plus hours, and you've already eaten at Pierre's, you've pretty much exhausted the nightlife."

"And each other?" This was asked so good-naturedly that Ezra smiled and tipped his head affirmatively. "Not," Susan added, "that she looks easy to exhaust."

"No, you're right, I think her body must operate on solar energy. Some infinitely renewable resource. But hers isn't the only body in question. Anyhow, it was high time we got out of the house and . . . Again, I don't mean this the way it sounds, but even an English Department do started to look like an attractive proposition."

"You dog. You've been fucking your head off, haven't you?"

No one at Beuhler had ever talked to him like this before. And she said it with a rather creepy relish, as if she were observing them at it in her mind's eye. He carefully chose from among about eight different responses, ultimately picking the least interesting but the most emotionally authentic: "What makes you say that?"

"Well, Jesus, Ezra, if my party appealed to you more than staying home with, with *that,* she must've pretty much wrung you dry."

He granted her a wan smile. "Pretty much."

She shook her head. "Now I guess it's *my* turn to tell you I don't mean this the way it sounds, but . . . Isn't she kinda, kinda *hot* for a guy like you? A little rich for your blood? Outta your league? Accustomed to a faster track? Able to—"

"I get the point, Susan! Christ." He refilled his cup. "And yes, she's all those things. What can I tell you?"

"Your secret." He laughed, but she went on, "You hiding something the department ought to know about?"

Which, to his mortification, made him blush. It wasn't the sort of secret Susan was getting at, his E. A. Peauhood, but any sort of suspicion directed his way, even in jest, was enough to remind him of the jeopardy he was risking.

Worse, Susan misinterpreted his discomfiture. "Oh my God, you mean it's true? You're some sort of anatomical outrider? A sport of nature? Why, Ezra Gordon—!"

Clearly, the Saltines and cheese represented a distinctly displaced appetite for Susan McGill. "Calm down, Susan."

"Will you at least show me? In the spirit of disinterested scientific inquiry?"

Perhaps she'd had too much Mountain Chablis. "I'm gonna go mix, okay? I've been hugging the refreshment table too long anyhow."

"Tease. You can run, but you can't hide."

As he slipped away, he noticed she was reaching for more cheese.

Now, where in the world was Tessa? Wandering into the living room, he couldn't see a sign of her, and this emphatically wasn't the result of her blending in with the prevailing fauna. In her brief black Betsey Johnson spandex dress—far too, too, well, too *everything* for this company and this setting, but when she'd emerged from his bedroom in it she looked so magnificent he chose not to argue—with her golden tan and golden mane and golden aura, there was no way she could be hiding in plain sight.

But his search was interrupted almost before it began by Bob Dixon, who lumbered up to him as he was crossing into the living room.

"Ezra, old boy," Dixon said. Evidently he'd done more than his share of damage to the jug of Mountain Chablis: His eyes glistened, his color was high, and his accent had slipped farther than usual toward the British end of the spectrum (at least his consonants; his vowels retained their Midwestern flatness). And that ridiculous "old boy" nonsense, as if they were meeting for a drink in the members' lounge at Boodle's.

Or perhaps it wasn't the wine at all, perhaps it was residual awkwardness stemming from that contretemps involving the FBI agent a few days ago.

"Hello, Bob." Dixon's example—or was it his very presence?—inspired Ezra to take a deep draught of his own Mountain Chablis. He himself still felt some residual awkwardness—or was it loathing?

"Enjoying yourself?" Dixon asked pleasantly.

"Um."

"It's nice to see one's colleagues in an unstructured environment, no?"

"Well put."

Dixon lowered his voice. "I've just been talking to your friend," he confided.

Ezra saw warning flags going up all over the room. Oh shit. Maybe bringing Tessa here was even more reckless than he'd thought before he'd, rather desperately, proposed it. Eliza Doolittle terrors engulfed him. Had she been telling the chairman about her *Penthouse* spreads? About *Flight Attendants in Heat*? About the joke among her actress friends that the only dress requirement when auditioning was kneepads? Oh shit oh shit oh shit. "Oh yes?"

"Very attractive woman."

"Isn't she?" God, the sadistic son of a bitch was prolonging the agony. On purpose, no doubt about it.

"Rather—what's the word?—rather *unconventional* views on things."

"Yes. Indeed." And then he couldn't stand it any longer. "Like what things, for example?" Bondage? Analingus? Carnal relations with inanimate objects? Put me out of my misery!

"Well, this deconstruction business," Dixon said.

Ezra just stared; the man was playing with him like a cat with a mouse, revealing depths of exquisite cruelty one would never have suspected of him.

Dixon went on, "Quite took me aback, I must say, what with one thing and another."

"How do you mean?" Excuse me just a minute, let me slip my head into this noose. There. Snug as a glove.

"Well, I was telling her about my Wordsworth research—just cocktail party chitchat, you know the thing—and suddenly she hits me with this stuff about semiotics and encoding and something about Lincoln at Gettysburg. I couldn't exactly follow it, but, well, I can't follow that stuff in the best of circumstances." He shrugged. "And I guess I must be more retrograde than I give myself credit for, but somehow I don't expect a girl who looks like that to, to . . . you know. Where's she at? UCLA? USC? Cal Tech?"

"Pardon?"

"She mentioned she's from down south."

A bubble of admiration and affection for Tessa was expanding in Ezra's chest. The little sly-boots! "She's sort of between jobs."

"Oh yes?" Dixon's eyes widened predatorily. "You think there's a chance we might be able, we might be able to tempt her?"

Ezra laughed, two parts amusement and three parts relief. "I shouldn't think so."

"No, I suppose not. Can probably write her own ticket on the open market. Beautiful girl." Dixon sighed. "You don't see many girls like that in real life."

"We call them *women* now, Bob."

"Of course. Of course we do." He gave Ezra a rather hard look, as if reluctantly forced to reevaluate him. "Are you familiar with her work, by any chance?"

Her work? Like that four-page pictorial in *Cavalier,* for example? "She's shown me some of it," he answered carefully. "Informally."

"Rough draft sort of thing?"

"You might say. Raw materials."

Dixon nodded. "Any good?"

"Fabulous."

"Could you make hide or hair of it?"

"Both."

Dixon raised his eyebrows quizzically—perhaps Ezra had permitted himself a bit too much latitude in this little game—and then said, "Ah, here she is now."

Ezra looked up. Tessa was just emerging from the bathroom and heading their way. En route, she was waylaid briefly by Drew Hatton, who said something to her as she passed, and whom she answered without noticeably slowing down. Then she was upon them, all smiles and radiance. "Hello again, Bob," she said, and then took Ezra's hand and stood so close to him one might suspect that Einstein was wrong, that two different bits of matter can indeed occupy the same space at the same time. And what astonishing bits she possessed! Who could say how many physical laws her person contravened?

"I understand you and Bob had a literary discussion," Ezra hazarded.

Her eyes danced. "Just a friendly exchange of views," she answered. "Come with me, honey, I want a glass of wine."

"Sure," Ezra said. He had noticed Dixon wincing when Tessa said "honey," which was gratifying. No doubt the chairman had been hoping that Tessa and Ezra weren't lovers, and the word "honey" dashed those hopes. Good. Fuck you, Bob. Eat your heart out.

"You'll excuse us, won't you?" she inquired graciously.

Dixon inclined his head with equal graciousness.

As they passed through the archway into the kitchen, Ezra said, "I don't know what you told him, but he was considering hiring you. Any interest in teaching? If my experience is any indication, you've got a gift."

"I just mostly fed him back what he was saying to me. Plus a little that I picked up in your class the other day. Just buttering up the boss for you. I'm good at that."

"And you impressed him. As well you might. What have you been up to for the last fifteen minutes?"

"Oh, talking to people. Looking around. Stuff."

"Like what?"

"Listening, mostly. Somebody was telling me about all these nineteenth-century novels about adultery that all have the same plot. Said something about how all of Europe contributed rough drafts and Tolstoy finally got it right. You know what he meant by that?"

"*Anna Karenina*."

"I've heard of *Anna Karenina*. It's good?"

"Oh yes."

"I probably should read it, huh? Anyway, then somebody else was explaining the Baptist connection to Beuhler. There was all sorts of stuff like that. It was neat."

"Neat?"

"You know. Different. Interesting. And then . . . this was weird, but when I was looking for the bathroom, I accidentally went into the bedroom. And there were all these bookshelves, but the only books around were paperback mysteries. I mean, thousands of 'em. Isn't that strange? I mean, this place belongs to an English professor, right?"

"Yep."

"So shouldn't there have been . . . I don't know, stuff like *Anna Karenina?* Or, I guess that's Russian, not English, but you know, classics? Shakespeare or whoever? Keats and his urn? What were all those mysteries doing there?"

Ezra nodded. "The thing is . . . See, Susan, that's our hostess, she spends her life taking texts apart. Being clever with them. Trying to demonstrate they actually do something different from what people think they do. I'm sure she got interested in books because she liked reading them, but now . . . The way the profession works, it becomes almost impossible to read for fun. Except things like mysteries, which have no point besides entertainment."

"But that's so sad."

"It's my life too. It's the way the profession works now. What was it Drew Hatton said to you back there?" He asked this question casually, but it had been on his mind since he saw Tessa cross the room, saw Drew say something to her, saw her answer him without perceptibly slowing down.

"Who's Drew Hatton?"

"The guy who said something to you."

"A lot of people have said things to me tonight, Ezra."

"Just before. When you were coming toward Bob and me."

"Oh. I know who you mean. He asked me if I'd made up my mind yet."

"About what? What was he getting at?"

They had reached the refreshment table. Susan was still there, still working on the cheese and crackers. She looked up and smiled at them. "Please have some food," she urged. "Everyone seems to be boycotting it. Except me. I'm doing my part. Is there some political dimension to cheese I've missed? Are the cheese-growers on strike or something?"

Ezra was feeling just fluttery enough to accept the offer. It wasn't oysters, but it would have to do. While Tessa poured herself some wine, Ezra sliced off a bit of the beige stuff—it seemed the minimally less risky of the two cheeses—and said to Tessa, "Go on. Have you made up your mind about what?"

"You mean that guy?"

"Yeah. Made up your mind about what?"

Tessa glanced at Susan, hesitated, then said, "About going home with him tonight."

Susan didn't miss a beat, didn't blink, didn't even observe a decent interval to allow this—to Ezra—extraordinary intelligence to register. "Who?" she demanded. "Who was it?"

"No!" Ezra exclaimed, authentically shocked. "Not really!"

"Don't be a child," Susan said to him, and turned again to Tessa. "The name, babe."

"Wait a sec, Susan." Addressing Tessa, he said, "He's married, you know. It's just incredible!"

"As long as we're shattering belief systems, the tooth fairy is a myth too," Susan said.

"Does this mean," Ezra wondered, "that I have to, to, like *hit* him or something?"

"Dontcha just love testosterone?" Susan inquired of Tessa. "I adore it, I really do. It's such a *cute* hormone, you know?"

"You don't have to hit anybody," Tessa said. "I took care of it."

"But, I mean . . . How'd you take care of it?"

"I said no."

"That's all?"

"It seemed to do the trick."

"But he asked if you'd made up your mind. That suggests it was an open question."

"Who?" Susan demanded again. "Who is this awful cad?"

"It wasn't an open question, Ezra. Except to him. He asked me twice. I said no both times. I guess he didn't believe me the first time."

"Well, gee, maybe I really *should* like, you know, give him a knuckle sandwich. Or at least talk to him. Give him a good firm talking-to. The verbal equivalent of a knuckle sandwich. Let him know there's a knuckle sandwich with his name on it if he doesn't straighten up and fly right."

"You go get him, champ," said Susan.

"Susan, do you mind?"

"Look, how about you just tell me his initials, I'll take it from there."

"Susan!" Then, turning back to Tessa, "I mean, I understand you handled it and everything, and I'm sure you handled it fine, and, you know, I recognize you're an expert at this sort of situation, but . . . I mean, there's also the insult-to-me sort of aspect, isn't there? He knows you're here with me. Don't I have some sort of guy obligation to punch his lights out?"

"Yes!" averred Susan. "Yes you do. But not near anything breakable, okay?"

"Of course, then he'll probably oppose my tenure case. Mustn't forget that."

"And besides . . ." Tessa took a sip of wine. "The thing is, once you go down that path, I'm afraid you're gonna have to beat up half the guys in the room."

"Wait! I know! It was Drew Hatton, wasn't it?"

"Half the guys in the room?"

"More or less."

"Am I right? Was it Drew?"

"Were they all that direct?"

"Some were direct, some hinted around. But it's no big deal. Happens all the time."

"Not to me," said Susan. "Doesn't happen at all. Except for Drew once."

"And I don't think it's really an insult to you. I mean, I see how you might take it that way, but . . . Basically, I think it's between them and me, you know?"

"His wife was away or something. Visiting her parents. It was around Christmas. The department Christmas party is when it was."

"Was Bob Dixon one of them?"

"No, Ezra, he wasn't. He stared at my cleavage pretty hard, but he didn't, he didn't, you know, he didn't make any improper suggestions. Okay?"

"And I said yes. Went back to his place and we got jiggy. I mean, what the hell, you know? Plus it was Christmas, and here I was all alone in Seven Goddamn Hills, family back on the east coast. And of course I'd had quite a bit of eggnog, not that that's any excuse. He just caught me at a vulnerable time."

"You *sure* it wasn't Bob? Him I'd positively enjoy hitting."

"Took him about forty minutes to get it up and then maybe forty seconds to get off. Said it was the alcohol. And the next time I saw him, it was like it hadn't even happened. You know how that makes you feel? Like *dirt.* He just nodded, said hello, and passed me in the hall like I was some sort of, some sort of *colleague.*"

"No, except for those saucer eyes, Bob was a perfect gentleman."

"And that's not all, either. I have it on good authority he voted no on my tenure case. Men are disgusting, you know?"

Ezra and Tessa suddenly both became aware of Susan's contributions at the same time, and turned to her. "They are, aren't they?" Ezra heard himself conceding. "But then, women aren't exactly a frolic in the park either."

"I bet things like that never happen to you," Susan said to Tessa.

"Sure they do."

"Yeah, right. You're saying you've slept with guys and then they haven't called?"

"Hundreds of times."

"*Hundreds* of times?" Ezra parroted unhappily.

"Butt out," Susan instructed Ezra, and then said to Tessa, "You're not just saying this to make me feel better?"

"Absolutely not," Tessa answered. "Take this one right here, for example." She put a hand on Ezra's shoulder. "A perfect case in point."

"Now wait—"

"A couple of thrill-packed encounters in Marina Del Rey and then—nada."

"You bastard," Susan said to him.

"I was scared, for Christ's sake."

"Well, okay, I can see that."

"You can?"

"I'm not blind, Ezra."

"'Hundreds of times' was an exaggeration, okay?"

"A guy like you would have to be nuts not to be scared. It's like, are you ready to go one-on-one with Michael Jordan?"

"It's not *exactly* like that, Susan."

"Well, nothing's exactly like anything else. But it's a good comparison. After all, you're, you're who you are, with, you know, all that that entails, while this gal here—"

"My name's Tessa."

"Susan. Nice to meet you." She shook Tessa's hand. "While Tessa here was clearly intended by God for the big leagues."

"But," protested Ezra, "it's different. Tessa and I weren't engaged in a competitive activity."

"Yeah, right. And it don't rain in Minneapolis in the summer time."

"Trust me, he's ready for any team in the conference," said Tessa.

"You know, I'm starting to believe it." Susan smiled. "But I'm not sure *he* does, yet."

"That's what makes him so nice."

"Yes, I can see that too. Some cheese?"

Tessa gave the cheese a quick glance and shook her head. At the same moment, Drew Hatton approached the table to refill his glass.

"Hello," he said to no one in particular, not meeting anyone's eye.

"Here's your chance, tiger," Susan murmured to Ezra.

Tessa giggled, and then bit her lip. Drew glanced up, puzzled, at which Susan laughed too. "Am I missing something?" he asked.

"You bet," said Ezra. "And always will."

Drew colored. He filled his glass quickly and scurried back into the living room.

"I guess I showed *him*."

"My hero," said Tessa.

Susan looked at Ezra speculatively, then turned to Tessa, then back to Ezra. "It's curious," she said. "You actually make a cute couple."

Tessa put her right arm through Ezra's left. "Don't we?"

Susan was still staring at Ezra. "I never noticed it before," she mused. "His appeal, I mean."

"Susan, please."

"*I* liked him right away."

"That was awfully clever of you."

"We must be going," said Ezra.

Susan smiled. "All right, all right, we can drop this."

"No, Ezra's right, we probably should be on our way," Tessa said.

"Back to bed?"

"For God's sake, Susan!"

"His batteries should be recharged by now," Tessa added.

"Too bad. This is fun. Hardly like a department party at all."

"I've enjoyed it too," Tessa said.

"Look, how long are you in town for?"

Tessa glanced at Ezra before answering. "I'm leaving tomorrow."

Susan's look of disappointment seemed genuine. "I was going to suggest lunch."

"That would have been nice."

"We have so much to discuss." Laughing at Ezra's stricken look, she added, "Relax, cutie. It was a joke."

A few minutes later, walking down Main Street in the warm pinkish twilight, Ezra asked, "Did you mind leaving?"

"The party? Not really. I was having a good time, though."

"You were?"

"Very."

"How is that possible?" He shook his head. "Besides, I was starving. Running on empty. And that cheese—"

"Yeah, the cheese wasn't a plus. But it was great to be with people who really *talk*."

"Oh, they talk, no question."

"I mean about something real. Something besides movies and money and, and, cars and clothes and personal trainers. And I liked Susan."

"She's a good sort. You have any philosophical objection to hamburger?"

"Nothing I can't ignore."

"There's a kind of miserable little burger place not far from here."

"Sounds perfect."

"I was beginning to find her curiosity a little creepy."

"Susan's? I thought it was sweet. She likes you. What's her work like?"

"Susan's? Angry. Angry and incomprehensible. At least to me. All about encoded modes of oppression."

"I wouldn't have guessed that."

"Listen, it's touching you still have this notion about intellectual integrity and all, but there are market forces at work in universities too. Fashions, trends, styles. We're no different from the folks who write for *Vanity Fair*. We need to publish, we need promotions, we need to make our reputations, we need to satisfy the commissars who pay our salaries and decide our fate. Susan was *hired* to be angry. She's doing the work she was hired to do."

"You don't think she means it?"

"She may. There's a lot to be angry about. And as for her Marxism . . ." He shrugged.

"She's a *Marxist?*"

He grinned. "You're actually surprised, aren't you?"

"Well, of course. It seems so . . . what's the word? It seems so *quaint.*"

"What can I say? A small coterie of American intellectuals may be the last holdouts, the world's last little enclave, they may stick with it even after China and North Korea and Cuba move on. I have no idea what Susan really thinks. I'm not even sure *she* does. I mean, if you *want* to feel alienated, if it's in your *interest* to feel alienated, God knows it isn't hard to feel alienated. And you're right, she doesn't have an embittered personality."

"And you don't have a cynical personality."

"I'm not a cynic."

"You *sound* like a cynic. I've never heard you so sour."

"Go figure."

She took his arm and tugged, bringing him to a stop.

"What?" he said.

"I keep trying to get a fix on you, but every time I think I've got you pegged, I find out I was wrong."

"I'm a very simple soul."

"Why do I doubt that?"

"Maybe you have a stake in doubting it."

"I don't even know what that means." He started to answer, but she put a finger on his lips, forestalling him. "And I don't want to hear some cynical explanation either. Why don't you kiss me instead?"

He smiled, took her in his arms, and, indifferent to the pedestrian traffic around them, kissed her. She melted against him. He had never held a beautiful woman wearing a Betsey Johnson dress in his arms before: Another inaugural experience surpassing all expectations.

And then he heard a voice: "Ezra?"

He recognized the voice, and stiffened. The voice belonged to Carol.

He and Tessa separated and turned to face her. She was wearing torn jeans—not stylishly torn, just old—and a shapeless much-washed Beuhler sweatshirt, she held a plastic bag from Longs Drugs in her right hand, and she wasn't wearing any make-up. Her hair was wet and stringy, probably from a recent shampooing. She looked as bad as he'd ever seen her.

"Carol," he said.

Her eyes, wide with astonishment, were on Tessa, traveling slowly down that voluptuous body encased in its tight tubular black wrap. When they reached the ankles, they blinked once, but they weren't any narrower afterwards.

It occurred to Ezra that he had seen a whole lot of widened eyes in the last few days.

Carol looked up. The expression on her face slowly gelled into one of utter dismay.

Ezra should, perhaps, have found this gratifying, but somehow he didn't. At all. Instead, he wished that at least one of the three of them were elsewhere. But there was no graceful extrication from the situation, short of bracing oneself and passing through its rigors squarely, with dignity more or less intact.

So he took a deep breath and made the introductions. Each woman offered assurances she was delighted to meet the other, and after an awkward few seconds, Carol proceeded on her way.

"That couldn't have been easy," Tessa said a couple of moments later.

"No." Then, a second later, "How do you mean?"

"Give me some credit, Ezra."

There was little conversation during dinner, and later, back in his apartment, he lay on his bed in his navy blue jockey shorts—the night was really very warm, even by Seven Hills standards—lazily watching while she silently packed. His one offer of assistance had been declined, laconically if not curtly. Something tense and unsettled had arisen between them, no doubt about it. Finally, after waiting more than ten minutes for her to break the silence, he said, "Is something the matter, Tessa?"

She looked up from her suitcase. "The matter? I wouldn't say anything's the matter." And then the kicker: "Exactly."

"Okay . . . so what exactly *isn't* the matter?"

She smiled thinly. "It's just . . . I mean, I am leaving tomorrow, and we don't seem to be taking account of that fact."

He rose up on one elbow. "I see what you mean. It's hard to know quite what to do about it, though."

"Just some sort of not pretending nothing's been happening here."

"I didn't think we weren't pretending that."

"That's how it seemed to me."

"You can navigate through a thicket of multiple negatives better than I can."

She didn't smile. Whoops.

"What should I do, Tessa?"

"Say something. Say how you feel about my being here and about my leaving."

"Well, I'm sorry you're going." This sounded pretty lame, but the fact is, he hadn't let himself think about it. There would be plenty of time after she was gone.

"Really?" Kneeling down there on the floor, she stopped packing and looked up at him. Sheenah the Jungle Girl, drinking from a stream but suddenly startled by the distant sound of a ravening beast.

"Of course."

"You liked having me here?"

"It was great."

She rose and came toward him. "Are you just saying that?"

"Hardly."

She planted herself beside him on the bed. "'Cause I had a wonderful time."

"Really? I thought you were gonna be bored silly."

"What you don't understand is, that's what I *wanted*."

"Glad I could oblige."

She grimaced. "You know I don't mean it like that. I didn't want to be bored silly, I wanted a different *pace*. Slower and quieter. Less traffic, less people, less tumult. I wanted to kick back, take some slow deep breaths, smell some hay, and make love nonstop."

"We managed some of that."

She began running her fingers through his hair. "It was lovely."

"Maybe you'll come back sometime soon."

"Maybe I will. What I was thinking . . ."

"Go on."

She hesitated. "I need a shower. It's such a hot night. Wanna join me?"

"I think I'll sit this one out."

"Lazy."

"I'm beat, Tessa."

"Okay, okay. But don't you dare fall asleep!"

He smiled. "Haven't I earned the right?"

"That isn't how we measure our obligations, buster."

She slipped out of her cut-offs and her tee shirt—amazing how he barely bothered to watch, so accustomed to her had he grown in the past few days—and left the bedroom. He shut his eyes, feeling very peaceful. The window by the bed was open, and a warm breeze was blowing through, carrying the delicious scent of jasmine with it. A few moments later, from down the hall, he heard the white noise of running water. As his muscles eased, his thoughts began to drift and scatter . . .

The next thing he was aware of was his own raw, distantly pained, bone-hard erection secured in Tessa's throat, and of a low groan emanating from his own. He lifted his head and opened his eyes; the room was dim— the overhead light was off, but a little illumination bled in from the hallway—and Tessa's shape was at the foot of the bed, leaning over him.

"If G.E. marketed this as an alarm clock, they'd have a winner."

She made a sound that might have been a stifled laugh.

"Wouldn't even need a 'Snooze' button. How much have I missed?"

Her mouth slipped off him. "Only the tuning-up," she said. "The overture's about to start." She returned to what she'd been doing.

"I'm not sure the fat lady's gonna sing."

"You leave that to me."

"Laryngitis. Doctor told her to give it a rest."

"Oh, shut up."

He did as he was told, lying back and relishing her expert ministrations. And it was exquisitely pleasurable, drifting passively like this, carried aimlessly along on the buoyant surface of sensation.

After a few minutes, he felt her release him, felt her body slide up along his, felt her fingers grip him and ease him inside herself.

He expelled a sibilant breath. She reached for his hands and put them over her breasts.

"How'd you get so wet?" he whispered.

"The power of positive thinking."

She leaned down over him and kissed him. Then, as he slid his mouth down her cheek and nuzzled her neck, she whispered, "I adore this."

"It's a miracle," he answered.

"That I adore it?"

"Yes. And that it's happening."

"It's yours for the asking," she said. Then she said, sounding slightly surprised, "I'm going to come."

"I'm not."

"Better still." Then she did, almost noiselessly, but with a general stiffening of her body, and some seconds later she collapsed against his chest. But she resumed moving almost immediately, an intricately frictive circling and snapping. He placed his hands over her tight buttocks, as much to trace the virtuosic choreography as for the tactile pleasure of touching her.

"When you're not in me, I feel empty," she murmured into his ear.

"You want to take it home with you? It's probably going to fall off soon anyhow."

"No, I like the accessories too." She shifted her balance so that she was over him again, her hands on either side of his head, the weight of her breasts on his chest, and then began a squeezing series of contractions which made him take the lord's name in vain. "Listen," she said, her face so close to his that he could smell her sweet breath, "I don't have to leave."

"Huh?"

"What I mean is, I can drive home and get some stuff and come back."

"But—"

"We can do this every night."

"I wanna live to see forty."

"Ezra!"

Despite the groundwork she'd been laying, he was taken by surprise. "You're getting me at a vulnerable time."

"That was the plan."

"Can we—?"

"Drop it?"

"Table it."

"One thing at a time?"

"There's a lot more than one thing going on here."

"Okay." She hoisted herself upright. "Tell me," she said a moment later, her back arched, her face constricted in concentration, "can you feel this?"

"Yes."

"How about *this?*"

"Oh Christ."

"I think I'm gonna come again."

"Be my guest."

"What about you?"

"In the fullness of time."

"Music to a girl's ears."

It was almost an hour later before they spoke again. Tessa was lying on her back, her hair spread over the pillow, and Ezra was on his side, his left arm under her neck, gliding his lips over the sheen of perspiration glistening on her chest. Her breathing was still labored, but she was the one who broke the silence, saying simply, "So?"

"So?" he echoed.

"Don't play dumb."

"No, I wasn't. I was, I was returning to earth, is what I was doing. Were you always this orgasmic?"

"Pretty much. I probably ought to tell you it's only with you, but I'd be lying."

"That's okay, I don't have that kind of vanity. I was just curious."

"My mother says she's the same way."

Ezra raised his head, disbelieving. "Your *mother?*"

"Uh huh."

"You talk about orgasms with your *mother?*"

"From time to time."

"Jesus." Ah, the mysteries of family life. Tolstoy didn't have a clue. Of course, considering the results, the Miles way of doing things had plenty to recommend it.

"You don't? I mean, with your parents?"

"We don't have that sort of relationship. It's more a name-rank-and-serial-number sort of deal."

"My mom's one of my best friends. We talk about everything."

"And she has lots of orgasms, huh?"

"That's the story."

"And it doesn't bother you to, to think about it and so on?"

"Of course not."

"And that's like, like a bond between you or something?"

Tessa smiled. "I wouldn't say that, no. It's more, it's probably just, you know, geography. Or is it topography? Anyway, it's this genetic quirk we share."

"You're very fortunate in your genes."

"And out of them, ha ha."

"Ha ha."

"Okay, have we vamped enough? Can we talk now?"

"Sure. Isn't that what we've *been* doing?"

"Not exactly, no." Her tone changed, became almost businesslike. "Here's the deal. I'm sick of L.A. I'm sick of the parties I go to and the work I do and the lines of cocaine I snort and the career-building blow-jobs I perform and being a piece of meat and dealing with assholes. I actually sort of dug it at first—even the blow-jobs had a kind of outlaw thrill, a kind of fuck-you dirtiness, you know?—but now I hate the whole game. I wake up every morning dreading what the new day's gonna bring."

Ezra ceased his nuzzling. He suddenly felt like just another coarse male appetite. She noticed, and said, "I'm not talking about *you*, honey. I'm not talking about people I *want* to be with. I'm talking about, there's a, a, an assembly-line sort of feeling . . . And it isn't just, it isn't even *mostly* the sex part, that's just a small aspect of it. I know it's the interesting part, the glamour part, but . . ." She shrugged. "What gets to me finally is how *dehumanizing* it all is."

"You're a sex object?"

She made some sort of impatient gesture in the dark. "That's such a dumb expression," she said. "We're born with those appetites. You might as well attack somebody for getting hungry."

"But you still have the right to insist on good table manners."

"Well . . . you can try. But I'm talking about something different. Until you've been to an audition, given the best reading you know how, and heard someone say, in this really bored, really dismissive tone of voice, 'Thank you,' you can't understand what I mean. In a way, it's *worse* than giving a strategic blow-job. I once heard there was some German general during World War One who cleared mine fields by ordering his soldiers to march across them. *That's* what my life is like."

"Jesus."

She rolled over to face him. "And the other thing is, I like it here. I like being with you. I think it's neat you're a professor, it's neat you're a poet. All those people at the party you think are boring, I found them refreshing. At least they're interested in something."

"You give them too much credit."

"You don't know what I'm comparing them to. So listen . . . I'm ready to move in with you if you're ready to have me."

So there it was, on the table, glowing like pig iron. "Tessa—"

"I have some money saved. Quite a bit, actually."

"Please, Tessa, a dowry isn't the question here."

"No, I meant we could get a bigger place."

And then Ezra was silent. In fact, Ezra was struck dumb. For all her hinting around, it remained inconceivable, literally incredible, that this paragon wanted him. Even at his most grandiose—and, a small grace, grandiosity wasn't his stock-in-trade—it made zero sense.

"Aren't you going to say anything?"

"What have I done to deserve this?"

She smiled. "Nothing. God knows." She hesitated. "I know you've been hurt before. Is that the problem? Your marriage?"

"Oh, my marriage . . . I try not to think about it." Try not to think about Helga's affair with Klaus, another Swiss graduate student in Ann Arbor. After God knows how many others, Isaac apparently included. Try not to think about *that,* either. And try not to think about her solemn unforgivable request that he step aside and permit their still-unborn daughter to believe Klaus was her real father. And especially try not to think about his acquiescence. Which he could never not think about.

Apparently, at least as far as he was concerned, psychobiology had it wrong. He'd passed on his genes, all right, and he'd been spared having to take responsibility for the care and feeding of his own offspring. But it didn't feel like a victory. Far from it. It felt like a catastrophe, the worst of his life. One he tried not to think about virtually every waking hour.

He shook his head to banish these thoughts. To try not to think about them. "What occurs to me, Tessa . . . You know, all this time, I felt you were a figment of my fantasy life. What occurs to me now is, maybe I'm a figment of *yours.*"

Which produced a sudden frown, visible in the gloom. "What do you mean?"

"I'm not who you think. I'm a schlemiel stuck in a dead-end job. I'm mediocre at what I do. If there's anything I'm *not* mediocre at, I haven't found it yet. I flatter myself I have a relatively rich interior life, but let's face it, most mediocre people tell themselves the same thing. It's how we justify our miserable existence."

"Are you saying you don't deserve me?"

"Oh, that's a given. I'm saying sooner or later you'll make the same discovery. Then you'll wonder how you got stuck here, and what's the quickest way out."

"Can't we cross that bridge when we come to it?"

"It'd be a very difficult crossing. Better to plan an alternate route beforehand."

"I get the feeling you spend too much of your life trying to anticipate and avoid pain."

"Ouch."

"You have a real self-esteem problem, Ezra."

"Maybe. Or maybe I'm just honest with myself." Or maybe I'm a dope. Mustn't discount that possibility.

"So, let me get this straight. Are you, are you *turning me down?*"

Am I? "I don't know."

"You're turning me down because you think I'll grow disillusioned later. Have I got this right?"

"I've expressed myself badly. I think you've invested me with all sorts of excellence I don't possess. You want, and I mean you *deserve,* some sort of life which I really can't begin to give you. I've come to represent *deliverance* to you, somehow. I feel like a total fool saying this, but, but, it is the impression I get. And, you know, I *need* deliverance, I need it more than anyone, I can hardly provide it."

"Maybe we can deliver each other."

What's my problem? he thought. Every instant I've spent in this woman's company I've spent doubting myself.

Maybe that's my problem.

"Do you love me, by any chance?" he heard himself asking.

"You want me to take all the risks," she said, and there was, for the first time, anger in her voice.

"Just asking."

"You're beginning to drive me crazy," she said.

"See? It's happening even sooner than I thought."

"Ugh!"

"Look, Tessa, I'm not trying to be difficult, and you mustn't think I don't know how astonishing it is that a woman like you has set her sights on a guy like me. But there's an element of projection here—a big element—and it's introduced a false note between us. I have this feeling that if I said yes, I'd be as corrupt and dishonest and, and, and as *opportunistic* as those L.A. guys you talk about."

She fell back on the pillow. "I give up," she announced. "Let's go to sleep."

"It isn't that I, that, it's, I mean you've given me more joy than I've had in my entire adult life, so I mean—"

"I understand. Good night." She rolled over toward him, kissed him on the lips, and then rolled away again.

He felt as if he should say more, but he couldn't think what. And soon the various phrases colliding in his mind stopped making sense. But, strangely, just as consciousness was irrevocably departing, he saw Carol's face in his mind's eye, as she had looked that night, plain, unadorned, unkempt, wearing an expression of dismay, and it brought him back to himself with an unpleasant jolt, a surge of what felt like some foreign substance along his spine. He sat up, troubled, heart racing, and shook his head. But then he lay back, took two or three deep breaths, and soon thereafter sank into a profound dreamless sleep.

When he woke up almost nine hours later, Tessa wasn't in bed beside him. He propped himself up on one elbow, and noticed that her suitcase wasn't on the floor where it had been the night before.

"Tessa!"

No answer. He rolled out of bed, grabbed his bathrobe from the closet, and, slipping it on, padded out into the hall.

"Tessa!"

The bathroom was empty. The kitchen was empty. The living room was empty.

Which meant his apartment was empty. Unless he counted himself.

Something he wasn't in the habit of doing.

Then, standing in his living room, feeling, if not exactly forlorn, then at least a little lost, he noticed a sheet of yellow legal paper on his desk which he hadn't put there. He walked over and picked it up. Tessa had written a note on it with one of his felt-tipped pens.

Dearest Ezra,

I decided to get an early start. Might as well beat the traffic.

You're an honorable man. I can hear you saying, "I'm not honorable, I'm just terrified," but in your case maybe the two things have something in common.

You should have more respect for yourself, though. Maybe then you wouldn't be so afraid.

No hard feelings.

Love, Tessa

P.S. I hope you'll write about me some day!

He stared at the paper, waiting for some strong emotion to visit him. It didn't.

Well, he thought, all in good time.

He put the paper back on the desk. Then he noticed his new computer, barely touched during the last few days. He stared at it for a moment, and then, acting on impulse, switched it on.

Chapter 7

In the five days after Tessa's departure, Ezra continued to wait for a strong emotion to overtake him. He felt it gaining on him a few times—a sinking, lurching sort of sensation, a sudden acute awareness of her absence—but it never got close enough to take him down. Probably because he was otherwise engaged. Boy, was he otherwise engaged.

He barely left his apartment, so indefatigably was he addressing himself to *Every Inch a Lady*, so extraordinary was the progress he was making. He even cancelled a seminar session, a rare professional lapse he considered forgivable under the circumstances. During these exhilarating oblivious days, he systematically, if not quite sentiently, managed to eat his way through the provisions Tessa had purchased during her stay. It was only on the late afternoon of the sixth day that he realized his cupboard and refrigerator were laid waste.

His needs were simple now, almost monkish, but they hadn't disappeared utterly. And so, irked at the exigencies of a bodily existence that required him to abandon his post for any reason whatsoever, he drove to the Seven Hills Market in a kind of fog.

The fog didn't lift as he pushed his cart along the narrow aisles of the small dusty store, grabbing several cans of tuna, a loaf of white bread, a jar of mayo, a head of lettuce, some diet drinks, and a large package of Oreos. The necessities. He was making his way to the checkout stand when he became aware of a commotion in the next aisle over.

Commotions were rare in Seven Hills. Some vestige of ordinary human curiosity, abstract and attenuated as it might be in his present state, must still have dwelt in him, because he pushed his shopping cart down the aisle and around the corner to find out what was up.

At first, all he could see was a group of people and a collection of shopping carts jamming the aisle. But moving closer, he suddenly recognized Reverend Dimsdale, writhing on the floor and emitting a harsh desperate rattling noise, his face purplish, his thick hands desperately grasping at his throat. The people in attendance seemed paralyzed, standing immobile, staring at the beached whale in their midst, doing nothing.

Perhaps being in a fog helped. Ezra didn't do any conscious processing—which was in any case beyond him—but pushed his way through the assembled bodies and shopping carts, heedlessly shoving the latter out of the way (sometimes into the former) as he approached. His manner must have appeared authoritative; people readily stepped aside and allowed him access to the struggling Dimsdale. They probably assumed he was a doctor of something more impressive than philosophy.

"Someone call 911!" he shouted. The first words he had uttered aloud in almost a week. "Hurry!"

He knelt beside the minister, roughly pulled off his clerical collar and ripped open his black shirt. Now what? Overcoming a spasm of distaste, he bent down and applied his mouth to Dimsdale's. The man's breath, he noticed without surprise, was noxious. But the fact that there *was* breath had to be interpreted as a positive sign. Decay but not morbidity.

Ezra had never learned CPR, assuming, like everybody else, that he would never need it. But at a summer camp ages ago, during compulsory swimming lessons conducted at a scummy pond known, optimistically, as "the lake," he had been taught the rudiments of mouth-to-mouth resuscitation. There was no way of knowing whether it was appropriate to Dimsdale's current condition, but it was the only technique at Ezra's command. Better to try it than to do nothing, than to stand around gaping inanely like the others.

Not sure why it was deemed effective—wasn't he merely blowing carbon dioxide into the minister's lungs?—he still did as he had been taught, spreading his mouth over Dimsdale's and blowing, then turning away, counting to four, and applying his mouth once again.

Several minutes into this exercise, he noticed that Dimsdale's eyes had opened wide, and were looking into his own with an alarmed expression while their mouths were meeting. This came close to shattering Ezra's concentration and undermining his will, so intimate did the process suddenly seem. But he forced himself to persist.

It felt like hours before he heard the distant siren of an approaching ambulance, although probably no more than a few minutes had gone by. And even after, it still seemed to take an endless interval, at least fifty kisses' worth, before the medics finally burst into the market and up the aisle where Ezra and Dimsdale lay with their mouths locked.

As the medics hoisted Dimsdale onto a gurney, the watching crowd, silent until now, burst into sustained applause. It took Ezra a few moments to realize the ovation was for him.

■　■　■

"You're mad at me."

Ezra's coffee cup was halfway to his mouth. He put it back down on the formica table. "I don't think so, Carol." In a way, it was a relief, this accusation. He had assumed *she* was angry with *him.* It did, after all, number among the world's safer assumptions.

"I know you don't. That's kind of the problem."

"I didn't think there *was* a problem."

"Which is *another* problem."

"I'm not sure I'm following."

"I'm sure you aren't."

She had arrived at the hospital a half-hour after the ambulance, which was perfect: By the time she found the attending physician, Dimsdale was out of immediate danger, and so she could be reassured on the spot, without some ghastly interval of pacing and brooding.

After looking in on her father—he had been sedated, and was now sleeping—she found Ezra in the waiting room, giving an interview to the *Seven Hills Sentinel.* This story would doubtless make tomorrow's front page, alongside some crop reports, news of the Seven Hills mayoralty race just gearing up, and a handful of national stories off the wires.

She embraced him, thanking him tearfully, while the reporter looked on and the photographer took pictures. His answering modesty was unfeigned. No doubt he'd be called a hero in tomorrow's paper, that was standard journalese, but he hadn't done much, certainly nothing requiring courage, no courage beyond what was needed to kiss Dimsdale. Which meant Carol's late mother had been far more heroic than he, and over a much longer period of time.

"The doctor said you probably saved his life," Carol told him.

"It's lucky it worked out that way. I was flying blind."

"I can never repay you," she said matter-of-factly, without any histrionics.

"No debt's involved."

She wiped her eyes with a handkerchief. Her tears had stopped. Casting an uncomfortable glance at the reporter and photographer hovering nearby, she suggested Ezra accompany her to the hospital cafeteria for a cup of coffee. He didn't feel he could refuse. Nor, he realized, did he want to; after five days cloistered in his pornographer's hermitage, human company—any human company—had some appeal. And after what had just happened, simply going home would feel anticlimactic.

"Why should I be mad at you, Carol?" he asked now, looking up from his coffee cup.

"Because I—"

"And are you sure," he interrupted, "you aren't mad at me?"

"Oh, that too. Of course. And we're both justified."

"You seem to have given this some thought."

She smiled. Winningly. "Yep."

"I suppose I can take it. Shoot."

She picked up a plastic spoon and worried it a little before answering. "The thing is, though, I want to talk seriously. I've been *thinking* seriously, more seriously than I've ever thought about anything, and, and, this way we have of dealing with each other, this *irony*, this kind of buried anger masquerading as, as what?, as, you know, amused impatience, well, frankly, it isn't worthy of what I have to say. So unless you're prepared to take me seriously, let's forget it."

He stared at her in surprise. She said all this with a manifest absence of acrimony, with measured calm, and it introduced a new note into their dealings, it made him feel as if he were losing control of the discussion. Why did he find this feeling pleasant? "You've busted me," he conceded.

"I've busted us both. I'm guiltier than you. But neither of us is blameless."

"What's brought all this on?"

"What do you mean by 'all this'? My thinking about it or my telling you about it?"

"Both, I suppose."

"Oh, various things."

"Give me an example."

"Well, my father just now must be one. Something so near real disaster . . . It kind of makes you impatient with trivialities. That's probably why I'm telling you this stuff. I didn't plan to. As for thinking about it . . ." She shrugged. "Lots of things. Like, well, the other night, seeing you with that, that—"

"Tessa?"

"That Tessa."

"Now listen, if you're angry about—"

"No, no, how could I be? I mean, aside from anything else, aside from the fact I don't have the right, I mean, my only reaction is, Holy cow!" She smiled again, just as frankly and winningly as before. It was impossible not to smile back.

"I may be more competitive than I care to admit," she went on, "but I can't compete with that. Not in the holy-cow arena, anyhow. Maybe in the courtroom, if she ever decides to become a litigator. Is she the woman you, you . . . in L.A.?"

There was no reason to deny it. "Uh huh."

"Holy cow!"

"I felt the same way."

"I'll bet. And you even enticed her up to Seven Hills. Boy. I've underestimated you."

"You know, everyone's been acting like she's some sort of trophy. It wasn't like that."

"Wasn't it?"

"Well, maybe at first. But she's, she's more than—"

"The sum of her parts?"

"Right."

"That's saying a lot. Those are remarkable parts."

"This is a very weird conversation, Carol."

She waved this aside. "I want to be friends. We can have this conversation. We can change the rules about what's permissible. I was trying to do that when I came over that time. When you read me the, the Icelandic thing."

"You disappeared."

"Yeah, well, I was still working through some stuff."

"'Working through?' Are you in therapy, Carol? Is that what this is about?"

She colored, which Ezra initially assumed to be confirmation, but then she said, "Nope. But it isn't a bad phrase. That's what it feels like."

"And you think you've got somewhere?"

"I do. Isn't that interesting?"

"You *seem* different." Perhaps just because she was saying what she meant. On balance, this counted as a distinct improvement, and, against all odds, he was enjoying her company—enjoying *her*—quite a bit. But this new mode, if it was real, would clearly take some getting used to.

"I've been trying to grow up. I can see I must have driven you crazy before."

"Is that why I'm supposed to be mad at you?"

"To simplify. Drastically."

"Okay, so what's supposed to happen now?"

"Nothing." She had a humorous, sly look. "Why? You *want* something to happen?"

He thought he recognized the rhythm. "Are you *sure* you haven't been in therapy?"

Which got a big open smile. "Positive. Okay, what happens now is, we can try to be honest with each other. We can see if there's any basis for us to be friends." She snuck a look at her watch, and frowned. "Oh fudge!" She compressed a lot of irritation into the ridiculous expletive. "I've got to run, Ezra. There's a lot I want to say, but it'll have to wait. Daddy and I were expecting some church-types for dinner tonight. I've got to make some calls."

She stood up. Ezra did too. "I'm glad . . . you know . . . this didn't end tragically and everything," he offered.

"Yes," she agreed, "on the whole, this was the preferable outcome." Then she took his hand. "The doctor says Daddy'll be fine. You should be proud of yourself." She hesitated. "Where . . . where's Tessa, anyway?"

"L.A." Responding to the look on her face, he went on, "She was just visiting."

"Aha." Her expression didn't change. "Like jail in Monopoly?"

"She probably saw it that way."

Her eyes betrayed amusement. Leaning in, she gave his cheek a quick peck, and then walked away. He watched her leave and inhaled deeply, thinking, Not a bad afternoon. Saved a life and had a pleasant conversation with Carol. Two things that don't happen every day. Was it her or me? She seemed . . . is "terrific" too strong a word? Maybe she's easier to take if I'm not trying to get her into bed.

The word "bed" reminded him of his book, and brought with it a flush of pleasure. Much more intense pleasure, if he was honest, than having saved a life. That was a fine thing, no question, but it didn't seem *important.*

The ground he'd covered in the last five days was little short of incredible. There was light, blindingly bright light, at the end of the tunnel. He had tried to suppress the thought, but now it peremptorily insisted on announcing itself: Completion was three or four days away at most. The last section was already blocked out in his mind. Finishing it would be almost entirely mechanical, transcription rather than composition.

Coupled with the thrill of recognizing this fact was a spasm of anticipatory depression. It would be great to finish, but he knew already he'd also feel bereft; not having it to work on would be like losing a best friend. While he fished in his pocket for change to pay for the coffee, he wondered if this wasn't somehow a displaced despondency at the way things had ended with Tessa. The days she'd been around, she'd been *so* around, he couldn't deny that her absence left a huge void. Or would have, if his consciousness had space for a void. Tessa, beautiful, sweet Tessa . . . He sighed. It had no future, that relationship, but what a present. Which was now all in the past. When he thought of her at all, it was always with ambivalence and regret. So it was probably just as well he didn't think of her too often.

Unlike the book. Strange how much pleasure he'd found in writing a stupid little dirty book; it had actually reawakened his joy in literature, reminded him why he'd gone to graduate school in the first place. Strange too was the fact that, once he mailed it off, the thing would be over. The usual payoffs that novelists can at least dream of, chancing upon the book in bookstores, inscribing copies for friends, awaiting favorable reviews, entertaining (however briefly) hopes for good sales and personal fame, all these would be denied him. The Isaac Schwimmer Press was governed by a different set of rules and customs: Charlotte Rouse wasn't interviewed by Charlie Rose, Jack Gough didn't give readings at Borders, Tranh Long

Dong searched in vain for his standings at Amazon. No, whatever thrills the book had to offer, Ezra had already enjoyed. But to the max. No complaints.

He drove home quickly, even though, on signs displayed at the city limits, Seven Hills was proud to boast, and not idly, that traffic laws were strictly enforced. He put his two bags of groceries, a gift from the Seven Hills Market in recognition of his heroism, on the kitchen counter, fished in one for the pack of Oreos, tore it open, ate a couple without tasting them, and headed into the living room.

He flicked on his computer, accessed the appropriate file, and, without bothering to read what he had written earlier that day—no need, he could easily recite it from memory—he immediately resumed exploring Nora's complicated relationship with her former high school English teacher.

His style had loosened up perceptibly since Tessa's visit. He wondered, very briefly, if any reader would notice the change. The place where it happened could be precisely pinpointed, a sweetly melancholy souvenir of a delicious interlude.

That was the last conscious thought he had for many hours.

Time presumably passed. He couldn't have said how much, but time does have a way of passing, even, perhaps especially, when one is unaware of its doing so. Insofar as he measured it at all, it wasn't in minutes and hours, nor even in words and paragraphs and pages, but rather in scenes and couplings (and triplings and morelings). He knew he had turned on the light at some point, although he couldn't remember doing it, so it was reasonable to assume it had grown dark outside, which suggested that quite a bit of time had in fact elapsed.

He was describing an encounter in a hot tub—trying to evoke the heat and the bubbles and the buoyancy and the sharp smell of disinfectant along with the more directly sexual stuff—when his doorbell rang. The phenomenon was so foreign to him in his present state, came from such an alien plane of existence, he didn't recognize it at first, indeed actually said, out loud, "What?" As if some explanation might be forthcoming from the ether.

The doorbell rang again. He shook his head to clear it. Which didn't quite do the trick, but he nevertheless had the presence of mind—or had sufficiently drilled himself on security procedures so it was automatic—to execute a save-and-exit command before he rose to answer the door. He checked his watch en route; almost eleven o'clock! Where had the evening gone? And what nutcase was dropping in on him at eleven?

"Who is it?" he demanded through the cheap pine.

"Me. Carol. Hope I didn't wake you."

His mood instantly soured. Didn't he have some say in scheduling her visits? He opened the door, and was suddenly aware of a certain gaminess about his person. His armpits were damp, his underwear felt adhesive. "I was working."

She strode in. She was wearing a long, full, blue print cotton skirt and a ruffled white blouse. She looked as if she'd come straight from a barn raising. As Agnes De Mille's date. "I was at the hospital with Daddy," she announced, perhaps by way of explanation. Could her cowgirl rigging be an outfit he favored? "He's awake and alert, he even ate some dinner. I thought you'd want to know."

"Good." She came for this?

"The doctors say if he watches his diet and starts exercising and learns to control his temper, he should be as good as new. I've been after him about those things for years. A medical emergency can be a blessing in disguise."

Except he survived, is what Ezra thought, although all he said was, "Glad to hear it."

"I told him what you'd done. He was very impressed. Deeply moved."

Enough to favor my tenure case? Ezra thought, unworthily. But contented himself with saying, "Anybody would have done the same."

"Only they didn't. And you did."

"What can I say? I'm a hell of a guy. Maybe I'll get to sit beside Hillary at the State of the Union."

She grinned. In the past, she might have chastised him for his levity. "You don't want to talk about it."

"There isn't much to say. That he's alive is a big deal, not what I did. I was in the right place at the right time and accidentally did the right thing."

She rolled her eyes, but dropped the subject for another. "Listen, I think we still have a lot to talk about," she said, "that's why I risked coming over so late. Hope it's okay."

"Sure. Why not?" On the other hand, she might have phoned. Given him a chance to shower and change out of his raggediest corduroy pants and most washed-out Gap tee shirt. Or—just as plausibly—to say no. "Sit down."

"What were you working on? Song of Iceland?"

"Right."

"It's taking forever, isn't it?"

"Poetry is a serious business." His pomposity sounded authentic, at least to his own ears. Good. Better pomposity than incipient panic.

She seated herself on his sofa, smoothing her skirt around her.

"Can I get you anything to drink?"

"A glass of wine might be nice. To toast your good deed."

"I'm sort of out of wine at the moment. Maybe your father will open some of Aunt Goldie's stuff when he gets home. You can toast me then."

"A cup of tea?"

"Well, the truth is . . ." He shrugged.

"Out of that too?"

"Not sure I was ever *in* it."

"Men," she snorted.

"How about a Diet Coke?" He had brought home that six-pack this afternoon.

"That would be fine, thank you."

He stepped into the kitchen, hoping there was still some left. He dimly remembered having drunk several during the last few hours, but doubted it could be as many as six. He opened the refrigerator. Three. Phew! He grabbed one, working it out of its plastic holder.

He decided he couldn't just hand her the can. That wouldn't be gracious. Which meant he'd have to wash a glass. He did, calling, "Hold on!" He quickly dried the outside of the glass with a paper towel, then pressed the last two cubes remaining in his baby blue plastic ice tray into the glass. Then he popped the can and poured the nauseous concoction in. How could anyone, himself included, drink this stuff? Bubbles exploded against his nose, as if announcing, It's party-time!

"Here I come!" he called. "Sorry to take so long." He stepped into the living room, the glass of fizzing brew in hand.

And was startled to discover Carol, wearing nothing but white panties, standing in the middle of the room. "Oh," said Ezra. Her skirt and blouse were folded neatly over the back of the sofa. It struck him that he'd never seen her naked before, not like this—not frankly and entirely exposed—

but only in bits and pieces; their lovemaking, when it occurred at all, was furtive, and took place in the dark. She had a very good figure, he noted in passing: small-breasted, trim, defined, shapely. Her rib cage made one of those nice tomboy six-packs.

She wasn't smiling. Nor did she say anything. Fair enough. The ball was in his court. "Do you still want your Diet Coke?"

She frowned.

Bad move.

He set the glass down on a side table and approached her. Is this a good idea? he asked himself. In one sense, the answer was clear; perhaps as a result of the erotic atmosphere in which a pornographer constantly enshrouds himself, perhaps as a result of five days with no sexual activity to speak of, especially in light of what had preceded them, perhaps (and it's funny, he thought, that I consider this possibility *last*) as a straightforward reaction to the attractive woman standing nude before him, but for *some* reason, he was suddenly quite aroused, easily as aroused as he was surprised. But on the other hand—

"Let's fuck," she suggested.

She had never before used the word "fuck" in his hearing, in any context, in any way. Not as a noun, not as a verb, not as an expletive, not in its adjectival form, certainly never as a synonym for sexual intercourse. Still, it might be a mistake to make too much of this; she could hardly say, "Let's fudge."

"But—" But what? No further words offered themselves.

"Nope. No ands, ifs, or buts. Well, maybe a few ands, but no ifs or buts." Now she smiled. "See, I've been thinking about *this* too. It'll be good preparation for a discussion about our relationship, don't you think? The whole exercise'll go down easier. Come kiss me." As he took several steps toward her, she went on, "Then take me and, and *ravish* me."

When he took her in his arms, she added, "I intend to ravish you too, by the way. Equal-opportunity ravishing." She was laughing when he kissed her.

Later, lying together in his bed, his arm under her shoulders, her head nestling against his neck, she said dreamily, "You know, I've finally begun to understand why people devote so much of their lives to this. Doing it, thinking about it, talking about it . . . I see how it can drive everything else. I didn't used to. I mean, it was nice sometimes, but . . ."

"Tonight was different?"

"Couldn't you tell?"

He could. He'd been slightly apprehensive, before they began in earnest, that after Tessa he'd find Carol cool and passive and not very interesting, and the thought unnerved him, gave him a sinking feeling, like someone suspecting for the first time he might be suffering from an addiction that could bedevil the rest of his life. But no such problems arose. Carol may have lacked Tessa's virtuosity, but sex, at least according to Norman Mailer, is for amateurs. A comforting sentiment. Everything felt sweet and tender, and the unexpected intensity of her ardor, and the unprecedented insistence and duration of her climax, were downright astonishing. He turned his head to look at her. She was smiling, shyly but proudly. A very appealing look. "What happened to you?" he blurted. "Read one of those self-help books?"

"Nope."

"It's a miracle."

"That's closer to the truth." She didn't say this lightly. "It *is* amazing, isn't it? I mean, it kind of does have the force of divine revelation about it." She snuggled closer.

"Not really my line," Ezra said.

"No, I realize. You're a secular humanist agnostic atheist or something. It's more *Daddy's* line. And I don't imagine he'd see it the same way, do you?"

He kissed her nose, a spontaneous show of tenderness that felt surprisingly natural. "No, I suspect he's more likely to give credit to the other side." He was feeling very benign. "So, to what do we owe this miracle, then? The power of prayer?"

"You shouldn't make fun of that. I accept you for who you are, you owe me the same courtesy."

"You accept me for who I am?"

"That's right."

"When did that happen?"

"Recently." She smiled. "It's all part of the same process. A number of things have fallen into place. Way late, I admit. I know I haven't been an easy person. I wanted to tell you about it back at the hospital, but, well, there wasn't time, and besides, it's a hard thing to discuss in the abstract. By which I mean, with our clothes on." She snuggled closer.

"This has to do with our being angry at each other?"

"Are you being sarcastic?"

"Uh uh. I'm trying to put things together."

"Okay, let me say this as clearly as I can. I've been a total pain. I know that now. I was censorious and withholding and cold and judgmental. Okay? I admit it. All of it. But I wasn't the only one at fault. 'Cause you *let me get away with it.* You acted as if you deserved no better. Not much of an inducement for me to change."

Where the hell had all this come from? Who was this woman? "Go on."

"That's why it might be healthy to admit you're angry." She gave him a twisted smile. "I'm not asking you to spank me. Necessarily." Before he could react to this last surprise, she plowed on, "But you ought to try a little candor, seeing as I'm right here and everything."

"Yes, okay. The thing is, Carol . . ." He considered. It would be easier to go for something facile and evasive, but maybe her earnestness merited an honest response, maybe this was an opportunity he'd be foolish to pass up. "I'll say this. My life at Beuhler hasn't been a bed of roses, and you haven't been much help. Instead of giving me support and reassurance and, and, and simple companionship, instead of being on my side, it was like you were adding to the misery, and, and blaming me for a lot of it."

"So, you mean like . . . What was that thing you told me? I wasn't part of the solution, I was part of the problem?"

"Like that." He braced himself; if this was a trap, he'd well and truly stepped in it.

"Well, good call. You're absolutely right."

He waited for the kicker. It didn't come. "Jeez, Carol, I thought you were gonna take my head off just now."

She nodded seriously. "I know. But I'm not. Maybe it's time for a little honesty. I think we've both been terrified without realizing it. Given my background, you can maybe understand why I might be. And you . . . I don't know, maybe it was Helga who did the damage, but you've never stood up for yourself, you just . . . floated along. It was unfair to expect you to rescue me, especially since I wouldn't admit I needed rescuing, but I was in quicksand, and you . . . you just sort of watched as I flailed around and kept sinking."

He continued to stare at her, not knowing what to say.

"If that Tessa woman got you mobilized, then you owe her a debt of gratitude. You seem very different to me."

"Me? *You're* the one who's different."

She ignored this. "And it's a decided improvement. Even when you were telling me off in the Cabbage Patch . . . Remember?"

"I remember."

"I was thinking, Gee, he's so attractive."

"You were?"

"I was. You seemed . . . strong. I don't necessarily want it to become a habit, but it felt . . . it didn't feel *good,* but it felt *just.* It got me, you know, a little excited, to be honest."

"Where does all this come from, Carol? I know there's something you're not telling me. If not therapy . . . what?"

She colored; even her shoulders showed bright pink. She turned away from him and spoke quietly. "Like I said, I started doing some thinking over spring break. Began to realize what I'd been avoiding. I pretended it was out of principle, when really it was fear. And then, seeing you with Tessa, I mean, that kind of accelerated the process. Like—I know how crass this sounds, but—like if you could score with *that,* then maybe I'd been undervaluing you. Taking advantage of what I perceived as weakness. But you don't seem weak anymore. Anyway, where it comes from doesn't matter, does it? I mean, here it is, here I am, you can take it seriously or not."

"Oh, I take it seriously."

"Well, good. You should." She kissed his shoulder. A second or two later, she murmured, "Listen . . ." Her hand was searching for him. "You think we could maybe do it again?"

Who is this person? What incubus has taken possession of Carol? And is it a long-term lease? A freehold? "Well, we *could*—"

"See, the thing is . . . I mean, you know, Daddy's in the hospital, sedated, more or less unconscious, so I don't have to account for my time. It's kind of a golden opportunity."

"What the hell has gotten into you?" he demanded. And then, after a moment, "Wait, let me rephrase that."

She laughed, a great hearty belly-laugh. "This is more fun than arguing, isn't it?"

As he leaned in to kiss her, a great wave of tenderness washed over him. Was it like this when they started dating, another lifetime ago? He couldn't remember anymore. Too much damned water under the bridge. But it didn't seem likely: Despite having known her for three years, he felt as if he were kissing her for the first time.

Chapter 8

THE END

Ezra leaned back in his chair and rubbed his eyes. He rubbed his eyes because he was tired and because they ached, but he might as well have been rubbing them because he couldn't believe what he saw.

THE END

Every Inch a Lady was finished, coming in at a streamlined 66,000 words.

Nora, contrary to his expectations, contrary to his plan, had turned her back on the SoHo artist who had always been the love of her life and opted instead for a life of adventure. Well, Ezra wasn't sure he approved, but the decision wasn't finally his to make. Nora was a big girl; at a certain point, you just had to give her your blessing and your love and hope she knew what she was doing.

His back was killing him, he realized all of a sudden. His head was throbbing. He had a genuinely nasty taste in his mouth, as if a tomcat had been in there delineating its territory. His stomach was making peculiar noises. His Casio informed him that it was just after five on a Friday morning. Two days ahead of schedule.

He stretched, feeling as if he had just gone through some elaborate, painful, sustained puberty rite. The world would never be the same, *he* would never be the same. From now on, henceforth and forever, he was Ezra Gordon, novelist. Ezra Gordon has written a novel. Millions try, but Ezra Gordon has succeeded. He's done the same thing that Honoré de Balzac did, not to mention William Faulkner and Jane Austen. And he hasn't merely *started* a novel, mind you; anyone can *start* a novel. No, Ezra Gordon has *finished* a novel. No, he hasn't finished *reading* a novel, which, at least to judge by his students, is a rare enough accomplishment; no, Ezra Gordon has finished *writing* a novel, one with lots of words in it, and characters and events and all those other things that novels have. And those words and characters and events and so on were all invented by Ezra Gordon. Himself. The world would never know it, only two people *in* the world would ever know it, but by God, it was so.

Every Inch a Lady, a novel by E. A. Peau. Who was, even though the world would never know it, Ezra Gordon.

He stood up and stretched again. Everything hurt some more.

Everything felt great.

Today was a very big day in his life. Today, Ezra Gordon, novelist, was going to *deliver his manuscript.* To his *publisher,* which was a thing that novelists are supposed to have, although, tragically, many do not. He was going to take the *novel,* which is the thing a novelist produces, and which had once been only a series of electronic impulses in his *brain,* which is something a novelist needs in order to produce a novel, and this novel, which now was a series of electronic impulses in his *computer,* a device to facilitate the production of the novel, would soon be turned into a *manuscript,* the term for a series of ink markings on paper, by way of his *printer,* a so-called *peripheral* to his computer. And then he, the novelist, was going to arrange to *transport* the collection of ink markings to his publisher. This would complete the process known as *delivering the manuscript.* He had planned it out carefully.

Which was a good thing, because now, he noticed, he was feeling increasingly befuddled.

My brain is gone, he thought. I used to have a brain, it used to work more or less the way a brain is supposed to work, whiling away the hours conferring with the flowers, but now my brain is gone. He didn't find the thought particularly disturbing, however.

My brain is gone, and I don't care.

Which is my prerogative. It's a free country. People are allowed to care or not, and about whatever they choose. Some people, for example, don't care about crack corn. Take Jimmy. He couldn't care *less* about crack corn. Whereas *I* don't care that my brain is gone. I'm not exactly sure how I feel about crack corn. If the Gallup people asked me my opinion about crack corn, I'd be stumped. I *suspect* I'm against it, but I haven't really given the matter a lot of thought. I actually haven't given the matter *any* thought, to be entirely candid.

And, seeing as how my brain is gone and all, I probably never will.

But that's okay. I don't need a brain anymore. Why? you no doubt find yourself asking. Because I've *written a novel.* My brain has served its purpose. So long, brain, it's been good to know you, I must be rolling along. Thanks for everything. Don't be a stranger! Y'all come back and see us again real soon, ya hear?

But, he suddenly realized, I must have a little bit of brain left, because otherwise I can't do all that stuff I have to do, all that delivering-my-manuscript stuff. I may not need my *higher cerebral functions,* as they're called, to deliver my manuscript, but I can't be quite so cavalier about, say, my *limbic system.*

My limbic system may be the best friend I have.

Other than my publisher, to whom my manuscript must be delivered. My publisher, right along with my limbic system, is my best friend. They can fight it out for the title. In this corner, in the pink ooze, my limbic system, and in *this* corner, wearing black bikini briefs, Isaac Schwimmer of the Isaac Schwimmer Press.

Ezra, acting on impulse, staggered down the hall to the bathroom. While urinating, a process that seemed to take an unwontedly long time, a new thought—if thought was the medium the remainder of his brain was working in—struck him: What isn't really fair, he realized, considering how they're *both* my best friend, and my limbic system is already fully apprised of my recent accomplishment, is that Isaac Schwimmer of the Isaac Schwimmer Press remains blithely ignorant of the fact that Ezra Gordon has entered the novelists' ranks.

This is wrong. This is a gross miscarriage of justice. This must be remedied.

After what seemed an eon of further urination, he wobbled back into the hall toward his telephone. Oh sure, it was doubtless a little early to phone someone, but hell, it isn't every day a fellow emerges from a long painful puberty rite, Isaac will certainly share my joy, and anyhow, the birds are singing outside, so looked at in a certain way it qualifies as daytime. The birds, closer to nature as they are, understand these matters better than we. They don't have those pushy higher cerebral functions to confuse them.

He dialed Isaac's number, which presumably must have been stored somewhere in his limbic system, contrary to what the neurologists might posit. After three rings, he began to have second thoughts. Perhaps the birds don't provide the best yardstick for determining how late a human being should sleep. This was another way of looking at the question. But just before he could hang up—guiltily but at least anonymously—the receiver was lifted at the other end of the line.

"Hello?" said a woman's voice, clogged with sleep.

"Oh, whoops," said Ezra, who suddenly had to acknowledge that his limbic system might not provide the best guidance for certain fine motor tasks, such as dialing a telephone. "I, I'm sorry to wake you. Do I have the right number? I'm trying to reach Isaac Schwimmer."

"Ezra? Is that you?" Now, as the voice became clearer and more focused, he was able to recognize it. It belonged to Tessa. "He, he's still asleep. You want me to wake him?"

"No, that's all right," Ezra said hastily, all at once feeling very alert indeed. "Just, just tell him I called."

And he hung up quickly, without waiting for her response.

Chapter **9**

Friday was a vague haze. Friday, as soon as it ended, would largely be lost to conscious memory. Ezra had to take it on faith that, like a sleepwalker, he was following the steps he had worked out for himself back when he was compos mentis. If that wasn't too flattering a self-assessment even at the best of times.

This hazy semi-consciousness wasn't, in truth, completely unwelcome. At least he was too brain-dead to examine the implications of Tessa's answering Isaac's phone before 6 A.M., and doing so, by all indications, from out of a deep sleep. Not that a dim sense of this disturbing fact was ever totally absent: All day he found himself experiencing a nagging sense of troubled confusion somewhere in the nether reaches of consciousness. And you didn't have to be Sigmund Freud to know that, while the nagging might be kept submerged for the present, sooner or later it would insist on coming up for air.

Nor, as a result of his zomboid exhaustion, could he worry obsessively over his having "seen"—a euphemism for fornicating with—Carol Dimsdale on every one of the last four nights. Ditto the potentially even more disturbing fact that he had enjoyed these encounters more than he had any business doing, and additionally, and despite the freedom to write it allowed him, how much he hated it when she left his bed in the middle of the night and went home to care for her father, now returned from the hospital, hearty if not quite hale.

Everything in his life was happening too fast, without his volition, almost without his permission. Now, these mostly seemed to be *good* things, which at least had the charm of novelty about it. But it would have been nice to be consulted. And kept apprised.

Take this Carol business. Although he was still mistrustful—and nothing in their history suggested he should be otherwise—there was no denying her attitude toward him had undergone a breathtaking improvement. She seemed cooperative, accepting, accommodating; she'd brought picnic dinners, good ones with pâtés and cheeses and fresh-baked breads and wine, the best the valley (the Loire as well as the San Joaquin) had to offer, every night they'd gotten together, and, despite his protestations that he'd come into some money and was happy to contribute, she refused; she'd spared him any contact at all with her father, barely made reference to the man's existence (an existence, it's true, which persisted only because of Ezra's actions); she hadn't mentioned his tenure case, not even once; and then there was bed.

As Hemingway might put it, Now bed. Well, bed. Yes, bed. Hm, bed.

Carol's transmogrification in bed was something he found hard to grasp. Let alone credit. Where had all this libidinous bravura come from?

The question seemed to engage her as well. "Do you think I'm a nymphomaniac?" she asked him on the second night, while they lay in bed basking in postcoital languor.

"I don't think there *is* such a thing," he answered. "It's a discredited myth. Invented by guys who weren't getting any."

She stretched. "But I mean, it just strikes me as incredible that sex *exists*. You know? It's at least as much fun as, I don't know, dessert or, or television, it's available pretty much whenever you want it, and it's *free*. Why don't people do it all the time?"

"I think they do. Some people, anyway."

"So what was I missing before? It's like 'Amazing Grace,' except I wasn't blind. So it's really mysterious."

"That bothers you?"

"What bothers me is the time I wasted. The opportunities. And even more how I used to feel *superior* to all this."

"Rest easy. According to the experts, you're just reaching your peak."

She turned around to face him. The look on her face had become thoughtful. "When I married Buddy, looking back, I think it was mostly just to get out of the house. Away from Daddy. And I suppose Buddy was acceptable to him because we met through church. And because he seemed so . . . *unthreatening*. Which is probably another way of saying sexless. I think that's why Daddy approved. We were just kids, really. And Buddy was even more uptight than I was. Our wedding night was a disaster. We never recovered."

"You didn't try again?"

"Oh sure. Even succeeded. Sort of. But not . . . I mean, the notion that it might be . . . whatever . . . we never got to that point. And so it was easier to think you had to be sort of coarse to enjoy it than to think there was something lacking in him or me. It was more acceptable to regard it as an aspect of hygiene. To admit we were inept and to acknowledge I wasn't letting myself feel anything, well, it was much easier to consider myself being above the animal passions. And that proved to be a remarkably tenacious belief. As you may have noticed."

"And you're telling me that's changed?"

"Along with a lot of other stuff."

"So where do you end up?"

"Here, in your bed." And then, lest he find this alarming, she added, "I don't mean *end up* here, necessarily, but it's where I seem to have alighted for the moment. It's almost as if I'm starting from scratch. I feel a little like one of those bad girls in high school, the sluts, the ones I used to hold in such contempt while pretending to want to pray for their souls."

"Does that make you uncomfortable?"

"Less than you might think. It's kind of fun. Fun to be a bad girl for a change."

"Oh, you'll never manage *that*."

"I might surprise you."

This exchange left him somewhat disquieted. The coincidence between what was happening to Carol and what he had caused to happen to Nora seemed almost uncanny. But her candor, her newly sunny nature, her frank pleasure in his company, were things a fellow could get used to. And she was in his bed every night, and he wouldn't have wanted her to be anywhere else.

Not that she ever spent the night. "I can't," she'd say, although he hadn't in fact asked. But he didn't have to; getting out of bed was so contrary to every impulse, the invitation seemed inherent in the situation. "I have to go home. If I don't, Daddy would, he'd—"

"Shit a brick?"

In many ways, the situation suited Ezra perfectly. On each of those nights, after she finally left, he dragged himself, spent, sore, rank, and content, over to his computer and immediately lost himself in composition. Recovery of energy was almost instantaneous. In some way, on some level, he was probably running on empty, getting by as he was on only four or five hours of sleep a night max, but for some inexplicable reason, he'd never felt better in his life. As Isaac would say, Go figure.

This Carol business was a genuine puzzlement. Just two days ago, working feverishly, eating up the pages, he had taken a little Diet Coke break and impulsively phoned her office. Ostensibly it was to tell her not to visit that night, he had too much work; but part of him suspected it was primarily for the pleasure of hearing her voice. When she answered, he could hear considerable background hubbub.

"Is that you, Ez? It's a madhouse around here. We're having a meeting. I can't talk about it now."

"The computers?"

"I'll explain tonight."

"Well, that's what I'm calling about."

"Oh Ez—"

"I'm sorry, Carol. I can't. The next day or two is going to be very difficult."

"Why?"

"Uh . . . I'm trying to finish." He hoped she wouldn't press.

"Reykjavík hayride?"

"I think I see light at the end of the tunnel."

"So that means I can finally read it."

"Maybe not *that* much light." Whoops. He still had to proceed with caution.

"It's been an awfully long tunnel."

"Yes it has."

She lowered her voice to a barely audible whisper. "How about a, you know, a *quickie?*"

He laughed. "You're a wonder."

"To prevent my doing something wanton. Go out and cruise for sailors, maybe."

"In Seven Hills?"

"Don't underestimate me."

All at once the threat sounded credible.

And now, standing by his new printer, his knees buckling, waiting as it

spewed forth hard copy, he decided that things with Carol were so confusing, so deeply unsettling, it was just as well he was too tired to think about
them. Just as it was fine he couldn't think cogently about Tessa. For the
time being, instead, he'd sleepwalk through his novelist's duties.

First, he finished printing his manuscript. This was a boring and time-
consuming task. He even nodded off a couple of times during the process,
but then the memory of what he had accomplished brought him back to
startled wakefulness with a sudden jolt of adrenaline.

He had no intention of xeroxing the pages. They were already on disk,
and he didn't want any other evidence of his association with the book
anywhere in his apartment. Indeed, he briefly considered erasing all of his
files too, but then relented. He'd never be able to take such a drastic step.
Those files would soon be his only tangible connection to his book. They
were like love letters saved from an intense but short-lived affair.

Like the one with Tessa.

But he was too tired to think about that.

After the printing was complete, he put the manuscript in the oversized
manila envelope he had bought several days before from the codger at
Seven Hills Stationers. The envelope was still blank, with no address on it.

He drove to campus, the manila envelope on the seat beside him, pray-
ing out loud to the God he didn't believe in that he be spared a major col-
lision en route, and that, should such a catastrophe befall him, he neither
become comatose nor lose the use of his hands. The manuscript had to be
protected from discovery at all costs, up to and including prayer.

There are no atheists in foxholes, and there aren't any at the Isaac
Schwimmer Press.

He walked from his car to the Student Union, descended the stairs to the
post office in the basement, and had the package weighed. Then, after buying the requisite stamps, he walked back to his office and addressed the
envelope to Isaac's office building, doing what he could to disguise his
handwriting. Then he affixed the stamps he had bought. He didn't write a
return address.

He trudged back to his car—weariness was overtaking him fast—drove
into Seven Hills, and deposited the envelope in a mailbox on Main Street.
He had hoped for some sort of large emotion consequent upon this action,
but none came. Perhaps he was simply too tired.

He drove home, took the phone off the hook, undressed, leaving his clothes in a pile on the floor, and climbed into bed. He fell asleep almost instantly, and didn't wake up again until Saturday morning.

Now, a few hours later, a warm late Saturday afternoon, clad in a Beuhler College tee shirt and old sweat pants, he sprawled on his living room sofa, sipping bourbon—the bottle of Makers Mark was a little celebratory present to himself purchased at Seven Hills Liquor, along with a bottle of champagne, after a huge pancake breakfast (another little celebratory present to himself, eaten ravenously at Mom's, one of the few remaining nonfranchise coffee shops in town)—and preparing to read Henry's novel. It was well past time for that. And reading Henry's novel seemed preferable to starting a journal article; he felt he had earned a weekend off before he had to confront his life in earnest once again, said weekend off being one final little celebratory present to himself (a rather dubious one at that) for a job, if not well, then at least incontestably, done.

Ten pages into Henry's book, agreeably unbored, he suddenly noticed he missed Carol quite a lot. This presented a practical problem. It also presented a *philosophical* problem—if he missed her so soon after having seen her, what did that suggest?—but the practical problem took priority. She had been conscientious about following his instructions and not phoning him, which demonstrated a forbearing and trusting nature, and that was good; but now, because he had finished his book ahead of schedule, his time was free and he was eager to see her, but it was still the weekend and so she wouldn't be in her office, and that was bad.

That was bad because if he wanted to talk to her, he would have to phone her at home. And if he phoned her at home, there was a fifty percent chance he would have to talk to the Reverend Mr. Dimsdale first.

A fifty percent chance isn't so terrible, he assured himself. It's like flipping a coin. That's better odds than you get in Las Vegas.

But in Vegas, he next told himself, if you lose, all that follows is utter destitution. You still don't have to deal with Mr. Dimsdale. They arrange it that way on purpose. Otherwise the gaming industry would go bust.

This must prove how much I want to see her, he concluded as he rang her number. And that raises a philosophical question I'll leave for another time. Or maybe another lifetime.

"Hello?" intoned the Reverend Dimsdale.

It had come up tails.

"Uh, hello, sir. This is, uh—" A rogue notion of giving a false name entered his mind, but was immediately rejected; Dimsdale knew his voice. "—Ezra Gordon. Is Carol there, please?" He held his breath.

"My boy! How are you bearing up?" Dimsdale, incredibly, sounded warm and affectionate and *concerned*.

What the hell is going on here? Ezra wondered. "Bearing up?" he echoed.

Dimsdale launched into an extravagant speech of gratitude for Ezra's having saved his life. Phrases like "underestimated you," "hate the sin, not the sinner," "the Lord works in mysterious ways," and something about "casting the first stone" were sprinkled liberally throughout the oration.

Ezra waited until Dimsdale paused to draw breath—a long wait indeed—and then said, "I'm glad I was able to help." He may have spoken a little more sharply than he intended.

"Yes," the minister said, "Carol warned me you don't enjoy talking about it. Which shows a humble heart."

"Yes," said Ezra, "my heart's my most humble organ. And speaking of Carol—"

"I know, and it's a real shame, son. Not that I think you two were right for each other, the match wasn't what I'd call made in heaven, and I don't use such an expression casually. I've made no secret of my opinions on that score. But the way she's gone about this is brutal, and my heart goes out to you. For whatever consolation this provides, I believe Carol to be a headstrong, stubborn, imprudent girl—always has been, and I reckon I have to accept some of the responsibility for that, along with her dear departed mother—and it's clear she still has a fair amount of growing up to do. This new one she's got herself is a chastisement, that much I'll say, a chastisement to me for every mistake I made along the way. So you may not feel it now, I'm sure you don't, but in the fullness of time you'll regard it as a blessing you got yourself a small injury now, one that smarts like the dickens but'll eventually heal, instead of a maiming down the pike."

"Right. Thank you." Had oxygen deprivation during his ordeal in the grocery store cost the man his wits? "Uh, is she there? Can I speak to her?"

"You sure you want to put yourself through this? Break and break clean is the best advice I can give a young person in your situation. Do it all the time, too. You'd be amazed how many come to me for guidance."

"Yes."

"Pardon?"

"Uh, I'm, uh, prepared to, to take the risk, sir. Even though I may, as you say, I may . . . uh . . . May I speak to her?"

"Every generation has to learn the hard way, I suppose." Dimsdale sighed, then added, "Hold the wire, son. If you want to talk afterward, I'm available."

"That's very comforting."

A minute later, Carol said, in a cool, neutral tone of voice, "Hello, Ezra." Then, a moment later, suspiciously, "Daddy, are you on the line?"

There was an answering click.

"Hi, Carol. Is there something going on I should know about?"

"That's a two-part question."

Her voice was more animated now, but Ezra felt concern. "Your father just told me how he shares my pain. Which might have been more comforting if I'd known I was *in* pain."

"We're all in pain, Ezra. Because of man's fall."

"Carol—"

"It's a long story, Ezra. I'll explain later."

"Tonight?"

"Sure."

"What's going on, Carol?"

"Nothing to bother yourself about. I'll be there at seven, okay?"

She hung up before he could confirm. Well, this was odd. He went back to the sofa, took a good strong pull of bourbon, settled back along the armrest, his knees bent, his feet on the sofa cushion, and hoisted the immense weight of Henry's manuscript onto his lap. Judged solely in terms of heft, Henry qualified hands-down as the superior novelist. On the other hand, E. A. Peau's sex scenes were more vivid. Call it a draw so far.

Ezra chided himself for not taking Henry's effort seriously enough, and settled in for some concentrated reading.

When the doorbell rang about three hours later, Ezra was still in his tee shirt and sweat pants, still reclining on the sofa, still reading Henry's book. The binding of the manuscript had come apart, and the book was now in two pieces, one an unruly mountain of already-read pages on the floor, the other a neater pile on his thighs. Ezra now knew two things about Henry he hadn't previously suspected: Henry was very talented, and he was homosexual. No wonder the previous summer had changed the boy's life so dramatically; that's when he'd finally found the courage to admit his sexual nature to himself. In a way, Ezra had been right about the source of Henry's change of identity, but he hadn't had the vaguest notion of what the boy had gone through, how much pain, how much loneliness, how much genuine (as opposed to literary) alienation. The book, Henry's book, made it dramatically, and movingly, clear. Well.

The doorbell rang again. Ezra crossed to the front door and admitted Carol. She kissed him, then regarded him with bemusement. "Dolled yourself up for me, did you?"

He glanced down at his clothing. "I'm sorry, I, I—"

"It doesn't matter," she said. "No buttons to unbutton, fewer obstacles between my hands and you."

She was already at work on his sweat pants. "Hey, wait a sec," he protested.

"You've been drinking. I can smell it."

"Nothing to speak of. I'm sober."

"Too bad. I was hoping to take advantage of you."

"Just a little bourbon. Want some? Or should we go right to champagne?"

"Are we celebrating?"

"I just thought it would be a nice idea."

"What are we celebrating?"

"I didn't say we were."

"Ezra, give me a break, usually I'm lucky to get a Diet Coke around here."

He laughed. "Well, okay. I finished my poem. And no, you can't read it, don't even ask."

"Why not?"

"I need to live with it a while, then we'll see." He had been lying about the poem on such a regular basis that he could do so now with effortless, unstammering facility. "Tell me what your father was going on about. Why I'm in pain and everything."

"Okay," she said as she unhanded him and sashayed into the room. "The thing is, I'm gone so often these days, I've had to tell Daddy *some-thing*. You know? And I thought it was a good idea to take the heat off you. So I told him I'm seeing this other guy. In the long run, I figured you and I'd both benefit."

"Uh huh." Ezra felt wary. "And in the short run?"

"Well, there *is* another guy, Ezra. I've been looking for an opportunity to tell you. I haven't slept with him yet, and I don't have any strong feelings for him or anything, but . . . I mean, I don't have a clue where things stand between you and me right now, and this guy, he's kinda cute, it's real flattering the way he's been after me."

Ezra felt a bubble of hurt rising up inside him. Why hadn't he seen this coming? What madness had let him think the course of anything might run smooth? "Who is he?"

"An FBI agent, believe it or not. How about that?"

Ezra felt a rush of blood to his head. "An FBI agent!" A wave of nausea followed the rush of blood. "Not Dan McGruder!" Nah, it couldn't be: She'd said he was "cute," hadn't she? Not revolting. Cute. It must be some other FBI agent.

She was looking startled. "You know him?"

Whoops. No accounting for taste. "I've met him." I've met the fascistic son of a bitch.

She smiled hesitantly, then went on, "It's supposed to be very hush-hush. I mean, even the fact that he's here."

"I guess it's not as hush-hush as you think."

"You know why he's in Seven Hills?"

"The computer stuff."

She looked very surprised. "Yeah. And I'm liaison with the Bureau. They think it could be serious. The hacker's MO—that's what they call it, his MO—is similar to some guy in Germany who got into the Defense Department computer a couple of years ago by entering the network through a small college in Arkansas and proceeding from there. Just a matter of mastering a few passwords and so on, and then—"

"You seem to know a lot about this," Ezra interrupted testily.

"Well, Dan's been explaining it to me."

"'Dan?'"

"What am I supposed to call him?"

"'Asshole' suggests itself."

"You're jealous!"

"That's not the point. You sure you haven't slept with him?"

"Well honestly, I think I'd know if something like that had occurred, don't you?"

"You're nothing but trouble, Carol."

She smiled. "You know, I think I will try some of that bourbon, thank you very much. I seem to be adding new sins to my repertoire at an alarming rate."

As he got up to get her some, she called into the kitchen, "It's really your fault, Ezra."

"*My* fault?"

"For two reasons. First of all, I'm in a state all the time because of you. That makes me vulnerable. And then, we haven't talked about what's happening between us. You obviously don't care to. That's the other reason it's your fault. With so much ambiguity, it's hard to decide where the boundaries are."

"That sounds like emotional extortion," he called out.

"I guess it does, in a way. I suppose it *is*, in a way. But I'm not doing it to manipulate you. It just worked out like that."

"So you plan to sleep with this guy?" Ezra returned with a glass of bourbon over ice.

"Well now, I don't *plan* to, no. But things happen. As you know better than I."

"Oh, I get it," he declared. "You're punishing me for Tessa."

"Good heavens, I'm not punishing you at all, and certainly not for anything that occurred before . . . you know, before things changed between us. That wouldn't be fair at all." She took the proffered drink from him and sipped. "Hmm. Sort of medicinal."

"That's a great American whisky!"

"I didn't say I didn't *like* it, did I? Now how about we drop this other little matter and go to bed? You're the one I want to be with right now. I'm exactly where I want to be."

"I'm not in the mood."

He was back on the couch, and she abruptly sat herself down on his lap, causing him to grunt involuntarily. "Are you grumpy?" she asked. She put one hand around his neck. "Is that what's happening here? Is Ezra grumpy?" She bent down and nuzzled his ear. Her lips were cold from contact with the ice in her glass, and gave him a chill. Then she repeated, in the voice one uses with a baby, "Aw, is little Ezra grumpy?" only she pronounced the last word "gwumpy."

"Go away."

"What's the matter, wittew Ezzie?" Still speaking in the baby voice.

"This is exceedingly annoying."

She laughed.

"I'm serious. I just finished, I just finished this thing of mine, I was hoping we could celebrate, but instead—"

"Fine idea," she interrupted, using her normal voice again, "I'm all for it. *You're* the one who's spoiling things by being grumpy, not me. I'll do anything you want." And then, her pitch lower, "I will, you know. No fooling. Just name it. Ooh, you wanna know something? It's exciting just to say that. It is. I'm excited. I really am. Listen. Teach me something new. Something really dirty and perverted. I'll do *anything* you want."

"Tell it to the G-Man."

"Don't be an idiot." She put her glass on the side table and kissed him. When she finally pulled away, she said, "If you want to negotiate some sort of arrangement where we don't see other people, that's fine with me. It really is. Dan, except as far as Daddy is concerned, can go jump in a lake. If that's what you want, say so. But otherwise—"

"What's your father got against this guy? An FBI agent should be right up his alley."

"Yeah, except when I get back from being with him, which of course is really with *you,* it's late and my hair's mussed and my make-up's smeared and my clothes are disheveled and God knows what else Daddy notices. I don't even want to think about it."

"But you like this guy? I mean the real one, not the make-believe one?"

Carol sighed. "I'm going to try this one more time, Ezra. No pretense, okay? The guy's cute. He likes me. He likes me a lot. It's flattering. That kind of attention is very nice. He's not at all like you, and I'm sure he isn't anybody you'd cotton to or respect, he's not especially educated or sophisticated, and he isn't . . . you know, he doesn't have all that irony and everything you seem to value. But for a girl like me, a simple country girl like me, he seems pretty neat. He's a country boy, he's from Tulare originally, so our backgrounds are similar, he reminds me of the boys I went to school with, only, you know, he's in the FBI, which means he made something of himself. And, the thing is, what I've discovered with you, it's all sorts of things, but among them is, is, it's like a new toy, I can't help being curious about what it would be like to be with someone else. Someone completely different. Heck, I sometimes wonder what it would be like with *Buddy* if he and I bumped into each other again. I don't *need* to know, but I'd be lying if I didn't tell you the question occurs to me now and then and kind of intrigues me. Okay?"

Christ, she sounded like Nora in Chapter Three! Where would this end? "It still feels like blackmail," he complained.

"Ugh!" She hopped off his lap. Her irritation was real. "I wish Daddy had kept his fat mouth shut. Soon as he thinks somebody's weak and powerless and, and *useless,* suddenly he becomes an angel of mercy. Usually, he's an angel of *vengeance,* which suits him much better." She rounded on Ezra. "But at first I thought maybe it's for the best anyway, his blabbing. I thought being honest was getting us somewhere, so maybe this would help us take the next step." She picked up her drink and took a swallow. She seemed to be growing angrier, or at least more vehement, with each passing second. "But you know what? Forget everything I've said. I take it back. You want me to be faithful while you offer nothing in return? While you just passively accept everything I give you? You think that's a reasonable arrangement? Okay, you got it. It's yours. You win, I lose." She put the drink down. "Are you satisfied now? Have I capitulated enough so you'll deign to come to bed? Or do you need more? I don't know what's left, but if you've got a list of demands, let's hear 'em."

Ezra rose and took her in his arms. For awhile there it had seemed as if she was going to cry, but now she no longer seemed near tears, although she was still pretty wound up. "Listen," he began, but now it was her turn to try to wriggle out of his grasp. "Listen," he repeated, "this is so new, I'm still not completely sure how I feel, I'm kind of a wreck today anyway, not that I'm using that as an excuse, but the last few days have been sort of *extreme.* But I know I don't want you to see Dan anymore. So what do you want in exchange? What's your price?" He got down on one knee and took her right hand in both of his. "You wanna go steady?" he asked. "Wear my ring around your neck to show the world I'm yours by heck and so on and so forth?"

She looked down at him and laughed. "Why don't we just go to bed. Let's take it from there."

But for the first time in the last five days, their lovemaking was out of sync and unsatisfying. "What were you thinking about?" she asked afterward, breaking a long silence. "Dan? Your poem? Your mind was somewhere else."

"I was thinking about one of my students," he said.

"What's her name?"

"Henry."

She smiled, then said, "Maybe I should spend the night."

"What would Daddy say?"

"He'd shit a brick. But the way I see it, it's about time he got that brick out of his system. Might improve his disposition."

"I guess this calls for champagne."

So they had their celebration after all, toasting his poem, toasting her spending the night with him, finally even toasting the antique tradition of going steady. And when they returned to bed, the mood was more amorous, the lovemaking more satisfying. They fell asleep with their arms around each other.

At five-thirty the next morning, he woke to find her dressing. "Where are you going?"

"Shh. Go back to sleep."

"Aren't you gonna spend the day with me?"

"I have to get to church."

"Are you nuts? He'll fulminate at you from the altar."

"No, his sermon's already written." She laughed. "Anyway, maybe I'll get home before he wakes up."

"So the brick will remain in place."

"There's no big rush about the brick. Time's on our side."

"What's his text?"

"Deuteronomy. 'I have set before you life and death—'"

"'Therefore choose life.'"

Carol was startled. "You know it? You?"

"Oh yes. Wouldn't expect that passage to appeal to your father, though."

"He interprets it in the Christian sense. You know. *Eternal* life."

"Little anachronistic, isn't it?"

"Moses was a prophet, is his feeling, so he wasn't constrained by the dimension of time."

He was about to speak, but she forestalled him with, "Don't start arguing. *Please.* Take it up with *him* if you want. I've got to go."

She gave him a quick kiss and was out the door, leaving him to ponder the mysteries of existence in the pre-dawn half-light.

Chapter 10

"How's your friend?"

Susan McGill had been leaving her office, briefcase in hand, as Ezra passed by en route to his own. After a perfunctory exchange of hellos, he continued on his way, but she detained him with her question.

"My friend?"

"Your bosom buddy. Tessa. Heard from her lately? What's the good word?"

He must have winced, because she immediately got a shrewd look in her eye. "Trouble in Paradise?"

"Well . . ." He liked Susan well enough, but didn't really feel she was an appropriate repository for any confidences. "Something like that."

"It's to be expected, I guess." And then, perhaps fearing that he might interpret this as an aspersion cast on his general sexual worth, she added, "These long-distance romances are a bitch, aren't they?"

"Something like that."

"You grieving?"

"I wouldn't put it that way, no."

"But you must miss her."

"Well . . ." God, she was persistent. "Sure. Now and again."

"I'll bet. What a babe."

"I thought you were supposed to be a militant feminist, Susan."

"Militant feminists don't necessarily deny the validity of the sexual instinct. We simply seek to domesticate it."

"Thereby ruining the fun."

She broke into a broad smile. "Ah, Ezra, you have unexpected depths," she proclaimed. "Really. Your demeanor is like totally effective camouflage."

"You do me honor. The fact is—" He shrugged. There was no point try-ing to explain that it was the camouflage that was real, while the unex-pected depths were about an inch deep, an illusion resulting from unsought and unearned happenstance, accidental glory dimly reflected. "There's less here than meets the eye, Susan."

"Yeah, right. Listen, you free for dinner some night this week? I'm a good cook. Don't judge by those cheeses I laid out the other night, that was just counting pennies. We'll get nice and potted and you can tell me all about it."

For some reason, he wasn't unprepared for this. "Well now, the thing is—"

"Don't judge by externals," she interrupted. "Deconstruct me, you'd be amazed what you find."

"I never doubted it, Susan. But I'm sort of back with Carol Dimsdale now."

She blinked. "Jeez, the grass doesn't grow under *your* feet, does it?"

"No matter what you're thinking, you've got this wrong."

"Any port in a storm, huh?"

"No, that's what I mean. It's so much more complicated than that, I can't even begin to tell you."

"The Don Giovanni of Seven Hills. I'm speechless."

"That'll be the day."

She laughed, letting it go. "Okay, Ezra. Whatever. If things with Carol don't work out, or you find you've got a stray urge to spill the details, or maybe spill something else, give me a call. Dinner's a standing offer."

"You'll be the first to know."

"I'm on tenterhooks."

Amused, and relieved at getting away so easily, he resumed his progress down the hall and up the flight of stairs to his office. As he was reaching for his keys, he heard his telephone ringing within. He scrambled to get through the door in time, and, untypically, did, grabbing the phone in mid-ring, without shutting the door behind him, and gasping out a sharp "Yes?"

"Ez? Isaac."

Ezra felt himself tense. "Isaac. Hi." It was a genuine pleasure to hear his friend's voice, but there were other emotions as well.

"You sound outta breath. Doing something you shouldn't?"

"I just got here, that's all. Rushed to get the phone."

"Okay. Now. Couple things."

"Go on."

"First, are you fucking *nuts*?"

"Huh?"

"You used the *United States Postal Service* to deliver a manuscript?"

"You got it already?"

"Against all odds. It arrived this morning. Please, please, *please,* pal, next time, if there is a next time, use a courier service. The post office is like something out of fucking Mack Sennett, nobody in his right mind uses the fucking post office."

"Okay. What else?"

"Get yourself an answering machine, okay? This is the twentieth century, for Chrissake. I've been trying to get hold of you for over an hour. The switchboard people at Bollocks are retards."

"Beuhler."

"Whatever. Pop for an answering machine, you owe it to your friends."

"I'll think about it. Anything else?"

"Do we have a problem?"

"What do you mean?"

"You know. About Tessa. Is there gonna be any friction? I mean between you and me, of course." He laughed, then said, "All right, that was in bad taste, I admit it. But are we okay about this?"

"Of course." Were they? It was hard to know, but it *wasn't* hard to know he had no right to complain. He was also relieved to notice he felt no irrational, unjustified rancor toward Isaac. Which isn't to say he felt . . . *normal,* exactly.

"You're sure?"

"Absolutely." Well, maybe not absolutely. "How is she, by the way?"

"Terrific. She asked me to give you a message, in fact."

"Uh huh." Very wary.

"Said you were right. Showed a lot of maturity. She's glad you were so sensible."

"Well . . . good." The bitch! He assumed she'd be there in case he changed his mind.

"I didn't ask her what it means, and I don't intend to. We're sort of going together."

"You and Tessa?" Gulp.

"Uh huh. Just sort of happened. One of those things."

"This is, like, serious?"

"Too early to tell. Maybe."

"Well, congratulations." Gulp. "Say hello for me."

"Let me get back to you on that."

Ezra laughed, flattered, as was no doubt intended, by the suggestion of jealousy. "Anything else?"

"Yep. Your check is in the mail. That's one of the three most frequently told lies in Hollywood, as you may know, but in this case it happens to be true."

"Via the U.S. Postal Service?"

"Don't sweat it. I was only talking about manuscripts. You should get it in the next day or so. The envelope's addressed to 'Occupant,' just like you wanted."

"Great. Anything else?"

"Just one."

"Okay."

"Great job."

Ezra felt something flutter inside his chest. "You mean you've read it?"

"The minute it came in. Dropped everything. And you did great. Knew you would, but you did even better than that."

"It's really okay?" Ezra wanted more. Lots more. Now that he was assured the book wasn't a total botch, his feelings had gone from simple relief right to aching greed for praise.

"It's great, Ez. It has something special. Some distinctive quality. I can't even explain it. But I've got a nose for this kind of thing, you know? It has a sort of *sweetness,* somehow, a tenderness. When I was reading it this morning, I got hard maybe seven times, and that's saying something, man, I'm *immune* nowadays, these books are like *technical manuals* to me. If you want to do another, just say the word. As many as you like. You've skipped to the head of the class."

"I'll think about it. When's it going to appear?"

"Couple weeks."

"Couple of weeks?" Ezra echoed incredulously.

"We're not Oxford University Press, buddy. Our goal is to move inventory. We're gonna rush this sucker into the stores as soon as the printers deliver it. I've already put Winkler to work on the cover."

"Personal favor, Ike? Ask him to tone down the boobs. Keep 'em to 50-Double-D's or so. Nora's not a bimbo."

"Isaac Schwimmer doesn't potchky with an artist's freedom of expression, pal. Besides, tits move inventory. The bigger the tits, the greater the movement. Listen, I'll get you some copies soon's they come in. And come visit. Door's always open. So's Lucy, if that's an inducement. She sends regards." So saying, he abruptly hung up.

Ezra kicked his office door closed, sat down behind his desk, leaned back, clasped his hands behind his head, and laughed. If only *life* were this easy.

Which reminded him—the word *life* was doing this more and more frequently—of his need to write an article. Okay. No prob. Just do it. If he could write a novel in sixteen days, he could do anything. He decided he wouldn't leave his office until he found a topic.

Later that day, he devised, if not a topic, then at least a title: "In/Signification and Dys/Lexicography: A (Mis)Reading of Nabokov's *Ada*." Later, he'd have to figure out what it meant. Now, though, it was time to search for Henry. He felt an obligation to Henry, a debt for not having taken him seriously enough.

After nosing around campus for over an hour, he found him in the editorial offices of *Les Mots,* the college literary magazine, on the top floor of the Student Union. Henry was sitting on a vinyl sofa with two other students, all three smoking Gitanes and reading manuscripts. The noxious clouds of smoke were like something out of Wilfred Owen.

"Can I speak to you a second, Henry?" He made an effort not to cough; he didn't want Henry to think he was making a point.

"Sure thing."

Henry excused himself and joined Ezra in an empty room just off the editor's office. Before Ezra could speak, Henry blurted, "I should've called. You went out on a limb there, and I do appreciate it, especially since, since I know you have doubts of your own."

Ezra dismissed all this with a wave of his hand. "How'd we do?"

Henry graced Ezra with a thin smile. "You made an impression, no doubt about that."

"Good."

"But you didn't *sway* them. Don't blame yourself, they don't sway easy. Gale-force winds wouldn't sway them. You did yeoman's duty."

"I'm sorry, Henry."

"That's why I didn't call. Kind of discouraged, you know?"

"So what happens next?"

"Well, I guess I come back in the fall as an engineering major." He shrugged. "Not much alternative. I don't feel quite ready to support myself. Not in the manner to which my folks have let me grow accustomed."

"Writers don't have to be English majors," Ezra said gently. "Lots of 'em studied something else. You could do a whole book on the writers who went to medical school, for example. Keats. Chekhov. Maugham. That bastard Céline. William Carlos Williams."

"Yeah. Except, it won't work out that way for me."

"Don't be so sure. I've read your pages, Henry."

"You have? You did?" Henry's eyes widened.

"Yes. I'm sorry I took so long."

"And?" Before Ezra could answer, Henry plunged on, "Go ahead, be as scathing as you like, I'm numb, I won't even feel it. What's the verdict?"

"The verdict is, everything I told your parents is true. Even though I thought I was bullshitting at the time."

This was so unexpected to Henry that his mouth literally dropped open, which was gratifying. Ezra went on, "When do you think you'll finish?"

"Before the semester's over." There was a quaver in Henry's voice, of excitement, or misery, or hope, or some volatile combination of all three.

Ezra reflected, We have so much more power over these kids than we realize, so much more than we have any right to. "Good. Don't stop. I doubt there's anything I can do to help, but I'll do whatever I can." He awkwardly patted Henry's bony shoulder, suddenly terribly aware of his fragility. "It's been rough on you, hasn't it? I mean, everything, your whole life's been hard?"

"It's had its ups and downs."

"Well, you've taken the grit and produced a pearl. Maybe that's compensation."

A little embarrassed by the emotion he was feeling—the intimacy—and by the difficulty of giving praise in any natural way, he quickly turned, walked through the door and down the corridor. Before he reached the top of the stairway, he heard a great loud whoop of joy coming from the room he had just left. He shook his head and laughed as he descended the stairs. Today, he thought, I've done a good deed. It felt better than saving Dimsdale's life.

Emerging from the Student Union Building into the hot spring sun, he realized he did feel pretty damned good, pretty okay about things. His book was done and Isaac liked it. He had done a—what was the word Isaac sometimes used?—a *mitzvah* on Henry. The thought of Tessa didn't automatically turn him into an Edvard Munch etching. He and Carol were somehow hitting some kind of stride. Tomorrow or the day after, in his box in the post office in the basement of this very building, there'd be a check for $5,000. He had even come up with an idea, well, okay, a title, for a horseshit article that might just pry open the department's mind, at least as wide as this particular department's mind would ever go.

After two or three years thrashing about in the muck, he thought, things are coming up roses. I've hit bottom and bounced back. I've weathered the storm, bit the bullet, seized the day. And now life is spread out before me, a feast, a banquet, a buffet table of possibilities.

Got my gal, got my Lawd, got my song.

So why was this feeling of well-being almost instantly succeeded by a strange, niggling, nagging anxiety? Why a tiny distant intimation of dread just over the horizon, a peculiar conviction that life was going to turn complicated?

Was it simply the low self-esteem everybody seemed to be accusing him of lately? Was he one of those people who just can't accept their good luck? Or did some part of him know something the rest of him didn't?

Part 4

The Hunt for E. A. Peau

Chapter 1

T he first hint that something strange might be going on occurred in Ezra's Victorian novel seminar. And in retrospect, he couldn't say it was paranoid of him to find the incident unnerving, although he did misinterpret its significance.

The course had suffered a drop-off in the weeks since Tessa's visit—two students had quit, citing the ongoing computer confusion as their reason, complaining that the department wouldn't let them know if they were eligible to attend, and therefore whether they would ultimately get credit—and was now down to five. Fine. The fewer the better. However, as Ezra could have predicted, among the undiscouraged were Jack Scheer and Mindy Dunkelweisse. So the size might have improved, but the pain-in-the-ass density decidedly had not.

One hot afternoon in May, during a desultory and unilluminating discussion of *The Way of All Flesh* (a great title, Ezra had recently decided, sadly wasted on Mr. Butler's little effort), Ezra noticed something alarming in the pile of books and papers Mindy had on the table in front of her. It wasn't at all obtrusive; it was near the bottom of the pile, calling no attention to itself. It was easy enough to miss so that for the first hour or so Ezra *did* miss it. But once he saw it, there was no unseeing it.

It was a copy of *Every Inch a Lady.*

When he first noticed it, he gasped audibly, so audibly that the students all looked up, concerned perhaps that he was about to succumb to heat prostration (not a farfetched fear in the overheated, unventilated little seminar room) and they might have to cope with a medical emergency. No question who would provide mouth-to-mouth, slipping him some tongue while bringing him back to life. Another sexual harassment charge would inevitably follow, and his defense—that he was legally dead at the time—would butter no parsnips.

He succeeded in allaying their fears simply by not keeling over. But his heart wouldn't stop racing. He tried to make eye contact with Mindy to let her know he had caught her signal, to concede she had him over a barrel and he was prepared to sue for peace from the position of the vanquished negotiating with the victor, was willing, indeed, to meet her in General Foch's private train car in Compiègne to discuss terms; but, although he did succeed in making eye contact with her, and received full-blast the same yearning cow-eyed look she'd been directing his way for over a year, he could discern no sign of anything unusual, nothing teasing, nothing sinister. On the contrary, she seemed genuinely intent on discussing *The Way of All Flesh,* more so than anyone else in the class, himself included, and was doing it seriously and intelligently, single-handedly elevating the level of the seminar. The cow-eyes focused his way sought acknowledgment and approval, not surrender.

But that damned paperback, with the detail of Winkler's lurid illustration on its spine, had him in its grip and wouldn't let him go. The thing had been published about two weeks before, and though Ezra kept his own copy, sent by Isaac to his post box, under literal lock and key, he regularly took it out to gaze and wonder at. "This is mine," he would tell himself, "I made this." And so seeing it now among Mindy's pile of books, he could entertain no doubts about its identity, not with that grotesque rendering of Nora-as-Anita-Ekberg holding him in its double-barreled stare. It made him feel like Joan Fontaine in *Suspicion,* obsessively watching the glass of milk glowing ominously on her nightstand.

When the seminar finally ground down to a close, Ezra had to risk it. "Mindy, would you stay behind for a moment?"

"Of course."

She spoke with such alacrity, such eagerness, that Ezra recognized his error and suggested they leave the building together instead. It was prudent policy never to be alone with her, certainly not within the confines of four walls.

As they descended the stairs together, the other seminar participants just out of hearing range, she said, "What is it, Ezra? Is there something I can do for you?"

"No, no, absolutely nothing you can do for me," he said, and immediately hoped he hadn't sounded insultingly definite. "But I was wondering . . ." God, this was difficult. How do you ask someone if she knows your dirty little secret without letting on that you *have* a dirty little secret? "Is there anything you want to discuss with *me,* by any chance?"

"Discuss with you?"

"Is there something, something you think might, might *concern* me in some way? Something you want to *share* with me?"

Her eyes glowed. "You mean . . . you mean those *three little words?*"

"No!"

Hurt: "Then I'm not sure what you do mean." She continued to stare at him, inviting him at the very least to explain himself, probably inviting him to do a lot more than that.

"Never mind, Mindy. I must be mistaken."

"If you could just be a little *clearer* about what you want . . ."

"Nothing, nothing, forget it."

"Is it an apology you're after?" she demanded, her mood, not uncharacteristically, taking a nasty turn; she had raised her voice sufficiently so that some of the students on the stairs below them looked up. "Is that it? Is that what you want? As if! I don't owe *you* an apology! You owe *me* an apology! You can't play with hearts like they were toys!"

Ezra pasted a neutral smile on his face and avoided meeting anyone's eye. Damn. This little outburst should give fresh life to the old scandal, and just when its reverberations were finally fading. But the mystery persisted. Ezra was reasonably certain Mindy wasn't withholding damaging information for a more propitious moment, when it could work optimal mischief: Such calculations required a more organized emotional life than she was capable of leading, and besides, she really seemed not to understand what he was trying to elicit from her. So what the hell was she doing with his book?

This question might have continued to haunt him, except, as he crossed the campus, puzzled and upset, he was startled to see, in the middle distance at the other side of Gardner Field, Carol and FBI Agent Daniel McGruder walking by the stables. They weren't touching, he noted, although they were quite close to one another. Now he was even more puzzled and upset than before, and the question of what Mindy was doing with his book suddenly took a backseat to this new puzzle.

After a brief internal tussle, he decided not to hail them, just ask

Carol—all right, all right, *grill* Carol—about it later, but then McGruder, that eagle-eyed guardian of our liberties, spotted him and shouted a greeting. Now Ezra had to deal with both of them; to do otherwise could only be construed as a deliberate snub, and though he had no compunction about snubbing McGruder, indeed rather relished the opportunity, he needed to be surer of his ground before he tried anything similar with Carol.

He started toward the stables, and Carol and Dan moved—more slowly, he felt—in his general direction. He noticed how brown and desiccated the field had turned in recent weeks, as if spring hadn't really come at all this year, merely dropped by momentarily to usher in summer. If Vivaldi had composed in Seven Hills, he could have spared himself a season.

They met in the middle of the field. Ezra pictured the encounter as a scene in a movie, a high aerial shot of the entire field, the three figures miniscule and insignificant amidst the ineffable immensity of nature, with its dead grass and indifferent meadow muffins.

"Well," Carol said, "you don't say."

It seemed to Ezra she looked uncomfortable. He didn't volunteer anything.

"I was just showing Dan the horses. He expressed an interest. Have you two met?" She surely recalled they had.

"Some weeks ago in Professor Dixon's office," McGruder said. He offered his hand. Ezra didn't see that he had any choice, although there were at least three good reasons *not* to shake. As he dutifully took the man's hand and winced in anticipation of the agony in prospect, McGruder went on, "Fact is, I've been meaning to talk to you again, Professor." Then, right on schedule, came The Grip. It was bone-crushing all right, as bad as Ezra remembered. He hung on for dear life. At least the ordeal was brief; evidently, McGruder wasn't too crazy about touching him either.

"Oh," said Carol during their handshake, with a stab at airiness, "don't call him Professor. Everyone calls him Ezra, even his students. I don't know why he puts up with it, no other instructor on campus would, but that's just his way, I guess."

"Professor is fine," Ezra said coolly, while surreptitiously flexing his right hand a few times. In fact, he never gave permission to his students to address him by his first name. They simply presumed—something in his appearance or his manner must have suggested it was okay—and he couldn't gun up the requisite pomposity to correct them.

"I wanted to let you know, you're no longer an active suspect."

"Well now, that *is* good news."

"Thought you'd be pleased." McGruder seemed not to notice Ezra's irony, nor to intend any of his own.

Carol looked from one to the other of them with a tentative, worried smile on her face, as if nervously aware for the first time that this could get out of hand. "You suspected *Ezra?*"

"I wouldn't say we *suspected* him. He was one of the people we were looking at."

"That's the stupidest thing I ever heard."

McGruder didn't like her saying this, which cheered Ezra considerably. "So," he said to McGruder, "you boys making any progress?"

"I'm not really at liberty to discuss it."

Ezra knew they *weren't* making progress, or at any rate very little. They still weren't even completely sure that the sabotage originated on campus. This too was supposed to be secret, but Ezra had a mole in the counsel's office.

"So anyway," Ezra said, "I guess you sort of owe me an apology, don't you?"

McGruder looked at him unblinkingly, and there was just the slightest hint of something in his eyes: Contempt, was it, or incredulity, or simple incomprehension? "For asking you questions? That's my job. I don't guess I owe you much of anything."

"Now now," said Carol.

"Anyway," McGruder went on, "you're not exactly *cleared*. You're just not under active suspicion. We're looking into a few other areas that show promise. And that's already telling you more than I should, so let's drop it, okay?"

"You brought it up in the first place."

"Come on," said Carol, "this is getting childish."

"Is it? I think I have the right to be interested in the progress of the investigation. It's affecting Beuhler's ability to administer itself, which is having a deleterious effect on my classes."

"You'll be informed in due course."

"I can hardly wait." And then, after staring into Carol's eyes until she looked away, Ezra said, "Anyway, Dan, you keep up the good work," and walked off. What was niggling at him? Was it Dan's manner toward him, or the story Carol had told her father? Whatever. His feelings of unease were growing.

■　　■　　■

That night, in the kitchen of his apartment, while he and Carol were silently putting together a chef's salad, having barely exchanged a word since she'd arrived, she suddenly said, "You really need to have a little trust, Ezra."

He looked up from the ham he was dicing. "Why is that?" He didn't bother to pretend not to understand.

"Because I tell you to, that's why."

"That's enough?"

"It's what trust is," she said. "Faith. The evidence of things not seen."

"I don't share your faith. I believe what I do see."

"Too bad for you." She dropped the head of lettuce she had been tearing. "Look, I spend a lot of time with Dan. It's my job. This computer stuff has legal ramifications that could literally destroy Beuhler. And yes, I also happen to like the guy."

"He's a schmuck."

"I know you feel that way. Maybe it's some big-city prejudice."

"For God's sake, Carol, can you drop this silly farmer's daughter pose? You spent three years at Stanford Law, you're not some inbred dueling-banjos rustic."

She laughed at that. "Okay, okay. But we do disagree about Dan. I think he's a decent person. And I know how hard he's working to break this case."

"Spare me."

"And he's trying just as hard to get into my pants. So what? Susan McGill's trying to get into yours, I don't hold it against her."

"What makes you think that?"

"Beuhler's a small community, word gets around. But I'm not worried."

Ezra began chopping turkey breast. Time to regroup. "He considered me a suspect!"

"And that was idiotic. As I told him. But he questioned *me* pretty closely too, at first. He doesn't want to leave any stone unturned, is all."

"He's a Nazi goon."

"Now you're being childish again."

"Does he know you and I are—?"

Before he could figure out how, in order to frame the question, he should characterize their relationship, the phone rang. Ezra swore, put down the knife, and went to grab it.

"Hello?"

"Ez, it's Isaac."

"Oh, hi."

Isaac must have heard an edge in Ezra's voice, because he said, "This won't take long. I'm about to call it quits for the day myself, I'm pretty eager to get out of here."

"You're still at the office?"

"No rest for the wicked. I was wondering, you making progress on your next book?"

Ezra lowered his voice. "I haven't given it any thought at all."

"What are you waiting for?"

"Well, I'm, I'm trying to write an academic article."

"Yeah? How much they pay you for that?"

"That isn't the point."

"Just what I thought. Zip, right?"

"That would be a ballpark figure."

Isaac laughed. "We have to get you started on Opus Two, pal. For your own good."

"Eventually."

"Why wait?"

"I'm just not up to it right now. I don't have the time."

"You can knock off one of these suckers in a couple weeks."

"Nah, I was inspired before."

"So get inspired again."

"It doesn't work like that."

"What if I send up Lucy?" And then, when Ezra failed to laugh, he went on quickly, "You want more money? Is that it? You got it. How's fifteen? Does that inspire you any?"

"When the time comes, *if* the time comes, I'll take it."

"Jeez, Ez, work with me here. What if I go up to twenty?"

Isaac's tone was uncharacteristically wheedling, and it put Ezra on alert: "There's something you're not telling me."

"What do you mean?"

"Don't bullshit me, Ike. It isn't seemly."

Isaac's expulsion of breath was audible over the line. "Okay, fair point. I'll level with you. The thing is, we're having a little, a sort of run of luck with *Every Inch a Lady.*"

"Run of luck?"

"We've gone into a second printing. That's never happened before."

"A second printing?"

And then Isaac could no longer contain his excitement: "The orders are pouring in, it's unbelievable! We can't keep up with 'em. I don't know what it is, I mean it's got to be word of mouth, God knows we don't do promotion, we don't have the budget. But your book . . . We're out of copies. The distributors are howling. They want more. They want 'em *now.*"

"My God."

"We're making a killing. It's a beautiful thing to behold."

"You mean, it's like a—" He couldn't bring himself to say the word, even in the whisper he'd been using.

Isaac had no such hesitation: "A best-seller. It *is* a best-seller. Within its own terms, of course. It's a breakout d.b., maybe the first since *Story of O* or one of those dopey books from the sixties. You hit a home run, pal. And I want you at bat again. In clean-up position."

"I have to think about it."

"You keep saying that. What's to think?"

"Just give me some time to absorb all this."

"How much absorbing is necessary, for Christ's sake?"

"I'm going to have to call you back, Ike."

"Okay, twenty-five. But that's my best offer."

"I have company."

"Oh! Why didn't you say so? Go to it! Take notes!" Once again he waited for laughter that didn't arrive, and then, unfazed, continued, "I'm serious about this, I want you to start writing. The iron's hot. The iron won't ever be this hot again. E. A. Peau better strike!"

"Yeah, I'll think about it."

"Say that one more time and it's your ass, buddy. I mean it."

Isaac hung up, leaving Ezra staring in bemusement at the telephone. He finally pulled himself together and put the receiver back in its cradle.

When he returned to the kitchen, Carol looked at him curiously. "Who was that?"

"Oh, it was, it was, uh, an old friend."

She wrinkled her nose. "*Her?*"

"No, Carol, not *her*. Another old friend. Male. From way back."

But the expression on his face must have really been something, because she suddenly looked concerned, and said, "Was it bad news?"

"No, no, not at all." And then he shrugged helplessly. "I don't think."

Chapter 2

"A very provocative piece of work."

"'Provocative.' Is provocative good?"

Dixon smiled. "Well, I meant it as a compliment." He swiveled in his chair and looked out of his window at the grass and wildflowers. Ha! Ezra wanted to exclaim. Caught you! "I'm very pleased," the chairman continued. "A few more like these, your tenure case could have some life in it."

"Well. I'm delighted."

"Couldn't make any sense of it, of course. But that's rather the point, isn't it?" Dixon smiled puckishly, the wrinkles in his beefy face deepening and shifting. "Don't get me wrong, I'm not promising anything. Couldn't if I wanted to. I'm just saying this'll give your defenders something to point to." Tactfully failing to specify whether he himself could be found in this camp, or indeed whether the camp had any members at all. "You did say it's been accepted?"

"At *Representations*."

Dixon's eyebrows went up. He was impressed. "Ah. Very *comme il faut*." Followed by another puckish smile, another ballet of wrinkles. "And do you have another one—what was that expression?—'in the hopper'?"

"I'm toying with a few possibilities."

"Excellent. By all means keep toying." Dixon swiveled his bulk—and his glance along with it—away from the window and back toward his desk. He put on a pair of wire-rimmed glasses and began peering at the neatly squared stacks of papers and journals and books which checkerboarded the surface. "I should return it to you. It's here somewhere."

"No rush."

"No, no, I've got enough junk here already, there's no need to—" He caught himself. "Not that your article's junk, of course."

"No offense taken."

"Let me see." He began moving stacks of things around, putting one stack on top of another, rifling through a third, always taking care to square each stack again after having touched it. "Damn, I know I—" And then the incredible happened; as he lifted half of a stack off its base, there stood revealed a copy of *Every Inch a Lady,* with its unmistakable Winkler portrait of Amazonian Nora rampant. He hastily put the top half back where it had come from, and then stole a quick glance at Ezra; a quick glance was all that was needed to confirm that Ezra had, beyond a doubt, noticed the book. Dixon laughed self-consciously, caught in the act as it were, and held it up. "Seen this?" He seemed to be blushing—he was so ruddy you couldn't be sure—but in any event he had evidently decided the most dignified course was to fess up and bull through.

"Um." Ezra tried to look judicious and nonjudgmental.

"Read it yet?"

"Uh. Not really."

"Total merde, of course. My wife gave it to me. Not sure how to interpret *that,* unh?"

Ezra smiled, as he knew he was supposed to, and then asked, as casually as he could, "How'd *she* happen to hear about it? Any idea?"

"Not really. Might've read something somewhere, I suppose. I think I saw some sort of squib in the *L.A. Times* or the *Bee,* can't remember which."

What? The *Los Angeles Times?* The *Fresno Bee?* Obviously, Dixon was mistaken.

"Or," he went on, "she's in one of those reading groups, you know the sort, where they read anything that chubby little black woman suggests. Could've been there. The fair sex do seem to have taken the book to their bosoms, for reasons I can't fathom. Anyway, it's sort of fun, actually. Not too bad. Quite elegantly written, not at all what you'd expect."

"Ah ha." Ezra looked down at his shoes.

"Author calls himself E. A. Peau. Bit of blasphemy, what, a pseudonym that's a homonym for America's greatest poet."

"Who also happened to be a pedophile and alcoholic, of course."

"Yes, I take your point. Not quite like calling himself Emil Dickinson or some such. Anyway, *entre nous,* I recommend it. It's better than you'd expect. But don't tell any Beuhler brass I said so. Not really up their alley, if you know what I mean. And for goodness sake, don't read it alone, ha ha ha. Ah, here we are!" He had turned back to his desk, and now had located Ezra's article. He proffered it to Ezra. "There you are. Thanks for the look."

"Pleasure. Thanks for reading it." By now it was Ezra who was blushing, furiously. Fortunately, Dixon was still so embarrassed himself, and so preoccupied squaring all the documents on his desk, he didn't notice.

This is getting out of hand, Ezra thought several minutes later, as he entered his own office. It's nuts. Dixon must be wrong about the *L.A. Times* and the *Fresno Bee,* those are simply out of the question, but still, he heard about it *somewhere,* he has a copy on his desk, he's *read* the thing. The conclusion was inescapable: People, normal people—if you considered Beuhler people normal—were buying the book.

Why, on his desk right now was a publishers' trade publication Isaac had sent him a few days ago, proclaiming *Every Inch a Lady* number eighteen on its fiction list. And, as Isaac pointed out in an accompanying note—right after the ritual insistence that Ezra set to work forthwith on his next book—in reality it must be doing much better than that if a trade publication acknowledged its existence. "They don't poll the whack shops that move most of our product for us," was how he'd put it. "We've just started getting orders from the major chains. If you want a surprise, check out Amazon."

Which Ezra did, at the first opportunity. To his amazement, he found the book was listed at number twelve, and had garnered eight readers' reviews, six positive, the other two rabidly, wonderfully negative. The negative ones were more likely to sell books than the positive, since they stressed the novel's disgusting sexual explicitness.

He regretted having checked the page, though, because, now that he knew it was there, doing so became an addiction. Every hour or two, he went online to check his standing at the web site. There was a disconcertingly wide fluctuation from visit to visit, but he never fell below twenty, and once he even reached three. Incredible!

He felt like one of the dead in *Our Town.* He could see the effect he had on everyone, he could witness the stir eddying around his book, but no one could see *him,* no one knew of his existence.

I'm E. A. Peau, he assured himself. My book's at eighteen according to *PW* and three at Amazon.com. Only nobody knows it.

And I'm not getting any royalties.

And I don't think I can write another.

It wasn't that he hadn't been trying. As he had told Isaac—Isaac was becoming a bit of a bore on the subject—he was devoting several hours each day trying to start something. Hours he should be using to come up with ideas for his next article.

He'd tried every which way to trick himself into getting going. Constructing a plot. Inventing a lead character. Sitting down at the keyboard and improvising. He swallowed some nauseous Chinese herbs he found at Seven Hills' only health food store, which were supposed to stimulate mental activity. They made him jumpy, but they didn't shake loose any serviceable prose. He'd gotten good and drunk one night in an attempt to release his inhibitions. Humiliatingly, he'd even considered the notion of a sequel. Above all, he'd tried, somehow, anyhow, by sustained effort, meditation, dogged self-discipline, to recapture that exultant mood of literary abandon that had carried him into and through *Every Inch a Lady.*

Diddley.

A single paragraph was the best he ever managed. And when he looked at it the next day, it was garbage. *Dreck* was the word that Isaac, in an untypically sympathetic mood (untypical where Ezra's failure to produce a book was concerned), had supplied. Following it up, of course, with a repetition of his customary marching orders.

"What do you care?" Ezra protested. "You're getting rich anyway."

"I want to get richer. And I'd like to put my press on the map. I want respect."

"Just a little bit?"

"Precisely."

"Let's not ask for the moon. We've already got the stars."

Isaac hurrumphed, a sound somewhere between amusement and indignation. Then: "What is it, Ez? You want royalties next time? Is that your aim? I told you already, it's a deal-breaker."

"I'm not *negotiating,* Ikey. I'm *blocked.*"

"You and me both, pal."

It was beginning to get him down. He couldn't even say for sure *what* was beginning to get him down, the absence of recognition or his literary impotence. But something was inarguably getting him down.

Maybe it was the prospect of having dinner at the Dimsdales' Sunday night.

You're clutching at straws, he told himself, you're trying to distract yourself. That's *bad,* no question about it, but it isn't what's getting you down.

This was a new inspiration of Carol's, and perhaps represented a first tentative stab at an eventual assertion of independence: She had decided to end the McGruder charade, which she felt had served its purpose. Ezra was of two minds: An assertion of independence was clearly long overdue, she should have moved out altogether a long time ago. But he doubted the McGruder charade had entirely served its purpose, since Dimsdale hadn't succumbed to apoplexy yet. He couldn't quite say this to her, of course, but having saved the man's life, he felt it was his to dispose of, at least in his imagination.

There *would* be a measure of relief in Carol's no longer telling her father that she was with Dan whenever she was off doing all those dirty things he didn't want her to do and occasionally threatened to throw her out of the house for doing. Although she hadn't dared repeat the experiment of spending the night at Ezra's place, so drastic had been Dimsdale's reaction, her subsequent activities still provided him with abundant opportunities to blow his stack, and, according to Carol, he energetically seized them all, despite his doctor's stern admonitions. He called his daughter a slut and a tramp, he repeatedly hurled thunderous anathemas in the direction of Dan McGruder, Louis Freeh, and Efrem Zimbalist Jr. But, even if pleased to have the man's wrath deflected, Ezra also had the uncomfortable notion that Carol derived some inexplicable amorous satisfaction from retailing the lie about McGruder and vicariously living it, and for that reason at least he was willing to see it retired. On the other hand, a useful buffer between Dimsdale's potential rage and Ezra himself—in abeyance these days, owing to gratitude and ignorance—was about to vanish. Sunday dinner was secretly intended to celebrate the occasion of its disappearance, but Ezra doubted this was *cause* for celebration; the event itself was sure to remind him why such a buffer had come in so handy over the last month or two.

Well, that ordeal was still two days away. Stupid to suffer through it in advance; he'd be suffering through it big time soon enough. And meanwhile, there were other concerns.

Like not seeing Carol tonight. In a sense, it was a relief; they'd been together every one of the last six nights, often, it's true, at Ezra's suggestion, but he was starting to feel *crowded*. Tonight she had chosen to stay home with her father, to prepare him for Sunday's dinner. Ezra imagined Carol stuffing the guy, sewing him up, and shoving him into the oven, but presumably those weren't the sort of preparations she had in mind, but rather, something on the order of explaining why Ezra was their guest. Anyway, it *was* nice to have a little solitude, an opportunity to do some reading. Except now he felt lonely. Interesting how that worked.

After eating lightly, and putting Beethoven's op. 127 on the stereo, and grabbing an Elmore Leonard paperback, and settling into the dust-encrusted wing chair he favored for such occasions, he took a moment to acknowledge he missed her. This wasn't necessarily *welcome* news, but there it was. Without *Every Inch a Lady* and without Carol, he felt bereft. And if one of those was irretrievably gone, the other was right across town.

It was hard to concentrate on the novel. Who cared about someone *else's* problems, even if they involved thuggery and mayhem? And in some ineffable way, the quartet reminded him of Carol. Especially the last movement, with its witty, dancing theme, a theme that undergoes so many transmogrifications before the end. Just like Carol. When the piece ended, he weighed the advisability of calling her, just to say hello, and finally opted not to. No reason to wimp out, not in such transparent fashion, not so pathetically, not because of *one night's* separation. It might give her the wrong idea. It might give her *ideas*.

It sure would be nice to talk to her, though.

He put on a Sibelius symphony next, the fourth. And regretted it. Not that it wasn't pretty, but Jesus, all those Nordic wastes—it was hard not to feel lonely in the midst of so much empty tundra. It made a person long for some sort of companionship.

Like Carol's, to pick one sort of companionship at random.

But it wouldn't do to call. That was the sort of gesture Carol might *misinterpret*. She might think it suggested he missed her. Which he did, maybe, a little.

Have we cleared that up?

It would be nice if *she* called, though.

■ ■ ■

When he got into bed, her failure to phone had left him too unsettled for sleep, so he flipped on the television. He came upon Jay Leno in mid-monologue. "You might have seen this in the paper the other day," Leno was saying. "How Al Gore isn't too happy with his speechwriters. Feels his speeches are kinda dull, is the problem. Gee, what a surprise, huh? Stop presses! So anyway, he wants to juice 'em up a little, and his staff, they've come up with a brilliant plan. They're gonna hire that E. A. Peau guy, see if that helps."

Ezra sat bolt upright. Had he dreamt this? No, he was awake—his heart was pounding—it was real. And the audience was *laughing,* so they recognized the reference.

"When he gives his next speech, they figure the Nielsons'll be through the roof. May even save it for Sweeps Week. And I betcha he'll find some reason to say 'Act of Congress.'"

Rim shot.

Ezra looked on, horrified and fascinated.

Then Leno asked the audience, "You read it yet?"

There was some applause.

"Oh yeah? Didja like it?"

There was more applause. To Ezra's ears, *enthusiastic* applause. And some hooting.

"Yeah, it wasn't bad. And now I hear there'll be an edition for fetishists. *Every Foot a Lady.*"

Rim shot.

Ezra flicked the television off with his remote. What the hell was happening here? It was unreal. It was *surreal.* Lying alone in bed, minding his own business, he had become the subject of a Jay Leno monologue. And the audience *got it.* Something was happening outside the Seven Hills city limits, something weird. The situation was Kafkaesque. Or was it Serlingesque? Or maybe grotesque. Whatever it was, it was undeniably esque. And he was pretty sure he hadn't heard the end of it.

Chapter 3

"Real sorry I didn't see you in church today," said the Reverend Mr. Dimsdale through a mouthful of baked ham. His napkin was tucked into his shirt collar, his knife and fork were clenched in either fist, his face was flushed, and there were droplets of perspiration on his forehead. He had evidently gotten past his recent medical scare.

"I'm not really much of a churchgoer," Ezra felt compelled to explain; this won him a warning glance from Carol, but also the reverend's thoroughgoing inattention.

"Yep, real sorry you weren't there. Unless I missed you?"

"No, as I said—"

"Or perhaps you're another denomination?"

"Nope, no other denom—"

"Because," Dimsdale plowed on, "I think you might've enjoyed my sermon. As a student of literature, you might've found it interesting."

"Ah ha," Ezra answered noncommittally, and reached for his goblet of Aunt Goldie's apple wine. He had been given to understand by the reverend that they didn't serve this stuff to just *anybody*, not a bit of it; Aunt Goldie's wine was reserved for special occasions, and for special guests like himself. Of course, this meant the rather expensive St. Emilion he had brought as a gift disappeared directly into the pantry, never to be heard from again, but that was part of the price one paid for Dimsdale's favor.

Ezra was beginning to wonder whether the reverend's former unyielding hostility wasn't preferable to this newfound fondness. (Or perhaps fondness was too strong a term, but his indifference had assuredly been rekindled, no small achievement.) In addition to Ezra's demonstration of good Samaritanship in the Seven Hills Market, Carol had been pleading his case, pointing to her own purported transgressions with McGruder to prove Ezra's forgiving and forbearing nature. Dimsdale was not unimpressed. He now regarded Ezra as a pussy-whipped sap, a sizable step up from the sin-steeped reprobate he had once considered him.

But whether this elevation in moral rank was an entirely good thing remained an open question. Even leaving the apple wine issue to the side. Hostility rendered the minister taciturn, and that was a distinct plus. Well, the good news was, since his present toleration of Ezra was based on an illusion, it was unlikely to survive concentrated exposure.

"You enjoying your apple wine?"

"Yes sir. It's very, it's very *tart*."

"Sort of like Aunt Goldie herself," offered Carol.

"Now," rumbled Dimsdale, "it isn't fitting to speak slightingly of kin, Carol."

"Okay, I'll pick a stranger next time."

She was playing with fire, but Dimsdale had too much of a head of steam to notice. "Now, where was I?" No one volunteered assistance. "Oh yes. My sermon today." He swallowed what was in his mouth. "I flatter myself you would've found it edifying."

"Do you?"

"Pass the peas, please, Carol. Yes I do. And the biscuits. Thank you. Yes, because I'm confident you share my concern at the parlous state of contemporary culture."

"That was your theme?"

"Indeed it was."

"Parlous?"

"Parlous is the word I used, yes." After a moment of focused chewing, Dimsdale went on, "Why, what with Negroes 'rapping' about violence on their record albums, and all that killing and nudity and profanity on television and in the movies, and all that filth in the art galleries . . . I won't even describe the type of thing they exhibit now, not at the dinner table, and not in front of a young lady . . . but, well, it just drives you to despair, don't you agree?"

"Well, I—"

"And then, this couldn't have been more fortuitous, I mean, my sermon was already written, but this was so apposite that as soon as I saw it I had to incorporate it into the text . . . I'm referring to, did you happen to see the *New York Times* today?"

"No sir, I didn't."

"We get it every Sunday. Still the finest paper in the world, even if it hasn't remained proof against the barbarian assaults of this degenerate epoch. That fine man, William Bennett, has written an excellent book on the topic, which I say even though I believe he professes the Roman faith. But today . . ." He shook his head. "Today it had something that sickened me."

"The real estate section?"

All right, it was just as well it happened now, that one learned at least approximately where the line got drawn, that one received some sort of indication how far one could go before that seemingly impenetrable obtuseness got penetrated. "Having a little fun at my expense, are you, son?" Dimsdale inquired as he wiped his mouth with his napkin.

"I suppose I was."

Dimsdale nodded. "That's okay," he intoned lugubriously. It clearly wasn't. "I enjoy a good laugh as well as the next body. 'Make a joyful noise unto the Lord,' we're admonished by Scripture. But I assure you, what's in the paper today is no laughing matter. Here, I'll get it for you."

Dimsdale removed his napkin from his collar, hoisted himself effortfully out of his chair, and trudged into the kitchen. Ezra turned to Carol. "Is this worth the wait?" he asked.

"How could it be?"

When Dimsdale returned, he was carrying the *Book Review* in his left hand. He proffered it to Ezra and resumed his seat.

When Ezra saw the cover, he gagged on a piece of ham. The featured review was of *Every Inch a Lady!* And—oh my God!—it was written by . . . John Updike! Ezra started to choke. Alarmed, Carol struck him on the back, and he grabbed desperately for Aunt Goldie's apple wine, he wheezed and gasped, he heard Carol shout out something about the Heimlich Maneuver. But he finally managed to get his esophagus cleared without external intervention.

"*Makes* you choke, doesn't it?" said Dimsdale, while Ezra struggled for breath.

Ezra, his face flushed, his breathing labored, scanned the review. And instantaneously, his heart started racing again. The review was *positive!*

Indeed, it could be termed a rave. *Every Inch a Lady* was compared to *Lolita* (more, it's true, because of the latter's original provenance, Girodias's Olympia Press in Paris, than on the basis of intrinsic literary quality, but never mind, he was still in awfully good company), its style was described as "graceful," its eroticism "refined, oddly delicate, and refreshingly novel," its plotting "competent," its characterization "compelling and coherent." Updike said the novel "lays fair claim to being counted among the more readable and accomplished published this season." The review ended, "We can now add to the list of celebrated literary puzzles—such as the identity of Mr. W. H., and the name of Edwin Drood's killer and the fate of B. Traven—a new mystery, namely: Who is E. A. Peau? It's a conundrum upon which much ink is likely to be spilt in the coming weeks."

"The man's a respected writer too, isn't he?" Dimsdale said, forcing Ezra to look up from the magazine.

He couldn't respond right away. His mouth was dry, his stomach aflutter. With enormous effort he finally managed to grasp out, "Very much so."

"Mind you, I'd wager cash money *his* books are pretty smutty too, am I right?"

"Well—"

"But still, to go into print in the country's best paper there and to *praise* an out-and-out piece of filth, a self-admitted work of pornography . . . and for the paper to publish it on the *front page* of their book magazine . . . it just makes you sick, doesn't it?" He narrowed his eyes at Ezra. "Are you all right, son? You're looking a little peaked."

"I, I—" Ezra took a big swig of apple wine.

"Mustn't take these things too much to heart. Too damned many of them, pardon my French, the world's going to hell in a hand basket, you have to inure yourself or you'll spend your whole life bothering about nothing else. Could you please pass the potatoes, Carol?"

"I suppose you're right." Ezra guessed he *was* feeling a mite peaked, or at least was unable to calm down; John Updike liked his novel! John Updike! And said so in the lead review of the *New York Times Book Review!* Hot damn!

Nicholson Baker, eat your heart out!

Dimsdale glared at Ezra, suddenly, inexplicably suspicious, perhaps finally recognizing that Ezra was, after all, a professor of literature, and hence potentially in the enemy camp. "You haven't read this book now, have you?"

After clearing his throat, Ezra replied, "No sir," in a strong firm voice.

"Good. Don't let fashion seduce you."

"Not much chance of that."

Later, in the kitchen, while Carol rinsed dishes and Ezra stacked them in the dishwasher, Ezra said, "Boy, your father's really on the warpath tonight, isn't he? Like he was going to call for a revival of the Salem witch trials."

Carol stiffened. "I don't deny he can get pretty pompous," she said, her tone suddenly steely. "And I admit he expresses himself in a kind of old-fashioned way. But that doesn't mean his concerns are, are, it doesn't mean you can just dismiss what he has to say."

Ezra felt as if his face had been slapped. Was this the same woman who seemed to be his ally only minutes before? "Oh come on, Carol," he said. It was more a plea than a rebuke.

Carol resumed rinsing the dishes, probably, or so it seemed to Ezra, to avoid meeting his eye, and said, "You really haven't read that book?"

"Why do you ask?"

"Well, it's generating a lot of controversy. Lots of people say it's offensive. Not just troglodytes, serious people. I saw something about it on *Nightline*."

"Offensive to whom?"

"To lots of people."

"Ah. And their sensibilities are the yardstick by which the question should be judged?"

"It's a consideration."

"So, for example, if I'm offended at the way English professors are portrayed by David Lodge, maybe *his* books should be banned too?"

"Let's not fight about it, Ezra. It doesn't have anything to do with us."

Like hell it doesn't.

Ezra was nonplused. Ezra was doubly nonplused. He was nonplused first because he realized how little he knew Carol: Was she Republican or Democrat? Did she prefer dogs or cats? Stick or roll-on? His ignorance was profound. And with regard to his book . . . Christ, if she ever found out, that might ruin everything.

And second, he was nonplused because his book had been discussed on *Nightline*. On *Nightline*! His book! Holy cow!

In the next few days, such shocks ceased presenting themselves singly. Something peculiar, and peculiarly American, was happening: Like the Hula-Hoop, Edd ("Kookie") Byrnes, the twist, "Who Shot J.R.?" the Pet Rock, Cabbage Patch dolls, Teletubbies, like any number of other fads and fancies over the years, *Every Inch a Lady* seemed to have worked its way into the national consciousness. Why not? The story was goofy enough to be amusing, sexy enough to be titillating, and mysterious enough to be intriguing.

WHO IS E. A. PEAU? was the *National Enquirer* headline greeting Ezra at the Seven Hills Market check-out stand on Monday, and that same night, Jay Leno announced, "My crack staff has done some research, and they've managed to ferret out the identity of E. A. Peau. It's Salman Rushdie, trying his damnedest to write an inoffensive book."

The mainstream press was also beginning to weigh in with reviews now, following the *Times*'s lead, and most were favorable; the *Book of the Month Club News* offered the book, recommending it with a caveat ("Not for the timid"), *Time* liked it, *Newsweek* didn't, the *Weekly Standard* condemned it, *Vogue* gave it a recommendation. Ironically, most of the negative notices tended to take a cluckingly disapproving tone that was guaranteed to intrigue potential purchasers. Gail Sheehy, writing in *Vanity Fair,* produced an article speculating that, because of the manifest sensitivity to and insight into female sexuality the novel evinced, E. A. Peau was almost certainly a woman. *People* magazine proposed a list of possible Peaux, repeating rumors that were supposedly circulating in New York publishing circles. The most plausible candidates were said to be John Updike himself, his review in the *Times* being part of the joke, and Joe Klein, playing another secret-identity game with the public.

The magazine also ran a sidebar about Isaac entitled "The Happy Schlockmeister." In it, he categorically refused to reveal E. A. Peau's identity—"I wouldn't divulge it even under torture," he was quoted as saying, "I gave a writer my word"—but did allow as how he was looking for promising manuscripts, including those of a nonerotic nature. He looked very handsome in the accompanying photos. Ezra felt a hot flush of jealous envy when he saw it: That should be me, he thought, they're using Isaac only because I won't reveal myself.

The temptation to do exactly that was a constant companion now, but Ezra resisted; it would be signing his own death warrant, indulging a silly lust for some short-term celebrity (or was it notoriety?) in exchange for long-term (or was it lifetime?) unemployment. Beuhler would fire him like a shot, and his prospects on the open job market were dim. Were *de minimus.* No, for better or worse, he was forced into the role of invisible onlooker during his own Warholian fifteen minutes.

It wasn't an easy or comfortable position to be in, though. He sat and watched an episode of *Larry King Live* devoted exclusively to various feminist responses to his book: There on one side were Andrea Dworkin, wielding her trusty meat cleaver, ferociously attacking the novel as pro-penetration propaganda, and Catharine MacKinnon, inveighing against the novel's inherent tendency to sully and degrade, squared off against Naomi Wolf and Susan Faludi, distressingly respectful of their nutcase antagonists but still waxing lyrical about the book's enlightened, egalitarian eroticism. Ezra sat on his bed, grim, frustrated, and disconsolate, watching the fatuous contention roll by.

On a Barbara Walters special two nights later, he saw Gwyneth Paltrow claim that if she were ever going to marry, it would be to somebody like E. A. Peau, somebody who was attracted to strong, intelligent, sexually independent women. "Here I am, Gwyn!" he wanted to shout, "Come and get me!" It might have proved cathartic; what stopped him was Carol's presence in bed beside him.

By the following week, the major best-seller lists all agreed *Every Inch a Lady* was number one. As confirmed by Amazon.com every one of the hundreds of times Ezra visited it.

IS E. A. PEAU AN ALIEN? the *National Enquirer* wanted to know, offering a $5,000 reward to anyone who could provide documented proof one way or the other.

Several booksellers in the Deep South were arrested on obscenity charges for carrying the novel, and the ACLU had offered to defend them, as had Alan Dershowitz and Johnny Cochran.

The citizens of several southern municipalities burned the book.

Which just goes to show, Ezra reflected, how artificial this whole phenomenon is. There are far dirtier books out there. But if anybody burned *them,* who would pay attention?

At a news conference, a reporter asked the president if he had read

Every Inch a Lady. To much laughter, he said no, one impeachment trial
per administration was quite enough, and besides, the only books his wife
would now let him read were the Bible and *Rebecca of Sunnybrook Farm*,
and she was considering revoking permission for the latter.

On Friday, at the monthly wine-and-cheese party the English Department held, Susan McGill commandeered the floor to joke that Beuhler
ought to consider giving E. A. Peau a position as Writer-in-Residence. Her
use of the word "position" provoked several further, and very lame (even
by department standards) jokes. "If only you knew!" Ezra wanted to yell.
The department seemed to be divided between those, largely the relatively
recently hired, who thought the book a hoot, and those, predominantly the
old guard, who regarded it as an abomination. Ezra was the only one present who didn't express an opinion, although he was asked several times.
This reticence was probably ascribed to tenure-case tact. The whole thing
was maddening. "If only you knew!"

He sat in a corner of the department office, a Dixie cup of wine in one
hand and a smoked oyster on a toothpick in the other, thinking bitterly, It
isn't just recognition that's passing me by, not just fame and public éclat
(although he, who'd never harbored that kind of ambition, found it surprisingly galling to miss out on the fame). But more galling still was the
fact that he wasn't making a penny from the sales.

Which was something Isaac, for all his professed loyalty-unto-death
toward his writer, had somehow neglected to tell *People* magazine. When
Ezra read in the "Show Business" section of *Time* the day before that a
bidding war was going on for the film rights to *Every Inch a Lady*, he'd felt
a sudden impulse to murder his best friend. Ezra had relinquished those
rights with a casual handshake, along with all other ancillary rights. He
had made Isaac a millionaire, probably several times over. What did he
have to show for it?

Ten thousand dollars and a problematical tenure case.

Finally finding the tension intolerable, finding every allusion to the
novel an assault, he left the department party early, well before the second
jug of Mountain Burgundy got opened. He just wanted to be alone. Or
with Carol. If I could tell Carol, he thought, that might make things okay.
But only if she takes my side. And there was no way of knowing if she
would. She was still a cipher to him in some ways, and goodness knows

she'd been her father's daughter a lot longer than she'd been his girlfriend. So it was a risk he didn't dare take.

They're laughing now, he thought of his colleagues as he walked wearily to the parking lot in the hot afternoon. They're laughing now, and if they found out I'm E. A. Peau, they'd be thrilled, I'd have to autograph all their copies of *Every Inch a Lady*. And then they'd watch me get kicked out on my butt without lifting a finger.

Driving home, he was feeling so bilious he tried arguing with himself: What's your problem? If you hadn't written the book, you'd have nothing. But you did, it was fun, it gave you a sense of accomplishment, you made $10,000, and the world has come to validate your most cherished dreams about it. So what if nobody knows it's yours? So what if it's making millions you'll never see? If you hadn't done it, would you be better off?

But these arguments didn't help. He was feeling ill-used, unappreciated, exploited, violated. Every mention of the novel was an affront, every reference to it a knife in his vitals. And it was almost impossible to *avoid* references to it.

Damn the fucking book. Damn the infernal American PR machine that elected it Flavor of the Month. And damn Isaac Schwimmer, damn his eyes and damn his press.

As he turned into his driveway, he noticed Isaac sitting on the front stoop of his building talking on a cell phone.

What?

Pulling into the garage, he told himself, "Okay, get a grip, it's perfectly natural to have hallucinations under these circumstances, it's a stressful time, calm down, don't panic, there's a shrink on duty at the Beuhler infirmary, emergency psychiatric care is covered by the college's health plan, they won't even stick a hand up your ass." But these reassurances were unavailing, and he felt shaky as he climbed out of his Tercel and walked around to the front of his building, apprehensive about what further phantasms he might find.

He found Isaac, still sitting on the stoop, still talking on the cell phone. And patently no hallucination, which may have been the only welcome thing about his presence. Unshaven, wearing faded blue jeans, a maroon Izod shirt, New Balance running shoes, and wrap-around shades, he was reclining comfortably on the front stoop of the building, his face turned toward the afternoon sun. He waved casually as Ezra came up the walk, murmured a few words into the phone, and then clicked it shut. "Howdy, citizen," he called to Ezra. "How you keepin'? This Seven Hills sure is one stinking town, don't you think?"

"Didn't expect to find you here," Ezra responded, none too warmly. "Last thing I expected."

Isaac noticed the coolness. "Having a bad day?" he inquired solicitously.

"Bad couple weeks." Ezra began fishing for his keys. "Might as well come on in."

"There're a few things in the car I have to get," said Isaac. "I'll be right along. But what do you mean, 'bad couple of weeks'? I'd have thought it's been a pretty good couple of weeks."

"What are you doing here, Isaac?"

Isaac took off his sunglasses. "Just dropping in on a friend." He had a wounded look in his eyes. "At least, that's who I *thought* I was dropping in on. Listen, is something wrong? Is something eating you? Tessa, maybe? What's on your mind, Ez?"

"Nothing. Absolutely nothing." He had the door opened. "I'll meet you inside."

Isaac nodded uncertainly, unfolded into a standing position, and headed down the walk. Ezra shook his head—it was hard to stay angry at Isaac when in his actual presence, but he'd give it the old Beuhler College try—and proceeded into the building.

Later, in the kitchen, both of them drinking beer out of the bottle, with Isaac sprawled at the kitchen table and Ezra leaning against the sink, Ezra said, "So, these are glory days for your press, mm?"

"Well, awfully busy, that's for sure. I've had to do a lot of hiring in the last few weeks. We're gonna move soon, too. And we're inundated with manuscripts. Incredibly terrible shit, you wouldn't believe it. What makes these people think they're writers? It's pathetic."

"I saw you in *People,* Ike. You seemed to be inviting the whole country to submit stuff."

"Yeah, well, I was young and naive in those days."

"Last week?"

"Things have been happening fast."

"You really plan to go legit?"

"Well, there are a few things in the works, too early to talk about 'em."

"'Cause I may have a book for you." The opportunity to do Henry a favor gave Ezra a sudden lift, his first in a long time.

"An E. A. Peau?" Isaac's eagerness was downright offensive.

"Uh uh," Ezra answered flatly. "It's not by me. A student of mine. It's almost finished. And *very* good."

"Is it dirty?"

"Not especially."

"Thank God. I'd love to see it."

"Remind me to give it to you. I've got a copy lying around here somewhere."

"Great. But don't think you can buy me off so easy. I'm still impatient for your next display of Peautency."

Ezra shook his head as he crossed over to the table. "I've tried. Believe me."

"Listen, pal." Isaac held his open palms up. "Next time you get royalties. Okay? A first for me. And I'm prepared to write you a check right now for a $75,000 advance."

"Is that what this visit is about?"

Isaac looked hurt. "I came to say hello. That's what this visit is about."

"Right, right. Look, I'll take the check. Happily. I just can't deliver the book." He sat down across from Isaac. "Now. Tell me what you're doing here really. It's good to see you, but . . . I mean, why didn't you call first?"

"Just an impulse. Wanted to see my pal."

"Ike—"

"Plus, I have some stuff for you, is another thing. I couldn't send it to your post box."

"Why?"

"Come with me, you'll see."

He rose, and led the way into the living room, with Ezra following several yards behind. Leaning against the front door was a huge gunny sack, perhaps three feet high, and stuffed as full as a Polish sausage.

"What's that?" Ezra demanded.

Isaac undid the string at the top of the sack and upended it. Paper started cascading out of it onto the floor. Isaac said, "It's fan mail. For E. A. Peau. Thought you'd get a boot out of it. Look at this stuff!"

It was making a mountainous pile in the middle of Ezra's rug. "Come look, Ez," Isaac urged. "You owe it to your admirers."

Ezra knelt down and stuck his hands in the pile, like a pirate with his treasure. There had to be thousands of envelopes and postcards, plus, amazingly, several pair of silk panties addressed to E. A. Peau, c/o The Isaac Schwimmer Press, written in Magic Marker or lipstick, with the postage glued near the waist band, and, in at least one case, a return address across the seat. The message on that one read, "Here's the wrapping, come claim the package."

"This is fantastic," Ezra said, laughing.

They spent the next hour randomly sampling the contents of the sack. Some—the majority—were innocuous fan notes, while a few threatened eternal perdition, and several were clearly the work of the criminally deranged. But there were also love letters; intimate confessions; accusations of plagiarism; accusations of Peau's having pilfered the facts of the assorted writers' life stories (and what exciting lives these correspondents must have lived! And how astonishing that they all should have been so similar!); a breathtaking quantity of Polaroids showing naked women of all shapes and sizes and degrees of attractiveness doing extraordinary things to themselves, to men, to other women, to various household appliances, and to their pets; plus a truly overwhelming number of lovingly adumbrated offers of sexual favors.

"Your book's touched a nerve," Isaac finally observed.

"A *cluster* of nerves."

"Shame about the anonymity. You could be cashing in from here to eternity."

Ezra stared hard at Isaac. Isaac looked back, unruffled. "I mean in quiff, of course," he said. "Not royalties."

Here it was finally, out in the open, and Isaac didn't seem at all perturbed.

"No kidding," Ezra muttered.

"Huh?"

"You heard me."

"Is that how come you're pissed?" Isaac continued to stare at Ezra, his eyes wide open and moistly innocent.

"That's part of it."

"Not Tessa?"

"No, not Tessa. If I have misgivings about her, it's my problem and I'll deal with it. But the fact you're making a killing off my book and I'm getting nothing . . . *That's* a tough one."

Isaac took a second before answering. "We had a deal. The standard deal. I didn't know your book was gonna do so well. Neither did you. For all either of us knew, it was just gonna sit there and gather flies like a matjes herring. You might never've even finished it. You think I would've asked for my advance back?"

"It's hard for me all the same."

"Well, I understand, but I want you to know, I've kept my side of the bargain. Like, those *National Enquirer* types came nosing around, they offered me big bucks to say who you are. *Big* bucks. Big enough so's I'd notice, even with all the shekels I'm raking in. They're hot to break this story, Ez, it's like Isikoff and Clinton. But I told 'em to go fuck themselves. I've done this straight-up all the way, you need to know that."

Ezra nodded. He didn't feel mollified, but his ongoing anger wasn't easy to justify. He didn't blame Isaac, really; he railed at the universe for putting him in this maddening position. John Updike hailing his talent! Gwyneth Paltrow seeking his hand! Thousands of women offering to do unspeakable things for him! Dueling feminists debating the correctness of his book! Money pouring in hand-over-fist! A tornado of attention and respect and controversy and riches was swirling around out there, everything he'd regretfully forsaken when he was still an adolescent and had come face to face with the implausibility of ever having any of it, and yet there it was, almost within his grasp, only he didn't dare seize it.

Of course the situation was intolerable. Of course he resented Isaac, even if Isaac had intended only to do him a favor, and even if Isaac *had* "done it straight-up all the way."

Who the fuck cares how you've done it? he wanted to scream in his friend's face. The fact remains, *you've done it!* You've done it and I haven't.

"And of course," Isaac said into the silence, "if you ever do another, it'll be dif—"

"Will you *please* shut up about that!" Ezra suddenly exploded. "I! Can't! Do it! If I could, you'd pay through the nose. I'd get the hottest agent I could find to negotiate our contract. I'm not a total imbecile, I'm sure E. A. Peau can write his own ticket on the open market. *Straight-up,*

Ike, all I contracted for was one book. If there's another, you can bid on it with everybody else."

Isaac now looked not merely startled, but injured. "I didn't realize you were this upset," he said. "It never even occurred to me."

"What did you expect?"

"That you'd be enjoying the fuss." He shrugged. "I even brought you a present today. Thought it would be a nice surprise, thought you'd say things like, 'Gee, Ike, you shouldn't have.' Now I feel terrible."

"What present?"

"I mean, it's not going to make anything better between us or anything. It's just, just a little something." He took out his wallet. "You'll probably be insulted, accuse me of trying to buy you off cheap. But I swear that wasn't my intention. I just wanted to show my appreciation." He opened his wallet and pulled out a smallish piece of pink paper. "Here."

"What's this?"

"Your present."

"You got me a piece of paper?"

Isaac laughed. "It's a pink slip, stupid. For your new Mercedes." He waited for Ezra's jaw to drop open, which it obligingly did. "New 450 SEL. Nice blue one. I drove it up, that's the reason I showed up unannounced. Supposed to be a big surprise." He handed the pink slip to Ezra, who took it and examined it. "But if you wanna tell me to shove it, go ahead. Not just the pink slip. The whole fucking Mercedes. We seem to have a sincere difference of opinion about the ethics of this situation."

Ezra stared at the pink slip for a moment. "This is incredible, Ike."

Isaac shrugged. "Just a gesture."

"No it isn't. It's amazingly generous. I mean, given your view of things." Then, seated amidst the debris of his fan mail like a child surrounded by gift wrapping on Christmas morning, Ezra reached over and embraced Isaac. "Forget it, Ike," he said. "Forget everything I said." He was feeling oddly sentimental. "I respect the, the delicacy of your feelings." Isaac looked at him skeptically, perhaps suspecting sarcasm, so he went on, "No, I do, it's exactly what I respect. With all the vulgarity you work so hard to cultivate, it strikes me your feelings are incredibly refined, much finer than mine, and I know you weren't trying to screw me."

"I don't cultivate vulgarity. It just grows wild."

Ezra smiled. "Well, the point is, you weren't trying to screw me."

"I was trying to *help.*"

"Yeah, I recognize that."

"Okay, good, I'm glad we talked this out." Isaac, probably from embarrassment, made his manner brusque. "Now, tell me, is there a good hotel in this shit-stick town?"

"You can stay here."

"Surely you're joking," Isaac said, looking around the living room with unconcealed distaste. "Tessa said it was a pit, but even in my wildest imaginings I didn't picture *this.*"

"She said it was a pit?"

"Words to that effect."

"Gee, she never said anything to me."

"She was your *guest,* for Chrissake. Now offer me an alternative."

"There's an okay hotel."

"Not that I can trust your judgment."

"There's a hotel. The Seven Hills Inn. But—" This just struck Ezra: "How do you plan to get home?"

"Tessa's coming up tomorrow, we're continuing on to San Francisco. Hey, wanna join us?" This last was evidently a sudden inspiration.

"Can't. I have a seminar to teach." And the caroming vibrations on such a trip might be a little extreme for my blood, he thought to himself.

"Too bad. Well, I hope you're free for dinner tonight." After a brief pause, "My treat, of course."

"I've got a date."

"Bring her along."

Ezra weighed the pros and cons of putting Carol and Isaac at the same table for an evening.

"What's the matter?" Isaac was sharp.

"I told you about her once, remember? The minister's daughter. Not sure what she'll make of you."

"Hey, you keep slipping into this deal where you think I'm some kind of Visigoth. I can be as couth as the next guy. Couther."

There was no gracious way out of it.

On the way to Pierre's, Ezra, after inventing a lie to explain his magnificent new car (the second installment of that same small inheritance which had come his way some weeks ago, he'd decided to splurge, etc.), and while driving with fanatical caution, tried to prepare Carol for what to expect: Old friend, not like us, very L.A., sometimes a little indiscreet, heart's in the right place, etc. Carol seemed to find the whole prospect an adventure.

And, in the event, things went perfectly smoothly, Carol was charmed. Ezra realized he needn't have worried; *everyone* was charmed by Isaac, charm was Isaac's stock in trade, if he passed out I LIKE IKE buttons, the whole world would be sporting them. And Isaac, except for one small lapse, was the very model of a gentleman, coping effortlessly with Pierre's recalcitrant service ("We'd like a little more attention here, please," he told the waiter in a firm, pleasant, ignore-me-at-your-peril sort of voice which produced instantaneous groveling), flirting in a flattering but patently unthreatening manner with Carol, regaling her with stories about Ezra that kept her amused and admiring, and generally maintaining a light and pleasant tone. His solitary lapse came at the end of the evening, when Ezra dropped him off at the entrance to the Seven Hills Inn: As he stepped out of the car, he leaned into the passenger window and said, "Listen, I hope this isn't outta line, but do you have any notion where a guy might hope to get laid in a backwater like this?"

Ezra was speechless. But perhaps Isaac had accurately gauged the effect of this one too, for Carol laughed out loud, and then, astoundingly, said, "There's supposed to be a whorehouse on Grant, the cabbies can direct you." Ezra turned to face her, and she met his glance, shrugged, and said, "Don't forget, honey, I went to high school here, the guys used to talk about it. Mostly to scandalize the girls, I think. And to brag. As if paying for a dose of clap was something to brag about." She smiled at the memory for a moment, and then went on, "And there's a bar called The Last Chance about a block from here, it's a kind of singles place, I think Beuhler students sometimes go there to, to make new friends."

"Um, coed cooze," Isaac said. "Have to check it out."

"Isaac—" Ezra began, exasperated and disapproving, only to be interrupted by:

"Happy hunting," Carol called. "Take precautions. And thanks so much for dinner."

Ezra turned incredulously toward Carol—no one could say *her* mind was tiny or had any hobgoblins—and then back to Isaac. "Wait," he said. He knew it wasn't his business, he knew the ice in this bend of the river was perilously thin, and that asking in front of Carol was singularly inappropriate, but, damn it, he was too curious to restrain himself. "What about, you know, your girlfriend?" He compromised by not saying her name.

Isaac smiled, unoffended. "Tessa?" Which got a startled reaction from Carol, but Isaac didn't notice, and went right on, "We haven't taken the pledge yet. We may get there eventually, but right now we're both allowed a little leeway. Don't ask, don't tell."

Ezra shook his head. Listen, he told himself, don't go there. Avoid the whole neighborhood. It's time to stop regretting the road not taken and be glad for the road less traveled. And Carol is indisputably a road *much* less traveled. So can we please drop the whole matter?

Okay, let's.

After Ezra slowly, painstakingly maneuvered the Mercedes away from the curb, ready to brake for any vehicle anywhere within the Seven Hills city limits, Carol said quietly, "Is it the same Tessa?"

Steeling himself for a possible conflagration, Ezra confirmed that it was.

But the fracas didn't come. Carol suddenly proclaimed, "Gee, what a neat guy! And *so* good-looking! Is he a Jew?"

The question—or at least the attitude that might lie behind it—made Ezra nervous. "Uh huh," he said uneasily. There was so much they'd never discussed.

"I don't know too many Jews. They don't exactly flock to Seven Hills, do they? There were some at Stanford." She shrugged. "I always figured Daddy was wrong about that stuff. And I had no idea you have such terrific friends."

"Well, no others like *him*. He's unique. To be honest, I was worried about your reaction. Did you find him to be a little on the crude side?"

"That's not crudity," Carol insisted, "that's *vitality.*"

"God," he groused, "if girls find you attractive, you can get away with *anything.*"

"But that applies to you too, honey," Carol said, sliding a hand up his leg.

But his relief at how Isaac's visit had gone proved premature. The next day, Saturday afternoon, while sitting at the kitchen table grading Jack Scheer's unbearably, gratifyingly awful term paper, he got a phone call from Isaac. "S.F.'s gorgeous, Tessa's happy as a clam, she tells me she hates L.A., says she never wants to go back."

"She *always* hated L.A.," Ezra said.

"Yeah? You sure?"

"Absolutely."

After a brief pause, Isaac responded, "Okay, let's not start comparing notes, bud. Might end in tears. Did you know she loves Frisco?"

"Uh uh."

"Well then."

"You should buy it for her. You can certainly afford it."

Isaac ignored the shot. "I liked your girlfriend. Sweet kid."

"She liked you too."

"Yeah, I could tell. Hope you noticed I was on best behavior."

"By and large. Any luck last night?"

"Did okay, as a matter of fact. Went to the bar she mentioned."

"And?" Ezra found himself grinning.

"Scored."

"You did?"

"Um hm."

"Good for you."

"Student at your college, as a matter of fact."

"Really?"

"Yep. I didn't tell her I knew you."

"Sound strategy."

"You can count on my discretion, you know that. Pretty girl. Asymmetrical tits. Fucked like a demon."

"Mindy Dunkelweisse!"

"You know her?" Isaac laughed, delighted.

"Enough to recognize her from your description," Ezra said, laughing back.

"Listen." Isaac's tone had modulated into High Serious. "Are we square now? Everything straight between us?"

"I think so."

"Good. 'Cause it's crucial you understand we're in this together."

"What do you mean?"

"Well . . . we may have a problem."

Ezra felt a nervous flutter in his chest. That was a phrase NASA might use to inform a team of astronauts their vehicle wouldn't be returning to earth in the foreseeable future. "What sort of problem?"

"Now don't go all squidgy on me, it's probably nothing. The hotel here had a passle of messages for me when we checked in, my office has been trying to get hold of me. I promised Tessa no business this trip—you can imagine what the last month has been like, and this is supposed to be a vacation—but this one sounded pressing, so I checked back. It seems the *Enquirer*'s looking to have a chat with me. Want me to *confirm* something. That's all I know."

"The *National Enquirer?*"

"Uh huh."

"Aren't they working the 'Who's Peau?' angle, isn't that what you told me?" Ezra's voice had gone up in pitch.

"Now don't panic, they're probably on the wrong track totally. I just wanted you to be prepared."

"'Confirm?' They said 'confirm'?"

"That's the word they used."

"Aw shit."

"Relax, okay? Don't give it another thought. *I* sure as hell won't. I plan to go out on the balcony with Tessa and watch the sun set while we do the warthog. Recommend you try something similar with *your* honey. She'll thank you, I guarantee it, and you'll enjoy it too."

Ezra couldn't quite "not give it another thought," although he managed to survive the suspense of the weekend more or less intact, managed to concentrate on getting his seminar's papers graded, even managed to do the warthog with Carol once or twice. But when he woke on Monday morning, the first thought in his mind was, Get up, rush rush rush, get your hands on the *National Enquirer.*

BREAK IN PEAU CASE! said an immense headline occupying half the front page. Underneath, the subhead explained: NOTORIOUS AUTHOR AT BAPTIST COLLEGE!

Head spinning, ears ringing, eyes smarting, Ezra scanned the page quickly under the censorious eye of the woman operating the cash register. Piecing together what had happened wasn't an arduous task, despite the obfuscatory and self-glorifying prose in which the article was written: The *Enquirer* reporters had evidently come around the Isaac Schwimmer Press with lots of cash in their pockets, looking for whatever tidbits were there to be gleaned. Fortunately, the conditions Ezra had imposed limited what kind of information the would-be corruptees, regardless of their eagerness to be corrupted, could offer the would-be bribers. But unfortunately, there was one Schwimmer employee who did know one thing deemed worthy of hard currency: The zip code where Ezra's check had been sent.

Ordinarily, this wouldn't have provided an investigator with anything very useful: If he chose to stake out the post office in question hoping to catch E. A. Peau visiting his box *in flagrante,* all he'd have learned for his pains is how boring a stakeout can be, since Ezra hadn't had any reason to check his post box in weeks, and consequently never did; and if this same investigator had sought to examine post office records in order to get the names of the post box renters, he would have found access denied him regardless of the cash inducements on offer; postal officials are, as a class, incorruptible. They may have a propensity for acts of insane violence, but, credit where credit's due, they remain true to their code.

But in this case, the information qualified as a genuine scoop, could be regarded as scandal-rag paydirt, because the zip code to which E. A. Peau's check was sent belonged exclusively to the Beuhler College post office.

Which meant E. A. Peau was a member of the Beuhler College community.

Beuhler was named in the first paragraph of the article, and described in generally accurate detail. That same *Enquirer* investigative team was certainly on its way to Seven Hills by now, in fact had probably been in town for several days already, digging around, asking questions, offering money, scratching for clues, in general upholding a noble journalistic tradition: *Exploit human misery.*

And other journalists were bound to follow. That was another noble tradition: *Hunt in packs.*

Ezra put the paper back in the rack, rubbed his eyes, and, looking up, met the gaze of the fierce cashier.

"This ain't a library," she sniffed.

"Right," he said. But what he felt like telling her was, "get yourself an umbrella. There's a shit-storm coming, it's going to engulf us all."

One of the challenges you faced on campus these days was avoiding an interview. Print and video journalists seemed to outnumber students and staff. As Ezra made his way from the parking lot to the emergency meeting of the full faculty, he recognized, among the many correspondents dotting the landscape, a few faces from the local Bakersfield news shows. Stars! Beuhler had finally made the big leagues, courtesy of E. A. Peau. Almost all the journalists seemed to have buttonholed some student, professor, or staffer, most of whom were apparently thrilled at the chance to see or hear him or herself on the evening news; those who hadn't were casting about desperately in search of potential interviewees. Well, thought Ezra, at least Peter Jennings hasn't seen fit to anchor a broadcast from Beuhler yet. Things still have a way to go before we rate alongside Baghdād and Belgrade.

"Excuse me!" someone yelled at Ezra as he walked by. "Could I just—?"

Ezra kept walking. Once you slowed down, you were carrion.

Another current trap, and one that sprung closed around Ezra now, was having the bad luck to encounter a demonstration. Demonstrations had lately become a daily occurrence at Beuhler, and though still peaceful, they were growing more strident and ill-humored with each passing day, and better attended.

Ezra in fact had the misfortune to encounter not one demonstration, but two, facing off against each other. One group of students carried signs saying things like PEAU IS POO-POO; PORNOGRAPHY = RAPE; and DON'T READ THE BAD BOOK, READ THE GOOD BOOK. It was one of the absurdities of modern life that the born-againers and at least one faction of the women's movement made common cause; if they ever stopped to compare notes, both groups would find themselves at mutually horrified loggerheads, but evidently the shared urge to repress and coerce took priority over the substance of their respective agendas.

The other group had signs that proclaimed FREE SPEECH ON CAM-PUS; COMMISSARS KEEP OUT; and—a popular one, reminiscent of the king of Denmark's yellow star during the Nazi occupation of his country— I AM E. A. PEAU. But maybe this last was merely a bid for Gwyneth Pal-trow's attention?

The two groups were exchanging catcalls, and a few from each side were shaking their fists in the other's direction. The confrontation was acrimonious and combustible; you could feel the barely suppressed rage in the air. Ezra followed a big circuitous loop in order to circumvent the melee, but both groups were maneuvering around each other to achieve optimal exposure to the cameras, and as a result he was suddenly in the middle of the action; shouting students from both camps surrounded him and shook their signs at him.

From out of nowhere, Paul Van Horne was in his face. "Ezra!" Paul, former captain of the tennis team, handsome, rich, stupid Paul, an affront to everything Ezra held dear, had taken a class from him last year and still resented the C he'd quite generously been given. He'd needed a B- to raise his GPA sufficiently to remain on the team. "Which side are you on?" he yelled now, inches from Ezra. Beuhler's own answer to that annoying scold Pete Seeger.

Which side are *you* on? Ezra wondered. In the confusion, the two crowds had intermingled, and you could no longer tell the players without a scorecard, or at least a placard.

"You don't defend porn, do you?" Paul pressed, which cleared up that little mystery.

Ezra, uncomfortably aware of the cameras recording this contretemps for posterity, tried to extricate himself, and found his shirt collar in the hands of Mindy Dunkelweisse. "Ban guns, not books!" she shouted.

He didn't much care for the facial spray of saliva that accompanied this expression of her personal credo, but he was pleased, even in an odd way touched, that Mindy, whose sentiments presumably could have inclined her either way, or indeed sent her skittering down some crazy ideological rabbit hole irrelevant to any recognizable issue, had come down on the pro-Peau side. "Please, Mindy," he shouted back, "I'm late for a meeting!"

"This is more important!"

"It probably is," Ezra agreed. "But—"

Then he felt a hand roughly grabbing his shoulder. He turned around, angry. It was Paul. "Ezra! Any idea who this Peau guy is? You owe it to us to say!"

Ezra knocked the offending hand away. The rage in the air was contagious; Ezra felt an adrenaline surge, a queasy fight-or-flight IM from his nervous system. It was particularly unwelcome right now, since the surging crowds prevented flight from being a viable option; the other alternative had never been his style. And Paul had inches, pounds, and loads of muscle tissue on him, so it was even less his style now than usual. But he couldn't resist its primitive imperative. "You're too fucking ignorant to have opinions," he growled.

Somehow, this proved to be audible. The pro-Peau faction gave a rousing cheer. Paul seemed to take umbrage at the phrase "too fucking ignorant"— could he be more sensitive than he seemed?—and colored angrily. When he reached for Ezra again, his intentions were unmistakably violent. Mindy, standing behind him, abruptly brought her sign down hard on his head. The boy staggered and dropped to his knees. Ezra turned to Mindy, and she smiled at him triumphantly. "Serves him right!" she said. "He exposed himself to me the other day! Revolting! Like a big ugly cobra!"

Ezra's second response, coming right after infantile male envy, was pure glee: Right on, Mindy! You go, girl! But he wasn't given much time for enjoyment, or even to wonder whether the accusation could have any basis in reality, because Paul was on his feet again, enraged and snorting, all but pawing the ground, and a second later he was making a flying dive for Mindy. Ezra was not being gallant, he simply happened to be in the way, but he absorbed the full force of Paul's lunge, and both of them fell over onto the grass.

Even through his anger and his fear, Ezra was aware the cameras were capturing the action, that it might be on television tonight, and that it wasn't exactly appropriate to his dignity as a molder of young minds. He even managed a stray hope the microphones hadn't caught his "too fucking ignorant" comment, which was unlikely to win the unequivocal approval of the Beuhler Board of Overseers. They were too fucking ignorant to see his point.

Now that Paul was on top of Ezra, straddling his waist, the younger man didn't seem to know what he should do next. Pummel him? Strangle him? Spit in his face? Overwhelm him with Socratic argumentation? All around, people were shouting and shaking their signs, and peripheral tussles were starting. This could get seriously out of hand, and soon.

"How about letting me up?" Ezra said, just loudly enough for Paul to hear, but not loudly enough to carry over the cries and shouts of the demonstrators, some of whose feet were coming alarmingly close to Ezra's head.

Paul looked confused, not sure what his next step ought to be. He stared at Ezra, his handsome face blank, his eyes flashing with savage vacuity.

"This isn't Wimbledon," Ezra went on. "Try to show some decorum."

Paul was about to say something, but Mindy's sign came down on his head again, hard. A moment later, down it came one more time, even harder, with an alarming thud. Paul yelped, blood began to trickle down his forehead, and his body went limpish. Ezra shoved him off—the fellow offered no resistance now beyond sheer dead weight—and pushed himself up to a standing position. Could Paul have suffered brain damage? Would anyone be able to tell?

"Thanks, Mindy," he said.

Her eyes glowed. "It was a pleasure, believe me." She looked vibrant, high on an adrenaline-and-madness cocktail. "You owe me your life," she added.

"Just pursue that indecent exposure case," he advised her. "I'm with you all the way."

Fights were breaking out to left and right. Ezra braced himself for a major effort, then pushed his way through the milling bodies, trying intently not to meet anyone's eye—there was no telling how someone might respond if he noticed Ezra as an individual rather than an anonymous body in the crush—and finally managed to fight his way through to open air. He brushed himself off, breathing hard, he made a stab at straightening his clothing—prominent and probably ineradicable grass stains now marred his best pair of corduroy trousers, he noticed unhappily—and trotted toward the entrance to Beuhler Hall. No one pursued him, but he could hear the sounds of the fracas behind him growing in intensity and volume. There was a good chance the county tac unit would have to be mobilized before the craziness ended.

Having run this particular gauntlet, Ezra hoped for clear sailing henceforward, but he encountered another obstacle on the steps of Beuhler Hall itself: The mayor of Seven Hills was holding a press conference. Although most of the national press were elsewhere, the man had somehow succeeded in attracting a smallish crowd of local valley media; possibly they'd been covering this story longest, had exhausted every other angle, and so had to settle for the "outraged bumpkin" slant. In any event, His Honor was doing his dead-level best to compete with the person-on-the-street interviews, the hand-to-hand battles among the demonstrators, and all those other sexy stories being offered just a few hundred feet away.

"This viper must be snatched from Beuhler's bosom!" the mayor was thundering, with lots of histrionic gestures. He was a freckle-faced man in his fifties; he looked like Howdy Doody gone to seed, with thinning hair and a paunch. "This wolf must be separated from these lambs immediately, and by force if necessary!"

Ezra stood and watched for a minute or two, fascinated. John Maier's November reelection prospects were considered poor, or had been up until recent weeks; having initially won office as a pro-development candidate, a sympathetic friend of the real estate interests, he had over the years repeatedly and victoriously taken on the environmental movement. At first it hadn't been any kind of contest at all, but recently town sentiment had been shifting away from him, and his days as mayor were generally conceded to be numbered.

"Once this filth is permitted in a fine upstanding institution like Beuhler, once even the Baptist Church finds itself powerless to isolate this scum and dispose of it properly, then we've come to the testing ground, and the American people—emphatically including the fine citizens of Seven Hills— have to take matters in their own hands and enforce the kind of rough justice to which the American West has always resorted in times of trial!"

Amazing, thought Ezra. You can read about historical demagogues and even exotic contemporary specimens like Slobodan Miloševíc, you can study the social conditions that make their emergence possible, but you can't believe it till you see it in person; and here it is, happening before my eyes, a sure loser catching a wave of public anger in order to hold onto power. And possibly succeeding.

And it's my ass he's after.

Disgusted, Ezra drew a deep breath and turned away, proceeding up the stairs and through the front door to the cool quiet of Beuhler Hall. After a few seconds to collect himself, he climbed to the third floor, where the Assembly Room was located.

He was over fifteen minutes late, but the meeting had just begun. Other faculty members had probably had as much difficulty as he getting into the building. No doubt many of them had taken a moment to share the fruits of their wisdom with the journalists outside.

The Assembly Room was shaped like a truncated bowl, perhaps 300 degrees around, the remainder consisting of a flat wall covered by a huge abstract wooden sculpture, a gift from a rich agri-biz alum. Tiers of seats lined the bowl; at floor level were a podium and a long table. President Matson was at the podium now, and the overseers, including the Reverend Mr. Dimsdale, were seated at the long table stage left.

Ezra walked down one of the steeply inclined aisles looking for a seat. The room was very full, today's meeting was unusually well attended. About halfway down into the bowl, he found a seat next to Hannah Jenkel and slipped in beside her. The grandmotherly Emily Dickinson expert smiled at him. She had taken an early liking to Ezra, and remained one of his few dependable allies in the department. "What happened to you?" she asked.

He realized he must look a wreck from the imbroglio outside. "Had trouble running the blockade," he said. "Have I missed anything?"

"Minutes and old business. They're just getting to the hot stuff."

President Matson, lean, ramrod-spined, thin-lipped, was speaking into a microphone. It was unfortunate, but he looked damned impressive. Matson was widely believed to harbor political ambitions, to be using the Beuhler presidency as a springboard for a future congressional bid. A valley native who'd gone to Harvard College and Yale Law School, he could switch from Bible-thumping primitive to smooth-talking technocrat with an effortless invisible shifting of gears. He was the most sophisticated spokesman imaginable for the most reactionary set of interests in the area, and Ezra was always intimidated in his presence. It would have been far more comfortable to dismiss the man with smug contempt, but only a fool would fail to notice his keen unctuous intelligence. Some of Ezra's colleagues contrived to treat him as joke, but they were consistently thwarted whenever an issue that concerned them reached the administrative level. Not just overridden, but routed.

"I'm aware some of you find the present situation amusing," Matson was saying in his mellifluous baritone. "Neither I nor the Board of Overseers share that view. We regard the book in question as a clear violation of the morals clause in the contract you all signed, and if the author of the book is one of our number rather than a student, which I'm forced to regard as likely, then that person won't be teaching at Beuhler much longer, you may rest assured of that. We anticipate litigation may result, but Carol Dimsdale assures me her office is prepared to pursue this matter as far as conditions require."

So Carol's my enemy in her official capacity? That's reassuring.

Matson peered around the room over the top of his designer glasses, as if daring someone to challenge him. "For those of you who think this is a relatively trifling matter, who don't share my feelings of moral indignation, let me tell you about some of the correspondence I've been getting, so at least you can understand there's also a practical side to this issue."

He riffled through some papers on the podium. "Yes, here. We've received—these tabulations were made by my assistant, Nancy Burnside, since, as you know, our computer system remains unreliable—we've received over forty-five letters from some of our most generous alums, telling us they won't make any further contribution until the situation is resolved. It's fair to assume there are many others out there who feel the same but haven't seen fit to write us about it. And as you know, contributions are a crucial part of our operations.

"Additionally, the registrar has estimated that applications to Beuhler are down 18 percent over the comparable period last year. I suspect there's a connection.

"The FFA has sent us a letter threatening to suspend our chapter.

"A number of national fraternities and sororities have done the same.

"Numerous clergymen have written us—not all of them Baptist, by the way, or even in every case Christian—demanding to know what steps we've taken in this matter."

Yeah, thought Ezra, I'm sure the ayatollahs are with you all the way.

"And then there's the mayoralty campaign. This may not be, strictly speaking, Beuhler business, but town-gown relations in Seven Hills have improved in recent years, and I don't imagine anyone wants to see them deteriorate. I'm informed the mayor is outside this very building right now, inveighing against us. So let me say to those of you who profess concern about infringement of your academic freedom, such infringement on *our* part is relatively benign compared with what you'd find outside this institution. I'd say we're your allies, and your last line of defense."

This won him some applause. Ezra glanced around the room. What are we coming to? he wondered. "What are we coming to?" he whispered to Hannah, gambling that she shared his feelings.

She shook her head. "There's always potential for something like this in a school like Beuhler," she whispered back.

Somebody shushed her.

"Let me also remind you that Beuhler's unhappy connection to this story is still new. All the problems I've outlined figure to get worse as time goes by, unless we take prompt action. For this and other reasons, it's my firm intention to find out who this, this 'E. A. Peau' is, and give him—or indeed her—his walking papers. Now, I don't suppose this is going to do any good, but I believe it's worth a try: Will the person who wrote the disgusting piece of trash called *Every Inch a Lady* please spare us the time and expense of a lengthy investigation and step forward and admit your guilt?"

A hush fell over the room. These sorts of moments, no matter how contrived, are always dramatic. Like during that moment in the wedding ceremony when the guests are invited to explain why the happy couple should not be wed or forever hold their peace, it's impossible not to feel an anticipatory thrill, to wonder if *just this once* somebody might leap up and narrate a chain of events with the convolutions and complexity of a nineteenth-century novel, the upshot of which is that the couple in question are in reality mother and son, and besides, both are in love with someone else.

Maybe elementary school might be an even better analogue. "We'll all put our heads down, and the person who stole Jennifer's eraser can come put it on my desk and no one else will know." Such moments have an effect on the guilty party, no matter how case-hardened. Ezra began to sweat. Ezra even felt a crazy urge to stand up, take that slow walk down the aisle to confess his culpability. It would be his contribution to the spectacle.

But of course he remained rooted to his seat, and exchanged a glance with Hannah.

"Like grammar school," she sniffed, reading his thoughts. "Utterly childish." The interesting thing to Ezra was that, with her gray hair in a bun, and her dowdy clothes, and her knitting, Hannah rather looked the part of an elementary school teacher herself.

After waiting about thirty seconds and letting the tension build—and build it did, with the silence stretching out ominously, and with much optimistic craning of necks, and a good deal of throat-clearing and shifting of weight—President Matson said, "Yes, I thought not. A coward as well as a degenerate. Those qualities go hand in hand."

Hey, hold on! I'm no coward, I just fought Paul Van Horne! Maybe I needed Mindy Dunkelweisse's back-up, but that doesn't make me a coward, just a wuss.

"I will entertain a motion about how to proceed."

What followed had clearly been choreographed. McClintock of the Theology Department, who'd been around Beuhler since its founding, raised his hand. "Move an ad hoc committee be formed to determine the authorship of the book."

"Second," somebody yelled.

"Any discussion?"

Nobody wanted to discuss it. No point. Everything had obviously been prearranged.

"In favor?" said Matson. There was a large chorus of Ayes. Of course. It wasn't only to avoid the effort of swimming upstream. Ad hoc committees were an ideal way to deal with this sort of thing. Once you formed an ad hoc committee, nobody had to pay it further heed. "Opposed?" Dead silence. Ezra and Hannah had both sat this one out.

"Now, as to the composition of said committee," said Matson, "if possible, I'd prefer participation to be voluntary. I assume there's enough interest so that we can get, say, ten faculty who'd be willing to serve. For what it's worth, I expect there'll be plenty of media interest. Not," he added with leaden irony, "that that's an inducement to any of you, goodness no. Anyway, if you're interested, speak to me or Nancy in the next day or so. But the *chair* of the committee ought to be elected by the full faculty. I welcome nominations for the position. I recognize the Reverend Mr. Dimsdale."

Dimsdale hadn't raised his hand. They weren't even pretending to spontaneity.

Dimsdale rose and waddled over to the podium. "Mr. President, I believe I have the ideal candidate to serve as chair. Someone whose objectivity and sound good sense will serve us well. Someone who cannot be accused of being in anyone's pocket. Someone respected by students and colleagues alike. My nominee will bring energy, gravity, and strong moral values to this endeavor—"

Ezra was nodding along, wondering what sterling character Dimsdale had in mind.

"—I nominate Ezra Gordon of the English Department."

It was like a sharp boot to the gonads.

"Second," yelled some person from the floor, a person who would certainly burn in hell for all eternity if Ezra had any say in the matter.

Hannah looked at Ezra quizzically. "Did you know about this?" she whispered.

"No!" Ezra whispered back. There was a tide of something bitter and acidic rising up along his esophagus, and a sickening sort of loosening somewhere in his lower intestine. He added, in a desperate voice that was no longer quite a whisper, "Help me, Hannah!"

She patted his arm in commiseration.

Matson stepped up to the podium. Dimsdale remained beside him. "Any other nominations?" asked the president. He waited. No names were offered. "All right. In favor?" A huge chorus of relieved Ayes.

Like Shirley Jackson's "The Lottery," Ezra thought.

"Opposed?" Dead silence. Matson didn't give them long to consider. "It's unanimous," he announced. "Ezra, are you here? Come down so we can get a look at you."

Uncertainly, Ezra rose to his feet. A huge wave of applause began to roll toward him. He looked down at Hannah beseechingly. She smiled, and shrugged helplessly. Then, like an automaton, he started down the aisle toward the podium. Damn, he was thinking, if I don't take this long walk one way, I take it another. Shouldn't a priest be shuffling along beside me, murmuring vain words of liturgical comfort?

When he reached the podium, numb except for a pointless self-consciousness about his unkempt appearance and the grass stains at the knees of his rumpled corduroys, President Matson took one of his hands and raised his arm, and Dimsdale took the other and did the same. It was like a political convention. Ezra felt like the briefly famous Vice Admiral James Stockdale. Who am I? Why am I here?

As the applause continued, Dimsdale leaned down and whispered to Ezra, "Wanted to do a favor for my favorite English professor." At first Ezra thought the man was cruelly rubbing salt in the wound he'd just inflicted, but when he looked up, Dimsdale was beaming beatifically. "Mentioned you to Matson a couple of days ago," the clergyman went on, "and though he couldn't quite place you, he took my word for it you'd be an excellent choice."

"I have to decline," Ezra whispered hoarsely.

"Nonsense, my boy, this is a great opportunity for you," pronounced Matson.

"But I don't—"

"You'll be terrific," interrupted Dimsdale.

"No, you see, I—"

"Do Beuhler this service and believe me, we won't forget it when your promotion comes up before the board," said the president, looking deep into Ezra's eyes, his inflection thick with meaning. "And bear this in mind: The board has the power to overrule your department's recommendations. *In either direction.*"

Ezra processed this one. Talk about your carrot and your stick. "But I've, I've never done anything like this. I wouldn't know where to begin."

The applause had died down by now, and Ezra was suddenly aware that they had over a hundred eavesdroppers.

"Just find the person who wrote the book," said Matson with grim impatience, clearly determined to terminate the conversation. "We've put our trust in you, boy. Don't let us down." He looked toward the assembly. "Do I hear a motion to adjourn?"

"So moved!"

"Second."

"In favor. Opposed. The motion is carried."

The faculty rose and began to file out, moving with the eyes-down alacrity of a tribunal that's ordered an execution. Ezra remained at the podium, paralyzed, and Dimsdale too remained behind, his heavy arm around Ezra's shoulder.

"Hadda pull some strings, call in a few favors," said Dimsdale, "but for a future son-in-law, it was worth it."

Future son-in-law. Did the man's presumption know no bounds whatsoever?

"A time like this," added Dimsdale, "is when you find out who your friends really are."

"That's for sure," said Ezra. What do I do now? he wondered. How do I handle this one? I'm riding at the head of a posse in hot pursuit of . . . myself.

"And," continued Dimsdale, his arm still oppressively around Ezra's shoulders, "don't you ever forget, it's me you've got to thank for it."

Nothing to worry about on that score.

C h a p t e r 5

"**Y**ou've been fucked," explained grandmotherly Hannah Jenkel. "Royally."

Out of the kindness of her heart—there was no other conceivable explanation—she had been the first to volunteer her services to the ad hoc committee, and now, back in her office next door to Ezra's, she was explicating the tactical fine points of the situation for him.

"Look at it from Matson's point of view. Now he can tell the alums and the press and the rest of the idiots on his back that he's taken concrete measures to solve the problem. If you fail to find the culprit—and I don't honestly see how you can do anything else—he has an expendable scapegoat he's happy to be rid of anyway."

"What if I succeed, though?" The question was purely academic, of course, but Ezra admired Hannah's ability to thread her way through Beuhler politics, and his curiosity was genuine, if also purely abstract.

"Well, for one thing, how can you? Short of some sort of Perry Mason denouement, an unexpected confession out of left field, this whole ad hoc committee business seems to be a nonstarter, doesn't it? The usual bureaucratic method, sweep a problem under the rug and hope it goes away. I mean, we obviously don't have subpoena power, which is the only way to get to the bottom of the mystery, although that probably wouldn't do the trick either. And anyway, listen, if you succeed, terrific, Matson can say the problem's been solved, he took the appropriate steps, put the right people into the right slots, etc. Either way, *his* ass is covered. And he's made *you* no promises, remember. When your tenure case comes up for review, whether you're a hero or a schmuck, he can still do exactly as he pleases."

"I've been fucked."

"Right up the ass."

"But Dimsdale—" Ezra couldn't believe the minister had been that Machiavellian.

Which Hannah confirmed: "Oh, I'm sure he believes he was doing you a favor. Played right into Matson's hands. Dimsdale may be a scumbag, but he's an *ingenuous* scumbag. Matson's a scumbag positively oozing guile."

"So what do I do now?"

"Honey, I wish I could tell you."

Ezra shook his head. "The press have been pressuring me for a statement."

"Stall 'em."

Ezra nodded. He'd been interviewed by the *Los Angeles Times,* the *San Francisco Chronicle,* and the *Fresno Bee,* but so far he'd managed to avoid saying anything to anybody. "We'll follow the evidence wherever it leads," was the sort of crap they'd been letting him get away with. He'd turned down several requests from the network magazine shows and the *News Hour with Jim Lehrer.* An extended interview might seal his death warrant.

"C-Span wants to broadcast our meetings," Ezra said.

Hannah's eyes widened. "You have to refuse."

"I may not have that choice. It was Matson who conveyed the message to me. He thinks it's a terrific idea."

"Jesus. He's playing the publicity angle the way Perlman plays the fiddle. And he's turning the heat up on you at the same time. It's a bitch, Ezra. I don't know what else to say."

He left Hannah's office a couple of minutes later in an even worse mood than when she'd invited him in, and headed next door to his own office. Back at his desk, he began to scratch notes for an agenda to the ad hoc committee's first meeting, scheduled for three days away. Why am I doing this? he asked himself. I mean, shit, *I* know who E. A. Peau is. And I certainly don't want anyone else to find out. So why am I going through this charade?

Because, dingus, he apostrophized himself, I have to do something, or at least I have to be seen to be doing something; because the best outcome I can hope for is an honorable failure, one in which I'll be perceived as having made a valiant effort against impossible odds; and because inertia, and everybody else's expectations, produce a powerful current that carries you passively along even though you know you're headed straight for the falls.

Do we understand each other, dingus? Good. Then let's have a little cooperation here. We have an agenda to prepare.

He picked up a felt-tip pen and wrote: *Stylistic analysis by computer.* A clear bullshit suggestion, but it had a nice earnest ring to it. Some of the committee members might even take it seriously, God help them. After all, *New York Magazine* had done the same thing with *Primary Colors,* and impressed everybody by fingering Joe Klein.

Then he wrote: *Does budget permit hiring of private investigator?* Of course, a private investigator wouldn't have anything to investigate; those jackals from the press had found whatever there was to be found. But this sounded very tough-minded. The name's Marlowe. Fifty dollars a day plus expenses. There's probably a dame involved.

Write to publisher for information. Oh yeah, Isaac is just falling all over himself to cooperate with our interrogatories.

Talk to Post Office employees. Who, tragically, are prevented by law from divulging anything.

Discuss television coverage. This sounded like a joke, but Matson had been insistent, and Ezra had a suspicion that a good many of the nine other members of the committee, probably all of them besides Hannah and himself, would welcome the chance to posture and prattle on the air.

Solicit other suggestions. Which, if I know my colleagues, won't be forthcoming.

There, he thought. Nobody can fault me for this agenda: It looks plausible, it shows I've taken my responsibilities seriously and done my homework, and it seems vaguely relevant to the designated task. It's not my fault it won't get us anywhere.

It *is* my fault that it *better not* get us anywhere, but that's another story. Not for public consumption.

These ruminations were interrupted by a knocking at his office door. "Come in, it's open," he called. He didn't expect anyone, but at this point, any interruption was welcome.

Well, not quite. When the door opened, it was Daniel McGruder who strolled in. "Can I talk to you for a second, Professor?"

Ezra rose with a sigh. "I'm kind of busy at the moment," he said, gesturing toward the notes he'd been writing. Kind of busy contemplating suicide.

"Well, when's a good time? Are you free tomorrow afternoon?"

Ezra sighed again. "What do you have in mind? Hot lights and brass knucks in some backroom somewhere?"

McGruder smiled mechanically, recognizing on some level of consciousness that this question wasn't intended literally, and thus might be construed as humorous or ironic or mordant or one of those other things which made certain types of people smile. "Nothing of the sort, Professor. Not that we actually use those methods, of course. But in addition, you're no longer a suspect."

"Hasn't that been true for weeks?"

"Wherever did you get that idea?"

"From you."

"Uh uh. You misunderstood me. You were on our inactive list, but you were still on a list. Now you aren't."

"Well that *is* good news. Even at this late date."

McGruder inclined his head slightly, pleading nolo contendere to the implicit reprimand. "In fact, that relates to what I want to talk to you about. But not in pursuit of my investigation. Which is going well, by the way."

"Is it now?"

"Um. People get impatient, we understand that, but nuts-and-bolts investigative work takes time, and it's what pays off in the end. Not hot-dogging, but sustained patient effort. We're going to break the case real soon. Matter of days now, I'd estimate. And when we do . . . well, the Justice Department's gonna make an example of this particular perp, they're gonna see to it he sizzles like a cat in a microwave. But what I wanna talk to you about is more, well, I wouldn't, I wouldn't want to call it *personal* exactly, but—" He shrugged, helpless before the befuddling nuances of language when applied to human affairs.

"It's sort of almost personal, would you say?"

"Yeah, that sums it up pretty well."

"Well, I can probably steal a little time tomorrow afternoon. You want to meet for a drink?" Ezra sighed yet again, and silently cursed his own weakness for making this proposal. Isn't my plate full enough? Isn't my cup already runnething over? Maybe, he reassured himself, just maybe I'm not being a good guy, maybe I'm just plain curious: What could this doofus possibly want with me now?

"That would be great. 'Course, I'm not supposed to drink when I'm on duty, but—"

"But this is sort of almost personal?"

"Right. Exactly. You know the Last Chance?"

"Only by reputation."

"Nice place. You'll like it. Five-thirty okay?"

"It's a date."

After submitting to a handshake considerably friendlier, hence even more agonizing, than its predecessors, Ezra came out from behind his desk to show McGruder to the door. But as he opened it, McGruder suddenly slapped the side of his head with the heel of his palm, a goofily literal charade of a man who's remembered something important in the nick of time, and exclaimed, "Oh, I almost forgot! There's something pretty funny I've been meaning to tell you, and I almost left without mentioning it."

"I can hardly wait."

"I mean, this is gonna slay you. Since you're the head of that committee to find E. A. Peau and everything."

Ezra felt his blood start to run at an appreciably lower temperature, but forced his face into a mask of eager anticipation. "Yes?"

"This is really something. It's supposed to be a big secret, but, well, with your being on that committee and all, we're kind of working the same side of the street now, so . . ." He lowered his voice, and his eyes sparkled, full of fun. "As I'm sure you can imagine, our lab's been going through the computer system with a fine-tooth comb."

"Bit by bit," was Ezra's jocular contribution, though his heart was feeling anything but jocular. He smelled danger, and the rough beast was slouching closer with every passing second.

"Bit by bit. Very good. And it's a fascinating process, kinda creepy, almost like brain surgery. And for a long time now, weeks and weeks in fact, we've been finding the damnedest stuff scattered among the files." He grinned. "At first we didn't know what the hell it was, and since it didn't have anything to do with our investigation, we weren't paying it much attention. And everything's so disorganized in there, such a godawful mess—like the machine's gone totally wacko—we didn't have a clue what it could mean."

"What sort of stuff?" Ezra asked, because he knew he was supposed to, and because he knew McGruder was going to tell him whether he asked or not.

"Well, that's the thing. Most of what we found, as you might imagine, was fragments of academic work, that was the main thing, tons of it, of every description, along with bulletin-board postings, E-mail, etc. But the stuff I'm talking about was just, just pure *smut*. Incredible. I've been an FBI man for a long time now, but I was still completely shocked. Anyway, at first we just assumed these were isolated pieces of E-mail, like maybe a couple of people using the system were, were, you know, were romantically involved, and they were kind of sending spicy messages to one another. Something of that nature. So we got a couple of laughs out of it, same as we do from phone taps sometimes—you'd be amazed what people say to each other on the phone—but we didn't pay it much mind."

He was enjoying himself, telling this story. He was taking his time, savoring the narrative experience. And Ezra, standing paralyzed by the door to his office, felt like a small succulent rodent hypnotized by a python. "And then?" he prompted.

"And then. And then that story broke in the *National Enquirer*. You know the one."

"E. A. Peau at Beuhler."

"Exactly. E. A. Peau at Beuhler. Which gave me a hunch. Just a hunch, but then, experienced investigators learn to trust their hunches."

"I'm sure."

"So I went out and bought a copy of the book. Just on a hunch, not 'cause I had any interest in reading that sort of trash. And guess what I discovered."

"The stuff on the computer was straight out of the book."

"Exactly." McGruder was impressed. "Very sharp. From the first few chapters of the book. It didn't take a prolonged search, thank goodness."

Ezra's knees were starting to buckle. He leaned against the doorframe for support. I erased those files! he wanted to scream. I was so conscientious! I've been betrayed!

Apparently some residue of his work had remained in memory. Perhaps the machine automatically performed some sort of back-up function without being instructed to do so. No doubt there are times when this feature is a lifesaver.

But not this time!

Even the fucking computers have turned on me! Is it too late to form an alliance with the Unabomber?

The answer, all but audible, was: It's too late for *any*thing, Rodion Romanovitch.

"Well," he said, his voice amazingly steady, "what do you make of it?"

"I'd bet my shirt this E. A. Peau character wrote the book, or at least some of the book, on the college computer system. That's what I make of it."

"Gee."

"So I guess that makes us rivals, unh?"

"What do you mean?" His voice wasn't quite so steady when he asked *this* question.

"I guess it's just fate, you and me. Not that I believe in that kind of stuff."

"But, what do you mean?"

"I mean—" And here McGruder interrupted himself to laugh gaily. "I mean we're sort of in a race, aren't we? It isn't the FBI's mission, but there's a good chance that while we're solving this hacker business, we'll get to the bottom of the E. A. Peau mystery too. I'm not trying to steal your thunder, I swear, but it may work out that way. Score a twofer. Quite a feather in my cap, as you might imagine."

"What, that is, how would you rate the chances?"

"Hey, professor, don't take it so hard. I'm prepared to work with your committee, share the credit, et cetera."

"Yeah, well, that's, uh, very decent of you."

"Don't mention it."

"Right. But, uh, the chances? What do you think? I'm, you know, I'm just curious."

"Oh, the chances are better than good. We're basically assembling a jigsaw puzzle. It takes time, and there may be a small gap or two, but the pieces are gonna fit together."

"Ah *hah*."

"Right. So may the best man win."

"As you say."

"Funny old life, unh?"

"It certainly is."

McGruder checked his watch, which, considering Ezra's eagerness to see him leave, added insult to injury. Then he announced, "I'd love to stick around and jaw, but I gotta go. Tomorrow at the Last Chance, right?"

"You can depend on it." What could he have in mind? Blackmail? He didn't seem the type, but which of us ever seems the type to do anything?

Who, for example, would expect a mousy little junior professor to find himself in shit as deep as this?

McGruder extended his hand once again, but Ezra had endured enough pain for one day. He shut the door in the FBI man's face.

Chapter 6

"You're awfully moody tonight."

"Am I?"

"And you've barely touched your fish."

Perhaps because of her father's attack, Carol had been concentrating on low-fat cooking lately. Her recent culinary choices would not have endeared her to the ranchers of the San Joaquin Valley.

Ezra looked at the pan-fried trout on his plate and felt a brotherly bond. Bobby Burns had his field mouse, I've got you. Baited, hooked, reeled in, and fried till your eyes pop.

"What's bothering you, Ezra?"

It would have been a relief to unburden himself, but he didn't dare. Carol's job required her to work hand-in-glove with Matson and the Beuhler administration on the Peau case, and she'd given no indication she found this aspect of her work uncongenial. Nor had she said anything further about the book itself. It seemed safe to assume she strongly disapproved. At any rate, you'd have to be a fool to gamble the other way.

Which meant, aside from having no one to confide in, if—or, to be hardnosed and realistic, *when*—the E. A. Peau shit hit the Buehler fan, Carol would drop him like a white-hot briquet. Would turn on him with the same remorseless fury as her employer. Greater fury; she'd consider his failure to tell her, in the face of their intimacy, some ultimate sort of betrayal, absolute proof of his irremediable degeneracy. And maybe she'd be right—he was uncomfortably aware his actions compromised her almost as much as they did himself—although it was equally true that nothing in her attitude invited confession.

Damn it, he didn't want to be dropped like a white-hot briquet. Not by

Carol. That was the interesting emotional discovery engaging him now. He obviously didn't want to lose his job, didn't want to be publicly humiliated, didn't want to be ridden out of town on a rail; those were all experiences he'd just as soon forgo, thanks all the same. But losing Carol resided in a deeper circle of hell.

"Something to do with the committee?" she pressed.

"Something along those lines."

"I guess your position isn't especially comfortable, huh?"

"No." He broke eye contact with the trout and turned to face her. "What do you mean?"

"Well, you know, my dad kind of roped you into this. He thought he was doing you a favor, but I'm aware you don't share his views."

"No, that's true, I don't."

"You're kind of out of sympathy with what you're meant to accomplish."

"I am."

She nodded. "It'll all be over in a little while."

Yes, he thought, it will. All of it. The good, the bad, and the ugly. The long and the short and the tall. Every little thing that constitutes my existence. I'll be—I'll really be, it won't be some sort of trope—I'll be like a survivor of some major catastrophe, an earthquake or tornado or civil war. Nothing left but the clothes on my back. Starting over, building a new life from scratch.

Well, why worry? I did such a great job with this one, the next should be a breeze.

It was clear he wasn't going to get away with it. McGruder's little news flash dashed any lingering hopes he might have had. Decisive, damning evidence was in their possession, and they were sifting through it. McGruder made it sound like a matter of days, no more. There was no escape. The necktie party was assembling, and he would be the guest of honor.

They were going to lynch a white-hot briquet.

"Honey," Carol said, intruding on these melancholy reveries, "I get the feeling you'd rather be alone. Would you? I won't be offended if you want me to go."

"Well . . ." As he was trying to assess the sincerity of her offer, and disentangle the complex knot of his own feelings (he wanted her to stay, but mostly because, any day now, she'd never want to speak to him again), the phone rang.

"I'll get it," she offered, rising and heading out toward the hall phone.

A landmark in their relationship had been reached a few days ago, when he told her to feel free to answer the phone when it rang. It was a peculiar sort of symbol of commitment, this offer, as was her willingness to act on it: It proclaimed he didn't expect to receive any calls she shouldn't know about, and equally, that she didn't mind if someone discovered her in his apartment at some putatively compromising hour.

Which realization made him sigh; they'd come so far, she'd been so willing to meet him halfway, more than halfway, she'd really traveled an immense distance in order to make things work, and now . . .

She returned from the corridor. "Somebody named Henry," she said.

"Oh goody," said Ezra.

She smiled at his undisguised sourness. "I'm gonna clear the dishes and clear out, okay? If you want me back later, just give a whistle. You know how to whistle, don't you?"

He nodded without acknowledging the allusion, and headed toward the phone. It was indeed Henry, wondering whether he could come by and discuss something.

"Can't it wait?" Ezra asked.

"Sure. I'm just kinda psyched, is all."

Ezra considered: Maybe it would be better to deal with Henry than brood alone. Maybe it would be tonic, under the present circumstances, to focus on somebody *else's* life. "You know how to get here?" he heard himself asking.

"Yep. I'll be over in two shakes," Henry said. "Two shakes" seemed an odd colloquialism for a Chinese boy to use, but perhaps growing up in the San Joaquin Valley had made his acquaintanceship with lambs' tails more real than metaphorical.

Less than ten minutes later, while washing the dishes Carol had cleared, Ezra heard the doorbell. He dried his hands on the dishtowel hanging from the refrigerator door and crossed quickly to the front door to admit Henry. The boy looked radiant, if also a little nuts. "Hi," he said, his eyes dancing, "I got here as fast as I could."

"There wasn't any rush," answered Ezra.

Henry entered and, when Ezra gestured to the sofa, waltzed over to it and flopped himself down. "So," he said, as Ezra took the wing chair opposite. Nervous energy seemed to pulse from him; he was almost writhing, unable to keep still in his seat.

Ezra smiled at him fondly. "What's on your mind, Henry?"

"Way-ull . . . I was wondering, did you happen to, did you happen to do anything with my manuscript, by any chance?"

"Why do you ask? Need it back?"

"Uh uh. It's just, I have this suspicion I may owe you a sorta huge debt of gratitude. See, I got a telegram this morning. You wanna hear something strange? I never got a telegram before. In my whole life."

"Poor you. It's a shame they abolished the peacetime draft. Draft notices used to come in the form of telegrams."

"Wouldn't have made any difference. I'm exempt."

"Yeah, right, don't ask, don't tell. So who was it from?"

Henry glowed. "*A publisher!* They're gonna *publish my book!*"

"That's wonderful, Henry. Congratulations. I'm delighted." Ezra found himself grinning back at the boy. Sometimes it did feel gratifying to do a generous deed. Good old Isaac had come through too.

"I know you had something to do with this. You're the only one who's read it. And you said you liked it. And you had the only copy besides my own."

"Well . . ."

"This is just so awesome, so *magisterial* . . . I mean, I don't know what to do with myself. Or how to thank you. I've been caroming around my apartment like a billiard ball all day. I can't figure out what to do next."

"Let me give you one piece of advice. Have an agent negotiate your contract."

"Why? Are these guy sharp dealers or something? The Isaac Schwimmer Press?"

"It isn't that. It's just, they have their interests, you have yours. It's your job to protect yourself. That isn't their responsibility."

"Right. Say . . . the Isaac Schwimmer Press . . . that rings a bell." Henry scrunched his face up, trying to remember where he had heard of it.

Ezra wasn't eager for him to succeed. "Have you told your parents yet?" he asked, to encourage the boy's hyperactive mind to scamper off in another direction.

"Not yet, uh uh. I've just . . . God," he said with sudden vehement glee, "they're gonna be *furious*. Well, fuck them, right? Wait till they *read* the thing! Can you imagine? That'll *really* drive them nuts. Their faggot son! Their dope-smoking, poetry-reading, pud-sucking faggot son! Oh, this is *soooo* great! This is truly . . . *righteous!*"

There was something in the quality of his joy, something in the scope and ferocity of his rage—tiles of a Rubik's cube suddenly aligned themselves neatly in Ezra's mind. So sure was he, it amazed him that he'd taken so long to figure it out.

"Henry?"

Henry heard the change in Ezra's tone, and grounded himself midflight. "Yes?"

Engineering. English Department target. All that free-floating rage. Ezra leaned forward. "It was you, wasn't it? Who fucked with the computer system? Right?"

Henry blanched. There was a sharp intake of breath. His mouth opened, but nothing came out.

"You want to tell me about it?" Ezra waited, but Henry didn't speak or move. "Come on, Henry, your silence is already confirmation, so you might as well say something."

Henry remained motionless, looking down at his hands. After a few moments, he mumbled, almost too quietly to be heard, "There's not much to say."

"Oh, I think there's plenty to say. You must have been pretty angry."

Henry looked up. "I guess I must've been."

"At your folks? At Beuhler? At the world?"

Henry nodded. "All of those, I guess. For a start. Lots of others, too. I was getting dicked from every direction." His voice quavered. "*You* know. You read the book. But . . . "

"But—?"

"These viruses, they're, they're, I didn't mean for it to go this far. They sometimes develop a kind of life of their own. It wasn't supposed to . . . it was just . . . " Another sharp intake of breath. "It was just supposed to create a little hassle, it wasn't supposed to—" He was starting to hyperventilate. He still didn't look up. He was obviously fighting tears.

"A guy from the FBI had a chat with me a little while ago, Henry."

"This is Federal?" Henry gasped.

"Of course. Computer sabotage has a political dimension now. It's a big deal."

"Do they know it's me?"

"Uh uh. But the guy indicated it wouldn't be long. And he said the prosecution plans to play rough. That means jail time."

Now Henry did look up. Ezra had never before seen such naked terror on anyone's face. Henry moaned softly, and then, barely managing to keep the sobs at bay, said, "What should I do? What should I do? Get a lawyer? Turn myself in?"

"Here's what you should do. Since you asked. Get lost. Withdraw from Beuhler."

Henry searched Ezra's face, not daring to believe what he had just heard. "You aren't going to report me?"

"In a way you're lucky, nobody's paying much attention now to anything but E. A. Peau, even the computers are on the back burner, so nobody'll connect your leaving with—"

"Hey, that's where I heard of Schwimmer Press!" Henry interrupted triumphantly. "They published *Every Inch a Lady!*"

Amazing, thought Ezra, not without irritation. Even in the midst of his terror, even staring down the rifle barrel of a jail sentence, Henry could still experience the eureka thrill.

"Please, Henry, let's keep focused, okay? If you withdraw because you got a novel published and you want to devote yourself to writing, no one in the department'll give it a second thought, no one'll connect it with the computer business."

"But why aren't you gonna—"

"Listen," Ezra interrupted brusquely, "you covered your tracks pretty well, right? With the trail cold, and you elsewhere . . . What do you think, will it lead to you anyhow?"

Henry shook his head. "I don't know. It could. But the way they do this . . . they lay traps, they monitor phones, that sort of thing. And I haven't logged on in almost a year." He grimaced. "It was a time-release virus. Kind of like HIV, if you see what I mean. And I never used my home phone. They may figure out when, they may figure out how, they may figure out where. They can certainly narrow it down to a short list of plausibles they want to interrogate. But if I'm not around . . ." He shrugged. "I never cast much of a shadow here. They might just overlook me."

"Good. Excellent. Something else I'd like to know. This thing *was* an isolated aberration, right?"

Henry managed a smile. "Depends how you define 'aberration.'" He waited for Ezra to smile back, which did finally occur, although barely. "But if you mean, am I some kind of serial saboteur—" He laughed woodenly. "I'm a nice well-brought-up Chinese boy, Ezra. I've been a nice well-brought-up Chinese boy my whole life. This was just a sort of crazy desperate prank that got out of hand. All I want to do is write. And be left alone."

Ezra nodded. "I'm going to gamble you're telling the truth. So get out of here, Henry. Go through the right channels, file whatever petitions and bullshit paperwork the college requires. The computers are so screwed up it'll probably all get lost, but go through the motions, don't attract any undue attention, and for God's sake don't create the appearance of haste. But *hurry*. And if anyone asks, this conversation never took place."

Henry stood up. "So now I owe you *two* huge debts of gratitude, don't I?"

"That's right."

"Can I ask why? Why you're doing this for me?"

Ezra hesitated. "I don't know, exactly." He considered. "I like you. I don't like them. I suspect the punishment they're planning for you wouldn't fit the crime. You ought to keep writing. And maybe I'd like to think there's still a bit of outlaw left in me." He shrugged, and thought, Or maybe it's because they're after me as well. And they've got me cornered, I'm a goner. At least one of us should get away. "Lots of reasons," he continued. "No reason at all. If I examine my reasons too closely, I may change my mind."

Henry laughed. "Then I withdraw the question." Then, suddenly grim, he said, "I basically owe you my life, don't I?"

"Something along those lines."

"I don't see how I can ever repay you."

"Hard for me to picture too."

"Too bad you're not queer. 'Cause if you were—"

"I'm not, Henry."

Henry nodded. "What if I dedicate my book to you?"

"I'd be honored." And then Ezra had an inspiration. It hit him like a line drive straight to the temple. A good thing he was already seated, or the idea by itself might have sent him sprawling. Now calm down, fella, he instructed himself silently, you're clutching at a very thin reed here, it's probably not going to support your weight. He took a deep breath and said evenly, "You know, there *is* one thing you might be able to do for me."

"Anything."

"Never sign a blank check."

"All right. What is it?"

"That's better. Tell me, is there any way you can log on one more time, and erase absolutely *everything* on the system? Everything on the *network?*"

Henry was startled. "Everything? Just clean it right out? Why would I do that? Why would you *want* me to do that?"

"Don't ask me any questions. Just tell me if you can do it."

"That's tough. Jeez, it never occurred to me to wreak *that* kind of havoc." He thought for a moment. "Computer security has gotten more sophisticated lately, as you might imagine. I'm very good, but . . ." He considered the question further. "You know, I should've thought of it myself. If I can pull it off, it'd go a long way toward protecting my own sorry ass."

"Fine. An incidental benefit. So . . . can you? In a way that can't be traced?"

"Let me think . . . If I route the call out-of-state and come in through another system—"

"You're telling me more than I want to know, Henry. Just tell me if it's doable."

"I don't know. I can try."

"Then try. If you succeed, we'll be dead-even."

Henry looked dubious. "After finding me a publisher and keeping me out of jail? I don't get it. I mean, what's in it for you? This whole thing, as they say, doesn't compute."

Ezra glowered dramatically. "I'm starting to have second thoughts . . ."

"Okay, okay, I'm outta here."

"I'd recommend it."

Henry was already at the door when he turned around and faced Ezra. "Just one more question, okay? Whatever led you to Schwimmer Press?"

Ezra shrugged again, hoping it looked as casual as he intended. "Shot in the dark, that's all. They've been in the news. I read in *People* they were looking for legit manuscripts. Seemed worth a try."

"That was clever."

"You don't seem to have gone yet, Henry."

"It's just, it's just, for one crazy second, I thought, what if—?"

"For Christ's sake, get lost!"

Henry suddenly grinned, enjoying his second eureka of the evening. "Why, Professor Gordon. You rascal!" He winked, giggled, and was out the door in less than a second.

Chapter **7**

Dear Member of the Beuhler Community:

As you are probably aware, there is considerable public controversy currently surrounding a book entitled Every Inch a Lady, ostensibly by one E. A. Peau. It is now a virtual certainty that this name is a pseudonym, and, further, that the actual author is in fact an employee of Beuhler College.

It is President Matson's firm belief that authorship of this book represents a violation of the morals clause in the Beuhler employment contract. He also believes that anyone in possession of information that might have some bearing on the identity of "E. A. Peau" is obligated, legally and contractually, to volunteer that information to the proper authorities, and believes further that failure to do so may constitute grounds for dismissal.

As Beuhler College Counsel, I have informed President Matson that in my opinion this position is legally tenable, and is likely to survive a court challenge.

I therefore urge all members of the Beuhler community to cooperate fully with any inquiry into this matter, either currently taking place or as may take place in the future.

Very truly yours, Carol Dimsdale
Counsel to Beuhler College

Ezra had found this note under the door to his office when he returned from lunch midafternoon. So, presumably, had the rest of the faculty. The witch hunt is picking up steam, he thought. And Carol is providing guidance to the Grand Inquisitor.

He sat at his desk, his head in his hands, and tried to think his way through the next week of his life. It was a week that obviously was going to leave every aspect of his existence altered, and yet he had no plan to cope with it, nor even resources to help formulate a plan.

What could he possibly do? What options did he have? Look for a job at a private school somewhere? Who would hire him once it was revealed he'd been fired for moral turpitude? Especially with that Mindy Dunkelweisse episode in his file as well. No one would take the risk. No reason they should. Sure, he could explain, but hell, everyone's got a story.

Clerk in a bookstore? That wasn't a career, it was a summer job. Reference librarian? Researcher? Personal assistant?

If only he were able to write . . . that would almost qualify as deliverance. But it was also a pipe dream. He'd had one lovely, fluky success, but laborious effort had failed to produce anything further. Even produce something bad. Well, he wasn't the first writer to discover he had only one book in him.

Of course, he could sign a contract with Isaac and then simply fail to deliver a book. With careful husbanding, the advance might buy him a year or two, and it was unlikely Isaac would ever demand it back. On the other hand, that was a shitty thing to do to a friend. And if he tried it with a publisher who *wasn't* a friend, he'd end up in court. Who would defend him then? Not Carol.

Carol.

Since McGruder was sure to discover his secret any day now—any moment—and would take great delight in announcing the discovery to a waiting world, why, Ezra wondered, had he failed to tell Carol everything himself? Withholding the truth till she heard if from someone else was bound to make things worse. What possible motivation could he have for it? Only cowardice, fear of that awful moment of confrontation, fear of the pain he would inflict and the pain he would consequently endure. Along with a clingy sort of weakness, a spineless desire to delay the inevitable moment of separation as long as possible. But for what? What happiness could he be finding, or hoarding, by wallowing in the dregs of a relationship whose days were obviously numbered and whose intimacy rested on deception?

The phone rang. He picked it up and grunted a melancholy hello. It was Carol. "Speak of the devil," he said.

"You were talking about me?"

"No, I was, I was *thinking* about you."

"Oh! I hope it was something pleasant. Or even, you know, *lascivious*."

First he smiled, and then his heart sank. God, he was going to hate losing her. "Pleasant," he said. As big a lie as he could manage under the miserable circumstances.

"Then you'll just have to try harder. But this isn't a social call. Jim Matson wanted me to contact you. Bet you love hearing that."

"Oh yeah. I already read your letter."

"It gets better. He's scheduled a press conference Thursday morning to introduce you to the press and public. He'll make some remarks, then you."

"What's the deal? He's jealous of the attention? Wants to leave his scent on the fire hydrant?"

She sounded less friendly when she answered. "He's concerned about the tone of the coverage. He wants to contextualize things."

Whatever that meant. But her sudden shift of verbal gears was, he recognized, a harbinger of the death knell he'd be hearing from her soon. The shape of things to come. She never evinced anything but respect for Matson and loyalty to his policies. Her irony stopped at the office door.

"This is a command performance?"

"Of course. You can't skip your own press conference."

"It's not my press conference. I'm just a supernumerary in Matson's show."

"And there's a prep session in his office tomorrow at three." Chillingly businesslike.

When he rang off, he noted with interest that his heart had sunk even lower, although he'd thought it was already as low as it could go. Not a good sign. A small foretaste of what losing her would be like. Maybe there were no limits at all to the pain in store for him.

Was it the word *pain?* He suddenly recalled he had agreed to meet Dan McGruder at the Last Chance. And he was already late.

Fuckfuckfuckfuckfuckfuckfuckfuck.

Dan McGruder sucked thick tan glop—ostensibly banana daiquiri—through a hot-pink plastic straw and grunted contentedly.

"You come here often?" Ezra asked.

"Now and again." He patted his mouth with a small damp paper napkin. "I'm not much of a drinking man, but this posting can get a little lonely."

"I imagine."

"And Seven Hills isn't exactly lousy with night spots."

"With or without, I'd have to disagree."

This was lost on Dan. "Anyway," he said, "I while away the odd evening here."

As if to confirm this, their waitress, whom Ezra thought he recognized from one of his classes last year, asked, "Ready for another, Dan?" as she brushed by their table.

"Not just yet, Bev, thanks."

"Gee," said Ezra after she'd passed by, "no flies on you."

McGruder looked puzzled. "Why should I have flies?"

"No, I mean you work fast. Knowing her name and everything."

The FBI agent blushed a deep scarlet. Evidently Ezra had tweaked a nerve. The fellow's manifest discomfort tempted Ezra to probe the issue, and in as crudely off-putting a manner as possible; it would be fun to see McGruder really squirm. But on reflection he decided not to yield to this particular temptation. It might offend McGruder so greatly that he'd terminate their interview, and if that happened, Ezra's one reason for agreeing to it in the first place, his curiosity, would remain unsatisfied. Additionally, in the unlikely event that some variety of blackmail really was on Dan's agenda, it could go worse for Ezra if the FBI agent felt personally vengeful.

Ezra leaned back against the cushions of the love seat he occupied—McGruder was in its twin, catty-cornered to Ezra's—and felt the irritating caress of fern leaves in his hair. He brushed them away, shifted position, and decided the preliminaries were over. The weather was probably next in McGruder's arsenal of ice-breaking gambits.

Ezra reasoned the ice was thin enough already, no need to go out of their way to break it.

"So," he declared, his tone decisively closing the chapter entitled "Dan McGruder's Social Life in Seven Hills." And then, opening the next, he asked, "What's on your mind, Dan? I may call you Dan, mayn't I?"

Another splash of red suffused McGruder's cheeks. Hadn't they taught him to control that reaction at the Academy? It certainly diminished whatever air of authority he hoped to project. "Of course. Please." He cleared his throat. "Well . . . it's just . . . Ah, Bev, there you are, I *will* have another, thank you."

The waitress nodded and turned to Ezra. "What about you, Ezra? Refill?"

"Ooooh sure." He didn't want to get drunk tonight—or to put it another way, there was nothing in the world he'd rather do than get drunk tonight, only he knew it wouldn't be wise—but on the other hand, you can nurse a drink only so long. Particularly in present company.

"That was a Manhattan up, no cherry, right?"

"Right."

She moved off. McGruder was regarding him curiously. "How come she knows *your* name?" He sounded aggrieved.

"I think she's a student."

McGruder nodded and sighed. It made sense to him, but that didn't mean he had to like it. "You're popular, aren't you? On campus, I mean."

"Oh, I don't know."

"Students like you and everything."

"My guess is, they find me unthreatening and mistake that for affection."

McGruder nodded again. It was a statement he was prepared to accept at face value. He seemed to accept a lot at face value, a peculiar quality in a criminal investigator. "Is that a good thing, do you reckon?"

"I can live with it. I wouldn't mind being an object of veneration, but intimidation for its own sake doesn't give me any special pleasure." The fellow seemed to want to prolong the foreplay forever.

"But I mean, don't you think—"

"Dan?" Ezra interrupted.

"Yes?"

"We can discuss my pedagogical philosophy if that's what you'd enjoy, but I was under the impression there was something specific you wanted to discuss."

Another blush. "Oh, yes. I see. Cut to the chase?"

"Whatever makes you comfortable."

"Certainly not this," the FBI agent answered, and laughed, briefly but apparently genuinely. The answer and the laugh were both startlingly out of character, and perhaps for that reason almost appealing. "Okay, look, what I wanted to say is, is . . ." He looked helpless for a second, and then tried again: "I guess I just wanted to give you that apology you asked for. Some time back. Demanded, really."

"I remember."

"Like I said yesterday, we know you're not the guy. Known it for a long time. I was being difficult for, for personal reasons, and that was unprofessional. It's been bothering me for weeks. I wanted to clear the air."

"Why now?" asked Ezra.

"I saw you on the *Today Show* the other day. Reminded me of unfinished business, you might say."

"That Katie Couric's cute as a button, isn't she?"

"Yes, she is. Very wholesome. What's she really like?"

"Beats me. You saw as much of her as I did, Dan. More. I just stared into a camera at the Fresno affiliate."

"Yeah. Anyway . . . I'm sorry." McGruder offered his hand.

Fearing the worst, Ezra took it. But this time, MrGruder's grip was surprisingly gentle. Could those earlier bone-crushers have been intended maliciously after all? "Well . . . no hard feelings," Ezra offered. Was this all? It hardly seemed worth a trip to the Last Chance.

"I mean, I don't expect you to like me, but I didn't want you to think I'm a really awful person."

"Nothing of the sort." Well, something of the sort, but there wasn't any reason to share that.

Bev arrived with their second round. As she reached for McGruder's empty glass, he held up a hand, took a last noisy slurp, and then leaned back to permit her to remove it. She vouchsafed Ezra a little raised-eyebrow look of amusement at this, deposited their fresh drinks on the table, and glided away.

"She likes you," McGruder said, with that same undertone of grievance, of personal injury. It occurred to Ezra that McGruder was feeling his banana daiquiri.

"Dan—"

"I bet Mindy Dunkelweisse did too. I bet that was the problem."

Ezra was startled. And mildly, distantly offended. "You know about that, do you?"

"Just the bare bones."

"There isn't much more to it than bare bones." Plus some very attractive fatty tissue.

"But am I right? I bet she came on to you pretty strong." His speech wasn't slurred, but he was talking louder than normal, and with greater animation.

"Let's just say my conscience is clear." Not, perhaps, in the cosmic sense, but granted human frailty.

McGruder took a long slurp of his fresh drink. "Women," he said.

"Can't live with 'em, can't live without 'em," Ezra said. And glanced toward the exit. Get me out of here.

The FBI agent looked up from his drink and stared directly into Ezra's eyes. And held them. It was disconcerting. "For a while there," he announced, "I really hated you. I freely admit it."

Ezra broke the stare with an effort, made a business of stirring his cocktail with the red plastic swizzle stick protruding from his glass. "You did? Why's that, do you suppose?"

"Why, Carol, of course. The way you came between us."

"What?"

"See, the way it looked to me at the time, I thought she was just gonna be another notch on your belt, you know? Can't blame a guy for resenting that."

"Wait a second."

"Use her and discard her kind of deal. And you know, a hound like you . . . one woman more or less, what difference could it make?"

"Can we maybe back up a little here, Dan?"

"But now I understand you weren't just casually fishing in some other guy's stream. I see that now. So I'm over it. I really am."

Ezra took a very big swallow of his drink. "Listen, Dan, you seem to be under the impression . . . I mean, Carol and I were dating long before you came along."

"Yeah, she told me all about that. Said she'd dumped you."

"She did?"

McGruder nodded. "Said you'd wasted some time together, then she'd had enough."

"That might be a little harsh," Ezra replied after a moment. Something about this conversation, some intangible something in Dan's tone, was decidedly unsettling.

"And then I thought we had something pretty good going, her and me I mean."

Ezra's mind suddenly lurched and reeled. Was it the Manhattan? Couldn't be. After all, he had nursed his first drink, hadn't he? But the exchange was beginning to get away from him, was slipping out beyond his control. "Something going? I thought—"

"She's *hot,* isn't she?" McGruder had lowered his voice, his tone was now intimate and confiding. "I mean, once you get past that Little Miss Prim facade, that minister's daughter crapola, she's like, she's like a *wild woman,* she can't get enough, those sounds she makes, you know what I mean? Wait, what am I saying? Of *course* you know what I mean."

Ezra put a hand onto the table to steady himself. "Listen, Dan, I'm not sure we should be having this conversation."

"Yeah, I know. But, I mean, you and me, we have this, this *connection.* And I don't know who else I can talk to about it."

"Nevertheless . . ." And then Ezra's growing doubts grew so fat, occupied so much space, exerted so much pressure, he couldn't help himself. Against every instinct he possessed, he asked, as casually as he could, "When did you two, you know, start—?"

"Keeping company?"

"As long as we mean the same thing by keeping company."

Dan leered, and said, "Oh, I'd guess we do. We're both men of the world. And from what I hear, you've kept lots and lots of company in your time." And then the bastard actually winked! Hideous! After which he finally condescended to answer Ezra's question, saying, "Over spring break, it was."

Ezra blinked, hoping his face didn't betray his anguish. "You sure?"

"Oh yeah. Hard to miss, if you know what I mean." He clapped Ezra fraternally on the shoulder, adding injury to insult. "The campus was kind of empty, all the students and faculty were gone, and except for this computer business, the counsel's office was, was, you know, nothing was going on. Kinda sleepy. Gave us time to get to know each other." His voice was dreamily nostalgic for a moment.

"Right. But what I'm asking is—"

"And you wanna know the stupid thing?" Dan interrupted, bitter, voice rising. "You wanna know the really stupid thing? I mean, I guess this just proves how dumb guys are, right? How vain. What suckers. But I got the impression—you're gonna laugh—I really got the impression I was, I was turning her on for the first time. I mean, you know the drill: 'Oh Dan, I never felt this way before.'" He sneered, outraged anew at Carol's perfidy and his own gullibility. "'Oh Dan, I never knew it could be like this.' Total doody. But we fall for it every time. We want to believe it so much. We *need* to believe it."

Ezra signaled for the check. He needed air.

■   ■   ■

Driving home, he found his emotions too chaotic to disentangle. *How could she?* was his first thought. But that required fine-tuning. How could she what? Sleep with Dan? Lie about it? Be, in Dan's quaint '60s locution, "turned on" for the first time by such a gargoyle? Keep both of them on a string for some undisclosed period of time? All of the above?

And then he cursed himself for failing to ask McGruder when she had ended things between them. For how long had he, Ezra, been a blithe dupe? And then cursed himself further for torturing himself with that kind of detail. The next step would be agonizing pornographic images: *Oh Dan, I never knew it could be like this.* That way lay madness.

Besides, maybe Dan was lying. Sure. Ezra seized on the notion eagerly. It was all a vengeful, malicious lie.

The mendacious son of a bitch!

But he knew immediately he was grasping at straws. Dan was too much of a lummox to make this stuff up. Dan's credulous blank earnestness was beyond question.

So what would he say to her when he saw her? What *should* he say? Should he phone her the moment he got home and launch into some extempore tirade? Or would it be better to prepare his bill of impeachment first, marshal his arguments, order his thoughts, and pick his way through the brambly underbrush of his emotions?

How could she?

By the time he pulled into his garage, he was no closer to clarity than he'd been in the Last Chance. There was one dim discomfiting notion that was attempting to insinuate itself into his consciousness, but the volitional part of his mind kept beating it back, desperately trying to hold it at bay: Something was whispering to him that, despite a massive effort of will to persuade himself he was angry, the anger was camouflage. He was, rather, *hurting*.

What the hell did that mean?

He *was* angry, he assured himself. That bitch! How dare she! I'll show her!

How could she do this to me?

It wasn't enough she'd be breaking his heart any day now. No, not content with that, she'd set about breaking his heart weeks ago, only he didn't find out about it till today.

He trudged up the steps to his front door, opened it, and trudged down the hall to his apartment. He'd show her who was angry, God damn it. Not hurting, either. You have to *care* to be hurt. Just plain old pissed-off, that's the ticket. He'd call her right away. Give her what-for. Or maybe he wouldn't. Maybe he'd nurse another drink first, put in some ferocious brooding, work up a really humungous head of steam. He slipped his key in the lock and opened his door. Well, at least this takes my mind off the E. A. Peau investigation. I haven't thought about *that* in, oh, forty-five minutes. He shuddered at the recollection.

Is this displaced anxiety? Or do I have so many sources of real anxiety that the whole concept of displacement is a pointless pathetic search for a silver lining? I'm a disaster magnet. A convergence point for bad mojo. Donnybrook Junction.

He stepped inside his apartment, into the living room. Something smelled odd. Odd and good. Like baking pastry. Strange. He flicked on the light.

"Honey! I was starting to worry about you!"

Carol had emerged from the kitchen and now threw her arms around him.

"What the hell are you doing here?" he growled.

Startled, she released him and stepped back. He noticed she was wearing a little blue apron. Where had she found a little blue apron? He didn't own a little blue apron. He wouldn't be caught dead with a little blue apron.

"I, I let myself in," she stammered, taken aback. "I've made you dinner. Not fish or skinless chicken or vegetable casserole, either. Something unhealthy. A treat."

He grunted. Something in him wanted her to resume the embrace. Just so he could push her away, he assured himself.

She examined his face. "Have you been drinking?"

"Yes."

"And you're in a foul mood."

"Something like that."

"Well, that's okay. You're allowed."

"I didn't ask permission."

"There, that's fine, you can take it out on me. That's what I'm here for."

"So *that's* what you're here for. Thanks for clearing that up."

"Well, that's part of it, anyway." Now she did embrace him again. And he couldn't quite force himself to push her away. It was too comforting, feeling her against him like that. But he didn't return the hug.

She'll get the message, he thought. I'm angry, *really* angry. Not hurt, mind you, but extremely furious.

"I was with Dan McGruder," he said.

She stiffened slightly, released him, and stepped back. "Were you? How come?"

"He wanted to talk to me."

"About what?"

"To apologize, is what he said."

She took his hand and led him to the couch. He followed her passively, a dumb tethered beast. We men *are* dumb beasts, he thought. For a brief uncanny moment, he even felt an affinity with Dan McGruder. Just two dumb beasts grazing stupidly side by side in the same barren pasture. My feeling superior to him is the emptiest, most unforgivable vanity.

"He's an idiot," she declared, seating herself beside him.

"You think so, do you?"

"A jerk. It took me a little while to realize it, but . . . well, I can be slow sometimes. And yet, you know, in a way, I think we may both owe him a vote of thanks."

Ezra looked at her strangely. "How do you figure?"

"Well . . ." She stared at the floor. "It's like . . . I mean, I know you don't much care for religion talk, but it's almost like a conversion experience. They happen in the oddest ways. The strangest places. You never know when you'll find yourself on the road to Damascus. Without Dan, I'd never have realized how much I, how much I care about you."

She looked up at him. Her face was radiant. She had never looked prettier. "I mean, you know how I . . . how . . . " She started over. "When you got back from L.A., you, you had changed in some way. You seemed different. Something had happened to you. Something *good*. I don't know how it worked exactly, but I have some idea, and I guess I don't need to know more, maybe at this point I don't *want* to know more, because I'm the beneficiary and we can leave it at that."

She took his hand. "And I just think our finding each other at this late stage, coming to care about each other like this, it's such a rare thing, it's so *improbable,* that whatever helped it happen is something to celebrate. So I kind of feel okay about L.A., and even feel beholden to that jerk Dan. Without him, I might not have noticed how special you are."

Ezra looked at her in silence and attempted to quell the flood of tenderness rising within him. When had she become such an extraordinary person? Something was happening behind his eyes that wasn't exactly tears, but bore a family resemblance to tears. This was so amazing, and so doomed. She'd feel completely different in a day or two, when everything came out. His name would be a curse. To have found her like this only to lose her . . .

There were a few moments of absolute stillness. She waited for him to say something, but he kept silent, and so she finally resumed, "This is an awful time for you, isn't it? Confusing and unsettling and disorienting and miserable."

He found his voice, unsteady though it was. "What makes you say that?"

"Oh, you know. We've talked about it some. I know you're not super-comfortable discussing it with me, but, well, there's your tenure case, and this ad hoc committee, and . . ." She hesitated, then went on, "And chairing the committee must be especially tough for you because, you know, because it's your book. I mean, that press conference on Thursday, for example, that's gotta be a nightmare, no two ways about *that*. And besides, it must be driving you crazy that it's a best-seller and you don't get any of the glory."

Something resembling an electric shock passed through him. For a moment, he even forgot he was sulking, forgot his feelings of betrayal. "What are you talking about?" he demanded. His voice came out in a croak; fortunately, it had been thick and gravelly already, so she wouldn't necessarily jump to conclusions.

"You know," she answered calmly. "I'm talking about you being E. A. Peau."

"That's nothing to joke about," he said. There. That sounded pretty natural.

"I've known for weeks."

He turned to face her. She was smiling broadly, grinning really. "What in the world gives you that idea?" he demanded. Don't protest too much. Remember your Gertrude.

"You might as well just admit it, 'cause it's not an open question."

"You wanna explain your thinking?" Careful. She may be teasing. Or fishing.

"Well, to be candid, I've been wondering what you were up to since that stupid Icelandic thing, so I was sort of on the lookout. And then, well, you suddenly had money when you came back from L.A. And your friend Isaac, I mean, I do read *People* sometimes, in the hair salon mainly, so I recognized him, and then, the day he showed up, you suddenly got this incredible car, so I would've been an idiot not to suspect something. And when I read the book, there was simply no mistaking it. I heard your voice."

"You read the book?"

"Yep. Just went to a bookstore and bought a copy. I was sooo embarrassed, as if everybody was staring at me. But I loved it. You know how I tried to be supportive with your poetry? Well, honestly, till I read the book, it never occurred to me you might be talented."

They seemed to have got past the point where denying it would serve much purpose. When had that happened? "Why didn't you say anything?"

"I was waiting for *you* to say something."

"I wasn't going to. Not with your attitude."

"What attitude?"

"You know, disapproval. Like . . . with your father, and that letter and on the phone today."

"I've got a job, Ezra. I'm a lawyer. I represent a client. Personally, I think Matson's a noxious gasbag."

Ezra barked a laugh, as much from confusion as anything else. He had been dreading this moment so fiercely. "Well, what about your father? When he—you know, that review and everything?"

"Well gosh, you were so smug that night, and so, so kind of sneer-

ing . . . That was my *dad* you were making fun of. He may be a Nean-
derthal to you, but he's kin to me."

"Like Aunt Goldie?"

"There you go. Even closer."

"So wait. The upshot is, you don't hate me?"

"I'm even willing to prove it."

They were facing each other, and he suddenly reached for her and pulled
her close. I actually love this woman, he heard himself telling himself.
Imagine that. I'm, I'm *besotted* with her. That's the word. Completely
besotted. It must have stolen up on me when my back was turned. The
Pearl Harbor of love. I never saw it coming.

He kissed her, a good long kiss. When they separated, she rose, took his
hand, pulled him up to a standing position, and began to lead him, with
what appeared to be considerable urgency, down the corridor to his bedroom. He followed without resistance. I may be a tethered dumb beast, he
thought, but at least I'm not going to be butchered. Out of the abattoir and
into the boudoir.

"Listen," she said, just before they reached the door, "I never got
around to asking, we kind of got waylaid there, but did Dan have anything
interesting to say?"

Ezra hesitated for the briefest of intervals. "Not really," he finally
answered as he reached for the doorknob. "Just that he was sorry. I told
him not to give it a second thought."

Chapter 8

Ezra wasn't admitted to Matson's office until almost three-forty. "I don't suppose you want coffee or anything like that," the president said when Ezra was finally shown in. He had risen from behind his desk, and approached Ezra, at the conversation group at the other end of the large room, with his right hand extended. "We shouldn't be long."

In fact, Ezra didn't want anything, but he was so annoyed at having been made to cool his heals, he said, as he shook the man's hand, "Coffee would be delightful, yes indeed." A petty method of exacting revenge, maybe, but the range of weaponry at his disposal was limited. And he'd increase the throw-weight, at least marginally, by not touching the coffee when it came.

Matson made no effort to hide his irritation, but he did say to his assistant, "Nancy, could you please bring some coffee for Professor Gordon and myself."

"I'll have to make a pot," said Nancy.

Ezra noticed the look Matson shot his way, but pretended not to understand its significance. "Oh good," he said, "I prefer it fresh."

Matson sighed, nodded to Nancy—both of them looked irritated now—gestured for Ezra to sit down on the sofa, then took the easy chair facing him. Ezra forced his face into a look of respectful attention while thinking, "My God you're a loathsome maggot."

Matson did not, however, *look* like a loathsome maggot, and Ezra had to concede, not for the first time, that the man presented an impressive appearance, with his thinning, sand-colored hair, his slim, serious face, his lean, straight body, and his stylish eyeglasses. Matson suddenly smiled, and that was impressive too, apparently personal, apparently genuine.

"So," he said. "You may be wondering why I've scheduled a press conference tomorrow." He didn't wait for Ezra to respond. "Some of the recent media coverage we've been receiving has taken a rather . . . a rather *facetious* tone, and I'm afraid we may be losing control of the story.

"A lot of people are starting to think Beuhler's a laughingstock. Those big-city types, those media honchos and so on—you know the element I mean—they think this whole business is one huge joke. Did you catch Brokaw last night? Smartass quip at the end of the broadcast? That's the sort of thing we're up against. But if we take the initiative tomorrow, I see it as an opportunity. Your actually identifying E. A. Peau isn't crucial, just between you and I."

"You and *me*," Ezra silently corrected him.

"But controlling the tone of the discussion, that *is* crucial. The point is . . . this must remain confidential, of course . . . " But he didn't wait for Ezra to offer any assurances. "I'm given to understand we shall soon learn the identity of E. A. Peau anyway, through means independent of your committee. Means I'm not at liberty to divulge. But I do think it would be in our interest, yours and mine, to get ahead of the curve."

He waited for Ezra to evince surprise. But Ezra felt no surprise. Horror, dismay, a sinking certainty of personal and professional disaster, but no surprise. He continued to look respectful and attentive. "What does 'ahead of the curve' mean exactly?" he asked.

"It means . . . well, for one thing, there's no reason the announcement of E. A. Peau's identity can't come from us. Even if the discovery did not. Do you see what I'm getting at?"

"Steal the credit?"

If Ezra hoped this baldly literal translation would faze Matson, he had underestimated his man. Matson grinned slyly, not at all put off by Ezra's candor. "Yes," he said, "that would be another way of putting it."

"Pretend we made the discovery?"

"No need to go that far. Finesse the issue. The important thing is that it comes from us."

"So we're ahead of the curve?"

"Precisely."

"Are you sure we'll have the information by tomorrow?"

"Reasonably. Even if we don't, there's still plenty of reason to hold this press conference. See, the way I see it, some of what we need to do is pure theater, is presenting our case in a compelling, media-savvy way. We'd be foolish to disregard that aspect of modern life. It's where we've been somewhat derelict. And we need to work as a team, you and I. We need to understand our roles in the show. As president of Beuhler, I'm the stern father figure, the unapologetic, old-fashioned upholder of traditional values. That's an easy role for me. It's also the easier part to play, I'm afraid. Your part is a little more difficult."

Right, thought Ezra, I'll be the drooling pervert.

"You must be the young, hip, sophisticated fellow who nevertheless adheres to the established verities. I'm being candid with you, son, because I believe you and I are on the same wavelength. Birds of a feather. But your role in these proceedings is more nuanced . . . you can be a little loosey-goosey. You needn't be afraid to tell a joke or seem amused by all this, as long as you also project an underlying seriousness. Too often, the good guys in this cultural war of ours come across as bigots and primitives, they look like medieval peasants. Your mission is to show that you don't have to be Silas Hayseed or sound like some sort of sky pilot in order to care about right and wrong. Got that?"

"I believe I do." Ezra, to his pain, believed he did.

"Yes, I believe you do as well. Which is why I'm sure you understand the need to keep this little chat private. People like Nat Dimsdale—a very fine man, don't get me wrong—they don't necessarily grasp the, the tactical requirements of complicated situations, they believe you go full-tilt all the way for what you believe without considering the consequences, they think the only way to proceed is full frontal assault and on to victory. Nat's a real Christian soldier of the old school, manly and militant, and you gotta love him for it. But people like you and I—"

"You and *me*, damn it!" Ezra thought.

"— who understand modern times, know you have to be willing to plan and calculate and strategize. The good lord didn't give us brains so we wouldn't use them."

"Very true."

"And just one more thing, son, and then I won't take up anymore of your time. I'm aware your tenure case is presenting some problems. But you and I both know Beuhler isn't where you'd want to end up anyway. I'm not saying your case is hopeless—you have some good friends in high places these days—I'm just suggesting you and I might both be moving on to greener pastures someday. Maybe heading out together, who can say? I'm always on the lookout for clever people."

From Ezra's point of view, there was only one satisfying thing about this entire awful interview: As he was leaving, he encountered Nancy, carrying in a tray of coffee things.

■   ■   ■

The damned phone would not stop ringing. As if Ezra's nerves weren't jangly enough without outside assistance, the phone insisted on ringing, making them do cartwheels and handsprings and backflips.

"Just take it off the hook," was Carol's sensible suggestion.

"I can't," he said, rising from the sofa. "It might be important."

"How important could it be?" she demanded, but he was already on his way to the phone stand in the hall.

Mostly it had been the press. Why so many reporters were phoning was a mystery; the press conference was tomorrow morning, and its ostensible purpose was to give them an opportunity to ask their dumb questions. But they seemed to feel a need to get a jump on things. Maybe Matson had leaked hints of a major announcement. That would explain it.

"Yes?"

"Ezra? It's Phil Bergland. Had a heck of a time getting through."

Bergland was one of the ad hoc committee members. Geology Department. Ezra had a vague recollection of having heard he was some sort of fundamentalist in his spare time. He probably devoted his professional life to casting doubts on the authenticity of the fossil record.

"Yeah, a lot of people have been calling. What's up, Phil?"

"I've been doing a little independent research, and I may have found something interesting. Might come in handy tomorrow."

"Go on."

"This Isaac Schwimmer fellow. Who published the book? It turns out he did graduate work at the University of Michigan. Isn't that where you got your doctorate?"

"Uh huh." Ezra's pulse rate began to accelerate once again.

"He was there in the mid- to late eighties. Weren't you there around the same time?"

"Somewhere in there."

"When exactly?" The man gave new meaning to the phrase "full bore."

"Oh, right in the middle, sort of." Lying outright about this one would be a serious blunder; Bergland could easily check the information, it was right in his file. In fact—the realization came to Ezra with an unpleasant little shock—he probably already had.

"My my! Did you know him?"

"I'm, I'm not sure. I can't remember." If memory served, that was the advice Richard Nixon gave his staff when coaching them about their testimony before the Watergate Grand Jury: Say you don't remember.

You can learn a lot from American history.

"Still, the thing is, *he* might remember *you.* I mean, I know he's probably a disgusting degenerate, but maybe he remembers you fondly." Bergland laughed. "I'm being facetious."

"Oh."

"But it's a connection we should explore, don't you think?"

"Yeah, maybe. Uh—" Christ. "Uh—" Was Ezra being paranoid, or did he detect a menacing undertone in Bergland's voice? "I've already made a note to myself about getting him to cooperate."

"Right. And now that we know you two have some sort of connection, maybe he'll be more coopera*tive.* Alma mater in common, maybe he'll feel some sentimental attachment to you, no offense. It's a lead we should pursue. I'm gonna keep pushing ahead with this on my own if you don't object."

"Thanks for calling, Phil." May you rot in hell. Ezra severed the connection with his middle finger. Then he left the phone off the hook. Carol was right. Any more calls like that one and tomorrow the manly and militant Reverend Mr. Dimsdale would be intoning a lugubrious benediction over his grave.

Ezra lumbered back into the living room. Carol was watching his arrival over the back of the sofa, and she had a look in her eye that was simultaneously sympathetic and humorous.

"How you feeling, honey?"

"How am I feeling? Like Woody Herman and his Thundering Herd are jamming in my duodenum, that's how I'm feeling."

"Nervous about facing the cameras tomorrow?"

"That's the least of it. Although, yes, I'm nervous about that too."

He sat down on the sofa beside her. She began to knead his back.

"You're not relaxing," she said.

"I can't. Woody won't let me. And the Thundering Herd is even worse."

"Worried you'll do a bad job?"

"I don't even know what a bad job is. Or a good one."

"Worried you'll say the wrong thing?"

"No, I'm pretty sure I'll strike the, the right note. I know what's expected of me."

"Worried you're working the wrong side of the street?"

"Sure. You know how I feel about that." He shrugged. "I felt a lot less sullied writing a d.b., to tell you the truth."

"Yeah. You probably find this harder than I would. You know, as a lawyer, I can differentiate between professional advocacy and personal belief."

He shook his head. "The thing is . . . what you should know . . . They're gonna nail me, Carol. I'm flailing about, but not because there's any escape."

"You're being alarmist. That's your style."

"Uh uh. Listen to me. Your friend Dan, his investigation of the computer virus . . . it's going to lead him straight to E. A. Peau. By accident. Just bad luck on my part."

Her hands froze on his shoulders. "You're sure of this?"

"Uh huh."

"No way out?"

"None worth thinking about."

"That's not good."

He turned to face her. She was frowning. "No, it's not good." She looked very concerned, which made him feel even worse. "So I'm going to go through the motions tomorrow, but only because I can't see any alternative. It's all gonna catch up with me soon."

"You'll do what you have to do."

"Only it won't be enough. And it's bad for you to be associated with me, Carol. I mean, Matson won't keep you on as Beuhler counsel if you and I stay together. Even your father'll be screaming for your head."

He waited. It was disconcerting, but she didn't respond right away, and it left him no choice but to wait. She seemed to be pondering. After what seemed like several minutes, but probably wasn't more than one, she announced, "I'm going to stay here tonight. With you."

He looked at her blankly. It seemed like a non sequitur.

She smiled. "You know, so Daddy will know what side I'm on when everything goes haywire. And even more, so you will. It's past time, anyhow."

"You're signing on with a sure loser, Carol."

"Makes the choice more romantic, doesn't it?"

A couple of hours later, lying beside her in bed, he thought he heard her mumbling. "Did you say something?" he whispered, quietly enough so as not to wake her in case she was talking in her sleep.

"Not to you," she whispered back.

He knew what that meant. He groaned.

She laughed. "Why does it bother you?"

"I just don't believe in it."

"I'm not asking you to. Yet. I'll get you eventually."

"You've already got me. Listen, if you have to pray, pray that the bastards *don't*."

■   ■   ■

He had set his alarm for six the next morning, but woke up several minutes before it went off. Carol stirred but didn't wake as he climbed carefully out of bed. He went into the living room to do some calisthenics, and then went on a five-mile run. The run was supposed to clear his head, but it didn't achieve its purpose; his thoughts skittered around in an anxious loop, going nowhere, accomplishing nothing. As he pounded through the streets of Seven Hills, his heart heavy, he kept reviewing the remarks he planned to make: We're moral guardians, standards have to be maintained, sacred trust, in loco parentis, eternal vigilance is the price of paranoia, etc. No dramatic last-minute improvements came to him. He obviously couldn't equal Matson's fulminating eloquence.

When he got home, Carol was up, fixing coffee. She kissed him, wrinkled her nose, and urged him in the strongest possible terms to take a shower. "You have two choices," she told him, "either take a shower or file an environmental impact study." He chose the former, managing to find some pleasure in the experience, then gave himself a fabulously close shave without nicking himself even once—a good omen?—then put on his new suit, which he had bought about a month ago in the first excitement of being able to afford it, along with three ties, a couple of shirts, a new pair of shoes, and four pocket squares (the sales clerk had pressured him shamelessly, and he had proved all too susceptible to the pressure). The suit was a conservatively tailored navy blue; when you own only one, he reasoned, you don't go for a major fashion statement. This was the first opportunity he'd had to wear the thing. One further small pleasure in what otherwise promised to be a grueling ordeal, a morning of hideous and unremitting self-betrayal. Well, he told himself, those are the wages of sin. It could have been worse. It will be.

He stepped into the kitchen and Carol rewarded him with a wolf-whistle. He grinned sheepishly. "I look okay?"

"Like a guy who could give E. A. Peau himself a few tips."

He couldn't face breakfast, but he drank several cups of coffee.

"You're going to be fine," she told him at the door while straightening his tie. "You're going to kick ass."

"My assignment is to kiss, not kick. Will you be watching?"

"Yep. I imagine every TV on campus is going to be tuned to it."

"Super. It should be quite a spectacle."

"You'll be fine. And when the day's over, I'll *really* show you a spectacle."

He was halfway out the door when the phone rang. He made a face. "Damn. Probably more press. Why can't they just wait a few minutes?"

"Ignore it," Carol counseled. "Leave."

"I can't," he said as he reentered the apartment. "I learned to use a telephone in Pavlov's lab." He grabbed the phone. "Hello?"

A foreign-accented voice said, "I have a collect call from Mr. Henry. Do you accept charges?"

"Mr. Henry? May I ask where you're calling from?"

"Mexico."

While the operator was giving this unexpected answer, Ezra heard Henry Ng shouting over her, "Take the call, Ezra, take the call!"

"I gave the operator that name as a precaution," Henry said, once the line was clear.

"Very clever. But make it quick, Henry, I'm late for my hanging."

"There won't be a hanging. You understand? Mission accomplished. I don't want to be too explicit over the phone."

Ezra caught his breath. His heart felt as if it had stopped beating. The tips of his fingers were suddenly cold and numb. "You mean you did it? What I asked?" He wasn't sure he would ever be able to breathe again.

"You wouldn't believe the difficulties, and I'm not gonna risk explaining now, even from a hotel room in Rosarita Beach, but the deed is done. There isn't one little bit left, if you catch my drift. Don't say anything. When I come back to the States to collect my Pulitzer, we'll get together and have a chat. In the meantime, I just wanna tell you I owe you my life and I love you. But not in a way that should make you nervous."

Henry hung up. A moment later, a little stunned, Ezra did too, and saw Carol standing near the door watching him strangely. "What was that?" she asked.

"That," he said slowly, "was deliverance."

"Deliverance? Deliverance is good, right?"

"Oh yes, it is good. Unbelievable, actually. They'll never catch me now."

"It involved Peau?"

"Partly. The part that concerns us."

"And you're certain? Last night you were certain they'd catch you."

"And now everything's changed." He shook his head. "It's . . . it's a miracle. And no, I don't mean it in a religious sense. Although, if I were ever tempted to offer a hymn of thanksgiving, this would be the time."

"You want to tell me about it?"

"I'm willing to. But you don't want me to. Honest."

She regarded him quizzically for a moment, then said, "You know what? I believe you. Don't tell me. Ever."

He collapsed into a chair. "I'm just . . . this is like . . . I can't believe it. I'm free. Out of the woods. I can sign my Faustian pact without let or hindrance."

"Whatever you have to do."

"That's what I have to do."

She touched his cheek. "It's the grown-up choice, honey. Any time you're tempted to tilt at windmills . . . just remember, the name of that song is 'The Impossible Dream.'"

He smiled at this, rose, gave her one last kiss, and was out the door in seconds.

■　　■　　■

When he arrived at Beuhler Hall, he found utter pandemonium, frenzied screaming pandemonium. Press, demonstrators, campus police, a deputation of county police, legitimate college personnel, and the idly curious were all massed around the entrance. Fortunately, a short burly campus policewoman recognized Ezra and offered to escort him into the building. Without her fearless blocking, he might not have made it. As it was, he was temporarily blinded by flashbulbs and temporarily deafened by the awful din.

"You okay from here, Professor?" she asked, her hand still gripping his arm supportively.

"Not really." He saw her hesitate, so he said, "I'll be okay. I appreciate your help."

"Listen," she said, "go easy on that Peau guy. All he did was write a book. It's not the worst thing in the world."

"I'll try to keep that in mind. Did you read it?"

"Hell no."

He made his way to Matson's office. When he entered, he expected Nancy to force a cup of cold coffee on him—he deserved no better—but Matson was already in the anteroom, pacing, obviously impatient to proceed. "You're nice and prompt," he said to Ezra. "I like that."

I was prompt yesterday too, Ezra thought, but you kept me waiting for forty minutes. Loathsome maggot.

"Let's go. We can talk on the way." Matson was always brisk, but there was something in his present manner that went beyond briskness. Perhaps it was merely pre-show nerves.

He led Ezra to a back stairway, away from prying eyes and ears. "Couple things," he said. He climbed the stairs quickly, with no sign of effort. Ezra had to scramble to keep up. "The first is the worst. We've been screwed, and I don't know how. No one seems to know how."

"Screwed?"

"Overnight. The computers . . . I can't even talk about it. Total disaster. Finding Peau, not finding Peau . . . that's trivial by comparison."

"But they didn't find him?"

"You're not listening. They can't find *anything* anymore. They can't find Beuhler's address. It's all gone. Everything."

Bless you, Henry Ng. "So maybe we should cancel the news conference."

Matson stopped climbing stairs and wheeled on Ezra angrily. "Listen. News of this is going to get out. No way to stop it. It's what you might call a black eye. A major black eye. Months of computer glitches, FBI intervention, and now total wipe-out. That's a black eye. Makes us look like incompetent idiots. And with this Peau shit already going on, a black eye is something Beuhler can't afford. You with me so far?"

The question wasn't rhetorical. Matson was staring at him, waiting for a response. "Sure," Ezra said. "Hard to argue."

"So we've got two black eyes right now, the computers and Peau. Anyone who wants to portray us as a clueless cow college—or wants to portray *me* as the clueless president of a clueless cow college—has an open field. And everyone does. If I just roll over and let 'em do it, I'm finished. Well, I don't intend to permit it. You still with me?"

"What do you plan to do?"

"Whatever I have to." He turned on his heel and started up the stairs once again. Ezra followed. "Somebody's responsible for all this, and it isn't me. Someone's going to be hung out to dry."

"Who?" By now, Ezra wasn't merely being sycophantic, he was honestly curious.

Matson spoke without looking back over his shoulder at Ezra. "Since Carol Dimsdale started letting all that riffraff into Beuhler, this place has gone to hell. We're going to have to clean house. We have to do it so the Justice Department won't be breathing down our necks, but there's gotta be a way. You keep company with her, isn't that so?"

"Yes."

"Good. Maybe she'll listen to you. Either she figures out how to make this work, or we'll find us a new counsel who will. You can pass that message along to her."

"Are you talking about . . . ethnic cleansing?"

"I'm talking about ridding Beuhler of a foreign element."

Otherwise known as ethnic cleansing. It was ironic, in a sick sort of way; while the person responsible for the college's computer problems did happen to be a member of a minority group, his group wasn't one of the ones Carol's policies had been designed to help. And the person responsible for Matson's other big problem was as much a WASP as Matson himself, namely Ezra.

"Don't you think that might just turn into another black eye?"

"Not among the people I care about," Matson said. Voters in the district primary, presumably. Matson and Ezra had reached the top-floor landing. Before opening the door giving onto the corridor, Matson said, "Okay, this is it. Keep your statement brief. Stay loosey-goosey. Be upbeat about finding Peau, even if, just between you and I, you don't think it'll ever happen. Atmospherics are more important than reality in situations like this, and besides, people have a very short attention span. And remember, unless a question is specifically addressed to you, let me field it. Got all that?"

"I'm not sure. Run it by me again."

Matson didn't know whether or not Ezra meant this seriously, but he had no intention of repeating himself either way. He opened the door and stepped through. He didn't hold it open for Ezra, just kept walking down the corridor toward the meeting room.

Jeesh! What a grouch!

But when they reached the door to the meeting room, he put an avuncular arm around Ezra's shoulders. Personal warmth, or preparation for the cameras within? "Ready, boy?"

"As I'll ever be."

"Good. Let's dazzle 'em with our teamwork." Matson pushed the door open. A riot of flashbulbs blinded them both. The room was jammed. Every seat occupied. Scads of people lining the walls. If the fire marshal ever found out about this, Matson would have yet another black eye on his hands.

Matson led Ezra to a podium, took his place at it, and indicated for Ezra to stand behind him. Gripping the podium with both hands, he faced the crowd—it was their cue to begin popping flashbulbs again—and said, "Ladies and gentlemen, I will speak briefly, and then Professor Gordon will say a few words, and then, if you have any questions, we'll do our best to answer them.

"We had hoped we would be able to use this occasion to inform you of the identity of the person writing under the name E. A. Peau. Our optimism in this regard wasn't blind, but it has proved to be premature. Professor Gordon promises me he's close to such an announcement."

When did I do that?

"His committee is pursuing a number of promising leads, and I have every confidence he will succeed. But in the meantime, I want to assure you that we at Beuhler don't regard this as a minor matter, no matter what the elites may think. We take our role in the molding and refining of young minds seriously, and we're sensitive to the fact that many parents entrust us with their children's well-being for precisely that reason. The notion that the author of garbage like this book might be an instructor here is anathema to all of us."

"Did you read it?" Ezra called out.

Matson stiffened, and turned to give Ezra a warning look. Ezra pretended to interpret the look as one of encouragement. "Did you?"

"Not all of it, no. I glanced at it. Enough to see—"

"Because sometimes it helps to judge something in its totality. You know? Like, if you opened *Huckleberry Finn* and just saw the word 'nigger,' you might get the wrong idea. Or glanced through *The Sun Also Rises* and chanced upon the word 'kike.' Do you see what I mean? Just glancing at something can be misleading."

Matson forced a thin, pained smile. "Nevertheless—" he began.

But Ezra was there to interrupt. "Unless you think those books should be banned too? Do you?"

"Now, Ezra, please, just wait your turn, yes?" Trying to sound affable, he turned to face Ezra again, and the look he directed his way didn't evince anger, but rather simple confusion: *What the hell are you doing?* He covered the microphone with one hand, and said quietly, "That might be a little *too* loosey-goosey, son."

"And then there's Chaucer," Ezra continued, as if he hadn't heard Matson at all. "I mean, jeesh, *The Canterbury Tales* has the word 'cunt' in it, for goodness sake! How crude is that!"

Matson blanched. The room itself seemed to emit a loud collective gasp. Then the flashbulbs started popping again. They think they have their lead, Ezra thought. Hah! We've got miles to go before we sleep. He pushed his way forward toward the microphone, literally elbowing Matson out of the way.

"What's the matter with you?" Matson hissed. The microphone picked that up. So must all the minicams. Including the one belonging to C-Span, carrying this live.

"I want to explain something," Ezra said into the mike, his tone conversational. "Earlier today, I had reason to believe my world was coming apart. And the odd thing is, I discovered I could live with it. I didn't like it, but I could live with it. And then something unexpected happened, and now I know my world *isn't* coming apart, but the really weird thing is, I find I *can't* live with it. Isn't that peculiar? Because my rescue has led me to this business we're conducting here, and it's just so goddamn distasteful, it's actually backing up on me."

The print journalists had begun scribbling furiously. Matson might be jealous, but Ezra knew he'd be hogging tomorrow's headlines: COMMITTEE CHAIRMAN SEVERAL SLICES SHY OF FULL LOAF. And then he realized—it was the first time he'd thought in these terms—that he had burned his bridges. There was no turning back. Well, in its own way, that was kind of liberating.

Matson was trying to wrest the microphone away from him, but Ezra gripped the podium with both hands, body-blocked, and held on tight. "Be patient, Jim, I'm almost done." He'd never called Matson by his first name before. He liked the implicit disrespect. What a shame there'd be no further opportunity to employ it.

"Earlier, Mr. Matson here—my friend Jimbo—told you we had hoped to announce the identity of E. A. Peau today, but then learned we can't. Well, he's wrong. About a lot of things, actually, that's only one of 'em. But I can tell you who E. A. Peau is."

That got their attention. Even Matson stopped maneuvering for the mike, and turned toward him in open-mouthed puzzlement.

"He's me. I'm him. He. E. A. Peau. I wrote the book."

Another collective gasp. Quite a gratifying sound, really. He took a deep breath, and it was a sensual pleasure to feel his lungs inflating, as if he were really breathing for the first time in months.

"You son of a bitch," said Matson. That was nice and audible too.

"Oh, and so there's no confusion, I herewith tender my resignation from Beuhler College. Let no one say I hang around where I know I'm not wanted."

A riot of flashbulbs was exploding in Ezra's face. And that's when—it was like a cartoon, those flashbulbs were like a pictorial representation of the event—that's when the idea for his second book suddenly came to him.

Chapter **9**

"I'll be sorry to lose you," said Florence Anthenien. "You've been a real good tenant."

"Especially when I paid the rent."

"Oh, I never doubted you, Mr. Gordon." She looked around the bare living room, containing nothing now but several cartons and suitcases. "I always trusted you. I mean, you were a *professor.*"

"Not anymore," he said.

She nodded unsmilingly. "No, not anymore. That's true." She glanced around the apartment again. "The next tenant's gonna be thrilled when they hear this used to be E. A. Peau's place. If I tell 'em."

"Why wouldn't you?"

"And you cleaned it up real nice, didn't you?" she said. "Reckon you'll get your deposit back."

"Well, that'll be welcome."

"I'll send it on to this forwarding address in, in—"

"Marina Del Rey." Where they'd be staying with Isaac and Tessa till they found their own place. *That* could get seriously weird. But it would be part of his next life, not this one.

"Yes, exactly, Marina Del Rey. Anyway, good luck to you, Mr. Gordon. If you're ever back in Seven Hills, stop by for some apple cake."

Ezra vividly remembered her bone-dry apple cake. It was unforgettable. "Thanks, I'll be sure to do that." An easy promise, seeing as how he'd never set foot in the town again. And then he took a small risk: "By the way, did you ever read my book?"

"Well now, yes, I certainly did." She had a quizzical look on her face, as

304

if two irreconcilable versions of reality were presenting themselves to her simultaneously. "You take care of yourself now."

She let herself out.

Well, thought Ezra, almost done. UPS had already carted off most of the little he wasn't simply jettisoning, his books and CDs and files and so on. His entire wardrobe fit into a couple of suitcases. The manuscript of his new book, *Dancing in the Dark*—all forty-three pages of it at last count, but with a bullet—was safely locked in the trunk of his Mercedes. I guess this is it, he thought. The ripeness is all.

There had been remarkably few good-byes to make. Professor Dixon had been pleasant enough, businesslike but uncensorious: Good-bye, good luck, no hard feelings. For a bad sort, he wasn't such a bad sort. President Matson refused to talk to him or even acknowledge him the one time their paths accidentally crossed, in the Student Union Building. Mindy Dunkelweisse had cornered him in his office to express the hope that his leaving wasn't a result of anything she had done. He assured her it wasn't, and watched her face fall. And then herded her out of his office as quickly as possible. His Beuhler reputation was raffish enough without further blackening.

A few colleagues had asked him to sign their copies of *Every Inch a Lady,* but had otherwise been awfully offhand about the whole episode. Perhaps they were afraid to be seen spending time in his company. Only Hannah Jenkel and Susan McGill had risked a more personal leave-taking.

Hannah came to his office while he was clearing out his desk, gave him a nice hug and a kiss on the cheek, and told him she was proud of him.

"How'd you ever get into this mess?" she finally asked him.

"You know," he answered, "I've thought about that a lot lately. It may have just been happenstance. Most things are. But it's possible I got into it because there was no other way to escape. Maybe on some level I knew I'd get found out. That could be why I wrote the book in the first place."

"Well," she said, "either way, congratulations are in order."

"Right."

"Maybe some day I'll get into a mess too. Keep your fingers crossed."

Susan also paid his office a visit, confessing unceremoniously, "You know, Ezra, I kept underestimating you. Every time I thought I had you pegged, I found myself eating your dust. I mean, what's next? The papacy? Movie stardom?"

He laughed. "Shouldn't think so. Don't have the right kind of experience for either. But who knows what fate has in store?"

"No, really . . . my image of you . . . I could just kick myself."

"Don't sweat it, Susan."

"Hey, I'm not *apologizing,* for God's sake. This isn't about you, it's about *me.* I would've set my sights on you when I first got here, only you seemed to be an ineffectual little shmegeggy."

"Pretty close," he told her. "That might even qualify as a bull's-eye."

"Nah, that was just your Clark Kent camouflage. I was too blind to see the rest. Now, do I get a good-bye kiss? Don't cringe like that, it'll be tongueless."

There wasn't much more. It was probably a measure of how little he belonged, the fact that he had so few people to bid farewell to.

Carrying his cartons and suitcases to the Mercedes took only two trips. Travel light, that's the ticket. Of course, in many ways I'm carrying a lot of baggage.

Before climbing into his car, he stood in the street for a moment and took one last look at his apartment building. Good-bye, apartment building. You've been my home for five years, and you're a real dump. And my *last* dump. No more dumps for me. I'm E. A. Peau. I've got a book contract. I've got a big advance. I've got paperback rights and film rights and all sorts of other rights I don't even know about. And I'm going to be on the *Tonight Show* tomorrow night to shoot the breeze with Jay Leno.

And I'm *rich!*

He got into his car, started the ignition, and slipped into gear. Here we go! Choosing life! Up the hill and across the old railroad tracks to Main, left on Main, right on McKinley, left on Grove. And there, looming ahead of him, was the Dimsdale house, or, as he sometimes thought of it, Manderley. He pulled up to the curb.

What, he wondered briefly, is required of me here? Face the music? Be a man? Take responsibility for my actions and decisions and confront the consequences?

Not when there's an alternative.

He gave his horn a prolonged beep.

Less than a minute later, the front door opened, and Carol appeared and waved at him. Then she staggered through the door with two huge suitcases, pushing three large cardboard cartons in front of her with her feet. Whoops.

Ezra bowed to the inevitable. Time to show a little gallantry. At least the reverend wasn't breathing fire right there on the path. He got out of his car and trotted up the flagstones to the front porch, calling, "Let me give you a hand."

"Kiss me first."

"Deal."

He did kiss her, and then piled the three cartons on top of one another and hoisted them up. Oof! Ah, he thought, great, perfect, herniating myself on the day of my elopement.

"I can manage the suitcases," she told him. "They're pretty light. I'm not bringing much. Figured we could hit Rodeo Drive tomorrow."

Is this the way a best-selling author's fiancée behaves, or what? Especially after negotiating a killer book contract for her husband-to-be and declining a commission.

When they were halfway down the path toward the car, she suddenly set down both suitcases and turned to face the house. Still carrying the cartons, Ezra turned around too.

There was a shadow in one of the upstairs windows.

"Good-bye, Daddy!" Carol yelled, waving. "I'll phone tonight to let you know we're safe!"

The shadow in the window didn't move.

"How's he taking all this?" Ezra asked, while squeezing all her earthly goods into the trunk of the car.

"Not too well," she said. "But, you know, it's funny, all these shocks and things, people adjust. He's pretty pissed, and he wouldn't give me his blessing when I asked, but . . ." She hesitated, then went on: "But, this is kind of bizarre, but he came into my room last night. Late. I pretended to be asleep, I thought he was coming in to yell at me one more time. That's what he's been doing for the last week, so I figured he'd see this as his last opportunity. And he stood in the doorway for a minute or so, and then he tiptoed over to my bed and kissed my forehead. It was very sweet, really. I mean, it was creepy, but it was sweet too. So I think he'll recover. More or less. He'll never forgive *you*, of course, but I'm sure he'll be an awfully darling old grandfather."

"Please, Carol, can we take this one step at a time?"

She laughed, and then said, "Come on, let's roll. It's a beautiful day for a drive."

They made only one stop, at a Denny's just off the highway, for what seemed to be an all-Velveeta lunch. Afterward, when Ezra went up to the cash register to pay the check, the cashier, while taking his money, said shyly, "I hope this isn't terribly rude, I mean, you probably deal with this all the time, but can I have your autograph? It's for my mom."

Ezra was startled, but Carol was delighted, slipping her arm through his in order to nudge him surreptitiously in the ribs. He signed both his own name and E. A. Peau on the napkin the cashier proffered, and then turned to leave. But before he and Carol were through the door, they overheard the elderly waitress who was standing by the cash register ask the cashier, "Was that someone?"

"Oh yeah," said the cashier.

Ezra and Carol waited by the door to hear the remainder of the exchange.

"Who?"

"You know," said the cashier, "that guy, the professor, the one who wrote the book."

"You mean the dirty one?"

"Uh huh. Seemed like a real nice fella."

Ezra and Carol exchanged a quick amused glance, and then continued out the door and into the brilliant sunlight.